CH00968133

The Luck
Weissenst

by

Christoph Fischer

To Francis
with best wishes

1

First published in Great Britain in 2012

Copyright @ Christoph Fischer 2012

The moral right of the author has been asserted.

No part of this book may be used or reproduced in any manner without permission from the author in writing. The book is sold subject to the condition that it shall not be lent, re-sold, hired out or otherwise circulated without permission from the author in writing

CreateSpace ISBN – 13: 978-1481130332

CreateSpace ISBN – 10: 1481130331

Cover design by Daz Smith of nethed.com

To my Amazement!

Dedicated to the members of my first family:

Gertha, Vilma, Eugen, Marile, Michael and
Susanne

and my new family:

Ryan, Molly, Greta and Wilma

www.christophfischerbooks.com

The Effect of the Munich Agreement on Czechoslovakia (Oct 1938)

Legend:
- Czecho-Slovakia: Territory after the Munich Agreement
- Sudetenland: Territory Annexed to Germany
- Territory Annexed to Poland
- Territory Annexed to Hungary
- Protectorate of Bohemia and Moravia

Germany

Carlsbad
Pilsen
Prague
Budweis
Brno

Poland

Slovakia

Kosice

Bratislava

Vienna

Austria

Hungary

Romania

0   50   100
Scale (miles)

Table of Contents

Contents

Chapter 1: Bratislava 1933

Greta Weissensteiner was a passionate and compulsive reader who spent enormous amounts of her time and money in bookshops and libraries - too much time if you asked the rest of her family. She spoke several languages fluently and was able to read her favourite Russian and German authors in their original versions. For her literary needs she frequently went to 'Mohr & Kling', a particularly renowned bookshop in the Bratislava city centre run by two German men. Greta adored their exquisite selection of beautifully bound and illustrated books, even though she could never afford such luxurious items herself.

The public library stocked mainly reference books and held only a minor collection of dated or classic fiction. In there she rarely found any of her favourite writers which were the more modern romantics such as E.T.A. Hoffmann, Heinrich Heine and Friedrich Hoelderlin.

"All starting with an aitch, I've noticed," a Prussian looking junior sales assistant commented one day while he wrapped her latest purchases. "Is that a coincidence or are you working your way through the alphabet?"

His name was Wilhelm. He had spotted Greta from the moment she had first come into the bookshop and was fascinated by her. He could hardly take his eyes of her while she browsed through both selections of delicate rare prints and the new additions to the stock, and he was astonished at her dedication as a reader. Her questions demonstrated a sound knowledge of literature and her choices proved that she could tell the good from the bad. She also had a slight hint of mystery about her and a set of dark, deep and penetrating eyes that suggested an extensive inner life and a seriousness of character; in many other regular readers, it usually merely signified a melancholic mood and pessimism. However, Greta possessed no such negativity, just pure enthusiasm for the written word and a clear focus on whatever she was doing. Wilhelm loved and knew all about German literature and welcomed a local girl taking such an interest in the excellent hidden treasures that this bookshop held.

Frequently there would be girls or young women trying to

engage him in conversations about books, but many used this only as a pretext for flirting with the handsome new assistant. Those silly and unworthy creatures soon exposed how little they actually knew about literature which put him off. His time was too precious for shallow discussions and idle chit chat. He could tell that Greta was the exact opposite.

She did not seem to notice him at all, her focus was always on the books and when she asked him or the other assistants for information, she hardly ever even looked up at them. That, for the first time in his career, had created a desire in him to take the attention of a customer away from the literary treasures and bring her focus onto him. He was a good looking young man with strong facial features. Pleasant to the eye and well groomed, he was not used to having to work at being noticed. He thought it was ironic how her aloofness, the one quality missing in all the other woman who admired him, was the very thing that made him invisible to her.

In fact, his looks had not passed Greta by at all but she was a little put off by his confident manner, which didn't live up to her romantic ideals of a potential suitor. Yet there was something delicate and soft about him, hidden underneath his confidence, that she thought was very appealing.

His eyes were full of mischief as he spoke to her and his smile was disarmingly warm and friendly. Greta was taken off guard and was almost lost for words. Whenever she had seen him before, there had never been a simple pretext for speaking to him and being not the most confident 21 year old, Greta would never have thought that she would warrant a second look from him. Behind her rigid posture was more fear and anxiety than an outsider could have detected. When Wilhelm addressed her at the counter she only just managed to hold his provocative gaze and smiled back at him.

"The aitch is a coincidence," she quietly got out before composing herself and stating with a bit more confidence: "All of the modern romantic authors are my favourites, really. There are so many, it would be hard to choose amongst them. I also love Dostoevsky and Gogol - Russians and Romantics. If I had more money I would probably collect their complete works."

"You have an exquisite taste in books young lady," Wilhelm complemented. "I would recommend you have a look at Hegel and his work. He is also a German romanticist beginning with an aitch and his work is very remarkable – that is if you were ever stuck for more inspiration – which doesn't seem likely."

"Thank you. I will keep that in mind," Greta said gratefully. Of her few friends and family, only her older brother, Egon, loved reading as much as she did, but he was solely interested in history books and was not very knowledgeable when it came to fiction or contemporary literature. Her sister Wilma often read what Greta chose for her but she lacked the ability to analyse and discuss the works in a way that Greta would have found stimulating. The young book lover was on her own in her quest for intellectual exchange and so Wilhelm's recommendations and comments were very welcome indeed. She wondered if she would ever be in a position where she could tell the assistant in a shop like this something he didn't yet know about books.

"If you wanted to, I could always lend you one of my books," Wilhelm offered, looking around him to make sure no one was listening in on their little conversation. "You know, so you could keep expenses down – if money is a problem."

Greta was taken aback by his sudden forwardness.

"Wouldn't that get you into trouble with your boss?" she said evasively.

"Probably, but only if he found out," Wilhelm said with his mischievous look again.

"I would have to give you the books outside of work of course, not in here. Maybe I could meet you somewhere for a coffee or a drink?" he asked with a little wink.

"Thank you," she replied. "But I don't have a habit of meeting with complete strangers. I am sorry." She made for the door.

"Wait! Wait! Well, maybe I could just stop by your house and deliver a few books to you sometime? We would not have to meet or talk if you don't want to. I would just give them to you and then leave. I promise."

He was insistent this man and Greta felt charmed and singled out, but she wondered whether this handsome German was a genuine admirer of romantic literature and her, or whether he really was just a notorious flirt.

"Why would you do that for someone you do not even know? What would be in it for you?" she asked, instantly regretting that she had given him a chance to explain his feelings, which she guessed were not of the purest type.

"Because I can tell that you really like our books," he said, becoming a little more uncomfortable and shy himself. "We don't get many young women in here that appreciate our treasures as much as you do. I would like to help you with that!" Wilhelm surprised her with his noble answer and the more genuine and kind tone he was now using.

"Maybe," she replied. "I am going to read these books first. Can we arrange the delivery of your loan when I come here next?"

"Of course. When do you think that will be? Are you a fast reader?" he asked.

Greta had to laugh about the sudden panic she detected in his voice.

"I am, but I don't always get much time to read. My father runs a weaving and embroidery business and we are always busy. As a matter of fact, I should be going right now. He sent me on some other errands and only allowed me ten minutes in here. He will be cross with me when he finds out how much longer I have been here and how much money I am spending."

"There are only a few weavers in town. Maybe I know the place. Which one is your father?" Wilhelm had left the desk and was following her as she approached the door to leave. "Just so that I can come by sometime for those books, then you would not have to leave work."

He felt he was making a fool of himself but now that he had already gone this far, he did not want to let her go. Normally it was he who set the boundaries for admiring ladies; now that the roles were reversed, he did not like it much.

"I am not sure that would be a good idea," Greta said to his great disappointment.

"Why not?"

"I don't think my father would like it if strangers came to the house unexpectedly. When we are busy I don't even know if I could come out and talk to you when you get there," she told him.

"I will take the risk. So which weaver is your father? Please tell me!" he said with pleading eyes causing her to finally relent.

"We are the Weissensteiners on Gajova, in the dead end part of the road."

Pleased with the small progress he had just made, he tried to engage her in further conversation.

"What other writers do you like?"

Greta hesitated a little, and then she replied briefly while looking towards the street outside.

"Schnitzler, Chekhov, Pushkin, Hoffmannsthal and Joseph Roth; the list has no end," she laughed. "But I really need to go now."

"What is your first name?"

"Greta. And yours?"

"Wilhelm. Wilhelm Winkelmeier." He extended his hand and bowed slightly. "Nice to meet you."

"Nice to meet you too. Goodbye then, Wilhelm."

When he first showed up at her father's workshop a few days later Greta seemed almost cross with him and acted very abruptly. Much later she explained to him that she was only worried at the time that she would get into trouble with her father or her co-workers about the unannounced interference with her work life. As the daughter of the owner, she had usually no more rights than any of the other employees were permitted; they didn't like it when she got preferential treatment and her father, Jonah Weissensteiner, did not want to alienate his work force by allowing his children any more freedom or liberties. Weaving had become a fragile business and with the continuing growth of industrialization in the sector – more so in other countries than in Czechoslovakia - competition was fierce. The Weissensteiners owned a few semi-automatic looms, which were already substandard in France and Britain but productive enough for the kind of work they attracted.

The income of the family fortunately did not entirely depend on those looms and the production of fabrics. Previous generations of the family had acquired traditional embroidery skills in the Ukraine and ran this part of the company as an artistic side-line. Numerous commissions for hand woven 'made to order' work - usually for the local nobility - was the most lucrative branch of the business and Greta's father was lucky to have made a good name for himself. While he designed and spent endless hours on individual orders, his children and staff had to take shifts in overseeing the looms for the production of blankets and fabrics. Even though this was less demanding than other work, everyone disliked doing it because it was incredibly dull, which was why Jonah insisted that everyone took a fair share of these shifts. He knew that disgruntled employees meant lower quality and damage to his own reputation. When Wilhelm arrived to bring Greta the promised books, she had been on one of those boring shifts and had to make one of the other girls take over for her which earned her a hateful look.

Wilhelm had brought her two books to start with. Of course, it had been a lie that he had his own private book collection at home. He had left all of his books back in Berlin from where the Winkelmeier family recently had moved. He had none of her favourite German romantics at his family home on a farm just outside of the Bratislava city limits.

He owned up to his lie right away and admitted that to impress her he had taken the books from the shop store room and he would have to ask her to be careful with them so that he could put them back on the shelves before the next inventory. Greta laughed and promised she would treat them with the utmost care, but she had to go back to her duties now and so the meeting was over quickly.

He swore he would be back the following week to see how she had gotten on but she did not hear him as she rushed back into the house to relieve her angry and impatiently waiting colleague.

On his next visit, only five days later, she had already read the first two books.

"I couldn't help myself," she told him. "I started before going to bed every night and I only meant to read a chapter or two, but I got so drawn into the books that hours passed before I realized how late it was and that I really had to go to sleep. Thank you Wilhelm, these were really a pleasure. Look, I made sure they are still clean and proper."

Wilhelm was impressed that she had such a passion for books and that she had been able to keep her concentration up till late at night. It appeared that she was having to work very hard at her father's company and yet her passion was able to overcome her tiredness.

Originally he had meant to wait much longer before coming to see her again to give her sufficient time to read the books he had brought, but he was so eager to hear what she thought of the books that he could not help himself. Besides, with no friends in this foreign land, he really had nothing better to do. 'Mohr & Kling' was far from his home and he spent a large part of his day commuting on foot. Frequently, he also worked right through lunch, completing orders and store paper work to impress the owners and secure his position. Usually he only had a little snack in one of the back rooms before being able to do a little reading of his own.

The owner, Herbert Kling, insisted that Wilhelm should go and stretch his legs and made him leave the shop for lunch at least a few times every week but Wilhelm was not grateful for the kindly meant gesture as it interfered with his precious reading time.

Hopeful that Greta had managed to finish at least one of the books he had brought with him the last time, Wilhelm had come with a few more treasures for her. He had managed to find her a book by Lessing. His own favourite, 'Nathan the Wise', had recently been banned because, as the German newspaper in Bratislava, Der Grenzbote, had quoted as the given reason, it 'practically put the Jewish faith on the same footing as Christianity'.

"It is such a shame that one possible interpretation of the book put it on the black list," Wilhelm complained. "You Slovaks are incredibly strict when it comes to religion."

"Do you think so?" she asked surprised.

"Oh yes, I do," came the instant reply.

"Who else do you like apart from Lessing?" Greta wanted to know.

"I do like the Enlightenment movement," he told her. "Do you know Schiller and Kant?"

"Yes, I do."

"Well, I have to say that although I am less worried about the religious implications of their argument, I share their belief in the greatness of the intelligent abilities of mankind. I like how Kant encourages people to make up their own mind and to take responsibility for their actions, rather than to look for already made up rules to live by," he said passionately.

"You are quite a philosopher I see." Greta observed.

"I guess I am. I like meaning in a book. Everything needs meaning!"

"What do you think about Romanticism then?" she asked. "That not always has a serious meaning."

"I also love passion which is in both the Sturm und Drang writings and the Romantic period," he consoled her. "It would be a

12

mistake to limit oneself by reading just one particular type of genre over and over again. I hope that this is not what you are doing by reading so much of the Romantics? That would be an insult to your potential."

Greta thought that this was a very nice thing to say and a valid point to make about her reading habits. She had been rather one sided in her choices and so from now on she encouraged him to bring something she had asked for and also something he had chosen.

The next time he visited she was pleased to tell him that she had liked the book by Lessing he had brought and she regretted having to miss out on the banned book, which sounded so very interesting. Fortunately he had managed to get her some early works by Goethe which she devoured with speed and passion. Even though he could not supply her with some of the literature she was looking for – Jewish writers for example were more difficult to sell and were often not even in stock anyway - she said she was always open to his suggestions. He rejoiced in her willingness to read whatever author he recommended and could not wait for her to have read the books so he could bring her some more. He considered himself extremely lucky that no one in the book shop seemed to notice his loans.

Jonah Weissensteiner was very happy for Wilhelm to come to the workshop and supply his daughter with books. He had words with all the employees and promised them that they too could receive short visits like Greta and thanked them for their understanding. Jonah could be very persuasive when he chose to be and with the other workers on board, it was occasionally even possible for Wilhelm and Greta to have at least a little chat about the books before she had to return to her tasks. Jonah wanted Greta to find someone that liked her for herself and not only for her noticeably good looks. This young man had things in common with his daughter and treated her with respect, which was the most important quality he searched for in any potential son-in-law.

Wilhelm with his good looks could have his pick of the girls and his eyes were clearly set on Greta, which secretly made Jonah a very proud father.

"Does he not mind you being Jewish, that German book boy?" Jonah asked her one evening over dinner.

"I am not sure he even knows yet," Greta told him. "The way

he talks about the Jews, it doesn't seem to have any reference to me at all."

"How does he talk about the Jews?" Jonah said with raised eyebrows.

"He just mentions them in passing, like ... so and so is a Jew so we do not have his books in our shop. I don't think he has an opinion about it himself," Greta guessed.

"But the name Weissensteiner, that is a Jewish name! He must know," insisted Jonah. "I often wished we could have changed that. It would make life easier, wouldn't it?"

"It only sounds Jewish to you because you know that it is," disagreed Greta. "It could pass as a German name to a naïve young man, which I think Wilhelm just might be."

"In that case you should bring the matter up soon before this 'book lending' goes any further," Jonah lectured.

"He seems very smitten with you my darling daughter. It wouldn't hurt to get it out of the way before you waste any more of your time on him or any of his time on you, unless of course you were only in it for the books?"

"No I am not just in it for the books father," she admitted. "I like him. I think I really like him. He is very interesting. He thinks a lot."

"Oh he thinks a lot does he?" Jonah said, with a little sarcasm in his voice. "Then it is important that he learns to do something as well, thinking alone will only give him a headache."

"Do you like him father?" Greta asked, ignoring his previous statement.

"Does it matter if I like him? You must like the goy and make sure he does not mind your family," her father warned. "I'll like him enough if he makes you happy; even if he thinks all day until his head hurts. If a thinker you want, then a thinker you shall have. You have the pick of the men, my beautiful. Trust me. Make sure you choose a good man and that you do really like him."

"I do like him, father. He seems such a gentle man from what I can tell from our short meetings but I still need to get to know him better," she admitted.

"You take as long as you like to make up your mind. I hope you realise that he has already made up his mind about you. It is written all over his face how enchanted he is. He could accuse you of playing with him if you let him visit this often and your decision is not the one he hopes for. You must not lead him on. Be careful, you know, because I don't think we need to wait much longer for a proposal from this one."

"I am not so sure. There are plenty of girls who make eyes at him, maybe he just loves talking about books. That could be all he wants from me," Greta said more to herself than to her father.

"Yes, if you were a fifty-year-old librarian that probably would be all," Jonah said with a roaring laugh. "Why is he not content talking about his Goethe with the old men in his book shop then? I tell you why, they are not his type. Always remember that men of his young age mainly think with their loins. Once they have satisfied such needs, they may not be interested in your views on books anymore and go back to the shop to discuss literature there. An attractive girl like yourself always needs to choose wisely."

"I don't think he is like that, he is so serious," Greta defended.

"Yes he is serious, the Germans often are. Now let's hope his seriousness is good for something and makes him worthy of you," Jonah laughed.

Like in other regions of Czechoslovakia, there were a lot of ethnic Germans in Bratislava at this time. They often appeared like a closed circle, even though that was far from the truth. One part of these ethnic Germans were Austrians, many of whom had only recently arrived here and now found themselves stuck in the remains of what used to be a part of their glorious Habsburg Empire. Other Germans in the region were settlers from the German Empire who had moved there over the course of many centuries. Both groups moved in separate circles.

Wilhelm's Teutonic family roots had helped him to get his job at 'Mohr & Kling'. The Slovak population was generally friendly, if somewhat distant towards the Germans, but the communities did not mingle much.

Formerly known as Upper Hungary, the eastern provinces of Czechoslovakia also harboured large numbers of Hungarians who were less popular with the locals, were seen more of a threat and were considered as unwelcome aliens. By the time that the new state of Czechoslovakia had come into existence, many of them had already returned to Hungary to avoid an existence as a minority. After the Great War, international lobbying by Czechs and Slovaks in exile had persuaded the Allies to create this new state. The massive German population in the Czech border regions needed to be neutralized which was why Slovakia was separated from Hungary for the first time in centuries and added to the new state, where Germans and remaining Hungarians were now comfortably outnumbered by the combined total of Czech and Slovak citizens.

For the first time, the Slovaks had their own recognised region and their politicians were eager to use this historical moment and achieve more self-rule than they had been used to under Habsburger rule. Understandably the Slovakians longed to become an equal partner with the Czechs. In their view, the Germans were a harmless minority and not a serious threat to their cause. Political parties representing the German minorities were becoming more vocal of late, but this was mainly felt in the Czech part of the country, especially Prague or near the borders in the Sudetenland. Bratislava was little affected by these politics and remained the somewhat sleepy capital of a Slovakia that was quietly focused on its overdue independence.

The problem of anti-Semitism had never been exclusively associated with the Germans and was present in all regions of the state, but Bratislava had a large Jewish population that seemed widely tolerated. It was certainly not a foregone conclusion that Wilhelm would object to Greta's roots. After the Great War many Jewish refugees had fled the Russian pogroms and had swamped Central and Eastern Europe where they had received few welcomes.

The way Wilhelm had spoken about the Jewish intellectuals and writers had been both respectful and factual, and made Greta optimistic about a future with him. Still she kept delaying telling him more details about her family. The Weissensteiners were originally from the neighbouring Carpathian Ruthenia, part of the North Hungarian Oberland, that since the end of the war belonged to the Ukraine. There the family had conversed in Yiddish in their settlement, or shtetl, and in German in their home, but they also had learnt to speak Hungarian and Russian. Jonah Weissensteiner had spent large parts of his childhood in a Jewish shtetl, which existed separately to the Russian, Ukrainian or Polish communities and villages in the region. His family moved to Slovakia long before the Great War because there was not enough demand for weaving work

16

and because it seemed wise to his father to be further away from Russia with its growing anti-Semitism and political instability.

As the only Jews in their new, rural setting the Weissensteiners were tolerated well enough. Jonah was a good craftsman and earned the respect of the villagers. He made sure to appear as unorthodox as possible. He celebrated only a few Jewish holidays, and unlike other Jews, he observed the Sunday and Catholic holidays. Jonah had picked up the local language in Slovakia very quickly. Greta and her siblings had already been born here and they were fluent in German, the Slovak dialect and learned Hungarian and Russian which helped with the business. The family observed the Sabbath because – as Jonah said - as long as he could afford it, he loved a day off.

Their diet was not kosher and they only sporadically went to a synagogue, which was too far away to attend the Sabbath service and not violate the travel restrictions. Some of the other Jews they had met at the congregation were outraged with the apparent lack of faith or discipline and accused the Weissensteiner family of opportunistic assimilation without acknowledging their own roots. Such disagreements were nothing new to Jonah and he had become an expert at avoiding answering any provocative questions. He knew that it was common in exile minorities to preserve their unity by sticking to the dogma because they felt they could not afford to deviate from it in hostile territories. Oberlander Jews were particularly notorious for their orthodox beliefs and many of them had pressured Jonah's father and his family to stick to their own kind and be part of their orthodox-leaning community.

Just like his father before him, Jonah refused to give in to such pressure on principle. For him, Judaism had always been a personal search to find the right way and whether it was a neighbour or a Rabbi, Jonah would always personally decide whether they were right or wrong.

After the war, Jonah had taken his family from the rural home in the Trnava province and had moved to Bratislava. Without the connections to the Hungarian trade across the border, he thought his business would be safer in a bigger city. Bratislava was not only the biggest city in the Slovak part of the new republic, it was also historically the only city - in what was then Hungary - that allowed Jews civil rights; everywhere else Jews were only tolerated or, at most, were given the right to practice their faith. Kaiser Joseph II had made protective statements for the Jews in Vienna and the Austro-Hungarian Empire; it was called the Edict of Toleration but executed law and order in the provinces had not always followed this liberal guidance.

Over the centuries Bratislava had become an island within widespread anti-Semitic sentiment and had attracted a large Jewish community from all over eastern Europe. Not trusting that deep rooted prejudice and hatred could be erased by modern laws, Jonah's main aim was to blend in when they got to the city and to not be noticed as Jews. Too close an association with the Jewish community might attract unwanted attention and damage his business, which was why he chose not to set up shop in the Jewish quarters of the city. In the 1921 census he avoided the issue by using a loophole; he did not declare his family as being of 'Jewish Nationality' but wrote that his mother tongue was German and so by the rules of the census form his nationality must be German.

Jonah was well informed about the political situation in Nazi Germany and its potential implications for Jews in Czechoslovakia. In his view it could only be advantageous for Greta to have a German boyfriend. The boycott of Jewish products was starting to make life difficult for Jews in Germany. If this started to spread over here, having a German passport and husband, especially one that did not seem to mind her heritage, could be good for the entire family.

Greta was a hopelessly romantic girl. Wilhelm knew this much from her book choices. When it came to girls he was admittedly less of a romantic at heart and more of a slave to his own raging and tormented hormones. He had convincingly played the enchanted lover to Greta, read her poetry and wrote passionate long love letters which he inserted in the books he kept giving her. Before long, he had managed to make her fall in love with him, yet his own feelings were still a little ambiguous.

Greta interested him as a person, that much was true. She was intelligent and wise but as important as her love for books was to him, he was becoming painfully aware that this had become an increasingly smaller part of her appeal. He respected her and found her ideas on literature very impressive but in his relationship with her his physical needs became soon the most important factor. So it turned out that he did not mind her Jewish heritage at all when she finally told him on his next visit to the workshop, following her father's orders to do so. She confessed that since the official census the family was officially known to the state as Lutheran Germans but there was always a danger that their lie might be uncovered.

To her relief Wilhelm was not in the least worried about any of this. When Greta commented how unusual it was to find a man who was so relaxed about the Jewish issue he curtly replied that he had once heard rumours that it was the Jews who had caused the crash at Wall Street but that meant nothing to him at all, especially since it was hardly Greta's doing what had happened over there.

Blissfully ignorant of most prejudices against the Jews he could not find anything wrong with his sweetheart. The closer and more 'intimate' the two of them grew, the less he wanted to hear about it. He knew that her family had not much money, so they had certainly nothing to do with the 'nasty Jewish financiers and bankers' that everyone so hated. She was simply the most attractive woman he had ever known, her eyes were seductive and her beauty taunting. All he wanted to talk about that afternoon was what it would feel like to be alone with her and spend a night with her. Nothing else mattered to him. At any other time she might have found his remarks rude or offensive but on that particular day she was too relieved to take offence and see the shallowness behind them.

He didn't have to wait very long for his 'curiosity' to be satisfied. Now that they knew he was kosher, her father encouraged her to progress with this relationship and she possessed none of the inhibitions other young women of her age were plagued with. Wilhelm bombarded her with compliments and declarations of eternal love and his hypnotic blue eyes made her melt in his arms. Before long they were kissing by the church wall after work. Soon kissing became only the first part of their amorous games and within a few months they consummated their passion, hiding in his family's farm barn on Sundays when everyone else in the house had gone to church. He claimed he had to go to work for an inventory which raised no suspicions whatsoever. Wilhelm was known as a keen worker and as he had not told anyone about Greta, his cover story was coherent with his usual dedication to the shop.

The Winkelmeiers were not even aware of her existence. Wilhelm did not want to become the laughing stock of his brothers, who were not very romantic and who would only talk dirtily about girls when they were in their own company. Wilhelm was far less romantic than Greta but compared to his brothers he was certainly a gentleman. Conversations amongst the siblings about his feelings were out of the question.

The length of his stay in Czechoslovakia had also never been decided, which made her being Jewish not a pressing matter. Wilhelm's family had come from Berlin to Bratislava in 1931 after the Great Depression. There were no jobs and no money for the men in the family in Berlin and so Wilhelm's father, Oskar, decided that the best place to survive would be with their relatives in the country where food was often more available in times of famine. Oskar had a cousin called Klaus Winkelmeier in Brno but Klaus and his family were struggling to survive and organized for Oskar, his wife Elizabeth and their children to live with another cousin, Benedikt, who owned a farm near Bratislava and who, assured Klaus, could easily accommodate and feed their Berlin relatives as long as they could help out on the farm.

Benedikt was an arrogant patriarch and anxious to preserve his status, from the very first day he treated the family as intruders. Initially, Oskar found that very trying but he managed to keep his head down and quickly began to enjoy the developing camaraderie between himself and Benedikt. Having been unemployed for a while, he appreciated the physical sensation of hard work and the way it made him feel like a real man again. He gradually earned Benedikt's respect for his strength and the effort he put into his work. Benedikt gradually started to trust him with bigger tasks and Oskar was always eager and proud to prove himself worthy.

Oskar's other two sons, Ludwig and Bernhard, were also a huge help to Benedikt, who had only two daughters and a teenage son, all of who could help with some of the lighter farm work but not with the really heavy loads. It was a relief for Benedikt not having to hire so many strangers for the season. You never knew how reliable these workers were and if any of them had long fingers or would try to get fresh with his daughters.

Benedikt's farm was in a good location and he was renting out some of his machinery to another farm which brought in additional income. Having family staying, for which he only had to provide food and accommodation, was very convenient. It also meant that

Benedikt's wife, Johanna, could stop wasting all of her time in the kitchen and do more of the regular housework like sewing and cleaning which she had lately neglected.

Oskar's wife Elizabeth was known for her expertise in the kitchen and took over those tasks. In addition, she taught Johanna's girls, Maria and Roswitha, a few tricks in that department that could come in handy when they were looking for husbands at some point in the future. The girls were still a few years away from the courting age but they had both inherited the good looks from their mother, who despite her sometimes harsh and bitter facial features was still able to turn admiring heads on the street.

Maria was the older of the two sisters and at seventeen probably the one Benedikt had to be protective over the most. She had completed her eight years of compulsory education at the German school in Bratislava and was now back at home helping full time on the farm. Her grades had been above average but Benedikt did not believe in educating her any further than necessary. She was beautiful enough to hope for a good marriage, especially with her links to a well-run farm and as the oldest child, he had naturally treated her with the harshest discipline so that she could be used as an example to the younger ones. The effect of this on Maria was that she had learnt to keep her mouth shut at all times and to always do as she was told. She spoke little, sat with her head down and appeared grateful for any attention she was given.

Any young farmer would be lucky to have such an obedient and hardworking wife, Benedikt often thought, and he felt incredibly proud of forming her character so successfully.

Maria however was far from being a happy girl even though she never complained. From early childhood, she had learned that this would get her nothing but a few slaps and humiliation from her parents. The rough treatment had beaten most of her personality out of her and unlike many of her friends at school, she felt completely useless and empty inside. Most of them were not the children of farmers but the offspring of rich landowners and skilled tradesmen. They never accepted this wallflower in their midst and ridiculed her for smelling of cows and horses. Even when she got good grades, the other students laughed about her outside the school building, screaming that she was empty in her head and that was why she could remember everything that they had been taught in the lessons so well.

21

In comparison, her younger sister Roswitha was outgoing, lively and always appeared to be happy, even though this too was not quite the case. At fifteen she had suffered two years less of the severe punishments than Maria and she had very quickly learned from her older sister's behavioural mistakes and become more compliant and submissive.

Roswitha was not as pretty as Maria and she was much slower at farm work and in school. She did however look much happier than Maria; she smiled more because she had realised that it was possible to charm people with a pleasant demeanour and they were more likely to give her attention if she seemed obliging. She enjoyed working as long as she was able to chat and socialize, unlike her sister who preferred to be left alone. Roswitha loved it best when the whole family was working in a field together and her happiest moments were the evenings when everyone was gathered around the wood stove in the living room and someone told tales or sang. She hated to be alone and when Wilhelm's family moved to the farm she was delighted to give up her room for the boys and to share with Maria.

Both girls were picture perfect blonde specimens of Aryan beauty, even though Roswitha's hair was much darker than Maria's. The sisters were not very close to each other which was due to Maria's almost permanent silence. Roswitha could talk for the two of them and would tell her sister everything there was to say about her life but she could not get through the quiet and blank exterior.

Maria was very grateful for the attention but somehow felt too timid, vacuous and uninterested to share much of her own life; she was often simply too unsure what would be expected of her and what might be an appropriate reply. Nothing ever happened to her anyway, so what could she tell that could compete with the elaborate stories of her sister?

Roswitha did not know how to read these silences. She carried on talking regardless and, in the absence of protests, hoped this to be fine but the one-sided nature of their conversation did not allow for much closeness between the two of them.

Now that both girls were back from school they were even less likely to have anything interesting happening to them. Their lives were dull and monotonous. A few excursions to the market with their mother were all they ever were treated to and even those trips

22

were performed under time pressure and strict adult supervision.

The local country youth was mainly Slovak and the girls would have felt out of place trying to socialize with them. Benedikt warned them to stay away from the boys in the village. His daughters should try and find German husbands and he was concerned that the youth around here might persuade them otherwise. To meet fellow Germans they would have had to go into Bratislava, here in the rural areas there were only Slav peasants.

Their brother, Gunther, was the youngest of the three children and at the age of fourteen he was already regarded as a weakling in his parent's eyes, much better off at school than inefficiently wrestling with the heavy and physically demanding farm work that he was so clearly not cut out for. Gunther was intelligent and would probably make a much better living than his father one day; he was best advised to earn his money with his brain rather than with his two left hands and with the arrival of the Berlin relatives there was an opportunity for the boy to fulfil this dream without causing a labour shortage on the farm.

Gunter was actually much stronger than Benedikt gave him credit for but in the latter's macho male ideas of a boy of his age, he would always fall short of expectations and without fail would be made aware of these disappointments. This permanent criticism had robbed the lad of all his confidence and without a chance of ever catching up with his father's demands, he had long stopped even trying. It had never been spoken about but it was clear that Gunter would neither inherit the farm nor even ever work on it later in his life. Benedikt had used him as little as possible as help, worrying that he would constantly have to check anything Gunter had done to ensure that no mistakes had been made. With the arrival of the Berlin boys the heat was definitely off him. Oskar's sons, Ludwig and Bernhard, filled the role of farm hands effortlessly and far beyond Benedikt's already high standards. The farmer loved to instruct the two physically strong boys in the farm work and to see finally the results of his coaching in the way he wished his own son could have done; the fact that the Berlin boys were much older did not matter. In his view, Gunter was a failure of the highest order, always had been and that shame would stay with his father forever.

Benedikt also thought that Wilhelm was a bit of a weakling and probably not much use at the farm. His mother, Elizabeth, had suggested right away that he should maybe find work in a library or a bookshop as he was so fond of reading and with the help of some people at the German club, Wilhelm was soon set up at the bookshop and even managed slightly to supplement the farm income with his salary. Wilhelm was away from the farm for most of the day and was hardly ever even noticed. That suited Benedikt very well; Wilhelm was the only handsome son of his cousin and he did not want his daughters to get any wrong ideas. Wilhelm was not ever likely to run the farm either, so the less the girls saw of him the better.

Despite their different backgrounds, the two Winkelmeier families bonded surprisingly well. Johanna was a very cold woman and not comfortable as the female leader of the clan but Elizabeth took on the role as the warm and giving heart of house and kitchen to whom the girls came with questions and their problems. For the first time in its history, the house started to have a friendly feel to it. Elizabeth hated shouting and arguing and she always tried to bring people back together rather than stirring things up like Johanna was used to doing.

The attention starved Roswitha loved that there was a person on the farm that made time for her and seemed to like her without any conditions attached. The more introvert Maria on the other hand was just relieved that she no longer had to help her mother in the kitchen. Although Benedikt had ordered the two girls to learn everything that they could from the new domestic boss, Elizabeth was not interested in pressurizing anyone into something they did not want to do and so she let Maria quietly steal herself back to the fields, where the girl could be as isolated as she wanted to be and so suffer less from the social pressures on the farm. Gunter was also extremely pleased about the new developments on the farm, mainly because of the superior cooking. All three children were content with the new situation and Benedikt's wife Johanna was relieved too that a competent woman had taken all these unwanted tasks off her hands. She did not form a strong bond with Elizabeth but was polite and thankful to her – much more than Benedikt would have expected from his otherwise cold and closed wife.

Oskar and his boys obeyed the laws of the ruling patriarch and accepted his role as teacher and leader without the slightest hint of questioning his authority, which pleased Benedikt no end. Everyone seemed happy.

After only a few times of her and Wilhelm meeting in the barn, Greta became pregnant and the young Prussian – despite his feelings towards her still being a little unsure - decided to do the right thing by her and proposed. Now that fate or bad luck had tied him to the bibliophile woman he became aware of the reasons behind his earlier hesitations.

Greta was more of a muse and a fantasy lover to him than a woman he would have chosen to marry. Too many practicalities were speaking against it and he did not even know if she could cook and be a good wife. It was his code of honour that forbade him walking away from her now. They got married in a civil ceremony in 1934 with little Karl already showing through her wedding dress.

Wilhelm's family was not particularly pleased with this marriage either but felt it only right that no Winkelmeier child should ever be brought up a bastard. When Wilhelm told the family about her background, Oskar had raised the issue of having a Jewish wife in these difficult times but Elizabeth made him see that the damage was already done and that there was no other Christian way out of this situation. A Christian solution was not necessarily something that would have mattered to Benedikt, but he was fond of the idea of grandchildren and the continuation of the family. The sooner this process began, the more he would be able to personally pass on and mould the next generation; a thought that was dear to someone who was so self-loving and arrogant, and so he gave his blessing. Besides, the bride was not an official Jew and her presence would destroy any ideas his daughters might have about the handsome young book seller.

After the wedding, Greta and Wilhelm lived together in a small room on the farm and soon after the birth of their son, when she was not nursing little Karl, Greta was called upon to help on the farm. Having been brought up so liberally by her father, she initially found it difficult to adjust to the new harsh climate where Benedict dictated what would be done and where she had the lowest part in the female pecking order. Working in the fields would have taken her too far away from Karl, so for most of the day she was made to cook and clean. Greta hardly managed to read, so exhausted was she in the evenings. She had to take orders from both Johanna and Elizabeth and while the latter was gentle and caring, the former could not have given a damn about the 'Jewish whore' who had trapped 'her' beloved handsome Berlin boy into marriage.

Wilhelm got promoted to assistant buyer at his book shop, a favour to the family out of respect for his new role as young father. He came home even later every day and then still had to read or work till late at night. Jonah had offered for them to live with him in Bratislava at the workshop, but Johanna and Elizabeth both were heavily opposed to the young family living with Jews. For the sake of peace and with one eye on the political situation in Germany, the Weissensteiners agreed that the farm would be a much safer place for the little boy to grow up.

Greta was able to see her sister and family at most once a week. When everyone else went to church on Sunday mornings, she was allowed to walk into town with the little one. Elizabeth and Oskar were not very religious but succumbed to the continuous social pressure from Benedikt and Johanna, who said that village life revolved entirely around church attendance. If you wanted to be part of the community, or at least find buyers for your goods, you had to stay friendly and always show your face at church. The rural population was incredibly devoted to Catholicism and it was best to go at least to be seen regardless of your actual beliefs, which in the case of the Winkelmeiers were Lutheran.

Hardly any of the locals knew them more than by name and no one ever came to visit apart from those farmers that borrowed or rented Benedikt's equipment, but keeping up appearances could never harm. Elizabeth and Oskar gave in to this logic and made their children go regularly to mass as well, but they didn't quite dare to ask Greta to come to church too.

Only Johanna tried to persuade Greta to convert. She found an unlikely ally in this campaign in Jonah Weissensteiner, the father of the bride. He felt that a family should be all of one faith and go to church or the temple in unison. When Wilhelm pointed out that the Winkelmeiers were actually not even Catholic but Lutherans, he shrugged and said why could they not convert, after all they were already going to the services, it should not make any difference to them.

Lutherans at that time were particularly unpopular in Slovakia because the politicians in Prague appeared to favour them. There was already a lot of ill feeling towards the government because it consisted mainly of members of the dominant Czech half of the country and the resentment was transferred to the innocent Protestants.

Johanna caught on to Jonah's idea and suggested immediately that her family should all convert together. It would ingratiate them deeply in to the local community and one could always do with some allies among the neighbours.

Greta refused to convert, saying that she felt it wrong to commit herself to a church she did not believe in, but since she was not a very committed Jewess either she declared herself happy to attend some of the church services. Since those occurred at the one time a week that Greta had been allowed to visit her family in Bratislava, she asked to be excused from at least a few services so she would be able to carry on with the visits to the workshop.

Johanna noticed how weak Greta sounded when she voiced this request and it seemed a good opportunity to try and bargain further with the young mother. Would Greta be prepared to have Karl baptised - after all it would do wonders for his future if he was raised in the predominant faith of the region? Greta said she would leave that up to Wilhelm. If he felt strongly enough to support Johanna's suggestions then she would happily go along with it. Secretly she was sure Wilhelm would never agree to such a silly idea and such an obvious sucking up to the local church members. However, to her surprise Wilhelm was very enthusiastic with the plan. His superior at the book shop, Herbert Kling, came from the Catholic Bavaria and had often commented on him not having had a church wedding. Wilhelm had laughed it off with much appreciated rude comments about the bride not being able to wear white at the wedding and refusing to walk down the aisle in a different coloured dress, but it was made clear to him that if he converted to Catholicism and baptised his son Karl, it would be appreciated and his career prospects would be much stronger.

To everyone's surprise the local priest seemed the first real hurdle. He was not particularly happy for any of them to convert and was certainly not prepared to baptise them without a series of harsh conditions. Father Bernhard Haslinger was of the old guard and demanded that they should all attend regular catechism lessons for several months during which he would test their current knowledge of the Bible and then teach them in detail the differences between the two branches of Christianity. He also scolded them for having gone to Catholic Church so frequently when in fact they were not of the right faith. In his book that was as blasphemous as eating meat on a Friday.

Benedikt found it hard to keep his anger in check and to let the priest carry on with his sermon, but Johanna and Elizabeth made up for his offensive body language by throwing admiring glances at the priest, playing up to his own grand vision of himself as the wise and charitable saviour of these poor souls before him.

Wilhelm and his father Oscar kept quiet and when put on the spot, they showed their lack of knowledge without any attempts to hide it or even make excuses for it. Father Haslinger was enraged whenever he saw the depths of their ignorance and ordered them to do homework. He knew that it was the women who were behind this whole conversion idea and if the men were ready to take on the new faith, he wanted to make sure they had to work for it. It shouldn't be made easy for anyone to convert and receive the reward of salvation. Baptism was a privilege and its right should be earned.

When the date of their baptism was near, Johanna mentioned little Karl to the priest and asked him if - after his father Wilhelm had become a Catholic – it would be possible to baptise Karl too? Father Haslinger thought about this for a while and then he said he would only do so if Karl's mother was a Catholic too.

Johanna immediately saw where this was going and in a desperate attempt to hide from the priest that Greta was a Jew she said, yes, the mother was kind of a Catholic, but she had only been baptised, had not been raised in the faith after that and had not received her confirmation. Elizabeth stared in disbelief at such speedy lying but Oskar punched her gently in the side to signal that she had to go along with it.

"I will personally see to it that she receives the sacrament if she is willing to. I can't have a little Catholic boy raised by a non-believer. It would not be in God's will," Father Haslinger stated with seriousness in his eyes and turned to leave.

Johanna rolled her eyes behind his back and then addressed him with as much humbleness that she could muster without laughing. "You are too kind. Of course you are right. I will speak to

28

the mother."

Greta was shocked when she heard the proposal by Johanna.

"You want me to pretend I am baptised so I can learn about Catholicism and convert, just so that my son can be baptised as well? That is a lot of lying and effort for something so unimportant. Will your God not punish you for all this deceit of a priest?" she said.

"It must be better in his eyes than remaining Protestant or Jewish," Johanna replied.

"Do you really think that it will make such a difference in the community? No one is interested in Germans, regardless of their religion," Greta guessed.

"I think it will make a big difference with the locals. It is not too much of an effort. We have all just taken that stupid course, so don't worry about the studying. We all can help you with the preparation. After that you only need to go to church once in a while, just like before," Johanna assured her. "Who knows when we might need the help of our neighbours. It can't be wrong to make more friends and get the locals to see us as peers and fellow church goers and not just as rich German land owners. The Catholics love seeing someone come onto the right path with them. We'd have the Father as an ally which is good and the congregation hangs on his every word."

Soon Greta gave in and went to the lessons, even though it meant she had to give up even more of her precious little spare time allotted to reading. Father Haslinger was less strict with her than he had been with the others. He was quite aware that Greta was not doing this for herself but for her son and he admired nothing more than a selfless mother. Unlike in his other lessons, he was incredibly patient and gave her much less homework than he had done with the other Winkelmeiers. He was content as long as she could recite some prayers and knew the main parts of the Catholic Church service and, of course, how to confess her sins. In his eyes, this woman had singlehandedly shown more dedication and Christian spirit than her whole family.

"Greta, the only thing I would dearly ask you to do now is to get married in a Catholic Church service. It pains me to see you living in sin in the eyes of God. Everyone in the village assumed you were married in a different church in town, but now that I know you only went to the registry office, I don't feel this is right. Once you are both

29

Catholic you should seek the right blessing for your union. I can do it secretly so you won't have the shame of being exposed. You know that in the eyes of your God it needs to be done."

"You will need to speak to my husband and his family. If they are happy with it then so am I." Greta said, quietly accepting her fate.

"That is very good of you. What about your own family? Why did they never carry on with their faith?" the priest asked.

"My father converted to Catholicism for my mother. When she died of the Spanish flu he was very upset and neglected his duties," she said, reciting her well-rehearsed lie. "He was very modern in his thinking."

"What a shame," Father Haslinger responded. "Especially when in the midst of pain and sorrow one should look up to Him for guidance and find faith, not lose it."

A few months later Greta went through the absurd charade of being confirmed one day and getting married the next, all in secret, and lacking all the formal foundations as well as all the ones of true faith. When she had her mandatory confession before both sacraments, she had to omit so much of her lying and other sins that she thought she should have been struck down by lightning if this Catholic God really cared that much.

Father Haslinger congratulated her with tears of joy in his eyes and welcomed the whole Winkelmeier family into the Catholic community. The whole affair had one big advantage, Father Haslinger gave Karl and Greta an official accreditation as non-Jews, adding their names into the church's lists of the faithful, something that was always handy in these days of potentially renewed pogroms.

However, Greta soon had a rude awakening when she found herself continuously pressured into going to church. This happened more or less every Sunday - despite the sworn promises that she would still be able to regularly see her family during that time. In their longing to become integrated into the community, Johanna and Elizabeth both insisted that the whole family displayed the strength of their faith and their belonging to the church. Nothing would make that point stronger than if they could all show up together every Sunday without fail. Johanna especially argued further that the locals had to know about young Karl and start to see him as one of their local church community. If the stigma of being a half Jew could be put to rest at all then it could probably only be achieved by showing him at church time after time. In trade for this concession, Greta was granted the right to see her family on some Saturdays which her father often still managed to spend in the Jewish tradition of not working or travelling.

Wilma was always incredibly happy to see her and the two sisters spent the days exchanging gossip. Greta told her about the Winkelmeiers and how their new belonging to the Catholic Church had probably made them more of a laughing stock amongst the local community than the respected citizens they had intended to become. Wilma laughed when she saw Greta impersonating her new family and their behaviour during mass, the over acted facial expressions, the loud singing of hymns and the passionate and exaggerated head nodding during the sermon. Admittedly, some of the other church members needed to express their faith with equal intensity and exhibitionism, but surely everyone else had to find this as ridiculous as Greta and her sister did.

Wilma told her about the news at the weaver workshop where business had picked up again. A former Hungarian countess had taken up residency in a large manor house outside of Bratislava and had ordered two massive hand-woven wall carpets, including one depicting her family history and another that displayed a variety of Bible figures. Jewish people were not supposed to be involved in the manufacture of symbols of the Christian faith as far as the Church and local law were concerned, so there was a little bit of a risk involved, but it was too much of an opportunity to turn down. The project meant that all three remaining Weissensteiners would have to weave continuously on these two commissioned works and leave the hired help to oversee the looms all by themselves. For the next few months the family would earn a lot and Jonah was positive that the display of his work in such a reputable home would bring in more custom, which was why they had to work doubly hard to make sure they delivered immaculate carpets to the best of their ability.

The Countess fancied herself as the sponsor of traditional and modern art alike and frequently came to the workshop to instruct Jonah with her latest ideas and last minute changes to the agreed designs. Despite being a tough business woman during negotiations, she also became a kind and a warm hearted friend, and she adored Greta and her little boy Karl. She took a strong personal interest in

31

the entire family without ever letting anyone come too close. There was never a mentioning of a husband or a Count and the ageing woman exuded a strong air of in-approachability on the subject matter and so no one ever asked her about it. Her status and riches were intimidating and helped her to keep a distance whenever she wanted.

One of the young girls in Jonah's employ had asked for a raise during that period as the work would be so boring. Jonah was outraged at her cheek, but the girl was sure that it would not be possible for Jonah to find a sufficiently qualified or trained replacement for her on such short notice now that the big order had been placed. Jonah had agreed to the raise but he had immediately written to some of his fellow tradesmen seeking to replace the cheeky and greedy woman. The Countess also supplied him with a few addresses of craftsmen she thought might be able to help him out.

The rich aristocrat loved to join Greta and Wilma when they talked about the books they had read or wanted to read and she frequently made recommendations. Sadly, Wilhelm only brought books home for himself these days and only occasionally did he keep them at home long enough for Greta to have enough time to read them too. Wilma was, by nature often too restless to sit down and read a book but if she did read, it was always something her sister had chosen. Occasionally the Countess brought books from her own large library for the two sisters to read, emphasising how important it was for young ladies to have a sound knowledge of literature and the arts. When they were on their own, Greta and Wilma were often rather unladylike. They started a silly competition between them about who would grow the longest hair. Greta had a slight advantage as her hair was less thick and therefore easier to look after. Wilma's hair curled slightly and never seemed as long as Greta's because of its structure. They even got their brother Egon to use a piece of knitting wool and measure each woman's hair; when pulled, Wilma's hair was longer than it seemed but she never caught quite up with Greta all the same.

While Jonah played with his grandson and tried to teach him to talk, the women braided their hair and tried out different hair styles. Egon usually read a book by the window or in the winter on a bench by the oven. He didn't make much fuss about his sister or his nephew. He loved his sisters in his own way but he wished he had a brother with whom he could share his more scientific interests or with whom he could have pursued more manly pastimes. His sisters were a disappointment in these areas and, in his opinion, they fussed too much about everything. They usually talked too much as well.

At school Egon had found it difficult to socialize. When the family moved to Bratislava, all three children had been admitted to the German school. Greta had found it easiest to make new friends there because of her good looks. She also had only two years left at school when they moved and found the girls her age surprisingly mature and reasonable compared to some of the girls at her school in the countryside. Wilma, only a year younger than her sister, found friends through association with Greta. Her class mates knew that she had the protection of her older sister's friends and left her alone - even during her last year when Greta had already left the school. Egon on the other hand was the youngest and had to spend four long years at the school. He was not a great athlete and unfortunately in his age group, that had been the only way to earn the respect of his class mates. He was considered odd and had it not been for his excellent grasp of science and his willingness to let other boys copy his homework, he would have probably ended up having a much harder time. There was an unspoken truce between him and his class mates that allowed him to exist quietly without being picked on, but to strike up a proper friendship with anyone was not on the cards.

While they still lived out in the province, Egon had developed a strong bond with a Jewish boy named Daniel and after his mother had died in 1918 of the Spanish flu, had spent a lot of time with Daniel's family. Egon had been impressed by the philosophical approach which Daniel and his family had to death. This was only the beginning of further spiritual inspiration Egon received from his friend and gradually Egon had developed a surprisingly strong sense of being Jewish. He felt he could never tell his grief stricken father or sisters about it, who seemed to be coping fine without religious guidance. On Jonah's instructions, Egon attended the Protestant religious education classes at the German school - just like his sisters - and he was immediately intimidated by the obvious anti-Jewish teachings and sentiments in these classes. He was mortified that he should be found out and this further added to his difficulty in making friends.

When Jonah and his parents had lived in the shtetl in the

Ukraine, they always used to light the Sabbath candles, a habit that the weaver had carried on, more out of a sense of tradition rather than out of actual belief, when he had moved into the Trnava province. The Weissensteiner family had moved there before the big waves of Jewish immigration and were accepted as just another Ukrainian family. When the big mass exodus of Jews expelled from the Russians happened, many of those who arrived in Slovakia were orthodox and very noticeable; the anti-Semitic sentiment began to grow.

Wanting a better life for his family and not being discriminated against as he had seen happening to the new arrivals in Trnava, Jonah decided to hide his already only lukewarm faith completely when he arrived in Bratislava. Since he and his family were coming from a Slovak province and not from Russia directly, they were never questioned when they called themselves Protestants and with their language being assimilated too, they found themselves easily separated from the Jewish community. As they were not living in a Jewish quarter, Jonah had to abandon some of the traditions like lightning the Sabbath candles - very much to Egon's regret. The Jewish community however did notice them all the same. Especially in the early days of the workshops on Gajova, Orthodox Jews would visit and try to persuade Jonah and his family to come to the synagogue regularly. Jonah always treated them kindly and with generous hospitality, but stood firm on his decision not to practice his faith. He knew how dangerous it was to offend the very faithful of any religion and so he offered donations to the Jewish community to maintain friendly relations, explaining that he just did not feel comfortable in any religious community. Of course, this did not buy him the respect of the Rabbis, but the donations lessened the frequency and intensity of their visits, which was important to Jonah and his plans to remain religiously anonymous. It was suspicious enough that they made the girls in their employ work most Saturdays on their own with only minimal supervision from the Weissensteiner family, but so far the plan had worked and their secret was safe.

Jonah was particularly pleased about Greta's conversion to Catholicism and the prospects this would bring to his grandson Karl. If this was what society demanded from his child and grandson to treat them with the respect they deserved, then lying was a minor price to pay. To Jonah, the only thing that counted was your inner life and that, no one could control. He wished his other children would do the same. Wilma and Egon were very lethargic and seemed to have no interest in either a good or an exciting life. If only they would be interested in the other sex or at least go out from time to time and experience things. It seemed they would be staying at home with him for quite some time to come. Greta however was his pride and joy, and his hope. She could not come home often enough to satisfy Jonah's longing for her.

Whenever Greta came back home from such visits to her family in Bratislava, Johanna couldn't help herself and immediately found as many tasks for her to do as she could, just to show that the time away from the farm was like missed working hours that needed to be made up for. Johanna hoped this would discourage Greta from going away as often as she did, but the young mother possessed an abundance of patience and never showed any signs of rebellion against these orders. Elizabeth however, had more understanding and always managed secretly to save some food for Greta and Karl, knowing full well that there wouldn't have been much food to be had at the Weissensteiner house, especially ever since that mad and disorganised sister Wilma had become the one responsible for the domestic duties.

While Greta was being fed in the kitchen, Roswitha was always keen to play with little Karl and to carry him around. She cherished these moments during which she could be in charge of the little child.

In exchange for a smile and a little warmth, Maria was also happy to help out and she would assist Greta with those tasks that Johanna had compiled for her on her return. Since the start of these arrangements, Johanna had unwittingly created a team of deceivers in the four women and instead of punishing Greta for leaving, she had given her an opportunity to grow closer to the women of the farm. A real circle of friends had developed from which Johanna herself was excluded.

Johanna however persisted in her campaign to keep Greta from leaving the farm so often and started to suggest that it should be the Weissensteiners who should make the journey from now on – if they wanted to see so much of their Greta. The Winkelmeiers could not afford to spare her for such long periods of time anymore and, as far as Johanna was concerned, it just was not natural for a married woman to spend so much of her time with her old family.

Elizabeth tried to intervene on Greta's behalf but Johanna was adamant, even though it was an obvious exaggeration. Benedikt could not care less and in order to be left alone he decided in favour of his wife's demands. From here on, the Weissensteiners would have to travel on the Sabbath to the farm or they would not get to see their beloved Greta.

Chapter 2: Bratislava 1935

Throughout the year of 1935, things started to change, both on the farm and in wider political life. The German Sudeten Party started a much more active propaganda campaign in the border territories for more autonomy. As a result, the relations between the Czechs and the Germans in the country became tense.

At its last elections, neighbouring Austria had become a fascist state and diplomatic moves from Germany were blatantly obvious in their aim for a Pan-Germanic dominance in Europe. As a result, Germans became much more prominent hate figures in all parts of Czechoslovakia.

The Czechoslovak elections in June voted for a coalition that left both German and Slovak parties without representation and spokesmen within the government, which created further resentment towards the Czechs of the country.

The economy in Germany itself had started to recover and the Winkelmeiers, who were originally from Berlin, considered moving back home. They had received encouraging letters from their relatives who said that with the preparations for next year's Olympic Summer Games in full swing, work in the construction sector was becoming widely available and both Oskar and Bernhard had been offered employment with such a company, owned by an old family friend.

Germans were not exposed to open hatred in the Slovak parts of the country; due to the political dominance of the Czechs all resentment was reserved for them. Oscar and Elizabeth both thought however that the time was right to take this opportunity to move back home. At least the idea was worth giving serious thought.

When she heard such plans being discussed, Greta asked Wilhelm if he too wanted to return to Berlin but he reassured her that he had no such intentions. He said he knew how much she preferred to live in the countryside and close to her family in Bratislava. He was far too involved in the bookshop and his advancing career to take much notice of the outside world and to base his decision on political developments.

Jonah Weissensteiner suggested they should stay since he had heard discouraging stories about the welfare of Jews and Germans in mixed marriages in the Reich. Admittedly it was hard to get an objective and representative picture of what life was really like across the border. Oskar on the other hand was of the opinion that these reports and rumours were all exaggerated and nobody should let such unreliable information dictate their decisions. He told his son that in almost every country of the world, the Jews had at one time or another been the object of temporary hatred and they had survived. He and his wife Elizabeth wanted their son and his new family to come home with them.

Wilhelm was however quite happy with his employment at the book shop. He knew that he would need a few more years of work experience in his current position before it would be possible for him to move on to a better job in a different firm. He decided to remain in Bratislava until it would be advantageous for him to change. Especially because there were so many Germans and Jews in the city, he felt no threat for his safety from the locals and stuck with his decision, even when Oskar made up his mind to move back to Berlin.

First to leave was Wilhelm's oldest brother Ludwig. He desperately wanted to join the army in Germany, which was recruiting. Becoming a pilot had always been his dream and this was his chance to be trained for free. One of his former school friends had already been accepted by the Luftwaffe and offered to help him with his preparations for the entry exams. His departure happened so quickly, that Benedikt did not even have the time to prepare for a replacement or organise the workload accordingly. Autumn and the harvest season were just around the corner and Ludwig's leaving could not have come at a worse time, the farmer complained. Johanna found the decision extremely selfish and before he left, scolded the young man for being so ungrateful. She and her husband had done so much for the almost unknown relatives and now they were being left high and dry.

Oskar and Elizabeth were extremely apologetic about their son's decision to leave and tried to play the incident down but Johanna would hear none of it. She hammered her point home several times a day and made the most of her role as a martyr.

Just as the atmosphere seemed to have reached its worst - and not two weeks after Ludwig had left - his brother Bernhard accepted a position he had been offered in the expanding construction company owned by the father of one of his former school friends outside Berlin. Additionally, he had been told, there was an offer for

Oskar to join the workforce. Bernhard's friends wanted to hire only people who they already knew, who they could trust to help keeping the business crisis proof and keep its uncontested reputation for quality and efficiency. Even before the offer, Oskar had always been optimistic that he could find lucrative employment back in Berlin, but the thought of being able to go home and work with one of his sons was just too tempting. Ludwig had already written to them during his first week in Berlin saying that he had found an apartment that was, incidentally, big enough for the entire family.

Johanna and Benedikt were speechless when they heard about these upcoming desertions as they were calling the announced departures. Oskar offered to stay and work for as long as it would take to find a replacement, but Benedikt was far too proud to accept 'charity' from such selfish and unchristian people like the Winkelmeiers were turning out to be. He wanted them all off the farm as soon as they could pack their belongings. After a fruitless attempt to make him see their reasoning, they left only a couple of hours later. Benedikt in his rage was visibly on the verge of using force to get them out of his property. Elizabeth had just enough time to write a short goodbye letter to her son Wilhelm and to kiss her grandson Karl goodbye.

Wilhelm was shocked when he came back from the bookshop and found that his family had gone. Benedikt and Johanna were not speaking to him that evening either, almost as if it were his fault; he was guilty by association. Greta explained to her husband what had happened and gave him the letter from his mother, which was uncharacteristically abrupt and bore no sentiment or regret. His mother must have been too excited about the prospect of going back to Berlin to think about her son and the situation in which she was leaving him. Wilhelm felt betrayed and it was his own anger that secured his existence on the farm. When Johanna finally spoke to him later that night to provoke some guilt in him, she was pleasantly surprised at his disapproval of their actions. She had always had a soft spot for this handsome young man but his current attitude brought him even closer to her heart. Wilhelm spoke disloyally of his own parents and shared Benedikt and Johanna's point of view that this departure resembled a very selfish abandonment of their benefactors. Of course he could stay, even with his secretly Jewish wife.

Johanna's feelings about the loss were actually more ambiguous than she let on. Elizabeth had been a great help in the house and, as such, would be missed but she had also always been the better cook, the better housewife and a better mother than Johanna ever was. Now the mighty Saint Elizabeth had fallen and in comparison Johanna could glow as the ever reliable and ever present woman on the farm and she loved Wilhelm for seeing it this way and saying so frequently.

Benedikt was very disgruntled by the sudden departures. He had banked on the possibility that Ludwig or Bernhard was going to stay at the farm and take over the business in later years. Ludwig especially was a good lad and would have made an outstanding farmer. He had a natural talent for planning and foresight, had known how to prioritise and had never once forgotten the daily routine tasks in the heat of other more pressing projects. That this capable young lad should be the first to jump ship was particularly painful.

Benedikt had at first tried to bully the aspiring pilot into staying and had threatened that should things not work out in Berlin he would no longer be welcome back on the farm; a threat the old man had considered rather grave so soon after the big economic crisis in Germany. Yet the effect of his speech had been disappointing and Ludwig left regardless.

When Bernhard mentioned his own plans of moving, Benedikt had had enough. Everyone knew how he felt about Ludwig leaving but that did not seem to matter to the Berlin strand of the Winkelmeier family; these town folk from the German metropolis. They seemed to have their heads and noses too high up to think of anyone but themselves, to feel grateful to their benefactors or to consider their relatives as equals. He suspected that this was also the reason why none of the boys had taken to his lovely daughters, a fact that had always been beyond him, especially as they would come with a great dowry.

Apparently, the otherwise so reliable Ludwig, had a lot of fancy ideas in his head about flying and seeing the world, and Bernhard missed Berlin and what he called real city life. What a bunch of weaklings.

"The younger generation is nothing like they were in our days." he lamented.

"At least there are fewer mouths to feed now," Johanna

consoled him. "And at least one of the Winkelmeier family has shown staying power. Wilhelm has no intention of leaving. In fact, he told me that he is quite cross with them."

"Be that as it may, he has got to go too," Benedict said. "He is no use to us on the farm. The little he brings in from the bookshop is not worth our trouble. That should teach the family a lesson on how you treat the hand that feeds you."

"Oh Benedikt, don't take your anger out on the boy. He is a young father. It is not his fault what his family has done. We are still relatives of his," Johanna insisted.

"He is only staying because his wife is a bloody Jew," Benedikt barked at her. "If she wasn't, don't you think they would have been on the very same train up north?"

"No, I think he would still have stayed here," she replied confidently. "He likes it here and he appreciates what you have done for him. If you don't want to let him stay for his own sake, then please let him stay for mine. Greta would be very useful to have as a help now that Elizabeth has left."

"I suppose you are right, there is not much harm in letting them stay. You just make sure that she pulls her weight and make it clear that they were very lucky we did not throw them out after what their family did to us."

"Don't you worry, I certainly will," she promised.

From the day of her arrival at the farm Greta had quickly got used to the hard work in the kitchen and on the fields. Once they had recognised her willingness and endurance, Benedikt and Johanna had started to become a bit friendlier towards her and later on to her son Karl. But it was only since her conversion to Catholicism that the Winkelmeiers had really taken to Greta and had started to treat her with genuine respect. They were also pleased with her moderate and obedient nature that never strained any one's patience. If encouraged, Greta could talk but she was mostly quiet and spoke usually only when spoken to, respectfully accepting her low place in the family hierarchy.

Since the departure of Elizabeth to Berlin, Johanna did not have to encourage Greta to work harder; the young mother felt the urge to prove her commitment and more importantly, lend her support to the farm quite naturally and made every conceivable effort to help wherever she could. Johanna had expected nothing less and started to invite Greta more frequently to accompany her to the markets in Bratislava. These outings were mainly functional to Johanna and showed more trust in Greta's abilities than personal favouritism as such but they still represented a step forward in their relationship. The two women never took the opportunity to go and see Greta's family because time was always scarce. Greta knew her companion well enough to not tempt fate by suggesting a detour to the workshop on Gajova and Johanna noticed and appreciated her restraint on that account.

On one of the colder evenings that autumn she finally allowed the young mother and child to join the rest of the Winkelmeier family in the big living room where, on such occasions, a big fire would be lit. This was a massive gesture. When Karl had been born, Johanna had argued that it would be too hot in there for the little boy and the room would be too crowded. All that time she had made the young family stay in their own room where there was no fire. When in a really generous mood she had sometimes offered them to stay in the kitchen where there still might be some heat left from the cooking. Through her hard work and her humble and quiet attitude, Greta had proven herself worthy to be included and to fill the gap that the recent departures had created. The old concerns about heat and space were no longer an issue and Johanna started to spoil her little Karl. The boy had grown quickly and now looked the spitting image of the handsome Wilhelm, a prime specimen of the adorable Winkelmeiers.

Johanna's own family had brought her up in a very strict way and her mother, in particular, had never failed to point out any mistakes the young Johanna made, resulting in the poor girl feeling very inferior and having little self-worth, a feeling that remained into her later life; she was never even aware of how attractive she was until Benedikt came along and courted her.

Whenever a boy had shown interest in her daughter before, she had laughed it off as a fluke or a prank. That was until she herself almost fell in love with the dashing Benedikt. She could not believe that her daughter could end up with such a strong and masculine handsome suitor. She was full of praise for Benedikt and in no uncertain terms told Johanna that she would be lucky if she could keep such a fine man. When Benedikt asked for Johanna's hand in marriage the young girl was overwhelmed and happy.

His choosing her instantly repaired some of her self-esteem issues. Instead of feeling inferior, she swayed to the other extreme, looking down on other men and women who, in her view, could not live up to the high physical standards of her husband and herself but there was something about Wilhelm that she adored completely. It had taken her a while to see through his quiet exterior and see his potential, but now she was a sworn admirer. He may not be as strong as her Benedikt but he was masculine in many other ways; a quiet authority, a leader and he was also the most attractive of all the boys. He would be the one to carry on the good looks of the Winkelmeier men.

Even his brothers looked passable compared to Gunther, her own son. If she was completely honest with herself, Johanna much preferred Wilhelm and she would even rather had Ludwig or Bernhard for a son in place of Gunter, the soft weakling with the crooked nose. Her daughters all had inherited Johanna's own pretty looks, but Gunter was not much to look at all. He had ended up with the features of Johanna's old father, whose most valued quality had been the possession of huge amounts of land - the only reason why Johanna's mother had been attracted to him at all. Later in life, after years of having to make do, this had pushed her to find satisfaction for her physical needs elsewhere. The resulting scandals were yet another reason for Johanna to distance herself from her own family and desperately wanting to feel as one of the Winkelmeiers.

Johanna gradually gave the young couple more freedom and treated them with the most attention. Despite Greta's questionable roots, these two were the couple of the future. Nothing they did was ever wrong in her eyes. Wilhelm lacked strength but in that serious face, Johanna could read an intellectual superiority and leadership skills just like those of her husband Benedikt. Once her infatuation had been established, regardless of evidence to the contrary, she projected more superior qualities onto his character.

However, Johanna did not approve of the frequent visits from members of the Weissensteiner family to the farm. They might be polite and nice enough as visitors, but they were dark, gypsy looking and much more obvious as Jews than Greta, who could have passed for a gentile woman at any time. The Weissensteiners had responded to Greta's less frequent visits to the weaver workshop in town by coming to the farm themselves, even though that meant they had to travel on a Saturday. Before the Berlin members of the family had left, it had been custom that whenever the Weissensteiners came to visit the guests would be well fed and, additionally, Elizabeth had always given them some food to take back home to the city. Greta had always appreciated this generosity and had seen it as a gesture of respect towards her. She had just got pregnant again and her family was so excited and pleased with the news that they seemed to visit almost every weekend now – very much to Johanna's annoyance.

Benedikt also worried that their reputation and standing in the community might suffer from a noticeable association with these Jews. Johanna was secretly more concerned that Greta's family would somehow lay claim to Karl and that she would have to share him with his mother's family. It was obvious that he belonged to the Winkelmeiers, blond and Aryan that he was. While she had previously always tolerated the Weissensteiners being welcomed warmly by Elizabeth and the big fuss the relatives had made when the Jews came, Johanna as the new hostess never offered them food or drinks when they arrived. Instead she emphasized loudly how busy she was and made sure that Greta had very little time to spend with her family. There were less people on the farm now with much more work for everyone and surely that had to be understood and respected. Greta's brother Egon seemed to take the hint immediately, coming less frequently to the farm; when he did come, he was naturally quiet during the visits, seemingly preferred to be left alone and somehow could never wait to go back home.

Her sister Wilma however noticed the wind of change in their reception and took great offence. Unwilling to be shunned like that, she would deliberately challenge Johanna by asking for drinks or food every time they came to visit, forcing the skinflint of a woman to cook up ever more outlandish excuses to deny these requests. Wilma enjoyed this game of childish revenge but did not realize how much damage she was doing to the fragile family relations. It was exactly this pushiness and noisiness that annoyed Johanna most and, she believed, was the main reason that so many people hated the Jews. What a shame that her handsome Wilhelm had not at least been able to find a rich Jewish woman – if his wife had to be one of those; a banker's or a lawyer's daughter would have been much more acceptable. The wealthy and established Jews in the west were usually so assimilated or westernised that only their physique could identify them as Jews. While Greta herself was very decent and not at all obvious, Greta's sister Wilma was – bar the black clothing - the stereotype of a poor eastern Jew, that even their own, rich kind did not want to be associated with. Admittedly, the Winkelmeiers were not particularly wealthy or posh but they certainly were far above such outrageous behaviour and poor standing.

The conversion of the entire Winkelmeier family to Catholicism had worked wonders for them and over the last year, the Slovak locals had become friendlier towards them, probably thanks to Father Bernhard Haslinger's encouraging word of mouth. This was still a new and fragile development and in Johanna's view, it had to be consolidated at any cost. The last thing they needed now was questions being asked about the young pregnant mother's Jewish visitors from town.

After the Great War, a lot of Jews from Galicia had been expelled by the Russian army and after unsuccessfully trying to establish themselves in Vienna many had opted for the Jew-friendly haven of Bratislava as their new residence. The local Slovak culture was already too 'unruly' for Johanna's Germanic taste, there was no need for any more of that kind and certainly not on her farm.

As for the brother Egon, on the few occasions when he did open his mouth, his whining, negative and always complaining attitude was another thing that she disliked of `the type`, as she loved to call the Jews. He was working with the father in the weaver's workshop in town and like the father was always busy. If any of them had to stay behind to supervise the workers, he would usually volunteer, probably too lazy to come all the way out to the farm.

Greta's father Jonah however, was a man to Johanna's liking. Completely untraditional and very aware of his low position as Jew in the Czechoslovakian society, he was mostly kind and humble and therefore very agreeable. He himself had suggested limiting the contact between Greta and her family as she was a Winkelmeier now, a 'Catholic' and a German. The less she was associated with her Jewish family the easier it would be to protect her. With the announcement of Greta's second pregnancy however he seemed, at least temporarily, to have forgotten his previous conviction but at least he knew that it was necessary to be careful in case the politics in Slovakia should develop in a similar way as in Germany. Especially now that there were less people living on the farm, any visitors would be more noticeable. A sensible man this Weissensteiner - if not somewhat pessimistic. Quite handsome for the type she had to admit. His wife Barbara had died of the Spanish flu after the Great War and he had never remarried, which was difficult to understand. If she would recommend any Jew, it would be him. Almost as respectable and proper as a German, if you could say such a thing but maybe that was why the women amongst his own people were not after him in the first place.

One Saturday when the Weissensteiners had come again and seemed to be set on staying the whole afternoon, Johanna had had enough and took Jonah aside.

"Jonah, your lot have got to stop coming here all the time," she said. "You know it is dangerous."

Jonah was a little surprised at her directness but immediately agreed with her.

"You are right. I should not have got carried away with the whole pregnancy spiel."

"I understand how you feel Jonah and I hate to take that away from you but if you had not mentioned yourself that the visits were too frequent, I wouldn't have known what to say to you but you know how it is these days. We can't risk any gossip about the family," she explained.

"Of course," he agreed. "Thank you Johanna. Say no more. We will be leaving shortly and I will make sure that we stay away for a while. After all, there is not much we can do for her while she is pregnant. Only fussing and that won't help you get the farm work done. I am sorry we were so thoughtless and thank you for reminding me of my fatherly duties."

As much as he realised that Johanna's concern was mainly for herself, he knew all the same that she was right. It would be hard for him not to see his daughter but she was a married woman now.

Johanna was relieved how easy it had been to see them out of the door. None of the arguing and pleading she had expected and feared of his type, no haggling and no discussion.

Greta was not aware of Johanna's resentments. Now that things between the two of them had finally improved she saw everything a little too optimistically to have a proper grasp on reality. To her, Johanna had always been a bit odd and difficult but completely harmless as long as you just let her be. Since Elizabeth had gone, they were almost becoming friends and it would have been completely inconceivable to the pregnant girl to think that the mistress of the farm had asked the Weissensteiners not to visit.

In the following weeks during which Jonah and Wilma stayed away, Greta missed her family but she regarded herself lucky to have found a home with the Winkelmeiers where she could blend in and bring up little Karl with so much assistance. She knew it was a great blessing that Wilhelm had not abandoned her when she fell pregnant out of wedlock. It would have been his fault, he had said he would take care of 'everything' (obviously not very successfully) but many other young men in those days would have denied their responsibility afterwards and not taken the firm and positive action in the way that Wilhelm had. She had married a good man with a great family which was going to grow again thanks to her. Johanna was so fond of little Karl and she had great expectations for the next child. It was no wonder she was fussing about the pregnant Greta and her little boy in the way she did. Secretly, Greta had always hoped that one day her sister Wilma might come and live with them on the farm; that would make her life just perfect. Several times, she had mentioned this idea to Johanna and Benedikt but got little response.

Wilma was currently running the Weissensteiner household but too often got things wrong to be called a good choice for the job, especially since Greta had left. She was a hard worker but not very organised and always in need of careful supervision and encouragement. Her involvement in the weaving business had turned into a disaster and had come to an abrupt end. Without someone checking up on her there had been too many mistakes, not necessarily big ones, but enough to bring the quality of their carpets into disrepute.

In her housekeeping similar flaws frequently showed up. She would start chatting and forget that the soup was boiling over, that she had left the front door open and when she went shopping for dinner, she often returned with only half of the ingredients. One thing or another was always happening to her which made her hard to employ anywhere, particularly when there were so many people looking for jobs.

Greta believed that if Wilma was working on the farm, that problem could be solved because she could work closely with her sister or under someone else's guidance and supervision.

With her pregnancy, Greta thought it was worth giving the issue one more try but Johanna would hear none of it and said they could not afford to take on someone with such a lack of concentration. Greta was upset about her little scheme failing.

Greta's new friendship with Johanna lacked a certain intimacy that she was used to from her own home and left her feeling empty. Maria and Roswitha had failed to transfer their warm feelings for Elizabeth on to her. The girls displayed a deep mistrust of other women and never opened up to her in the same way that Wilma did. Her husband Wilhelm was so busy at work that he often spent his entire evenings reading instead of playing with Karl or talking to her but she knew that reading was his passion. When Johanna criticised him for it Greta always defended him, saying that if he didn't read as much, he would not be able to sell books and make a good living. Deep down however, she was very lonely.

Wilma was upset about the separation from her sister, too. She loved Greta more than anyone in the world and being apart from her was very difficult to bear. She could see the reason for it but it was painful. All her childhood she had relied on Greta to support her. Greta had been the clever one in school, had helped her with her homework, had explained whatever Wilma did not understand and had made complicated things sound easy. Greta had been her extended brain and in return, Wilma being the stronger one, had always taken on the more physical tasks and in fights with other girls, Wilma had always defended the two of them - even though she was younger. The two sisters were as close as twins. Wilma could never wait for the next Saturday to come so she and her father would go and see Greta and Karl on the farm. On some Saturdays the workshop was too busy for them to get away but just the possibility of a trip to the farm was exciting enough to keep Wilma full of energy and optimism. All this was gone from her life now and the days were grey and monotonous.

Greta worked very hard on the farm despite her pregnancy. Benedikt had taken on some immigrant workers for the harvest but he frequently kept firing them because he either did not trust them or thought they were not industrious enough. At peak times, everyone on the farm could feel the strain of how short staffed they were and consequently, depending on the weather conditions, how difficult it was to get things done. Some tasks could only be performed if there had been enough sunshine and then the entire workforce may have to hurry if rain was on its way.

On one of those mad days when everyone was rushing to get the hay inside before an expected burst of rain, Greta lost her baby. It was Johanna's daughter Roswitha who detected blood running from Greta's legs and screamed; the pregnant woman had not even noticed herself that something was wrong. Concerned that he would lose all of the hay harvest, Benedikt made them finish the job before he put Greta and Roswitha on a cart and sent them off to the doctor. Everyone but him was upset about the incident and the atmosphere on the farm turned dark and depressive. Benedikt said coldly that these things happened and if the whole world stopped to grieve about a lost foetus then nothing would ever get done. Dying was just another thing in life. The baby would never have lived and to risk the harvest for that seemed a little extreme.

No one dared to contradict him but even the normally harsh and cold hearted Johanna disagreed with him and his actions. She thought he had unnecessarily risked Greta's life by delaying her trip to the doctor.

Johanna used this unique opportunity to stop finally all family visits from the Weissensteiners. She took it upon herself to walk personally into town and meet with Jonah, explaining how Greta had recovered well and just needed complete and total rest right now; how she appreciated how desperately they would want to see their darling Greta but with one working pair of hands down, the farm was now simply not in any position to socialise or receive guests. Besides, it already had been agreed that there should be as few visits to the farm as possible and the reasons for that should not be forgotten. Jonah knew better than to argue with the farmer's wife. For all his worries, he was sure that Greta was well looked after. Wilma offered to come and stay so she could look after her sister and help with the cooking, but Johanna said she would prefer to keep things as they were. The Weissensteiners surely must be very busy with their workshop too and needed her themselves.

Following the miscarriage Greta fell into a deep depression. She was allowed to lie down and physically recover for a week, but lying in bed and having the whole day to think about the loss of her baby just made things worse. Johanna had ordered Roswitha to look after Karl and restricted the contact between the boy and his mother drastically. Roswitha was great with the child but was kept under close inspection by her mother. Greta missed her little boy and tried to persuade Johanna to let her play with him more, but Johanna insisted that the poor boy would only be traumatized if he could see his mother so upset. It was an obvious excuse to spend more time with the golden boy herself and she deliberately neglected the care for Greta in the hope that this would prolong the mother's incapacity and foster Johanna's own relationship with little Karl.

The farm was missing three women doing work and Benedikt had to bite the bullet and hire more external seasonal workers. In the absence of a better alternative, he employed Jewish peasants from the east who were stuck in Bratislava, where even the large Jewish community could not help all of them to find jobs. Benedikt was very concerned about their work ethic and worried he might waste too much of his own productive farming time by having to control and supervise these 'shlemiels', but against his expectations the workers proved very experienced and efficient. They had to be desperate for more work in the future if they could overcome their lazy nature, he thought, but he still did not trust them enough to leave them to their work without breathing down their necks.

As things seemed to be working out, Benedikt did not put immediate pressure on Johanna to bring Greta or Roswitha back to do the farm work. Little Karl became the light of Johanna's life. Even on days when Greta felt physically strong, Johanna made her stay away from her own son until she had mentally recovered and was less miserable. The poor and isolated mother was too weak to successfully protest against the arguments and after hearing again and again how incapable she was to attend to her own son's needs, she started to believe that she was too fragile and even agreed with the separation. Without contact to the people closest to her, it took her much longer to return to her feet, exactly as Johanna had planned.

Wilhelm buried his grief about the miscarriage in a sudden burst of religious practice. He started to go to morning mass in Bratislava every day and left the house in the hours of darkness. When he came home he hardly spoke to anyone and just fell into bed. With both of his parents being unavailable, Johanna became the main adult figure in Karl's life and because her infatuation with him was so strong, he soon learned how to manipulate her to get his way.

Johanna's happiest moments were when she had succeeded in making him smile or laugh and he carefully used this tool to his advantage.

Greta found the situation increasingly difficult to bear. Her sadness and isolation drove her into a downward spiral and when she finally built up the courage to confide her feelings to Wilhelm, he was cold and unwilling to deal with her misery as well as his own. To get her out of his way, he suggested that she should go and stay at her father's place until she had recovered mentally. That should cure her isolation.

Johanna loved this idea and immediately suggested it to Benedikt who was happy to go along with it and ordered her to go and join her family in Bratislava. He felt that all the crying over spilt milk could become disruptive to his life and might demand too much of his attention which he exclusively had reserved for the running of the farm.

During his supervision of the new labourers, in two of the Jews he had recognised surprising talent and commitment to the farm. He now felt comfortable enough to entrust them with supervising the others. This had worked out very well and he calculated that it was worth the expense of giving them the little he had to pay them instead of returning the tasks to the cheaper yet more inefficient family members.

He chose Maria to work with them, knowing that her quiet and hardworking nature would be enough to keep them on their guard. The men were married and too desperate for work to get fresh with his daughter, but he often also showed up unannounced to impress on them that he was still watching them. Maria was pleased that she was permitted to keep working outdoors. She had expected and feared to be put back into the kitchen under the scolding hand of her mother. Since Elizabeth had left, the atmosphere in the house had lost its warmth and cosiness. The evenings were much quieter and the only thing that seemed to matter to her mother was the well-being of little Karl.

It was Roswitha who had to work in the kitchen now and do the housework more or less by herself, but she seemed to enjoy it. She had learned many tricks from Elizabeth and her efforts were now usually praised or at least not criticised any more, which already helped her with her feelings of self-worth. She drew a lot of

51

satisfaction from this and against character, Johanna made sure to show her appreciation - even though that was purely part of her plot to keep the daughters busy so that Johanna would have more time with Karl.

Her obsession with the baby upset her own children. They could not believe that the cold woman who brought them up without love could turn into such a caring mother figure and even neglect her own farm duties to spoil the little child. Benedikt was too much of a farmer to notice any of these things. He was certainly not a house-proud man who did not notice anything apart from the size of his nightly food portions. Housekeeping was for women and he did not waste his time keeping an eye on it. If Johanna said that things were under control, he was happy to believe it and any distraction, like the sick Greta, needed to be dealt with as painlessly and quickly as possible.

When Greta was finally considered strong enough to make the journey into Bratislava, she was allowed to say a brief goodbye to her son whom Johanna firmly held on her arm for the whole time. Karl was already so used to his 'new mother' that on the morning she was supposed to leave he seemed to take little notice of Greta. She felt a painful stab in her heart seeing him so happy on someone else's arm - as if he did not need her at all. She knew it was the best for her son, but it brought on another wave of grief, hurting as if she had lost now both children in such a short period of time. She managed to keep a straight face in front of Karl but when she was outside the house she could not control her tears. Wilhelm, who accompanied her to Bratislava on his way to work, did not console her. He handed her a handkerchief but said they would have to leave right away. They had a long journey ahead of them and, in her state, she was likely to slow him down. He carried the suitcase for her until near her father's workshop where their paths separated. Neither of them said anything for the entire journey and their half-hearted goodbyes were swallowed by the wind.

Wilma already stood on the street outside the workshop waiting for her sister when Greta turned into the dead-end road. She rushed towards her, took the suitcase, grabbed Greta by the arm and hurried her through the door. They fell into each other's arms and both simultaneously burst into uncontrollable fits of crying. The two had missed each other and the relief that surged through them was overwhelming. With Wilma by her side, Greta knew that she would learn to live with the loss of her unborn baby and would be happy again. She was sad that her own husband had not been able to support her at all in this dilemma but she appreciated that he had his own demons to fight over the tragedy. They had been very close and a real couple when they first started dating but now it felt as if they had drifted far apart. She blamed the hollow organising and the sober running of their life. The joint experience of their loss, which they dealt with so separately, showed how disjointed they had become in such a short time. With Greta back in her life, Wilma knew that nothing bad could ever happen to her either. While in many ways she had a strong bond with her father, the relationship with him was not a close one. Jonah was a cheerful man for a widower but it was obvious that the loss of his wife had taken its toll on his psyche. He lived more for his own company and his role as the family provider rather than for the pure joy of life.

In his younger years he had been as enthusiastic for life as Greta had always been but since his wife's death, Jonah had turned into an old version of his lifeless and ever so introverted son Egon. Jonah was asking the right questions and took an active interest in the life of his children, but he seemed not to be taking it in, and appeared mentally not really to be present when he spoke to them. It left his children feeling distant and disconnected. Wilma was also living in her own little world and usually too busy with whatever she was doing to take a look at the big picture. She did not have the skills necessary to reach out to him and bridge the gap between them. Greta was the only one who could sometimes bring him out of his shell and back into the family life. With her back in the house, the Weissensteiners had the opportunity to become a close unit again.

The task ahead of healing her hurt almost gave Jonah a new lease of life. He hated to admit it but of his three children, he favoured Greta more than he should; Egon was a good natured boy but very secretive and closed. The connection with Wilma was weak because she was an odd character that not many people could understand and sadly he was not one of those few. She was the middle child and had always hidden behind the bigger sister, a scatter brain who could not concentrate long enough to hear a story till the end and who could certainly not remember much of it an hour later, the impulsive breaker of things, the harsh and rude girl that upset people easily without even meaning to do so, and a young woman who did not really hold for any kind of tradition – it was hard for her father to form a close bond with her. She wore her heart on her sleeve and spoke before thinking things through. Too often she saw everything in black and white and could only see the surface of things. She was willing and eager to help but when she did, she did things so hurriedly and so carelessly, often making more of a mess than being a help. In comparison, Greta was so wise and he had to admit to himself that he did prefer her company to that of his other children.

Greta stayed for a few weeks during which she would sit reading by the upstairs kitchen window. Jonah and the Countess had gone to Wilhelm's bookshop and bought two brand new books for Greta, embarrassing her husband who had not thought of it himself. When asked he could not for the life of him think of which books to recommend for his grief stricken wife. He doubted that the romantic and passionate literature that she usually preferred was a good pastime in her current state.

Jonah settled for a collection of fairy tales and the Countess chose a collection of works by Eichendorff, who according to Greta, could always be relied upon for a very cheerful tone and a splendidly happy ending. Wilhelm was awfully quiet and uncomfortable. The Countess was appalled by the husband's lack of care and interest and threw him scolding looks. Her aristocratic authority intimidated the poor sales assistant and left him lost for words. Jonah had to make most of the conversation by himself, telling his son-in-law how sad Greta still was and how she missed her son. Jonah found it hard to hide his growing resentment to Wilhelm's self-indulgent grief and the neglectful behaviour towards Greta. That man had turned into a young spoilt child and hardly resembled the serious and mature man that had married his daughter. It was a sad development and Jonah could only hope that this phase would end soon and that once the couple was reunited they would work things out. After all, the doctors were hopeful that Greta should be able to have plenty more children. It was disappointing to lose a child but it had not even been born yet, not opened his eyes or said its first words. How could a young couple, with so much life and prospects ahead of them, be taken down by one minor setback like this? In his opinion, the young lovers should be together and comfort each other, like he would have done with his late Barbara. Maybe that was the price Greta had to pay for having a serious thinker as a husband prone to melancholy and depression?

Jonah would do anything in his power to bring her back to full blossom. When she was not reading, he made her sit down by his side in the workshop and they would sing a mixture of their favourite folk songs from the shtetl, cheerful tunes and some gruesome ballads as well.

Greta soon started to help with the big wall carpet for the Countess, feeling too restless to watch everyone else working hard without putting her hands to work as well. Additionally, every so often, Jonah would take his sad daughter to one side, hug her and assure her that all would turn out just fine. "Und es ward alles alles gut!" he would quote in German which was from the end of one of her favourite Eichendorff novels.

Had it not been for missing her little Karl, Greta could have stayed with her father for much longer. After three years with the Winkelmeiers she had forgotten how close a family could be. It was a real treat and did wonders for her but in the end the thought of her little one becoming alienated from his mother was too much of a burden. Johanna had asked her to stay away until she was feeling better and could give her son her full and cheerful attention. Greta thought she was ready for that now and one evening simply showed up at the bookshop with her suitcase so that she could walk home with her husband. However, when she got to the bookshop Wilhelm was not to be found.

"Excuse me," she said, addressing the grey haired man who appeared to be in the shop all by himself. "I am looking for my husband Wilhelm Winkelmeier. Could you please tell me where I could find him?"

"Oh you are Wilhelm's wife? How very nice to meet you. My name is Andrej, I am new here. So sorry to hear about what happened but God works in mysterious ways, you know. We just need to believe in Him and trust his gracious will."

Greta really wanted to spit in his face for springing his religion on her but somehow managed to control her anger.

"Thank you very much, Andrej, for your kindness," she replied. "Wilhelm has never told me about you. How long have you been working here?"

"About two months. Tuesday and Thursday evenings only when they leave me all alone here when they go to their meetings," he said.

Greta felt utterly stupid and humiliated by the fact that all this time Wilhelm was attending some clandestine meetings and she had no idea about it, let alone what kind of meetings they were. She had already embarrassed herself by not knowing about them in front of this new co-worker of her husband, it was too much to admit to her ignorance about the meetings as well, so she decided to pretend she did know.

"Oh yes, of course. How silly of me. The meetings. Could you tell me where the meeting is today, so I can surprise my husband and join him on his way home?" she asked.

"Of course. It is right next to the offices of the Grenzbote by the main station, the meeting hall of the German Sudeten Party," answered Andrej shyly. "I can take you if you don't know the way but I don't think you can go in there tonight, it is a members only meeting. The guards can tell your husband that you are waiting."

"Thank you so much, Andrej. I know where it is. I'm sorry to have troubled you."

"Any time Frau Winkelmeier. We rarely get to see such beautiful women in the shop."

Instead of waiting outside the party headquarters alone at night, Greta decided to go back to her father. How could Wilhelm never have told her about his membership at the German Sudeten Party? He had never taken any particular political views; he was too busy reading books. Admittedly he had always been interested in philosophy and finding the right way to live but why would he not have told her that he was turning this into an active political role? He had claimed to work late and to be busy at the shop, but he had lied to her and there had to be a reason for this secrecy. She was not going to confront him in front of his party members and when she arrived back at the workshop she just said that she had missed Wilhelm and was going to leave tomorrow on her own instead. Everyone who knew Wilhelm's committed work ethics had to be surprised at this statement and Jonah and Wilma certainly raised an eyebrow but they were happy to have one more evening with their beloved Greta and did not question her any further.

The next morning Greta walked back to the farm on her own and found nobody in the house but Roswitha, who was preparing lunch.

"Oh hello Greta. I did not know you were coming back today. Are you feeling better?" she asked while stirring the contents of one of the pots.

"Thanks Roswitha," she replied. "Yes I do feel much better. Where is Karl? Is he asleep?" she asked.

"Johanna has taken him to the lake to feed the birds."

"On a weekday?"

"Yes, I know it is strange, but she is completely besotted with the boy and she promised to take him out to see the birds if he manages to go potty by himself. He did it three days in a row and the silly woman thinks he is specially gifted. The boy is almost three," Roswitha said with rolling eyes.

Greta felt a surge of jealousy when she heard that she had missed such a stepping stone in the development of her child and she started to realise the extent to which Johanna had taken over the role of mother. She was close to tears but she could not afford to let them show. If Roswitha told anyone about her crying she would be banished from the farm again and from seeing her son and she couldn't let that happen.

When Johanna and Karl came home a few hours later Karl was too exhausted from the walk to take proper notice of Greta and Johanna took him to his bed for a nap.

"You don't have to worry about him," she assured the worried mother. "He is having a great time with his auntie Johanna. There is no need for you to rush back and make a big drama. It is better if you take your time and gather your strength. Losing a child is the ultimate ordeal a mother can go through and it must have taken its toll. I know Benedikt pushes everyone to go back to normal as soon as they can but I think it is wrong. Karl must never see you down like the way you were. Are you quite sure that you are ready to take him on again? He is quite a stubborn little prince. I am glad I had three children of my own to deal with his little schemes."

"I am fine, Johanna. I miss him. I need him back and he needs me," Greta said less confidently than she would have liked.

"I know that is what every mother thinks but it is not true," Johanna contradicted. "A child does not necessarily need his mother but someone who acts like a mother and knows what she is doing. You may need him but that may not be a good thing for him. He comes first," she said with dramatic emphasis and paused before adding, "... and then you. This is how we Winkelmeiers handle child rearing.

"That is a lie!" Greta almost screamed at her. "You brought up your children in exactly the opposite way. Your children are last by a long way in the pecking order and they always have been."

"They needed to be and they still are," said Johanna not in the least impressed by the emotional outburst. "If it was their life or mine to save I would always chose theirs. That is what I am talking about. You are no help to your son if you can't pull yourself together and put his feelings first. You are not thinking about his best but about your own best."

"Don't worry about that. I am fine now," Greta replied with as much strength as she could muster.

"We will see. Just don't let yourself go again, do you understand?"

Close to tears but determined not to let Johanna break her spirit she said. "Yes, I understand. So what needs to be done?"

Greta spent the rest of the afternoon in the cow shed.

"If you are as recovered as you say then that should not be a problem." Johanna had said triumphantly after lunch. "When Karl is up, I will tell him that his mother is going to bring him to bed tonight."

However, when the evening came Karl was not ready for his bed at all. Johanna had let him sleep far too long for his afternoon nap and he was cranky and wound up. Greta wondered if that had been deliberate to show her up as the bad mother Johanna wanted her to be. After several attempts to get him changed in to his night-gown had failed, Greta stood embarrassed in front of her smug audience and had to admit defeat.

"Maybe we can let you stay up until your Daddy comes home if you stop screaming and if you agree to put on your night-dress," Johanna negotiated, obviously knowing what offers did the trick because within a minute little Karl was changed and quiet.

"You'll learn eventually. Believe me, when you have the next child it will be much easier," Johanna said patronisingly. "If you are going to have another one."

Greta ignored the sting of that last remark and said. "The Doctor said I should be fine. We might have a whole bunch, lots of beautiful young boys I reckon."

"Of course that is what he said, the way you were screaming the place down he would have said anything to shut you up," Johanna said with a grin.

Shocked by the sudden nastiness in the person she had only recently started to think of as a friend, Greta was unable to reply and started to work on the dishes.

About an hour later Wilhelm finally came home.

"There you are my darling," he said. "I heard you were looking for me at the bookshop yesterday. Why did you not come and see me at the meeting?" he asked. "I was worried about you when I heard this morning. For all I knew you could have been attacked on the street."

"I went back to my father for the night," she replied. "It did not seem safe to be out in the streets on my own."

"You would have been fine," he said. "We have a lot of security guards at the meeting hall. It is the safest place in all of Slovakia."

"When did you become involved in the party?" Greta asked.

"How could you not know?" asked Johanna with a grin and poorly faked surprise in her voice. "He told me about it months ago. Do you not listen when your husband talks to you?"

"Wilhelm, when did you join?" Greta repeated her question when they were alone.

"Three months ago. I didn't have a choice really. One day Kling and Mohr, the owners of the shop, both grilled me about my political views, about a Pan German state and about the legitimacy of the Czechoslovak state. They can be very intimidating. So I stated my main concern as a German was the safety of us Germans here in Slovakia. Once I had said that, they led me with more and more questions into a corner where I had no way out but to ask to be accepted for membership at the Party. It was like in one of those dialogues of Plato. They kept asking leading questions and before I knew it I was stuck with a lot of answers I would never have given in the first place. Now I am even part of the local committee."

"Why did you not tell me?" she asked.

"I was too embarrassed," he said shyly. "You know I don't

really have strong political convictions but now I have a party book that begs to differ. It certainly secured my position at the shop that is for sure."

"What would they think if they knew that I am a Jewess? What kind of Nationalists are they? Are they like Hitler and the NSDAP?" she asked concerned.

"Don't be silly, of course not," he reassured her. "We are Nationalists and you are not a Jew any more. Remember? You are a Catholic now."

"But the Germans don't care about the Jewish faith, they care about the Jewish race," she explained. "I can never erase that and you know it."

"I don't think they will ever find out," he said. "Now, please let me sit down and read for a little while."

Chapter 3: Bratislava 1938

Once she had recovered mentally from the loss of her unborn child, Greta regained her positive spirit and learned to consider herself lucky that the Winkelmeiers had always treated her like a full member of the family. Johanna may have successfully secured the role as the predominant mother figure in Karl's life but now that she had achieved this goal, she had stopped harassing Greta. The phase of sniping remarks and continuous criticism disappeared as quickly as it had arrived and the two women were back on relatively good terms with each other.

Greta of course would never be able to forget the nastiness Johanna had been capable of during that period and remained on her guard, yet the extra time she had gained from Johanna's extensive involvement in looking after Karl became a blessing for her marriage. She was once again able to read a little in the evenings and share her views about books with Wilhelm. She was no longer reading her romantic literature but now joined his serious 'quest for philosophical wisdom' and late at night they would talk about what they had read. The entire family sighed with relief when Greta announced after only a few months that she was pregnant again. Everyone – including Benedikt - went out of their way to make sure she was always rested and fed, and that no harm could come to little Karl's future sibling.

Greta now worked exclusively in the kitchen. Johanna even gave up her favourite seat in the living room in the evenings so Greta could sit as comfortably as possible and not develop problems with her veins. Johanna had heard from a woman on the market that this could be a problem for pregnant women who worked physically. Secretly, she still wondered if Greta's miscarriage a few years back had been caused by too much farm work and if she herself was partly to blame for the misfortune. At the time she had made herself agree with her husband that the accident was just a sign of God's will and that it had nothing to do with Greta's farm duties. Still, Johanna felt a little responsible for adding so much to the woman's workload in those days and, as if to compensate for her previous neglect, she now ordered her to rest, gave Greta the biggest portions of food at every meal and worked extra hard to ensure that the young woman would not feel a need to exhaust herself.

The inclusion of Austria into the German Reich was a foregone conclusion and rumours were already running wild about the Germans invading Czechoslovakia once they achieved that goal. Every day more Jewish people crossed the border into Czechoslovakia from the neighbouring countries and the stories they told about life in Germany and Austria were frightening. Greta spoke excellent German which had been perfected during her time at the German school in Bratislava; she could easily pass for a German woman. The synagogues no longer held lists of their congregation so that an invading Nazi army would not be able to use them to round up the local Jews.

Being on the farm amongst a German family, she knew it would take a while before she could ever be uncovered as a Jew - if at all. However, in the event of a German occupation, despite her conversion her prospects were grim. She had big concerns about her family who were living and working in the middle of town and who were much more in the public eye than her. Were they on any list? Did anyone know about them? Did they have enemies who would tell on them? Were they in danger already?

Greta did not get to spend much time in town anymore and saw little of her family. She offered to help Johanna with the shopping and the trips to the market, but Johanna had almost become obsessed with the health of the unborn baby and considered such a trip too much of a hazard.

Wilhelm however had a lot of contact with the German community through the book shop and his party membership, and he was painfully aware of the growing tensions in the population of Bratislava and the anti-Semitic politics. Publications on the Aryan and Jewish Race were becoming popular and the shop started to stock some of this propaganda material. Although he was involved in the party at a high level, he did not know that much about racial politics. Reading these leaflets, for the first time in his life Wilhelm heard about the inferiority of the Jewish genes, a 'scientific' explanation for Hitler's racial politics. The pamphlets also mentioned the existence of a 'degenerate' gene in all Jews and claimed that most diseases were carried and transmitted only by the Jews.

While his rational mind found it hard to believe these accusations at first, he gradually succumbed to accepting these stories as truth - after all they were so frequent and consistent. He could not believe that nobody ever had told him about this before. Did people not know or had they carelessly let him marry a Jewess without as much as a word of warning? Well, he must have been very lucky then that his blond and blue eyed son Karl had not been affected. Wilhelm started to worry whether his next child, which currently was growing in his wife's belly and which should be born at the end of the year, was going to be so lucky and escape the nasty genetic predisposition.

Of course Greta seemed entirely healthy and sane, he could not imagine that she had inferior genes, but one of the pamphlets he had read stated that such genes could in fact be carried by the Jewish mother without her showing any symptoms and might still come into effect in her future children, casting a huge shadow over the life of his yet to be born baby. Then there was the issue of Greta's sister Wilma that concerned him. She didn't have any of the soft and beautiful features that her sister had at all. Wilhelm assumed logically that this was a sign of the Jewish genetic disease showing in one sibling and not in the other, as the pamphlet had explained could happen. If the theory of genetics was true it would all make a lot of sense. Greta carried but did not show the signs of those wrong genes and fortunately had not passed them on to Karl, but she already had miscarried one child and her sister was very visibly affected in her inferior looks. Greta was such a beautiful feminine woman, whereas Wilma had more mannish and harsh features. No wonder she had never been courted. Over the course of the new pregnancy he became increasingly worried about the health and looks of the child in Greta's belly and hid himself away in the book and party work to avoid letting his increasingly distant and anxious feelings show.

Greta on the other hand enjoyed becoming a mother again. Of course she had wondered if she would ever have another child after she had lost the last one and now that she had become pregnant she was quite concerned about another miscarriage. Relations with Johanna however were improving rapidly which made life a lot easier.

Her hostess could not do enough for her and even Benedikt was feeling very generous these days, content with the way the farm was running. Forgotten were the times of scolding, anger and shouting. Living here had once again become a blessing for Greta and being able to concentrate on her pregnancy without any worries made her very happy. It was easy for her to put her worries about the political developments to the back of her mind and think positively.

Wilhelm did not share her optimistic views. He clearly saw the writing on the wall and felt that living in Slovakia and on the farm was becoming the opposite of a safe place for him and his family. He had followed the newspaper reports and party rumours about the German tactics with Austria very closely and he knew that it was only a matter of time – and probably not that much of it either – until Hitler crossed the borders into Austria and Czechoslovakia and would implement his racial laws. Although these ideas were not the official party line of the German Sudeten Party, he only had to listen to his fellow party members to know that they were open to such policies. His marriage would be annulled and his son Karl would be treated like any other dirty Jew; there probably would be nothing he could do for Greta or her family once the Germans were here. The longer he thought about it, the clearer it became to him that he would have to try and see if he could save little Karl, get him out of the country and into safety, wherever that may be.

Wilhelm would worry himself sick about the dangers that lay ahead of him and his family, but then nothing would happen again for weeks and he would calm down and feel silly to have got into such a state of panic.

Then the news reached him that the Austrian Chancellor had resigned on Hitler's request and that the Austrian army had not offered any resistance worth mentioning when the German troops marched across the border in April. According to eye witnesses, the population had greeted the soldiers with flowers and enthusiasm. In Vienna there had been immediate acts of violence towards Jews.

It wouldn't be much different over here, he suspected, so he had to make plans. The summer had been surprisingly uneventful politically. Konrad Henlein, the leader of the German Sudeten Party, was strongly supported by German diplomats and was increasingly able to make more and more blatant demands to the government. An Austrian plebiscite gave Hitler a clear mandate as the new master of the Ostmark, as he renamed Austria, and that gave the Sudetengermans further encouragement to voice their demands for autonomy or inclusion into the German Reich. Even in those parts of Slovakia where few Germans lived, the campaign was vocal.

In September, it was announced that European leaders would meet in Munich to come to an agreement with Hitler about the future of the German minority in the Czechoslovak Republic. Greta would have to make up her mind soon what she wanted to do, stay here with her family and take a chance with their lives or flee with him and little Karl and seek safety elsewhere.

For some time it had been well known how horrendously the Jewish people in Germany were being treated and the reports about work camps had become more than just a vague and unconfirmed rumour. Hearing about deportations and beatings in Austria from refugees was particularly shocking because the anti-Semitic government had only recently been installed and was already very effective in persecuting Jews. Houses were raided, shops closed, officials dismissed or arrested and people were beaten up randomly in the streets. There was chaos and nobody knew if a missing friend had been arrested or had succeeded in fleeing the country. Soon the German tax for evading the country, a Reichsflucht Steuer, was introduced in Austria as well and now even the rich had difficulties raising the funds to be allowed out. Jewish passports were confiscated and returned with a "J" marked in it which was a request from the Swiss border police to make their life easier. Anti-Semitic sentiments were now more openly shown in Czechoslovakia as well; not just by Germans in the country but also by Nationalists and sympathisers within the Czech and Slovak community.

"Where would we go?" Greta asked Wilhelm when he broke the issue of leaving the country to her.

"We have a few options I think," he replied. "Our first step would be to cross the border to Poland and from there travel to England or France or wherever we can travel to. It is more difficult to get a visa now because there are so many refugees but it is not impossible."

"Could we not just stay in Poland?" she wondered.

"Poland is not safe either," he replied. "Silesia has a German minority population. Hitler must have his eyes on it already. Poland can only be a stepping stone to our next destination. Hitler is sure to follow there once he is done with Czechoslovakia."

"Where do you think we stand the best chance to live in peace?" she asked.

"Portugal, Spain and Italy are all dangerous places with their fascist governments. Sweden is trading with Hitler a lot, so Scandinavia seems risky too. That leaves Holland, France and

England. The best place would be America but we don't have the kind of money to make that a realistic goal. Besides, when things improve politically in Europe it would be difficult to return from there. It is far too expensive travelling even in one direction."

"Do you think it will ever become safe for Jews in Europe?" she asked.

"Yes, I think so," he said. "Sometime in the future it will be safe again. Right now of course that is hard to imagine but don't worry. You are not a Jew everywhere in the world."

"What about Wilma and the rest of my family?" she asked with concern.

"They should think about escaping themselves. I hope they are making enquiries of their own," he said coldly.

"Couldn't we get away all together?" she suggested. "Couldn't we help them?"

"We stand a better chance on our own," he said. "I am German. My passport is genuine. Every passport applicant in Germany has to prove their Aryan ancestry. It would be possible to get a forged one for you and Karl that won't identify you as Jews. We would cross the border as a regular German family. The fewer people in our group at the border the smaller is the risk of the patrol spotting a forgery. With Karl and me being blond I hope that we won't have any trouble."

"What about Wilma, Egon and my father? Do you think they could get false passports too?" she asked hopefully.

"I can make enquiries for them but with their looks they might have more problems and be subjected to a thorough inspection. It would be far too risky in my view for them to travel," he replied in a matter of fact manner.

"Will they get out with their own passports?"

"Officially yes," he informed her, "but you know the Polish are not very keen on their Jews either and might stop letting any more in at any time, especially as there are ever more of you these days. Every country fears being overrun if they let in just a few of you. For Germans travelling, it will be a lot easier."

"Are you suggesting that I should leave without them?" she said, realising what he was getting at.

"Of course I am suggesting that. A larger group is much more suspicious. We would endanger Karl," he explained.

"But they are my family. I can't just abandon them."

"I am your family now," came the curt reply.

Soon after this conversation, Johanna came back from a trip to the market in town and took Greta aside.

"I think you need to tell your family to get out of the country," she said.

"Why are you saying this? Has anything happened in town? What have you heard?" Greta asked worriedly.

"I have heard nothing, calm down," Johanna replied. "Nothing special has happened. Nothing needs to. The signs are all obvious. You don't see many Jews in the streets any more where there used to be so many of you. Now the ones that you do see don't seem to feel safe. The Germans are not even here yet and already it feels strange and dangerous in the streets. Don't your family tell you anything?"

"They have said nothing about that," Greta had to admit. "I am never in town, so I will have to trust your word. Wilhelm seems to feel the same as you. Maybe you are both right. I will speak to my father and ask him to consider it when they come here next."

"That is the other thing I was going to ask you," Johanna added. "I don't think it is wise for them to do that. They can no longer come here to visit at all. It is too dangerous for us and for them."

"Why?" Greta asked.

"It is a long way from town to here," Johanna pointed out. "They should stay indoors as much as they can. Bratislava is dangerous now. There are so many of you Jews, it has become the perfect place for excitable aspiring Nazis to stir things up. They are brutal and they are not scared of resistance, they want a proper fight and they know the police will look the other way."

"It can't be that bad, surely, I would have heard," Greta insisted.

"Do you think anyone would tell you about it? They want to spare you the pain of knowing, which is understandable. I, on the other hand, want to spare you the pain of seeing your family getting hurt, especially with the worry about your new baby. You lost the last one. You are safe here. We can cover for you and Karl, especially since you have rarely left the house in the last few months. If Jonah and Wilma come here and are seen, it will attract unnecessary attention and will refresh people's memory that you or rather that we know Jews. We need the neighbours to forget about that so if, or when, Hitler comes we won't get into any trouble. We keep agreeing to this and then we let things slide and the visits happen again. I'm afraid that we need to be more disciplined about it from now on. "

"Wilhelm thinks so too," Greta said with a sad tone. "He wants us to get away from here altogether before anything happens. He is looking for me and Karl to get clean German passports and leave via Poland.

"Thank God! That is an excellent idea," Johanna exclaimed. "I hope he does it sooner rather than later. There won't be much time."

"I just don't know where we would be going," Greta wondered. "We don't speak any other languages. He said he wants us to go to England or France."

"Why there?" Johanna asked surprised, as she knew little about International politics and other countries beyond Germany and Austria.

"It is where the biggest Jewish communities are," Greta explained. "France is especially liberal in its laws and has been so ever since the Great Revolution. He says that the political situation in most other European countries is not very Jew friendly or stable. He thinks it would be safety by numbers there. A larger community would be better equipped to help us."

"I see the logic in that but you must be aware that over there you wouldn't be Jewish. You would be German. They would look at your blond child and your passport and exclude you. How would you prove to them that you are Jewish if you want their help? They will never believe you. You never even practised your religion and you don't look your race. Even if the Jews abroad are willing to help you, they would not help Wilhelm. He can't prove he is Jewish and neither could Karl. You married a goy, how could they ever accept you as a family? You are too naïve my darling."

"But I am Jewish by birth and even more so by the German racial laws," Greta insisted. "It makes no difference to Hitler that I converted. In his society we are nothing. You think that any place that welcomes me and Karl as Jews won't welcome my German husband? That would be ridiculous. I am not the only one who is married to a non-Jew."

"You know your people better than I do," Johanna said with

doom in her voice. "I hope for Wilhelm's sake that you are right."

Greta sat down and stared into space. All of a sudden, life was so complicated. She was just a young woman trying to live her life without hurting anybody. Now the situation in countries that had nothing to do with her was changing and as a consequence she had become a pawn in a political chess game. Did she have to leave Europe altogether to escape that hateful Hitler? Suddenly, nowhere seemed to be safe anymore.

"Don't worry Greta," said Johanna. "Our Wilhelm will think of something.

When Wilhelm came home that night, the two women were busy giving little Karl his weekly bath. Greta withdrew from the room, gave her husband a kiss and started preparing the food, while he went to the bathroom to say hello to his little boy.

"How is my little Karl the Great?" he asked jokingly.

"I am cold Daddy. The water is too cold," Karl screamed playfully.

"Oh it is not!" Johanna disagreed. "Don't be such a wimp."

"How old are you now?" Wilhelm asked his son.

"Three. Three years old!" Karl said proudly.

"Well at that age you need to start being a little bit more tough my son. If the water is cold you have to be a brave boy and learn to tolerate it without letting on that you are cold. Then you will become a brave and strong man when you grow up," he told him.

"Why do I have to be a brave man, Daddy?" Karl asked. "Uncle Benedikt says he is strong enough for all of us."

"Yes he is but you want to be strong yourself so you don't have to rely on him all the time," Wilhelm replied.

"I'm not cold Daddy," Karl said with a cheeky grin on his face. "It is warm water, it is too warm. I need to get out."

"Nice try," laughed Johanna. "You are not clean yet.

Later when Greta took Karl into the bedroom to read him his bedtime story Johanna took Wilhelm aside for a little heart to heart.

"Wilhelm you need to do something about Karl. You need to get him out of Slovakia as soon as possible," she implored him.

"I know Johanna. I am working on it," he replied.

"I had a word with your wife today and she knows it will be difficult for you three wherever you go. People are either on Hitler's side or against him. The way he is acting, the countries that are against him might end up being invaded. I don't think there are any completely safe options for you," she said resigned.

"I know. I am trying to figure out what to do."

"Greta says you are trying to get forged passports for her. I hope you understand that together you are never going to be safe anywhere in his sphere of influence. Even your party membership won't help you," she said.

"The German Sudeten Party is not a Nazi party!" Wilhelm insisted.

"Not yet, but where else do you think he will recruit his helpers from? They will all be supporting the Nazis if they know what is good for them but whatever future you have, she will always be a liability," Johanna said with emphasis.

"Don't you think I know that?" he asked. "I have been over the options many times and I am not sure if anywhere but America will do for us."

"Oh my, that is a long way. You won't be coming back from there. We'll never see you again. Why settle there?" she asked.

"Because from what I hear, they have had civil rights for the Jews since the founding days and also because it is so far away. If anywhere is safe from Hitler these days it is across the Atlantic," he replied.

"Do they give out visas?"

"They do, but that is very difficult and expensive, as would be the journey. I am already spending a lot on the passports."

"Who is arranging those for you?" she asked.

"A communist who used to come to the book shop. We know a lot about people by the kind of books they buy. Now that the politics are turning so anti-communist, he has helped to get some of his comrades out of the country. It is expensive though," he said.

"Couldn't her family fork out some money for her passport? They are Jews, they must have more money salted away than they let on," Johanna said.

"I think so, but they will need their money for themselves. They too are refugees in the making. I don't want to involve her family. Jonah and Wilma don't want to be separated from Greta and Karl. They probably will want to go wherever we are going, so they will be the last people on earth I am going to talk about my plans with," he explained.

"Those Jews are a bloody pain in your neck," Johanna swore. "Listen Wilhelm, wouldn't it be much easier if you just took care of Karl?"

"How do you mean?" he asked.

"If you left her," Johanna suggested. "Just leave with Karl for Germany where she can't follow."

"That is absurd!" Wilhelm exclaimed. "How could I take him to Germany when he is half Jewish?"

"He is only a boy. There are ways of fixing him up with the right connections. If you can get him to Berlin on a fake passport you can make further arrangements there. I have heard there are ways," she said knowingly.

"What ways?" Wilhelm asked.

"There are forgers in Berlin too," Johanna explained. "New identities can be provided for children. I don't know, declare him the son of a deported communist and then adopt him. There are people who are experts in these things. Your son is not the only half Jew in Germany but he has the advantage of being born outside of Germany so fewer questions will be asked. Nobody would expect you to bring a Jewish child into Germany. You would have to be mad to do so. What is more, he does not deserve to be treated as a Jew. He has done nothing wrong and he looks nothing like them."

"Maybe you are on to something," Wilhelm admitted. "What would I do about Greta?"

"Nothing. Leave her here with us. She should not travel while pregnant anyway. We will look after her. If she knows what is good for her son she will not make any trouble. She is a sensible woman and I will talk sense into her if needed," Johanna promised.

"I would put her in great danger here," Wilhelm pointed out. "Karl and I would be of leaving because we all mistrust the future in Slovakia."

"We all agree that it is out of the question for her to come to Germany with you. Maybe she could leave with her precious family and go to England, France or even to America if she wants, or even Palestine. That decision is hers," Johanna said coldly.

"She probably would not want to be too far away from Karl," Wilhelm said.

"Exactly. If she leaves she will want to be able to come back

71

eventually. I think that if she stays here on her own she has a fair chance. We don't know how bad it really would be for her here as there are less Germans and less Nazis. The Hlinka Guard may act like Nazi police but they are soft on Jews that have converted," Johanna said persuasively. "They are more religious than racists."

"If she stays she would never agree to give up Karl," Wilhelm said suddenly.

"Then make her agree," Johanna suggested. "Make up a story or just take him and leave without telling her if you think she is going to kick up a fuss about it. It is your child's safety that is at stake. You know what is going on in town, it could get a lot worse and then what?"

"I know but she is my wife," he said. "It is not right to leave one's wife. We made vows and promises," Wilhelm pointed out.

"Do you want to have a dead wife and son or do you want them to be alive, even if it means you have to give up being together as a family?" Johanna asked him pointedly. "It may not be forever, just for now until we know more. She must see that it would make a lot of sense. She is a Jew, she has brought this on herself by marrying a German. She brought the danger to you and to Karl, now she should have the decency and make a sacrifice for her chosen family."

"I would be lying if I said I haven't thought about it myself," he admitted.

"Really?" Johanna almost cried out loud for joy. "Oh Wilhelm I am so relieved. I never thought you would."

"I never thought so myself but lately I have had my eyes opened," he told her.

"Your eyes opened?" she asked. "How come? What happened?"

"Just something I read about Jewish genes." Wilhelm replied.

"What about their genes?" she asked interested.

"They are meant to be faulty," he said.

"Is that true? I never heard about that," she admitted.

"Neither had I," he said. "In fact, I didn't know anything at all about the Jews before I married Greta. I wish I had known a few things. Now I am finding out more and more about them. Not only do they have faulty genes but they also carry diseases. I was lucky that Karl turned out this blond and healthy boy. Now remember the miscarriage. Did she really work too hard or was that her weak Jewish body that made the baby come away? I do wonder. This time I may well be unlucky again."

"Oh, you mean about the baby that's coming?" Johanna asked with such horror that the words came out far too loud.

"Quiet! Greta could be back any minute. Don't scream," he scolded her.

"Sorry. It is just that I never thought about it," she said, perturbed.

"Me neither. Now it is all I can think about. The new baby is a bit of a gamble," he said.

"So you think it might have the bad genes?" she asked.

"I don't know what the chances are. What if it did? If I stayed here and ended up with a child that looks like Wilma, Jewish nose, gypsy features? What on earth am I letting myself in for?" he said miserably.

At that moment Greta came into the communal living room. Johanna got up to give up the good seat to the pregnant woman and picked up her sewing kit.

"Benedikt is so careless," she mumbled as if only to herself, trying to give the impression that nothing important had been discussed while Greta was out of the room. "Hole after hole after hole. You'd think he could take a little care when he works, but no, he rushes and pushes and I have to mend the torn clothes, as if I had nothing better to do."

"Give me some!" offered Greta. "I can help you."

"No, you must only think of the baby," Johanna refused. "You must rest. I am just moaning about that husband of mine because he is so careless but really the mending is no trouble at all, believe me. I do enjoy the work. You should probably try and get some sleep, you have not had a quiet day either."

"Yes you are right but if I keep doing that I will never get to spend time with my husband." Greta said and squeezed his hand.

"Darling I know we see very little of each other at the moment but that will change. I am starting to get really respected at work now," Wilhelm said.

"You are not going to get any use out of your time with your husband if you are tired Greta dear," Johanna said. "Just go to bed, you have done more than enough for one day. You don't want to lose this baby too," she added, knowing well that the memory of this

73

still hurt Greta every time. It had become Johanna's magic response whenever she wanted to manipulate Greta.

"Thank you," was the predictable response. "I think I will just do that. I am exhausted. Good night you two."

After Greta left Johanna changed seats and again sat down next to Wilhelm.

"If you are worried about the baby, I can help. I can let you know when it has been born and if it is healthy I can always bring it to Berlin for you. If the child is too Jewish looking or unhealthy we can leave it here with her."

"Thank you for the offer. I will think about it," Wilhelm promised.

"Don't think about it for long," Johanna said with emphasis. "You don't have that luxury. A German passport is not going to be any use for her. I hope you have not paid for it yet. It would be a waste of money. The police know exactly what they are looking for and they can spot a Jew from a mile away. Just take Karl on his own and move back to Berlin. Our family will arrange the rest over there."

"I am scared for Karl. I am not sure it will be safe in Berlin for him. What if they take him away from me at the border?" Wilhelm worried.

"They won't take him away at the border. Not if we get him the right papers. I have a few friends in the right places for that. It would be fast and it wouldn't even cost you," she promised.

"Are you sure? Can we trust your friends?"

"Oh yes. I have a friend in Bratislava, Marika. Her husband is not entirely Aryan but she fixed that. I know she will help us. She and I go way back."

"Could she help Greta as well?"

"I will ask," Johanna lied. "I will come into town with you tomorrow morning and pay her a visit."

Johanna had no intention of helping Greta but decided to leave that discussion with Wilhelm for another day. His main concern was clearly for the boy. If he was prepared to risk his safe escape by taking his wife on a false passport across the border as well then maybe Johanna had to engineer a situation in which he would not have the luxury of such a choice. She hoped that once he and Karl had the opportunity to leave Wilhelm would see sense and go without the extra burden around his neck.

The next morning she knocked on her friend's door in Bratislava and explained that she needed Karl's Aryan status 'cleaned' up. Marika nodded and said with a business-like and pragmatic manner that she would contact Johanna on the farm within one week.

"Things are a little slow because of the many refugees," Marika explained. "Everyone wants papers. It took a long time for ours to come through and we did not even want a visa to get out."

"Is there no faster way?" Johanna asked impatiently. "It doesn't seem as if we have much time left."

"A good forgery takes time," Marika explained. "The good 'manufacturers' are all extremely busy right now. You mustn't upset or rush those guys, your life lies in their artistic hands."

"What do you mean?" Johanna asked confused.

"What would be stopping them to produce an inferior product that lands you in jail right away? Only the fear of being caught themselves. There are many tricksters out there who sell inferior papers and then move on to where they cannot be found. You are lucky that my guys are totally trustworthy and pressuring them would only defeat the objective. In the current market they can name their price and they can chose who they work for."

"I see, well I suppose when they see that we are trying to save a little boy they might feel a moral obligation to do the best they can," Johanna said hopefully.

When Marika named the price Johanna almost fainted. It would eliminate all of her savings and then some. There was no way that she could have helped with Greta as well even if she had wanted to. She agreed and said she would bring the money and the original passport later this afternoon. They could not afford any more delays.

Benedikt would kill her if he found out what she was about to do for his family. He would never agree that the situation was dire enough to justify such desperate measures and extravagant expenses. The farmer was much more concerned about the future of the business and his own children to give anything to Wilhelm and Karl. They were his family though and so she had to make that decision for him.

Wilhelm was overjoyed when she told him that Marika had promised to organise the papers as quickly as she could and that things had been set in to motion. He still had not heard back from

75

his own contacts. It had been some time and the communist seemed to have disappeared from the city. Fortunately, Johanna always seemed to know what she was doing. He trusted her sources much more than he did his own and never questioned her when she informed him that the forgers would only help Karl.

Wilhelm still had his doubts about Greta's safety in Czechoslovakia and had no idea how he would bring up the matter of leaving her behind; he could only hope that she would understand his predicament. They simply did not have the kind of money to travel to America, he could not possibly move to Palestine for her and any other place was questionable. For the time being, they would have to separate. Karl would be safe in Germany. They could wait this out, watch the developments in the world and plan further later. In the mean time she would be fairly safe hidden on the farm.

There was no use in upsetting her by telling her about it for now. Until he held the papers in his hands it would be easier not to trouble her at all, after all she was pregnant and emotional. Because of his wedding vows, he would never even have considered leaving her behind if Johanna and her forgers had not got him into this situation. Finding himself with the prospect of not having a choice about the matter he realised how comfortable this solution was. He had to admit to himself that he had simply fallen out of love with his wife. If things were different maybe he would not feel this way. She was lovely, beautiful and had a great mind but the circumstances which had come between them, showed that their bond simply had not been as strong as thought. All he really cared about was Karl. He wanted Greta to be safe and had enjoyed their intellectual discussions of late but he was not going to risk anything for a woman for whom he felt so little. No one could blame him for protecting Karl, the thing he valued most. His family was going to look after Greta now and there was nothing he had to blame himself for.

Karl's papers came at the end of September, the same day on which the European powers announced the secession of the Sudetenland to Germany. Nobody was in the least surprised by the development. The members of the German Sudeten Party in Bratislava reaped no immediate benefit from this development and their region remained in Czechoslovak territory. They still celebrated and were pleased in principle. Local politicians were already seeking independence for Slovakia and were rumoured to having been in touch with the Germans in Berlin to discuss that possibility, something which made the Czech politicians very nervous.

The political situation was most unstable and threatening. Many Germans living in the remaining part of Czechoslovakia were seen as hate figures and the discrimination of the remaining Czechs and Slovaks in the regions that were now part of the Reich did not help that sentiment. Public opinion continuously swayed between optimistic denial and pessimism. Supporters of either conviction were sure that the future was entirely predictable according to their gospel. Half of the population painted a doom and gloom picture with an end-of-times vision of an impending German invasion and the end of all good for the republic, while the other half stuck their heads into the sand and swore that everything would be just fine. The members of the latter group believed that the European powers did not want to upset the mighty Germans, but it seemed absurd to them to imagine that the world leaders would concede any more land to Hitler and allow him further aggressive moves.

Wilhelm didn't have the heart to tell Greta about his decision to go to Berlin without her. Johanna urged him on a daily basis just to go and leave and not to waste any more of the little time that was left.

Greta occasionally asked Wilhelm about his progress with the documents, meaning of course the German passports that would see them all into Poland together as one family, but her interest was only half hearted. She was preoccupied with her pregnancy and did not want to think about the future and the prospect of possibly leaving her family behind. Still remembering the pain she felt after her miscarriage, she was happy that this pregnancy had gone so well and that she had had so much support from Johanna.

Her siblings Egon and Wilma had not shown any interest in fleeing the country and her father too felt that his livelihood was to be found only in those two weaving frames and his reputation in the region as a craftsman. With the Countess and her circle of friends being such great customers, he could not see himself earning a similar livelihood and reputation by taking his family and his business across the border. He also felt too old to start all over again and wherever he would go he would have to do just that. So the Weissensteiner family joined the group of people in denial. Now that Hitler had the

German territories why should he bother with the rest of Czechoslovakia? If the three had had more contact with the Jewish community they probably would have been a little bit more informed and slightly more worried, yet even in those circles many refused to believe that it would ever come to an invasion of their country without an automatic massive foreign intervention.

By November the borders of the remaining Czechoslovakia that had not been swallowed up by Germany were redrawn. The new state was renamed into Czecho-Slovakia and - as had been decided at the Conference in Munich – further territories were lost to both Poland and Hungary. Large portions of southern Slovakia – home to more than 45,000 Jews – were annexed to Hungary. A new Slovak government was installed which possessed more autonomy from Prague. It was predominantly formed by right leaning Nationalists who immediately banned the Communist Party. As political scapegoats, the Jews got the blame for the loss of land to Hungary because of their alleged support for it. Thousands of Jewish families who held foreign citizenships were transported to the Hungarian and Polish borders in preparation for an expulsion from Slovakia. Very few of these deportees were permitted to return to their homes.

Jonah and his family were not amongst the selected ones even though they could have easily been included. According to the census information, they were not Jews and they had exchanged their Ukrainian passports for Czechoslovakian ones soon after the Czechoslovakian Republic had been formed. Yet many other families with similar official records and documents found their names appearing on the lists of the Hlinka Guards and ended up deported from the country. Wilma thought their safety had to do with one of their regular customers, the wife of a Slovak politician who had a soft spot for Jonah but he naively dismissed this idea as farfetched. He was confident that his far sighted decision to keep a low profile and to distance himself from the Jews in town had made a difference.

Greta had two weeks to go before she was due to give birth and Wilhelm knew he could not postpone his departure any longer. Any day now there could be either a civil war between Czechs and Slovaks or a German invasion. Either way, there was a sense of doom or negativity on the streets, mixed with an air of expectation and the possibility that literally anything could happen. He felt it was simply too risky to wait and see any longer. He actually scolded himself for having waited so long when he could already be across the border safely. He had done so because he was afraid that the emotional trauma of him leaving Greta would cause harm to the unborn baby, whose prospects were already in question as far as he was concerned. Now that Greta was at least so close to her due date, Johanna said the chances for survival of a prematurely born baby would be much better. Eventually he found the courage and told her.

"Greta I have something to tell you," he said with his eyes averted to the floor.

"That doesn't sound like good news. What is it Wilhelm?" she asked calmly.

"I have the papers we were waiting for," he said shyly.

"Oh," she said, sensing from his tone that this was not entirely good news.

"You don't seem very happy!" Wilhelm observed.

"I can't say that I am. No," admitted Greta. "It means saying good bye to my family and leaving everything and everyone behind us."

"Greta there have been some problems," Wilhelm said uncomfortably. "I was not able to get you a passport as well. The forgers refuse to help full blooded Jews. I did not know that. I tried but they said I could pay and get the papers for Karl or leave with nothing at all. So I took what I could get. I am so sorry my love."

"Oh dear," Greta sighed. "Well, you did the right thing, Wilhelm. At least our boy can get to safety. We really should have seen this coming. We can be so naïve. Well it does not matter, we can go across the border separately. Nothing must happen to our Karl. Once you are in Poland I will find a way in as well."

"You are right," Wilhelm agreed. "The problem is that Poland is harbouring a German minority as well. Politicians expect that Hitler will go there next and we would have gained nothing at all. I have thought about this long and hard and I think the best thing for me to do is to take Karl and go back to Berlin, not Poland. A blond boy with a German passport from the Czechoslovak Embassy has nothing to fear in Berlin. Johanna and I think that you are safest here on the farm. You are heavily pregnant, it would be a risk for you and the baby to travel now and probably for some time after it is born. Benedikt and Johanna can hide you on the farm, no one outside would even know that you are still here. We can wait and see what

79

happens to the country and its Jews and then make decisions how to reunite later."

"How long have you planned this?" Greta asked stoically, a sense of his deceit at last entered her mind.

"I have thought about it for a while. I was looking for alternatives. Leaving you behind was always the last resort. Now that the passport for you has not materialised the decision was made for me. We simply can't afford a journey to America. Nowhere in Europe is safe for us all together right now. At least here you have my family to support you."

"You are right," she agreed. "We have been fooling ourselves. It is really going to happen, isn't it? It is not just a rumour or a vague possibility. Hitler will swallow the country up."

"I think so," he said.

"Somehow I always doubted it would come to this. We have talked about it all the time but now that it is so close I am still surprised. If I am stuck on the farm it is going to be like a prison for me. I am not going to see anyone who means anything to me, my family, you or Karl," she said sadly.

"It won't feel like a prison," he tried to console her. "You will be busy with the new baby and hopefully the situation in Europe will be resolved soon. Johanna and the girls are also going to take care of you. Don't worry."

"When are you planning to leave?" she asked. "You'll miss the birth of your child."

"I know. Promise me you'll send me photographs of the new child," he said, now more confident since the emotional outburst he had feared had not occurred. "I have waited too long as it is. I am leaving tomorrow morning. I am really scared for Karl, Greta. More than you can imagine. If it was not for Karl I would wait but I must get him out of here. You must appreciate that."

Greta sunk her head onto his shoulder and cried.

"Just hold me Wilhelm," she begged him. "Oh what a disaster this continent has become."

Wilhelm was very pleased about the way Greta had taken the news. Better than he had ever could have hoped for. She was so calm and understanding and the conversation had not gone at all how he had expected. He was incredibly relieved that she had not queried his decision any further. He had had nightmare visions of having to

80

justify himself more and ending up having to talk about the Jewish genetic diseases and his worries about the new baby. She would not have believed him and tried to convince him otherwise. He was sure that the pamphlets were right, why else would Hitler be so obsessed with eradicating the Jews? The fear of those dreadful genes was the real reason why he was leaving and he had long stopped pretending to himself that he was ever going to come back to his wife. There was no future in a mixed marriage in these times. He had once loved his wife but he was no longer infatuated, naïve and uneducated. Now he knew the dangers he had played with and the miscarriage should have been a final warning to him; they should have stopped trying for another baby then. He felt bad about abandoning Greta like this but what he was doing was better than what some German men allegedly did to their Jewish wives to save their own skin. At least his family was offering to look after her. She was not left stranded and she was not being deported as so many Jews had been.

Greta in her naivety believed his assurances that this was only a temporary solution until the situation had changed and that he could not wait to be reunited. Once she had shown herself so calm and reasonable he felt safe to make her promises he knew he would not keep - anything to get away quickly and without a scene.

Next morning, after Wilhelm and Karl had left, Greta cried for a long time but Johanna scolded her and told her to pull herself together, which helped. They sent a letter to Jonah and informed him that there should be no contact between the two families at least until the birth. Four days later Greta went into early labour and delivered another Aryan looking little boy, whom Johanna insisted for good measure they christen right away. They named him Ernst (the serious) after Johanna's father as a thank you for all her help but also to impress on the little child the seriousness of the times he had been born into.

Johanna wrote to Wilhelm at his parent's new address in Berlin with the good news. His child was a boy, healthy and blond. Her prayers had been answered and Greta had even allowed them to christen him right away, so now even a priest could vouch for the little boy not being Jewish. Greta's father had agreed to the no visit policy and in turn, Johanna had promised she would soon take the new baby into town to the weaver workshop to show him off to his other relatives.

Wilhelm was relieved to hear the news but once he had arrived in Berlin and taken in its fascist climate, he decided to abandon any remaining link with Greta. There was zero tolerance for interracial marriages here and he was told that the only way to recover from such a marriage in the eyes of the authorities was to initiate the divorce proceedings and to do so immediately. Oscar arranged for Karl to stay with Wilhelm's brother Bernhard, who had recently got married. To muddy the waters, Oscar had come up with a complex plan in which Karl was to receive a new identity as the son of a communist. Then he would be adopted by Bernhard and his wife, while Wilhelm was handling the divorce. That way there would be no link to Greta at all.

When it came to annulling an interracial marriage, the German efficiency knew no limits; Greta did not even have to be consulted about it. The authorities sent a notification to Bratislava to inform her about her divorce on racial grounds but Johanna intercepted the letter and left Greta in the belief that everything was still fine. After a few weeks of no letters from Berlin, Greta was naturally concerned that Wilhelm had not written to her. Johanna calmed her down and explained that frequent contact could be dangerous. If the Germans ever did invade, an ambitious mail man would inform on her to ingratiate himself with the occupying force and tell the Hlinka Guard that she was still living on the farm. Greta continuously swayed between thinking that this was overly cautious and agreeing with Johanna. The times were unpredictable, that much was obvious.

The winter was hard that year. The thought of exposing her little new born boy to the harsh elements worried her, as did the idea of someone else taking Ernst to see her family, but Johanna insisted they must not take any risks and in order to avoid unwelcome visitors alone she took Ernst to the workshop to introduce him to his other family.

Chapter 4: Bratislava 1939

By the time the New Year had come, Greta could no longer pretend that everything was alright; there was a major problem in her marriage. Wilhelm had not been in touch with her, not even via a third party. Johanna kept reassuring her that this was all temporary and part of some plan to protect her and Ernst, but Greta knew Wilhelm well enough to sense that there was more to this than met the eye.

At first, she worried that father and son had run into trouble with either the border police or the authorities in Berlin but only a week after Wilhelm and Karl had left Bratislava, a letter arrived at the farm written by Elizabeth and addressed to Johanna. Wilhelm was mentioned in passing - enough to assure everyone about his health and well-being but without any further information. Most hurtful for Greta, there was no message for her and the new born baby. Johanna could talk all she liked about necessary discretion and secrecy but there would have been a way to communicate, either indirectly or in some understandable code, to get a message past potential censors. The way Wilhelm handled all this was nothing but a slap in the face.

Letters went missing or were opened by the Gestapo in Berlin and presumably by the Hlinka Guard here as well but it seemed extremely unlikely that Wilhelm would be under such observation. Greta could not help but feel that this excessive care was nothing but unjustified hysteria and way beyond what was reasonable. Johanna disagreed and defended Wilhelm and his caution. Their discussions were so focused on the issue of safety in Berlin that the subject of his willingness to write to his wife never came up.

Since the Sudetenland had become part of Germany, the Czech dominated government in Prague felt weak and insecure. Czechoslovakia was renamed into Czecho-Slovakia and the newly hyphenated Slovakia had been given more autonomy than it had ever had in its history. In the minds of the Bratislava gentry, complete Slovak independence became a real possibility and therefore a threat to the Czech politicians in Bohemia and Moravia. In the first two months of the year a lot of diplomatic and political moves were made, paving the way for an independent Slovak state. Party officials from the Slovak nationalist parties frequently travelled to Berlin and appeared to be on a good footing with the Hitler government.

At the same time, the Czech led federal government in Prague was misled by German diplomats who assured it of Hitler's lack of interest in the internal power battle between Czechs and Slovaks. So encouraged by the promises coming out of Berlin, the powers in Prague responded to the situation by invading the rebellious Slovakia in March in a pre-emptive strike. They declared martial law, had the army secure the country and arrested officials that were considered traitors.

This had given the Germans the excuse they were looking for and in "protection of the Slovak state" they invaded the Czech regions and declared it the Protectorate of Bohemia and Moravia. At last, Slovakia was declared an independent state and since it was an ally of Hitler, German troops could enter its soil without occupying the country.

Hoards of people took to the streets cheering. For centuries the Slovaks had been part of the Hungarian Empire until its fall in 1918. When the idea of Nationalism swept across Europe in the 1840s, the Slovaks were one of the few losing nations whose dream of independence had never come true. With the arrival of this independence almost a century of Nationalist frustration ended and the accumulated relief and joy was celebrated by the ones who cared.

For the Germans in the country this was also good news. Wheras in the past the Germans had been rivals to Slovak politicians for ministerial positions and power, they could now be considered allies and representatives of the great nation that had helped to secure Slovak independence.

However, huge parts of the population were too scarred from the countless reforms during the Austrio-Hungarian rule to believe that there would be real change. They feared that the cooperation with Germany was just a euphemism for a new kind of oppression and they were waiting for the catch in the new political environment.

Amongst the pessimists were forces such as communists and Lutherans who knew that the new leaders did not look favourably on them. The dominating force in the new Slovakia was the right wing Slovak People's Party, which combined both racist and religious forces under one umbrella and which was the political body behind

84

the much feared Hlinka Guard, named after the party leader Andrej Hlinka. Its religious wing was Catholic conservative and less concerned about the Jews in the country; the racist wing however was inspired by the nationalism and anti-Semitism of their German counter part and planned to work closely with Hitler's NSDAP.

This political situation worried Greta slightly but as Slovakia had been spared an invasion – like many Jews – she felt a little relieved. She was unaware that the Slovak People's Party had already begun to look into the Jewish question in Slovakia without any help or initiation from the Nazis. Jews who had converted before 1918 were not affected but spouses of Jews were being targeted in the drafts for future legislation and so were children where both parents were Jewish.

Johanna and Benedikt looked at the new laws when they were announced and they were confused. If it was discovered that she had never been baptised then Greta would be considered as Jewish but as she had converted – although after 1918 - there was still hope she might escape prosecution. Wilhelm would be safe if he was still here because of the divorce and so would Karl as only one of his parents was Jewish; these things considered, Johanna lamented that Wilhelm and Karl would be safer and better off here. However, nothing was straight-forward in the local bureaucracy and individual verdicts and circumstances depended on the good will and the efficiency of the processing civil officer.

The law proposed limitations for Jews who wanted to participate in Slovak social and public life, especially teachers, notaries, lawyers and civil servants. Anti-Jewish sentiment was increasingly noticeable but had still not come to the fore-front of public life in Bratislava. Since the beginning of the year, Czech government officials and civil servants had been expelled from their jobs and Slovak nationals had taken their positions. The establishment of a Slovak in contrast to a Czechoslovak identity was the main agenda on the political platform and so Jews did not feel the impact of the new legislation immediately. Things had never been completely easy for the Jews before but with the hate for all things Czech, the focus was not directed at them. Instead of persecuting or attacking Jewish people, the religious wing of the party used the predominant fear as an opportunity to persuade as many Jews to convert to Catholicism as possible. Jews who chose not to convert kept their heads down and tried not to provoke any attention. In this spirit of caution and safety Johanna declared it was only logical for her to stop even the occasional trips to town with Ernst to see Jonah and his children.

According to the new laws, Jonah and his family could also be considered both safe or in danger. They had been given Czechoslovak passports that did not identify them as Jews but gave away their Ukrainian origin. To people in the know, this fact always cast the doubt of a Jewish ancestry over a person because of the mass exodus of Jews from the region during Russian led pogroms. Civil servants, anti-Jewish police or border patrols would notice it and be likely to investigate the matter further. Jonah and his children were not in immediate danger but were well advised to act with caution.

Wilma was devastated over this. She had never been very fond of Karl but she had taken to Ernst like a house on fire and could spend hours with him. Whereas Karl was a very rational and clever boy who wanted to talk sensibly and who constantly asked questions, all of which Wilma was unsure how to answer, Ernst was a lovely and playful boy who related to her in a way she could completely respond to. He laughed at the silly faces she pulled and was always happy to play with her.

Johanna had taken offence when she saw the two of them together, feeling it was ridiculous how this spinster-in-the-making was more of a child at heart than the boy himself. That woman would be a bad influence on the boy and put stupid ideas in his head instead of educating him and teaching him how to be a functional member of the farming community. Johanna missed Karl more than she had thought she would and the growing feelings of longing and loneliness led her to have also more resentment towards Greta and Ernst and their strong bond with each other. The new child was not as responsive to Johanna's attention. She thought he was cute and adorable but he was not his brother and she could not be bothered to make much effort with him since it was clear he was so different in nature.

She wrote to Elizabeth several times to let her know about the progress of the little child but she never fulfilled her promise to Wilhelm to send pictures of him. In her letters she took a rather negative approach in describing the new-born and Wilhelm mistook this information as a sign that Ernst was showing first signs of the dreaded Jewish genes, just as he had feared. Any doubts he had had about leaving Greta behind were now erased.

Johanna's lack of affection for Ernst had made it even easier for Wilma to form a strong bond with her new nephew. She missed seeing her sister and when Johanna stopped coming into town with Ernst, Wilma felt her whole world collapsing. After a few months of trying to accept the situation Wilma decided to ignore the ban on visits and made plans to sneak out of the house and walk to the farm one Saturday afternoon when she was not required in the workshop.

She got on her way but as she was crossing the bridge across the river she saw a few uniformed boys coming from the opposite side. How odd, she thought, that boys that age would wear a uniform. She wondered what it stood for and stared at them a little too obviously and a little too long. When she saw the swastikas on their arms she turned her head but it was too late. The boys were a group of visiting German Hitler Youth and closely examined the girl who had so blatantly stared at them. They immediately recognised her Jewish looks and crowded around her on the edge of the bridge.

"Where are you going you Yiddish whore?" one of them almost shouted in German. He was tall but his limbs had grown faster than the rest of his body and in his short trousers he looked comically shaped. His short hair made his ears appear overly big. He seemed far too young and immature to use hateful language like that.

Wilma said nothing in reply and tried to get quietly past them but they blocked her way and forced her to stand with her back to the edge of the bridge facing their spotty and hateful faces.

"I asked you a question. Where do you think you are going?" the big eared youth continued.

"To visit relatives," she answered in a low voice, realising that she was outnumbered and that showing her raging anger or saying what she actually thought of these cowardly bullies would be a mistake.

"And where are these relatives?" another boy confronted her. He seemed to be the ring leader. He looked a little bit older and stood in front of the other guys. He had flaming red hair, cut short on the sides and had a long strand across his forehead, similar to the hair of Adolf Hitler. He was more muscled than the other boys and his posture displayed much more confidence and menace than the boy with the big ears could muster.

"Aren't you going in the wrong direction?" he asked her. "If I am not mistaken the Jewish quarter is the other way."

Wilma was at once struck with panic. She mustn't give away her sister's hide out by saying where she was going; she had to think of something to say quickly.

"I was just going to look at the river. I like looking at it," she said hastily.

"Oh you like the river. That's nice," the ginger boy mocked.

"Well I think maybe you want to have a closer look?" said the one with the big ears and while another boy lifted her legs off the ground pushed her face towards the river.

"Stop, please stop!" Wilma screamed. She was terrified of water.

"I tell you what," said the ringleader. "If we throw you in the river you can see it really close up and you could swim to your relatives in the Jewish quarter. That should be much quicker."

"I can't swim," she cried in panic. "Please stop!"

"You'll be fine. You can't drown. Shit floats," another one of them shouted.

There were two of them now holding one foot each. Wilma was scared for her life but she knew if she resisted the chances were even greater that she would not be thrown but accidentally dropped off the bridge and drown.

"Throw that ugly Jew in. I can't bear looking at her," demanded the ring leader and the two guys holding her legs lifted her higher so that the top half of her body was now hanging completely free over the bridge wall.

"Stop! Please stop!" Wilma cried.

"Time we let her go before any of the locals think he has to take the law into his own hands and tries to stop us. It would be a shame if someone wanted to risk his life for such a good for nothing Jewess," suggested another one.

"No, let's carry on. Let's hold her by her feet so she can have a real good view of the river. After all that is what she wanted," insisted the ginger one.

"Let's push her in." "Drop her boys!" other ones shouted.

Wilma was terrified. Were they really going to drop her or were they just playing? If it were a fight, one on one, she could have taken on any one of them easily and given them a good beating. They were young, green behind the ears and no match for her but in a group like this they were dangerous and the situation could easily end badly. Her father had always taught her to be careful and, while she usually did not take his advice, this seemed to be an occasion where it might be wise to take it and just shut up.

The boys pretended to drop her a few times but they always caught her in time. Wilma was scared and nearly soiled herself in panic but she also felt a slight sense of hope underneath her fear. They may not mean business after all? They would have dropped her by now, wouldn't they? The question was, should she show her fear and scream to satisfy their sadistic egos or be cold and calm to make them lose interest?

At that moment an old man approached the boys and asked them first in Czech and then in German what they were doing. Wilma wanted him to go away. She was certain the situation would only escalate if he was getting involved on her behalf and it would only stimulate the boys into doing worse. Nothing good could come from one fragile old man standing up for her.

"Oh we are just offering that dirty Jew a wash in the river," the red haired boy said casually. "Do you have a problem with that?"

"Not a problem at all," came the reply. "As long as you throw her in quickly. Don't get the wrong idea and think about raping her. You'll get your knobs dirty on that filth. Throw her in already," he sneered and turned away.

"Don't worry! She is too ugly for us to touch her. I would rather do it with an animal than with her," one of them shouted after the old man.

At that point, a group of slightly older Slovak boys came on the scene and started to confront Wilma's attackers.

"Let her go you idiots. That's not funny anymore," one of them told them in almost accent free German. He appeared to be a strong and confident looking young man with a very provocative and intimidating body language.

"Leave us alone," said the boy with the big ears defiantly. "We are just doing your job for you. You should be thanking us. Can't you deal with your Jews by yourself?"

"We don't drown our Jews," came the curt reply.

"Well you should and soon you will. Just you wait," promised the ring leader of the Hitler youth. "Do you really think that you can live under German protection and get away with treating your Jews like they were real people? How stupid are you?"

"Just let her go," said another of the Slovaks calmly and with an aura of authority and determination. He also appeared very strong and ready to fight. The Hitler Youth leader started to become unsure of him. He and his friends were clearly outnumbered and could not possibly win in a fight with them.

If there was going to be a clash he would have to go back to the youth hostel where they were staying and explain to his superiors and the party officials what had happened. It would be hard to justify how they had got into this fight in the first place when they had been sent to the city to instigate a similar youth organisation in Slovakia and should be making friends rather than enemies. His superiors would not be impressed. It was surprising that anybody should interfere on behalf of a Jew – obviously a lot of work had to be done here in Slovakia. Maybe the gentle approach of peer education and bonding with the local lads was not going to work if this was the case. After carefully weighing the best retreat he finally said:

"Okay, if you love this Jewish slut so much you can have her." He turned to his friends and ordered them: "Bring her back up guys."

"You better watch out," he warned the group of Slovaks. "Times are changing and next time you may not be so lucky," and the German troopers left the scene.

Wilma took a long time to regain her breath but despite these difficulties she managed to utter a wheezy thank you to her saviours. However, instead of the reassuring pat on the back that she expected from them, one of the guys walked up to her and struck her heavily with his hand across her face and hatefully said to her.

"You stupid Jewish bitch. What are you doing out on the street? Don't you know any better yet? Go back home and lock the door. We don't want to see your kind around here, is that clear?"

"Then why save me?" she asked without thinking that she should just flee while she still could.

"We don't like anyone telling us what to do. Not the Hungarians, not the Czechs and certainly not the bloody Germans. That's why. We were not saving you, we were showing them who the bosses are here. Don't think we wouldn't throw you in the river ourselves if we felt like it. This is Slovakia, not Palestine. Now go."

Wilma stood frozen for a second but then ran as fast as she could, back to the other end of the bridge and all the way home. She stormed through the front door of the workshop, ran up the stairs into the private part of the house, got to her room and locked the door. She had heard about such incidences before but somehow had always believed they had only happened because the victims had been too weak and frightened to turn the whole situation around in their favour; now she knew exactly how these apparently innocent scenes could rapidly get out of hand. Once she had seen the determination and hatred of those people she had known that her fate was entirely at the mercy of those thugs. She had always had a huge fear of water and unknowingly they had hit her weakest spot. Wilma hated to show weakness but she was too upset to be able to stop the tears flooding from her eyes. Those bastards, she thought, how dare they attack her for no reason at all. She had felt so helpless, completely different from any confrontation she had ever imagined she might have with Jew haters. It began to dawn on her that she was trapped in Slovakia as a Jew and in no better circumstances than the Jews who were in Germany. Those Slovak boys could talk about independence and autonomy with their big mouths all they wanted but the Germans were already here. They did not need tanks and guns to rule the country, they used ink and paper to write their own laws into the new constitution. How had anybody been so stupid and not seen it coming? Hitler was saving his bullets for a bigger fight but got the job done just as efficiently.

For the first time in her life, Wilma was really scared. Those guys had broken her spirit. She had always been so naïve and optimistic - so many of 'her people' still were - but now she felt the complete opposite. If the Slovaks who had helped her could be so hateful, what chance did she have? She and her family should have left while they still could.

Before today she had always thought that leaving was a gross overreaction, which naturally it would have been if Germany had not touched the Sudetenland, but history had proven her wrong. She wondered how she could have known it would really happen before it did. Just like her encounter on the bridge that could have easily ended in a different way? She could have been killed on that bridge or, if she had not looked at the Hitler Youth, she might have managed to get past them without any problems. In the big political arena she had always assumed that the European forces would refuse Hitler his demands. If that had happened he might have backed down and everything might have stayed the same. How was a young woman like her to know the future and how could she be judged for getting it wrong?

Without the incident on the bridge she would have carried on feeling confident and secure but now she stayed at home for months, either inside the house or at the weaver workshop, never daring to go anywhere alone.

Jonah sent the Slovak girls in his employ to do the shopping and run the errands - which they loved to do as a break from the boring work on the frame. Before the event on the bridge, Wilma had always been a little nervous, dropping dishes or books on the floor and bumping into doors and tables, but now those accidents happened much more frequently and even the smallest of noises made her jumpy. She never told anyone about the incident, feeling that by sharing her troubles she would make it more real. She did not want anyone to worry about her but she did start asking everyone to be careful and made her family promise to look out for each other, which amused them more than anything else.

Incidents like the one she had lived through were however not that common and the streets were still pretty safe. The delegates of the Hitler Youth from Germany did not reappear on the streets near her home but in Wilma's newly paranoid mind they were waiting for her everywhere.

Greta was totally obsessed with motherhood. Having lost her first born son to an unknown existence in Germany and with no immediate relief of the situation, she focused all of her energy on Ernst and spoilt him the best she could. This one would not get away from her, she would keep him close at all times. As Ernst grew older she saw less of Wilhelm in his features but instead she discovered a rather cunning resemblance to her brother Egon, especially the big nose. She was grateful for the blond hair that diluted the impression that Ernst might not be Aryan.

Apart from these slightly Jewish looks, the boy seemed however to be a lucky child, blessed with heavenly protection. He never had any problems with anything or anyone, he never complained and he rarely even cried or screamed. Instead, he smiled and laughed a lot and enchanted everyone around him with his cute smile, his curly blond hair and his engaging little games. Even grumpy old Benedikt could not resist Ernst's charm and spent time with him whenever he could, something he had hardly ever done with his own neglected children.

It was a blessing for Greta to have a son like this who even managed to make her forget her absent husband and first born for hours at a time. Every now and then a sting of pain came back but it was the not knowing that bothered her most. What had Wilhelm decided to do with the boy? Was he living with him or had they changed his identity? Was her son being brought up by someone else? What was life like in Berlin? Would there be a war or would this all blow over?

When she allowed herself to get worried and tried to project a vision of the future, Ernst would often come to her and distract her, demanding her attention, making her smile and forget all the doom and gloom. She was cut off from the politics in Europe and with Wilhelm no longer returning from town with all the news it could be days now before she heard anything about what went on in the country at all. It was so much easier and comfortable to get her head down in farm work and child care and lead her life day by day. Johanna and Benedikt never mentioned anything about politics to her and neither did their children. No news was good news she thought and while no news was forthcoming, she could enjoy the carefree existence she had come to lead.

In July the former priest Jozef Tiso became president of Slovakia. While the optimists amongst the Jews thought this would bring more humane conditions for them, the pessimists disagreed. Tiso was however part of the religious branch of the Slovak People's party and was rumoured to have a different agenda than the fascist wing. France and Britain initially recognised the new state and its elected president and temporarily established proper diplomatic connections. 'Nobody can deny that these are very positive signs', said one camp. 'What good can this really do?', questioned the other.

On September 1, Hitler invaded Poland and 50,000 Slovak troops in three divisions assisted the attack. The army had been mobilized within a few days and had been stationed in the North, under the pretext of regaining the territories that had been lost to Poland at the Munich conference. The campaign did not take very

93

long and shortly after German and Slovak soldiers halted their west and south campaigns, Russia also moved into Poland, from the east. As a consequence, Germany and Slovakia were now at war with Britain and things were escalating.

Greta and a lot of other people were shocked. Diplomatic actions and political chess moves between the European forces had preceded the military operations for so long that many had started to doubt that anything serious would ever happen at all. History again proved these people wrong. Greta believed that the invasion of Poland could have positive effects. Surely the rest of Europe would have to start an all-out war with Hitler and put him in his place. He could not possibly win against so many opponents; this had to be the beginning of the end.

Johanna and Benedikt left her in this hopeful belief and focused on their work. Compared to their cousin Klaus in Brno they were very lucky. Klaus had been a member of the German Sudeten Party and had immediately chosen to become a full citizen of the Greater German Reich. He had exchanged his old passport for a German one and within weeks of the invasion of Poland he and his sons had been drafted into the German army while the people that had kept their Czech passports were left alone.

The Germans who stayed behind on Klaus's farm were bullied and boycotted by the Czech villagers. In comparison to the atrocious climate in Bohemia and Moravia, life in Slovakia was heaven. Demand for farm produce was rising. Hitler had ordered its satellite state Slovakia to increase farm and industrial output to support the troops. With the focus on productivity, it was almost easy to forget about the war itself, especially since after the successful split of Poland between the Soviet Union, Germany, Lithuania and Slovakia, nothing major actually seemed to happen in Europe in terms of warfare. Everyone was surprised that, as yet, Europe seemed to accept the loss of Poland to Hitler without any actual military retaliation that had been expected immediately following the declaration of war.

Greta was very pleased because it meant security for her Karl in Berlin. She had to admit that Wilhelm had been right to move there instead of Poland, where they could have got stuck, and could have ended up being part of the Soviet Union or could be subjected to the thorough German search for Jews in the Western parts of the country. If Wilhelm had been right before, he probably knew what he was doing now concerning Karl as well and that thought comforted her as much as Ernst did with his smiles.

The best news was that the army had not sent her brother Egon into battle. It really was a miracle when she thought about it. He was inexperienced infantry, the kind she would have expected to be sent to the front line first as cheap cannon fodder that would pave the way for the more experienced soldiers whom the army needed and wanted to save. Immediately after the declaration of independence Egon had received a letter from the army requiring him to come for military examination. The new state needed to have its own security and since all the Czechs had been expelled, it needed more man power. Wilma had a fit of hysteria when she heard about it.

"They'll find out he is a Jew. That will be the end of us all. We have to flee. Let us pack our bags and run for it," she ranted.

"Where, may I ask, would we be going?" asked her father.

"We could try to get into Hungary. I have heard of a few who made it."

"If they have not found out we are Jewish yet they won't find out now. They would never conscript Egon if they knew he was. The new laws forbid him to enter the army. They don't trust Jews with their weapons," Jonah said. "In a very ironic way this is good news my dear."

"But when they look at his ..... you know down there .... is he not .... won't they see?" Wilma was beating around the bush.

"No they won't. We never made him Jewish that way," Jonah replied. "Why would we do that to him? We did not have a Bar Mitzvah for any of you. We are only slightly Jewish by our culture but not at all by religion, you know that. I never thought there was a need to make a sacrifice to God from Egon's body. Don't worry about that. If they take him he will be fighting with the Germans, not against them. Mazel tov to that!" Jonah exclaimed.

Egon himself was surprisingly calm about the draft letter. He agreed with his father that it was a good sign. At least the family had not come to the attention of the authorities. There was also a good chance that Egon's weak physical constitution might see him exempt from military duty anyway and even if he was drafted, he would be fighting with a winning army who seemed to be impossible to defeat.

95

Jonah was more worried about the future of the weaver workshop if Egon left. He and the girls could only do so much and Egon had an amazing endurance for the work.

Egon had to report to the military headquarters two weeks after he received the letter and after a very shallow and unsound examination was declared fit for all duties. His training commenced a further two weeks after that in the military academy buildings on the northern side of Bratislava. During his basic training, he was allowed one weekend leave a month and after that it would all depend on the state of politics and on his particular talents.

Sadly, his instructors found nothing special or likeable about the quiet and shy recruit and recommended him for infantry or worthless cannon fodder as it was becoming known. Wilma was the most devastated in the family when he announced the results of his examinations. The only glimmer on the horizon was that he needed far less training than he would have had if assigned to a different part of the army. After he had finished his initial training, Egon had been allowed to carry on working in the weaver workshop until further notice but in July he had been called back to duty to the infantry regiment.

In the barracks, one of his superiors noticed him reading books in his spare time and when examining the literate recruit further realised the potential of Egon's scientific mind. For a trial, he transferred him to the radio units and had him trained up quickly. During the invasion of Poland, private Weissensteiner was a safe distance from the front line and yet received praise for his exemplary military service. His superior was appalled that during the original examination nobody had noticed his talent or his incredibly sharp hearing. While many troops remained stationed in the formerly Polish territories, Egon was sent back to Bratislava where he received further training and was made to study on army grounds. It was heaven for Egon who, for the first time in his life, excelled at something and received such encouraging praise for it. He was well respected amongst his comrades and quickly learned all there was to know. It was confusing to him as a Jew to find himself fighting with the Germans or at least on their side, but this was his opportunity to learn and acquire knowledge that he would be able to use later on in a civilian career. The war in Poland had been about territories and not about the Jews he told himself. The Slovak nation had regained the land it had lost to Poland just the year before and surely Slovak involvement in the war would now be over.

Wilma scolded him for fighting in a war which, at least, indirectly affected the Jews. Nobody in her family quite understood why she was suddenly so concerned about the Jewish question. She had always been the one that laughed off reports about anti-Semitic incidents as exaggerated and avoidable, and she had never considered herself a Jew in the first place. She had not been brought up in any faith and had always ridiculed any believers, pointing out their irrational behaviours whenever she could:

"Oh yes, if he doesn't wear the prayer shawl his God won't listen to him," or:

"Does anyone actually really believe that that piece of dough turns into the flesh of Christ?"

Jonah had warned her several times how hurtful her comments were to believers of any faith and what a nasty and intolerant side of her such comments displayed. Wilma argued that these people had a brain themselves and if they chose to believe something that was so clearly against anything your senses told you, then they should have a thick enough skin to hear her bit of truth. However, when her siblings also asked her to stop, she promised not to make any more such statements in front of other people.

For Jonah and his family, life was busy but good and for the first year of the new Slovakian state they managed to stay clear of trouble. The business was doing very well. The increased demand for army supply meant that even the less efficiently produced goods were needed. Old stocks that had not found buyers could now be sold. The profit margin was not excellent but the workshop ran at maximum capacity. The buyers were either ignorant of him being a Jew or, for the time being, were too desperate to care. The Hungarian countess who had commissioned two hanging wall carpets a few years ago had brought a lot of new clients to his business. The carpets with biblical themes had ironically become something of a fashionable item with these customers, the one thing he was legally not allowed to manufacture.

On bad days he would be driven mad by fear that the public display of his carpets on so many walls would eventually lead to his downfall and identification as Jew; being talked about could attract the wrong kind of attention and without a reputation he and his

97

family could starve. However, when in an optimistic mood he would say that in the public opinion this speciality of his had made him believable and safe as non-Jew.

Wilma had come to think of the family's continuing 'slipping through the net' as the Weissensteiner luck. The family had left the Ukraine before it had become too dangerous and so had managed to settle in Slovakia before the big wave of eastern European Jewish refugees came after the Great War. They were not as thoroughly inspected when they came and were able to make it widely believed that they were Protestants. The German school where Jonah enrolled his children in the province had been almost completely Catholic and did not offer religious education for Protestants. The children had thus avoided showing their lack of knowledge in Catholic classes without being identified as Jews. Wilma insisted that it was nothing short of a miracle that this ploy had worked out. Then they moved to Bratislava soon after the big wave of Jewish immigrants but since the children spoke perfect Slovak and the family was coming from the province, yet again they were not identified as Jews. At the German school in Bratislava they could refer to the lack of Protestant lessons in the province when a teacher questioned their complete ignorance concerning religion. So far they seemed to be always one step ahead of trouble, Wilma said. The business was doing well, they were living in relative freedom and instead of being found out at the army, Egon had stumbled on a promising career without even looking for it.

Since the incident on the bridge Wilma had never repeated this statement in public, believing that maybe she had jinxed their good fortune by talking about it.

The rest of the Weissensteiner family still used the expression heavily to congratulate themselves and to keep their spirits up whenever things were looking difficult. Wilma could not deny that maybe it was also that famous Weissensteiner luck that had saved her from death on the bridge. It was far from a pleasant experience but she had to consider herself lucky to have walked away from it. The acknowledgement of this relative piece of luck however did not help her to overcome the new found fear and anxiety. She had started to suspect and mistrust everybody outside her family. She shied away from the other weavers and customers and hid herself away whenever she could. Jonah and Egon saw this behaviour as a sign that she missed her sister and got word to Johanna that they would like to see Greta but Johanna kept postponing contact until times were 'easier'.

At the end of the year, the English broadcasts on the wireless announced the establishment of a Czechoslovak National Council in exile in London and its diplomatic recognition by France, Britain and the USA. Johanna insisted that this was a sure sign that there soon would be a military intervention on behalf of the exiled quasi-government and it was worth holding out a little longer. Jonah realised that it was impossible to win an argument with this woman and, as much as it hurt him to see Wilma in such pain, he too felt it was safer to be cautious.

Chapter 5: Bratislava 1940

Christmas and the New Year had been a huge celebration at the Weissensteiners. They had completed another two huge wall carpets ahead of schedule for the Hungarian countess, who had generously shown her appreciation for the fact that she was able to install them ahead of the tree decorations in the main hall of her manor house. The Countess was very pleased with the result and Jonah was confident that after the big New Year's Eve ball at the manor house there would be further commissions from the gentry.

In January, new Military laws excluded Jews and gypsies from draft and service, and when the first two waves of expulsions had not affected Egon, the family felt reassured that their status in the country was safe.

Jonah worried much more about Wilma. She had taken to strange habits of late, running to the main door several times at night to check that it was locked and spending hours at the window. Her cooking had become more flawed than before and her dishes tasted as if she had used spices at random rather than following the recipes Greta had written down for her. Jonah realised that he could no longer blame any of this on the missing sister. Something was profoundly wrong with his daughter but she would not tell him what was troubling her mind.

Luckily the workshop had been able to replace the girl that had blackmailed him into a raise last year. When he had first written to other weavers he knew for recommendations, he had not been successful in his search. Even letters that the Countess had written on his behalf to put more weight behind his requests had yielded no success. When he wrote more letters to find a replacement for Egon, who was back full-time with the army, he had more luck and managed to hire not one but three new weavers. One of them, called Alma, was particularly talented with the artistic and manual side of the work. For most of her life she had lived as a Slovak in Hungary and had returned to her home country now that it was independent. She had moved to Bratislava especially for the job and offered to help out with the cooking in exchange for a free room in the house. She was incredibly hard working and efficient and it was only due to her interpersonal skills that Wilma could be sufficiently calmed and made useful in the kitchen at all. Jonah was however worried what the other employees and his customers would say about his hysterical daughter. The last thing he wanted was for anyone to report her as a mad woman to the authorities and for her to be locked away in some sanatorium. Her erratic behaviour could be very unsettling at times, even though it flared up very irregularly. Alma was a godsend in this respect and she seemed too content living with the Weissensteiners to be considered a threat.

At the farm the main event of the season had been the discovery of Maria's secret affair with one of the helpers. Marius was not only a Jew and a refugee with no money or future, but, adding insult to injury, he was also married with three children. Benedikt blamed himself for letting this happen right under his nose and Johanna could hardly stop her husband from throwing the 'rotten apple' from the farm.

Benedikt had been so conscientious in checking up on the work force when he hired them but when they had proven themselves worthy he had become complacent and was fooled into trusting them. They had impressed him as hard workers and Benedikt had forgotten about the other dangers they could bring to the farm. When he discovered Marius and Maria in the barn he hit and beat the dirty bigamist until his face was covered in blood. When he finally stopped and Marius lay doubled over on the floor he said nothing. He stared at Maria with a puzzled rather than an angry expression, turned away and left. All he had was contempt for the stupid girl and her misguided urges.

Johanna took on the role of the punisher for him. Even though she did not resort to violence she made sure that Maria's life on the farm became a living hell. Limited food rations, work in the kitchen rather than in the fields, additional house work in the evenings and no contact with the farm workers. Everybody was worried that Maria might be pregnant but luckily that worry turned out to be unnecessary when a few weeks later Maria's period came on time.

Benedikt of course threw Marius and his brother off the farm and hired two new people instead. He was gutted because Marius had been the best of the bunch. Maria was heart-broken. Marius had been her first true love. Nobody could begin to imagine what he meant to her and how special he had made her feel. Never before had she felt any kind of self-worth. He alone had given her this feeling and now not only was it taken away from her, she was also shunned and treated with the utmost disgust. Yet she was spared the horrors of finding out his sad future. Young unemployed Jews and gypsies – together with those who were expelled from the army earlier that year - were drawn into a forced labour initiative by the authorities, which later that year opened the first labour camps on Slovak soil. On the farm this was not known until much later.

For Greta the sad love affair was a very painful experience too as it gave her an idea of how little her new family thought of Jews. Nasty comments had mainly focused on Marius's class and the fact that he was married but there were enough allusions about his race to chill her to the bone. In the minds of the Winkelmeiers, Greta was hardly a Jew (because she was not a believer and did not look or behave the part) and so they did not think she would take any offence by what was being said. She could not have any loyalties in that respect and if she really did have any objections she would know better than to voice them. After all she lived on the family's mercy and good will.

Greta was indeed painfully aware of her situation and said nothing as expected. Had it not been for Ernst she might have considered leaving, but he was so well cared for here on the farm and she did not want to burn her bridges with the family in case Wilhelm and Karl one day came back. So she kept shtum and endured her life as single mother. She found her only good friend on the farm in Maria whose own isolation was so harsh that the two of them were almost naturally driven into each other's arms. They both felt more tolerated than welcome on the farm and were both grieving. For the first time in her life Maria had something that was so important to her that she found the strength to talk about it and opened up to Greta about her feelings. All of these were of course currently centred on Marius. Greta had been the only one not to judge her for the affair and the fact that Greta had been Jewish – just like her Marius – was another contributing factor for the new friendship.

Roswitha used this opportunity shamelessly for the purpose of becoming more accepted at the farm herself. She tried to shine particularly bright in contrast to her fallen sister and used every opportunity to complain about the Jews in general and about Marius in particular. She spoke with disgust about lying with a man before marriage and pointed out all the mistakes that Maria made in the home and in the kitchen. Greta who was not used to such horrible and malicious behaviour was shocked at the blatant attack on Maria, but Johanna and Benedikt found it surprisingly amusing and laughed at the sarcastic and cynical remarks of their younger daughter. Roswitha became quite a hit with the two of them and the family gradually settled into two camps.

In February, a land reform was implemented in Slovakia that made it virtually impossible for Jews to own land. Most land from Jewish farms was being confiscated, some of it got distributed to Slovaks and some of it was sold to the highest bidder, but the state kept the main share of these lands and leased it out to other farmers. To Benedikt's and everyone else's surprise one of his immediate neighbours turned out to be a Jew and the poor man and his family were stripped of their property. Government officials offered Benedikt to lease the land under very good terms and conditions, and by accepting the offer Benedikt suddenly became a farmer of much bigger influence in the region than he had ever dared to dream.

The former Jewish owner was allowed to remain on the land, now working under the obligatory labour directives for free. Benedikt enjoyed his new status as big shot immensely. With the new farm came also a bigger tractor that made working his fields easier. He didn't have to pay much to the government for the favour.

Johanna could not quite understand why the old owners wanted to stay at all – they had been given a choice - but Roswitha said they hoped to get their property back after the war and thought their chances were better if they remained in the vicinity. Besides, they had nowhere else to go now. They were land-locked between German and Russian occupied territory, both Jew hating countries, and the only possible escape route would have been via Hungary, who was however also sympathetic to the German Nation after it had helped Hungary successfully lay claims on southern parts of Slovakia at the Munich Conference in 1938.

Greta had to be more careful than ever not to be seen in public. Johanna was very worried that in revenge for losing their farm, the filthy Jews would try and take them down with them. Being associated with Greta and her Jewish family could be bad for them now that the farm had expanded and Johanna was always one to plan for all eventualities in life - just to be safe. She began to think that it would soon be time for the Winkelmeiers and Greta to part ways but somehow she could not yet make herself do anything seriously about it.

Jonah and his family seemed to have been blessed with luck once again. His workshop was somehow omitted from the list of companies that had to change to a 51% non-Jewish ownership in accordance with the April laws. Was this another sign of the famous luck of the Weissensteiners? Had someone really forgotten about him as he would have liked to think? Was it the interference of some influential client or friend, as Wilma's theory went? Or was his time still to come? As pleased as he was with the result, he felt it was not prudent to let down his guard and assume he and his family were out of the woods.

In April, Denmark surrendered to the Germans. Norway was being invaded rapidly and the successful end of the German campaign was only a matter of time. At last there was some action on the political chess board in Europe, the kind that everyone had expected after the Blitzkrieg in Poland.

The Phoney War or "Sitzkrieg" (sitting war) seemed to be over but unfortunately not in the way Greta had hoped. Instead of being attacked, Germany was expanding further with no real obstacles in its way.

Johanna and Benedikt as proud Germans were over the moon about the German success and the formerly so generous and hospitable Benedikt started to question whether they should risk their status and wealth for Wilhelm's Jewish wife and off-spring. Of course he liked Greta well enough and the boy was simply adorable, but realistically what chances did Ernst have now to be ever accepted in the new Aryan society that was forming in Slovakia? Should they really risk their livelihood for these two undesirables? Wouldn't it be better to dump them and let them fight on their own? In Germany Jews were deported and those who harboured Jews were prosecuted as well. If that happened over here they would lose everything they had, and in Johanna and Benedikt's eyes that was rather a lot these days.

Johanna had made up her mind to show Greta the divorce papers and ask her to move back in with her father in Bratislava but Benedikt still hesitated. The child was his bloodline, maybe slightly soiled by a Jewish mother but it was still a Winkelmeier child. Johanna was outraged at his attitude towards a mixed race child. He had hardly cared enough about his own children to spend time with them when they were young, but here was a mongrel and Benedikt was willing to risk their future for him, even if the risking was done out of ignorance rather than bravery. Johanna felt real jealousy and resentment. She had resigned herself to the fact that Benedikt was a farmer and not interested in family life, but his interest in Ernst was an insult to her own family and his neglect of it. Johanna's mind was made up. Greta had to go and take that little Jew bastard with her. Weeks went by during which she waited for the right opportunity to make this plan come true.

When Germany invaded the Benelux countries and France in May and had enormous success with its campaign, Johanna used the heightened expectation of a German "Endsieg" to put more pressure on Benedikt.

"No one can stop Hitler. The European countries all crumble under his thumb. What a great war, nothing like the last one. Aren't you proud?" she asked with an excited tone in her voice.

"Of course I am proud," he replied reluctantly. He could tell by that tone in her voice that this was a prelude to a totally different question, even though he did not yet know which one. "Every day I can hear another success story of the army on the wireless. It is amazing."

"Exactly, we are really going to win this war. This will be one giant victory, I tell you." Johanna said, pleased that he had replied as she had hoped. Now she leaned to him in a conspiratorial way and continued. "We have to make sure we conform to his policies Benedikt. The Jews can't be helped any more. Their time is up."

"I understand what you are getting at but Greta and Ernst are part of our family. We can't just drop them like hot potatoes. It was you who wanted them here in the first place, remember?"

"She is not our family anymore," Johanna protested. "You know very well that Wilhelm divorced her. The child is a bastard now and worse, he has the Jewish nose. They are a liability to us, we have to get rid of them."

"No one is even going to think about his nose with his blond hair and she can easily pass for a gentile woman too," he insisted. "No one ever sees them outside the farm. Who would be looking for them anyway? We are Germans, everyone knows that. They gave us the Jewish farm to look after, what more reassurance do you need? I have thought about this, I know that they are a small risk, but I want to keep them here, it is only right. At least for now."

"It has nothing to do with right or wrong," Johanna said agitatedly. "Have you not heard what is going on in Germany? Just because it has not happened here yet does not mean it won't come. Any association with Jews now could damage our prospects in the future, even though at the moment there are no explicit laws against what we are doing. In Germany we would be blacklisted and boycotted or arrested. Is that what you want, just because of some cute looking boy and his Jewish mother? Benedikt, please, tell them to go. We have our own children to worry about. She has got family in Bratislava, let them take care of her."

"I thought you liked her?" he asked, surprised at her vehemence.

Of course Johanna liked Greta but since Wilhelm had left she had found the woman more of a burden than a help. "I don't like her enough to risk my future in a new Germany, a new Europe, even a New World," she replied. "We are on the winning side. Let's not risk that. Think of your children and what they would have to lose. We have nothing to fear from the new government unless through our association with her. Wilhelm divorced her which means he is in the clear. I love Ernst just as much you do but he will never fit in with us here. Someone will find out eventually. We can't hide them forever. We always said we would look after them until we know where the Jewish situation is going. Now that we know, we have to go our separate ways. How can you not see this?"

"It is true, we only committed ourselves to look after them for a little while," admitted Benedikt. "That doesn't mean that we have to stop. I really doubt that anybody would be interested in our farm and a blond child on it. Everyone has seen them at church and gradually some of the Germans on this farm moved back to Berlin; that is all the Slovaks are thinking. They haven't seen her relatives here for years. I am not sure anyone has even seen her. You are hysterical. I don't know why you want her to hide, if you ask me, that arouses much more suspicion."

"Even the smallest of chances is too much to take, can't you see that?" she insisted. "We don't even know what connections the

Weissensteiners have to other Jews. Jonah claims they have none but who can be sure? What if some of our workers overheard us?"

"You are being too anxious. Greta and Ernst are safe here and so are we."

"If Greta knew that Wilhelm divorced her I swear she would want to leave here anyway," Johanna persisted. "She would want to be with her own people, not with the family of a coward who dumped her. What would she want from us now? I did not tell her because like you I felt responsible for Wilhelm and Karl leaving and because I care for her. We have done enough, let her family carry the burden now. We have to look after ourselves."

"We should at least tell her about the divorce and then see how she feels," offered Benedikt as a compromise. "If she wants to leave on her own accord then that would be fine. I will not throw them out."

"If she doesn't leave on her own account then we can at least suggest it to her. Gently shoo her on the way," Johanna argued. "She wouldn't want to be a burden, I am sure. She probably doesn't even fully grasp the situation. She is always so optimistic and naïve."

"She only leaves if she wants to," he repeated. "You will not suggest it to her, do you understand? There is something like family honour."

"If I didn't know any better I would start worrying that you have a crush on that woman," Johanna said and turned away angrily.

That evening Benedikt and Johanna ordered their daughter Roswitha to stay with Ernst while they sat down with Greta in the kitchen and broke the news of the divorce to her.

"Oh I feel so stupid!" Greta said, almost amused. "I should have known, I should have guessed. Of course he went to Berlin to divorce me. That is why he did not want to go to Poland. How could I have thought anything else? I can't believe I really imagined that a German would flee with his Jewish wife to Poland. To think he had it all planned and lied to me. I can't say I deserve any better for my naivety."

"Don't say that," Johanna comforted. "He spoke to me about going to Berlin and he never said once he was going to divorce you. They must have forced him to do that when he got there. You know about the laws about mixed marriages, it might have even been a deal to save Karl? He had no intention to abandon you when he told me

107

about his plans. He must have changed his mind," Johanna said.

"Greta, my love, it is better this way," Benedikt added. "You are better off without him. It is easier to be on one side of the fence than sat on it. Now you can be with your people and don't have to worry about your loyalties. As a Jewish family you can stick together and solve your problems together. It makes your life much less complicated."

"Oh! I see. Well in that case it will probably best if I pack my things and go back to stay with my father. Now that we are no longer family in the legal sense it would be unfair of me to compromise your situation. You have been kind enough as it is. Thank you for everything that you did," Greta replied.

"I wish things were different," Johanna said, acting so compassionately that she almost believed it herself. "You have been a great help, but we are busier on the farm now that it is expanding and there will be more visitors coming. It wouldn't be easy to have you here. We will pack you some food that you can bring to your family," Johanna assured her.

"I will send Gunter to tell your family that you'll be coming. I am so sorry things did not work out," Benedikt concluded the conversation.

Greta did not shed a tear for her marriage. The thrill of her first infatuation and the excitement of the early years had long gone. The harsh reality of farm life and motherhood had eroded the romantic notion of the happily-ever-after couple that she had envisaged that they would become. Their mutual interest of reading books had been buried under dirty laundry and his ever growing work commitments. They had not even talked to each other late at night in bed as they initially did, at least not about anything that mattered. When had their love become such a routine and joyless affair? At times she had been closer to Johanna than she had been to her own husband. He must have felt the same way and decided the best course of action was to leave. She did not blame him. If he had stopped loving her it was not his fault. Their union had only ever made sense because of their love. Take that irrational attraction away and it was suddenly a very inconvenient and very dangerous enterprise. To end it was the sensible thing to do. Were things different, it might be worth fighting for their marriage but under these loveless circumstances, had roles been reversed, she might have done the same.

Her grief about Karl was of course quite different; here she could not rationalize her feelings away. She missed that boy. No one could imagine what it was like to lose your own child until it happened to them. She wanted to cry but she was not just a woman any more, she was a mother and her emotional state had to be in top shape for her son Ernst. She could not let him see her sadness and her devastation. She would get over this and be strong for him; he was all she had now.

Two days later Jonah picked up Greta and Ernst. They moved back home and shared Wilma's room, who was full of joy to have her sister back. Of course the Weissensteiners were outraged that Greta and Ernst had been abandoned and that Karl had been taken away in such a sneaky manner, but at least they had their beloved Greta back with them.

There was simply nothing they could do to get Karl back. Wilhelm held all the trumps. The law, the politics and all circumstances made it impossible to even try. It was better to get on with their lives and be as quiet as possible. Over time they came to believe that Karl was probably safer in the hands of his German father anyway, even though Greta did worry how he could ever live safely in Germany as the child of a mixed marriage. She hoped that Wilhelm knew what he was doing.

That year saw the first wave of food shortages that would last well into the following year, mainly caused by the demands for food from Germany that had been agreed and guaranteed in a Treaty of Protection between Germany and Slovakia. However, a positive result was that the economy improved. Workers had been offered opportunities in the Reich and instead of unemployment there suddenly was a shortage of labour in Bratislava. Railway networks were extended and improved all over the country, new roads were built and the electricity network was also expanded, often thanks to the forced labour from the camps. To the general population this was of course all good news. War activity was far away from Slovakian soil and with the improvements in the infrastructure, one could easily be persuaded to think that the independent state had chosen wisely in becoming a close ally of Germany.

Even though the situation for the Jews was uncomfortable, it remained stable and less harsh than in Germany itself. Rumours spread about the dreadful conditions in the work camps erected in Poland and the deportation of many Jews from Western Europe into them. In Slovakia, the work camps were still mainly filled by criminals and political enemies of the state. Mass deportations of Jews without such backgrounds had not taken place and the development of ghettos was not as strictly enforced as in other areas of Hitler's influence.

In honour of its late founder, the ruling Slovak People's Party renamed itself into the Hlinka Party. Some of the Hlinka Guard, the military organisation of the party who was now properly organised and officially recognised, started to take to the streets to beat up and terrorize Jews. Nobody had to wear the Star of David yet and so occasionally gentiles were beaten up by mistake.

Greta and Wilma rarely left the house, mainly because of the Hlinka Guard, which had brought terror back to Wilma, but also because they were needed at the workshop. The Slovak girls who had been helping out at the workshop had found employment elsewhere that they said was better paid and less boring, and so the burden fell on Alma, their only employee now, and Jonah's children. Jonah was determined not to let the Countess, his great benefactor, down and worked as hard as he could.

Wilma raised the question of whether their employees had left because they knew the Weissensteiners were Jewish but Greta dismissed the idea as farfetched. Jonah said if their names had been on a hit list there would have been trouble already. During the autumn several laws and decrees were passed that ordered the transfer of all Jewish property into Christian ownership and Jewish bank accounts were frozen, but nobody had approached the Weissensteiner family.

They had survived for almost twenty years in Bratislava without unwanted attention, if they could survive this newest wave of discrimination without being detected it was not likely to occur after this. Just because two girls found a better job at a time when labour was short that did not mean an unprecedented anti-Semitic attack was imminent. However, secretly he did worry a little.

Alma had guessed their secret before she even got to the Weissensteiners. She had known some Weissensteiners in Budapest and she had not the slightest problem with Jews, as long as they were not too fanatic. The ones with beards and curls scared her a little although she could not say why. None of them had ever even as much as given her a dirty look. She appreciated the gentle nature of Jonah and admittedly had developed a little crush on this lovely and kind man. Wilma liked Alma a lot, but with all her hysteria and paranoia she was not sure if she could trust her yet

Johanna and Benedikt were enjoying their new existence as big fish in a small pond and became rather dictatorial with their staff. With Greta gone they felt no longer compromised in using their power and enjoyed inflicting their will on a whim. For years they had been a minority in the country and had to compete with the locals to sell their goods, now there was no competition as everything that was produced found buyers and Germans were much more accepted in society than ever before, although of course a slight reservation naturally remained.

To her own big surprise Johanna did feel a hint of guilt about making Greta and Ernst leave. She knew it had been an extreme precaution and every so often she wondered if she had done the right thing. Having gone so obsessively to church every Sunday she must have picked up the odd Christian doctrine without meaning to. When possible, she sneaked some food in a basket when she went to market in town and delivered it to the Weissensteiners. She knew it was risky and probably stupid after she had worked so hard to erase the connection with the Jewish weavers, but while her fear to miss out on the new opportunities in the new Slovakia had dominated her decisions before, occasionally now she was overcome by surprisingly affectionate feelings for Greta and Ernst. She reasoned with herself that in Bratislava she may not even be recognised and never stayed with them for long anyway. A few cuddles with Ernst and she was on her way again. Benedikt would be furious if he knew that she was feeding them after throwing them off the farm. He probably would have rightfully argued that this was much more dangerous and public than sheltering a secretly Jewish woman on their farm, but she could not help herself. She could have sent one of her girls to do it for her, but did not trust them enough with such a secret task.

Despite the increased violence against Jews, the Weissensteiner family had nothing to worry about in the year of 1940. Egon's career in the army had advanced rapidly and when he was on leave he always came in his uniform so that the neighbours would be reassured in their belief that the Weissensteiners were loyal to the Slovak Nation. Nobody in their right mind would think of them as Jews now. Even for the ones who noticed his nose and non-Aryan looks the uniform was a clear sign that they had to be mistaken. The army took on no Jews.

Slovakia was still far removed from any war activity. Italy, Japan and Germany formed the Axis and consequently Italy went to war in Greece and in Africa with the backing of its fellow Axis nations. The war even seemed to move further away and the Slovak army was not called upon to fight alongside the Axis powers.

Egon was safe and suddenly had a career and also had made some army friends, even though it gnawed at him that he had to compromise some of his opinions and feelings for the new career and friends. He was Jewish in some ways and in others he was not. He felt Jewish and he didn't feel Jewish at the same time. Many of his army colleagues were not really interested in the Jewish question, whereas others were. The barracks, despite belief to the contrary, were not a centre of anti-Semitism. Obviously many soldiers were racists, but also many were just proud to be citizens of a free and self-governed Nation, glad for once to fight for their own territory and lead their own war, not to follow some Austro-Hungarian order into some conflict that was of no consequence to the Slovak People. Slovakia felt an equal partner in a group of right wing Nations that was winning the war and if this war was the price for autonomy, these soldiers were happy to pay it. For some, the Jews were just a minor side issue in the battle for freedom but it left a bitter taste in Egon's mouth when he heard some of his new friends tell nasty jokes about the Jews.

There was an underlying assumption about him that had enabled him to become part of this circle of friends. Should it ever become known that he had Jewish roots he doubted these friendships would stand the test of time. It was hard because of all the Weissensteiners Egon felt the most Jewish, the only one who had even had contact with the Jewish faith after the death of his mother. Those days were a long way in his past now, but they were not forgotten.

Chapter 6: Bratislava 1941

Throughout the winter the country experienced severe food shortages, which everyone blamed on the aggressive demand from the Reich. While parts of the population appreciated the improvements their country had been able to achieve since its independence and the political leaning on Hitler, other parts were getting impatient with the dominant role which the Reich was displaying in its relationship with Slovakia.

Jonah and his family were grateful that Johanna still brought them the occasional supply of food. At first, they were suspicious about this charitable action, so obviously out of character for that cold woman, but over time they got used to it and wondered if they had been wrong in their judgement of her after all. Johanna herself was surprised over this inexplicable urge inside her to do good. Consciously she was not aware of any guilt or need for atonement. There was nothing that she should or could have done differently and nothing in her limited power that she had not done for that Jewish woman and her family.

For some strange reason these people had gotten to her and at home she often panicked and wondered if anything could have happened to them. It was a minor miracle that the family had survived all those anti-Jewish measures and seemed to be able to carry on as usual. It worried her deeply to think of them all in danger and it comforted her to think that at least they had enough food. Benedikt had no idea that she was still in contact with the Weissensteiner family. He did not really care about them anymore as he was too busy making profits from the confiscation of Jewish farms and, as Greta and her son were no longer living on the farm, he was not in the least worried about his previous connections to them.

Benedikt's confidence had always been based on outward success and the sole driving force for all his actions was his addiction to it. Ever since he had been a child he had enjoyed himself most when he could show off his newest achievements; excelling at running the family farm, marrying the prettiest girl and being able to harbour his relatives from Berlin had so far been the largest decorations on his chest. With the recent expansion of the farm he had surpassed his wildest dreams and even managed to outshine his own father. He felt invincible. Just like Germany and its Chancellor seemed to be, his farm was running like a machine. Seasonal workers were harder to come by these days because so many Czechs and Jews had left the country and many workers had been drafted to German factories, leaving Slovakia short staffed.

Of the Jews that had stayed behind many were interned in work camps like Terezin north of Prague or smaller ones in Slovakia. Peddlers, fixers and other 'unproductive' members of society were the main targets for selection. Benedikt's Jews had decided to stay with him instead of leaving and when the first internments of Jews occurred he was allowed to keep them. They thought themselves lucky compared to others and worked very hard to keep his goodwill.

In this moment of glory, he forgot all things unrelated to the farm and Greta and her problems had slipped from his mind completely. The running of the family was a trivial matter compared to his material progress and even his own children were of no interest to him right now.

Johanna in the meantime had a hard time keeping the younger generation on the farm under control. She had got used to the support of other women to help her in these matters and missed the emotional wisdom of Elizabeth and the efficiency of Greta. Ever since the discovery of Maria's shame with the married Jew, she was paranoid that something like this would happen again right under her nose. She could not rely on either of her daughters to inform on the other, at least not to her. There was no bond of trust with their mother and no obligation to share problems.

Roswitha had become a great help in the house and seemed a reliable worker but she was young and there was no guarantee that she would not make a similar stupid mistake as her sister. Johanna realised that she had no idea what was important in Roswitha's life and how she could manipulate her. She had only learned the 'cracking of the whip' to achieve results, but in Maria's case that had not led to success. How they were ever going to marry off either of the girls now was a big worry on her mind.

It was simply impossible to do all the work and at the same time check up on the girls. Yet rigorous control and detailed observation were the only things she could think of to prevent another scandal or wrong doing. She explained her dilemma to

Benedikt who thought these matters far too trivial to take them seriously. Why did women always have to make such fuss about everything? For years they had been able to run the farm and keep everything together.

They had disciplined the girl sufficiently, he was sure she had learned her lesson and besides, the size of the farm was an ever growing dowry that would attract attention for both girls despite an admittedly questionable reputation. There was no reason to get worked up about the future prospects, it was much more important to focus on the present and the continued success and expansion of the farm. If any extra time should be taken from the farm and house work it should be in aid of his contacts in the village, the farmers and party officials. He was a rising star and needed this kind of support, not foolish worry about the honour of a pretty but dumb daughter. Her looks would get her the attention of the boys but his farm would get the attention of the boy's parents.

Johanna disagreed with his optimism about the girl's opportunities for marriages but she knew when Benedikt talked as self-assured as he was now there was no getting through to him and all she could do was to side track the topic to get what she wanted. So she congratulated him for his far sightedness and agreed enthusiastically but she suggested that they should get the Jews to help her in the house as well so that she could try to see more of the villagers and neighbours. Surely it would be easy to persuade their Jewish servants to help her in the house, surely there would be no need to remind them what kept them safe from the work camps, they would not mind helping Johanna and the girls? They had to be thankful to their saviours and show their appreciation. Benedikt agreed with her view, excited that his wife for once had grasped the importance of his own plans and was willing to cooperate. The Jews working for Benedikt immediately sent one of their daughters to assist Johanna in whatever capacity she was required.

The girl's name was Sarah and she seemed very mature for her 14 years. She got busy scrubbing the floors and washing the large amounts of clothing and sheets for the family; all the while she kept her head down, was quiet and when she was spoken to she was polite and submissive to the point that it was almost embarrassing. She never seemed to tire and did every task that she was assigned with determination.

115

Johanna was pleased at how eager and keen the young girl was. Maria tried to befriend her, hoping to find out about her Marius and what might have happened to him but Sarah would not answer any of her questions, knowing full well that the relatively comfortable life of her family was hanging by a thin thread. Maria also tried to find out more about Judaism and the religion of her former lover but again she found herself up against the same stoned wall of silence from Sarah.

The two young women had however an amicable relationship, which was expressed in looks and gestures more than actual words and acts. Sarah knew that Maria meant her no harm and Maria felt that at long last there was a friendly face on the farm and that knowledge alone helped her to cope with the isolated position she had found herself within the family ever since the scandal broke.

Roswitha however did not take kindly to the Jewish 'slave girl' who pleased everyone else with her great work attitude. Sarah was a big threat to her only recently established role as the reliable female on the farm. It had not been easy to impress her parents after the industrious Greta had left and it had taken dedication to get recognised for her own hard labour. Outshining her mother and the simple minded Maria had been fairly easy, but it had taken time before she managed to reach the levels of Greta's efficiency. What if it turned out now that Sarah was not only a better worker than her but also better at cooking? Would the daughters have to take over the hard work instead? It was not the most likely scenario but she was worried all the same and so Roswitha decided to make Sarah's life as difficult as possible.

With an incredible attention to detail, she observed her 'rival' and found ways to sabotage her work, mainly by dirtying surfaces and clothes that just had been cleaned but also by calling her names and intimidating her when no one was around to notice. She discovered a nasty side to herself that she had not known was there; now that she had found an easy target, years of suppressed anger and frustration turned her into a sadistic bully.

Sarah let all of this happen, seemingly immune to the insults and stoically enduring the abuse. It was obvious who had messed up her work but instead of complaining about it to Johanna, she just apologised and did the work again. Johanna had her suspicions about Roswitha's behaviour but did not feel like doing anything about it. If

116

this was how her daughter was wasting her thoughts and energy there was nothing for Johanna to worry about. It might well be helpful to keep Sarah aware of her fragile position and she had far more important things on her mind than the Jewish kitchen help.

Benedikt had told her she had to make friends with the neighbouring farms to ensure there was no resentment against them and her husband was right; they had to demonstrate that their recent rise would be no threat to the community. Talking to the women of the farms might give her an idea how the Winkelmeiers could best ingratiate themselves with the community. However Johanna neither possessed the appropriate people skills to make new friends easily nor the endurance to wear down resistance. She quickly gave up and turned her focus back to her family.

The most recent worry was concerning her son Gunter, who was being drafted into the army. During the previous year, in response to what had happened to their relatives in Brno, the Winkelmeiers had decided to take Slovak Nationality. Cousin Klaus and his sons had taken German Nationality after the country had turned into the Protectorate, assuming that it would make their life easier but as German citizens they had been immediately called for army duty and were now stationed in France, leaving the women of the family to fight for themselves.

To avoid the same fate for Benedikt and Gunter they had made their decision believing that Slovakia's further involvement in war activities was unlikely and that their patriotic duties would be perfectly fulfilled by running food production on the farm.

Gunter spent most of his time at a boarding school and had done tremendously well in his exams. Initially his teachers had recommended that he should study Mathematics or Physics in Bratislava or even Vienna but he had broken a leg playing football against a local team and as a result he had to miss the admission tests at both Universities. He was still recovering in the sick unit of the boarding school when he was approached by one of the army recruitment officers. The army was looking for young intelligent men just like him and Gunter had been told that volunteering for the army would not only guarantee a future place at either University for him but would also positively influence his further career prospects later on. His protests that he was not physically strong enough for a career in the army were dismissed as silly imagination. Once his leg was healed what would he do with his time?

Having missed the boat to study this year, did he really want to waste a precious year doing nothing? He might as well do his duty for the country and egged on further by peer pressure at the school he was starting to seriously consider this option.

Johanna was both proud and worried at the same time. It was a relief that her son was not a coward after all and felt not threatened by the idea of physical fighting and a rough barrack life. She had secretly feared Gunter would turn out to be the weakling Benedikt had always made him out to be. She felt an unexpected surge of motherly pride swell up in her when he first mentioned the possibility in a letter to her but at the same time she was painfully aware that he was not the strongest of men and might not be suitable for warfare. They had not wanted him on the farm, what could the army use him for? She hoped her son knew what he was doing and was not trying to prove himself unnecessarily in the battlefield. Should she encourage or deter him?

Benedikt was of no help in answering her questions on that matter, he frankly did not care one way or the other. Should Gunter join up it would redeem him a little and it would save the family money. The army would hardly take him if they thought he was of no use to them. He might be weak but with his clever brain he could always do a desk job. Should he decide to study instead he would certainly excel and become an accomplishment of a different type for Benedikt's branch of the Winkelmeier family.

On Johanna's next visit to the Weissensteiners she decided to ask about Egon's career in the army. That boy was physically very weak, very inferior and if he had managed to secure a good position merely on intellect then maybe his father could give her and Gunter some insight into the situation. Johanna gathered some vegetables, eggs and a piece of ham, and put it all discreetly in a satchel, unaware that Roswitha had seen her through the kitchen window. While her mother was leaving in the direction of Bratislava, Roswitha wondered why all that food was being taken into town. Johanna had stopped taking food to the neighbours as a way of trying to improve friendships and she rarely went into town on her own. There was no denying that something out of the ordinary was occurring and since she had heard nothing about it there had to be a way to take advantage of it.

Johanna arrived at the workshop on Gajova just as Alma was coming back from the market and the two women entered the private quarters together. It was a little strange to her to witness the overly familiar way in which Jonah and his children treated their employee Alma. Johanna was surprised by the warm and close nature of their relationships with each other and she felt a little sting of jealousy that Jonah seemed to have an eye for Alma when she had always assumed he was holding a secret candle for herself.

When Jonah recognised Johanna he did make a huge fuss over her and thanked her many times for her kindness and the food she kept bringing. He got Ernst up from his afternoon nap and showed him off to their visitor but Johanna still was not overly interested in the boy; lately she could see both the Winkelmeier and the Jew in him. To many people this strange combination seemed cute or adorable but to her it was a little unsettling and disgusting. To see the handsome Winkelmeier features disfigured in such an ugly way was too much for her. Ernst was a freak of nature and a proof that humans should not mess around with the races that God had created. She could tolerate individual hard working Jews but as a whole there was something wrong with them and she had to make sure not to get carried away in her affections for Jonah and his family.

Greta and Wilma briefly came up from the workshop to say hello to their benefactor and to enquire about the news from the farm but they had to carry on working urgently on a carpet that was to be completed later that week and could not stay long for any more pleasantries. Alma got herself busy in the kitchen and left Johanna and Jonah alone in the living room to talk about Gunter's future.

"The army is the best thing that ever has happened to my Egon," Jonah reassured her. "I tell you, I hold a deep resentment to the war effort as you can imagine but I have never seen that boy happier in his life. They have made him a man. He is proud and purposeful."

"Our Gunter is such a weakling," Johanna said worriedly. "How will he even manage the initial training? Do you think he is as strong as your Egon? Is he as clever?"

"If my Egon has survived the initial training, then so will your Gunter," Jonah reassured her. "If they have singled him out at the school it is clear they want him. They are not looking for just anybody. It is not necessarily numbers that they want, they need clever people who can help plan and build up the army. The army is still in its infancy here. When it was the Czechoslovak army most of the leaders were Czechs, now they need to fill those gaps."

"Then how can we be sure that they know what they are doing?" Johanna worried. "Can we trust them?"

"Who can be sure in these times?" Jonah said. "No one can. They took Egon on and first made him infantry, pure cannon fodder. Then they discovered his brain and got him a good position. It will be the same for Gunter. Even if they just want anyone right now, they will see his potential and make good use of it. I am sure it will work out, Johanna. They are learning from the Germans and they seem pretty successful."

"Oh I wish I could be as optimistic as that," she said agitatedly. "He is so weak and so clumsy. If he does not get recognised for his brain and gets selected for an infantry job he will be amongst the first to die. I can feel it."

"Don't be silly woman. Where do you even think there would be such a battle or a war for him?" Jonah asked. "The Germans are doing fine without any help. Almost every country in Europe is occupied, is an ally of theirs, or is cooperating with them in one way or another. Let him train and reap some benefits for his patriotic duty, he will be stationed somewhere safe, I promise."

"I hope you are right," she said. "I am almost certain that Gunter will join up. These recruitment officers are very persuasive. He has to wait for another year to go to University and he hates it on the farm. He would do almost anything to get away from that."

"Can't you pull some strings to get him into University despite the time deadline?" he asked. "Bureaucracy has been established so that it can be overcome by favours and persuasion," Jonah said with a wink.

"Jonah, we are farmers. How would we have useful connections at a University?" Johanna said argumentatively.

"I thought someone at his boarding school might know someone. Isn't that how it always works?" he asked.

"If we knew someone they would not have let the army recruiters get hold of him," she replied. "We have no such help and he will sign up."

"If he does, I am sure it will be as big a success as our Egon. He is a smart boy your Gunter," Jonah said.

"If only I was as sure as you that being smart will be an advantage in the army," Johanna said without hope.

When Johanna got back to the farm Roswitha noticed the empty satchel and decided she was going to find out the secret behind it. Her mother was always so mean and stingy, it seemed impossible to imagine to whom she would give or sell food from their own larder. She decided not to ask her mother directly, but to use the food that had disappeared from the house as an attack on Sarah. Over dinner she would accuse her of stealing the food and her mother would either have to come clean about her activity and save the maid or go along with it and sacrifice her to keep the secret; either outcome seemed desirable to Roswitha and all afternoon she smiled smugly waiting for the big moment to come.

"I think Sarah is stealing food from us!" she blurted out at the dinner table a few hours later.

"You are ridiculous child!" Johanna cut her short.

"But she must do. There are two pieces of ham missing from the larder. Who else would take them?

"You don't know what is in the larder. Stop talking nonsense!" Johanna tried to halt the accusations.

"I do know," Roswitha insisted. "I was in the larder twice today. There were two pieces of ham the first time I went in and the next time I had to go they were gone. I swear!"

"Don't swear. You are imagining things as usual," was all Johanna said on the matter but Benedikt suddenly took interest in the matter.

"Did you see her anywhere near the larder?" he asked. His old mistrust of Jews – especially since the incident of his daughter with that married Jew – flared up immediately.

"I tell you that the girl is dreaming this up," said Johanna. "She has hated Sarah from the very beginning and is trying to get her out of the house. I won't have it. I'd rather believe that you ate the ham yourself so you can blame it on Sarah," she accused her daughter.

"Maria was in the fields all day. The only people in the house were her, me and mother," Roswitha claimed.

"Is that true?" asked Benedikt.

"I was in town, I wouldn't know," admitted Johanna. "Sarah works so hard for us I refuse to believe that she is a thief. I would know by now if Sarah was capable of such a thing. What I do know is that Roswitha has a vicious streak in her and never misses an opportunity to blacken Sarah's name. I know she is just making this up. Go to the kitchen and don't come back," she ordered her daughter.

Roswitha stormed out of the room stomping her feet like a toddler and the remaining family members could hear her clean up noisily.

"What is it with that girl?" sighed Johanna.

"She is a spoiled princess who wants to be the centre of attention. Maybe you should break her spirit a bit, get her to be tired in the evenings, work her harder so she won't dream up stuff like this," Benedikt suggested. "We have always been too soft on her. We don't need such childish games between young girls."

Johanna was relieved that Benedikt did not question her about the ham in the larder any further. She did as he told her and made Roswitha scrub the floor and help Sarah with the washing. She kept Roswitha busy as much as she could and hoped that by making her daughter spend time with the Jewish girl the two of them might start to bond with each other and stop the jealousy.

What was wrong with Roswitha anyway? She should have been pleased about the extra help, not feel threatened by it. Johanna failed to see that it was her own coldness towards Roswitha that had created the strong and urgent need for praise and appreciation in her daughter.

For the next few weeks however Johanna decided to refrain from raiding the family larder for the Weissensteiners. Too bad, she had so wanted to find out what was going on between Jonah and this woman Alma. She had never had a chance to ask, Jonah had discreetly steered the conversation away from it when Johanna hinted at her suspicions and he had changed the subject onto other business and family matters. He was a clever man that Jew. That was probably why he had done so well for himself.

That very week Gunter decided to try his luck with the army and to everyone's surprise was immediately required to report for duty in the barracks. His leg was still not fully recovered but he was able to attend theoretical training as well as shooting practice from a wheelchair. Within a few days it became obvious that he was an outstandingly good shot and would make a great sniper.

Before he even had the all clear for his leg from the army doctor, he was already trained on the Karabiner 98, the German sniper rifle, of which there were only a few in the barracks. His further training was rushed and superficial. As proud as he and the whole family were about his instant success at the army, they were also stunned at the sense of urgency around his training. Johanna fortunately did not comprehend that snipers were front line pioneers who often operated behind enemy lines and who were always in grave danger of being caught. She was so visibly relieved that he had not been assigned a common infantry position that nobody had the heart to tell her any differently.

In June the German army started its attack on Russia. Twenty Thousand Slovak soldiers supported the campaign in the Ukraine and the Caucasus. Both Gunter and Egon were amongst them. Egon's position was way behind the front line, whereas Gunter was right in the centre of the war activities. However, he seemed blessed with a sixth sense for enemy fire and was nicknamed the killing machine by his colleagues. The Russian army had significantly more snipers, most of whom were employed to keep the invading German and Slovak troops back while the rest of their own units reformed and positioned themselves ready for the attackers. Gunter's mathematical mind could instantly work out where the shots were coming from and he took out several enemy snipers before they could cause too much damage to his fellow conscripts. His letters to Benedikt and Johanna were full of success stories and his parents were too proud to think about the danger he obviously had to be in to kill that many enemies. Johanna had no concept of how the war was being fought as Benedikt had not seen much action in the last war.

The surprise attack on its former ally Russia was proving a big success for Germany and its troops quickly progressed deep into the Ukraine and the Caucasus. Egon was never far from the front line either, but he was working with the radio units which were usually stationed away from the line of fire. His sense of hearing was sensational and thanks to his great command of the Russian language he too proved an appreciated and valued asset to the offensive.

The Weissensteiners sadly were not aware of Egon's success in the army. Most of his work was classified and he was restricted to writing very few letters and even those were usually heavily censored.

All that his messages managed to convey was to tell his family that he was alive and well. As happy as they were for Egon to be in a safe place in the war, they could not help but worry about him. Wilma especially felt a deep despair that nobody seemed to be able to stop the Germans. Whichever direction one took from Bratislava, one could travel for a long time before arriving at a peaceful and non-fascist environment; let alone a Jew tolerating or friendly one.

Greta was keeping herself busy with childcare and weaving work to take her mind off her divorce and the loss of her son Karl. She also avoided talking about Egon and the war, leaving Wilma to worry all the more by herself. Jonah too was slightly distracted, in his case by a sudden attraction towards Alma, something which she seemed to be feeling too.

Jonah knew it was madness to get involved with her and so he had fought the feeling for as long as he could but their desire for each other was so great that they were spending more and more time in each other's company. Wilma and Greta had their fun watching the two love birds courting while pretending that that was not what they were doing. Neither Alma nor Jonah were particularly good actors and the excuses they used to be in each other's company were so farfetched at times that the two sisters started to imitate them behind their backs.

"Oh! What a coincidence!" Wilma would mimic her father. "I was just going to look for you to discuss the new carpet design. Shall we go upstairs and talk about it?"

"Oh there you are Jonah!" replied Greta, mimicking Alma. "Could you please show me the new fabrics in the workshop?"

"Alma you must come with me tomorrow when I walk Ernst to the lake."

"Jonah, Ernst would like you to read him his goodnight story tonight. Would you be so kind and accompany me to his bedroom?"

They would invent ever more bizarre chance encounters between the courting couple and laugh when once in a while the exact situation did occur as they had 'predicted' in their jokes.

One day in August Alma decided that the cat and mouse game had gone on long enough. She had noticed the girls giggling and knew that as far as they were concerned, she and Jonah were already a couple. She could not understand why Jonah had not made any move on her yet. She had given him all the right signals, surely he could not be that blind. He seemed to enjoy her company too and he was neither the type to be shy nor to be put off by her openness about her feelings. A different man might be deterred by a woman who shows her emotions but she could not imagine that to be the reason for his hesitation. She could feel the tension between them and he had to be feeling that too.

"Jonah, I think we really need to talk about us," she said to him one day in the kitchen. Wilma and Greta were already sleeping and she had just finished cleaning the kitchen and would not go to bed without bringing this issue to a head.

"Do we?" he asked nervously.

"Don't you think so?" she asked.

"Why do you think we need to talk?"

"We are too old to be playing games, Jonah," she said, looking him straight in the eyes. "Don't you agree?"

"I am old, that much is true," he conceded. "You have a long way to go before I would call you that."

"Don't try to evade the subject, Jonah."

"I am not changing the subject," he said smilingly. "We were talking about our age."

"Which leads us to the question of what we are going to do with the little time we have left? Are we going to behave like adolescent children and carry on our hide and seek game or could we be adults about our feelings for each other and do something about it?" she said forcefully.

"Oh Alma," he sighed, feeling the fight leaving his body. "So you know about my feelings for you?"

"Yes I think I do. Everyone else knows about them too. Haven't you noticed your daughters giggling and Johanna's pointed questions?" she asked.

"Yes I have and I have been worried it might upset you," he admitted.

"Why would it upset me? You must know about my feelings for you." she said.

"I was hoping you had feelings for me and I feared it at the same time," he admitted, but then carried on, looking sad and disillusioned. "What good could come of it? The times we live in, it is impossible for us to be anything else than what we are now. Just

125

look at Greta and how sad and lonely her life has turned out to be."

"I am different to Wilhelm," Alma replied. "I am a middle aged Slovak woman, not a young inexperienced German boy. All I want in my life now is some happiness, some companionship and some warmth. Jonah, you are the nicest and kindest man I have met in my life and I care very much for you."

"You don't know the half of it." Jonah said, his head hanging down.

"Well, I know you are Jews and I don't care," she stated forcefully.

"You must care," he warned her. "If we were to get married you would become a Jew yourself by law. I care for you too much to let you risk your life like that. My family has been lucky so far. Someone somewhere might know about us and one day that person might decide that we have been enjoying our freedom for long enough. If they come to get us I don't want them to take you with them as well. It would be irresponsible for me to get you involved, especially because I have these strong feelings for you."

"My love is too strong to let you get away, even if that means we will one day be taken away," Alma said passionately.

Jonah took a deep breath, exhaled very slowly and felt his shoulders sink further and further in resignation.

"Look, Alma, I saw my wife dying of influenza," he explained." The heartache it caused me, the guilt I felt for surviving it myself. I don't know if you ever experienced a loss like that but let me tell you it is harder than you think. I could not face to watch you being deported or hurt because you were with me."

"I don't care about that," she insisted. "I would rather have a few years of happiness with you now and face the consequences when they come than being alone all my life and missing the one opportunity for true love. If my life is going to remain loveless, is it really worth living?"

"Yes of course it is. There is always something to live for, experiences, happiness, and friends. Love is beautiful, but it is not the only thing in the world," Jonah insisted.

"If you did not have your children what would have become of you after the death of your wife?" she asked provocatively. "Do you think you would have developed the same strength and sustenance just for yourself? If you refuse me now all I will ever live for is to go to work, to sleep and to eat, without anyone else to care for. What life would that be?"

"You are simplifying things," he stated. "You have to be stronger than that. We both have to be strong. I have thought about us being together for a long time. After Barbara died, I decided to live my life for my children and the business so that I can support them. I never expected any more romances in my life and I have made my peace with it. I was very tempted to have another chance at love when you came into our lives but the circumstances speak for themselves. We both know it."

"We don't have to make things official," Alma suggested. "I am your housekeeper, you are my employer. I have my servant's room, you have your own. I am not asking you for the official status as a wife or marriage, I am asking for your love."

"You are seriously thinking of a secret affair? Alma, you cannot keep anything a secret. Nosy neighbours, informants, spies, censors. What chance would we have to hide a thing like our love for each other?" he said with bitterness in his voice.

"Little or no chance that is true but that proves my point exactly. If the Hlinka Guard came in here tomorrow to pick you up, they will already assume that I am your mistress and a Jew lover."

"Then you must leave at once, move somewhere else. I beg you," he said, panic filling his body. How could he have been so blind and not realised that what Alma just had said was true and that he had endangered the woman he loved by keeping her near him.

"You are right, you are already in too much danger. I am ashamed I failed to think of that myself. How neglectful and thoughtless of me," he reprimanded himself, starting to pace the room nervously. "What can we do, where could you live?"

"I will stay right here," said Alma firmly. "This is my place of employment, I am a weaver and a seamstress, and I work for a widower with grown children and a grandson. We can try and deny everything with the benefit of some credibility. After all, at the moment nothing is happening between us. Moving somewhere else now will not make a huge difference either. If we had spies or enemies after us, they will have informed on us already and if the Hlinka guard come they will have already made up their mind about me, even if I live somewhere else."

"Do you have any idea how hard people work in these labour

127

camps?" Jonah asked her with gravity in his voice. "Do you know how bad the living conditions are? At the rate that people are being taken away, those places must be already crowded. We are not married, we would also live apart from each other. No, Alma, the risk is too great."

"You can deny me in that way but I am not leaving. The workshop needs me and so does this house. If you take that away from me I will be left with nothing and I promise you I will throw myself from the nearest bridge," she threatened.

"Don't be stupid," Jonah said with panic in his voice. "You are a great woman and you will always have a new chance at happiness. You mustn't put all of your bets on a shlemiel like me. You can always find different work, another family who needs you and you can always find a better match than an old man like me."

"You should give yourself more credit, Jonah," Alma contradicted. "You are anything but a shlemiel."

"You still mustn't risk your life," he insisted.

"Should the day come when the Hlinka Guard knocks on our door, I am prepared to take the risk because it is worth taking. I have found happiness here that I have not known before. I promise I will not play the heroine and we can all try and deny that there is anything between us. My Slovak passport might be enough to save me. But now, behind closed doors, let us not waste any more time and let us be together," she pleaded.

"You are a brave and determined woman, Alma. I wish I could change your mind," he said defeated.

"Yes I am determined and you cannot change my mind," she laughed, then went up and kissed him.

"No Alma!" he protested at first and tried to get away, but his resistance was very half hearted; soon he kissed her back and that was the end of the discussion. Two decades of sexual abstinence made him less determined and able to control his desires than he would have liked to be.

After a week of spending every night together and failing miserably in hiding their feelings during the day, Jonah called a family meeting where he officially announced their relationship to his daughters and tried to impress upon his children the desperate need for secrecy for Alma's sake.

"You'll need to learn a lot more about keeping secrets and lying if you are serious about protecting Alma." Wilma said cheekily. "At the moment a blind man could come into the house and pick up that you two are lovers."

"Wilma is right. You are doing a terrible job of hiding it," Greta agreed. "Do you remember how persistently Johanna asked about the living arrangements in the house when she met Alma last time? She picked up on the sparks between you even before you did; customers and suppliers might have done the same."

"We will have to try harder then," Jonah laughed. He had always encouraged honesty and confidence in his daughters and could not now complain when this policy came back to haunt him. Besides, he had never been happier in the last twenty years than he was at this very moment and he enjoyed the surge of optimism too much to let it be dampened down by worry. There had been too much of that in his life recently, just for once he wanted to be able to enjoy his life and so he allowed himself to relax and forget about the dangers out there.

By September however, the high spirits at the Weissensteiners received a big blow when the Slovak government passed a further set of anti-Semitic laws, the Codex Judaicus or Jewish Code. To most citizens, it was a little surprising that it had taken so long for this comprehensive piece of legislation to replace the existing hodge-podge of laws and regulations discriminating against Jews in Slovakia.

The Codex Judaicus finally implemented the harder principles of the German Nuremberg Laws into Slovak society. It finally defined Jews on racial rather than on confessional grounds and required them to wear the yellow Jewish Badge. Jews were now banned from using cinemas, parks, cafes, restaurants and public transports; they were only allowed to walk in town at certain hours of the day and owning a wide variety of valuables such as cars, radios and cameras was also forbidden.

To Jonah this was a first real crisis of faith. The new laws demanded him to act and identify himself publicly as a Jew. He could either carry on as if nothing had happened and walk around town as the non-Jew people might have come to believe he was. This meant he was risking the punitive measures in place if he should be discovered as the Jew he really was. Or he could follow the laws and make himself recognisable as Jew, which could ruin his life.

129

Either option was a huge risk and after a long discussion the family decided unanimously that Wilma would best remain indoors as - because of her physical features - she was the most recognisably Jewish. Greta and Jonah were less obvious in their appearances and the family thought they should be able to walk around town safely without being identified as Jews, but only if they really had to and even then they should try to stick to the prescribed times for Jews as an extra precaution. To be completely safe, Alma would take over all of the outdoor tasks for now, until it was clearer how the new laws would be implemented and how violations of the laws were being punished. They could only wait and see.

Sadly, Alma reported to the family that her experiences on the streets were far from comforting. Transgressions against the Codex Judaicus were met with varying degrees of harshness by the police and the Hlinka Guard. Some offenders were beaten but then released on the spot, some were let go with a broken limb as a warning, others were imprisoned but released very soon and some were used to make big examples of. Entire families - over 6000 Jews from Bratislava alone as the newspapers announced triumphantly - were evicted from the city and sent to forced labour camps right away.

Policemen and members of the Hlinka Guard were out on the streets and would challenge Jewish looking citizens to produce their papers, but Alma said that the language of the people was still more important than those papers. She had heard Jews reply in pure German or Slovak to these requests, saying that they did not have the required papers on them. In such cases the officers were usually not interested any more, they were looking for the Jewish refugees from Galicia and Russia, who usually had a strong and easily identifiable accent. Any of those who were not wearing the Star of David or who were walking around town at the wrong time of the day were taken into custody and not seen again.

Deprived of any opportunity to earn a livelihood and dispossessed of their property, many Jewish families were now in need of aid and relief. This came from some Christian charities and the Centre of Jews, which had been established by governmental order. The Centre was the exclusive authority representing and governing the Slovak Jewry and was charged with organizing the Jewish life in the country for the government.

By October the newspapers proudly reported that the number

of expelled Jews had risen to 15000 and with help from the Jewish administration the Hlinka Guard compiled further lists of Jews for deportation. The main targets were those with enemies or aggressive business competitors and those resisting confiscation of their properties. Apart from the occasional and sporadic violence against Jews in the street by excitable youngsters, the impression was that those who kept their head down managed to be left alone.

In the Protectorate of Bohemia and Moravia, similar rules had been implemented a long time ago but people risked being shot on the spot for not adhering to them and rumours about the conditions in the Jewish Ghettos in and around Prague were so shocking that life in Bratislava seemed safe in comparison.

Alma was a godsend for the family. She was competent in looking after the private and business interests for them and could get supplies as well as represent the company in town with clients; always excusing Jonah's absence with his other work commitments and deadlines. The clients took no notice.

The first real challenge to the new routine of voluntary house arrest of the Weissensteiner family was an invitation to a Santa Claus party at the house of the Countess in early December. She had always treated Jonah more as an artist rather than a manufacturer and wanted to present the genius behind her beloved wall carpets to her guests.

A liberal but devout Christian and art collector, she had recently commissioned a few artefacts, such as a beautiful Crucifix and the picture of a Madonna. She was dying to exhibit these new additions to her collection and held the party on the name day of Saint Klaus. Initially Jonah refused the invitation and in an apologetic letter cited his many projects that needed completion before the end of the year, but the Countess would hear none of it and even came in person to the workshop to put more pressure on him, making it too hard for him to refuse.

Her manor house was outside of Bratislava, the same side of town as Benedikt's farm and Jonah hoped he might be able to stay at their farm, to avoid breaking the travel time restrictions imposed on Jews. It seemed unlikely to him that he would be discovered as a Jew on the street, but he had heard that if a Jew was found walking the streets without the Star of David on his clothes he was usually less severely punished if the offence took place during the hours he was allowed to be in public. That way one could always claim to merely having taken the wrong piece of clothing. Sticking to the allocated time demonstrated a compliance of sorts and made the missing star more believable as an unintended mistake.

Johanna was surprised when at the end of November Alma showed up on the farm unannounced and related Jonah's request. When she heard the detailed reasoning behind it she decided to allow him to stay. Benedikt was unlikely to approve, so it was best if she did not mention it to her husband and decided to put the secret visitor up in the barn. It would not be comfortable but it was the safest option. Johanna would make sure Benedikt and the girls would not go anywhere near the barn that night. The Jewish maid Sarah could look after him.

On the day of the Santa Claus party Jonah dressed in his finest clothes and nervously made his way to Benedikt's farm, hours before he was due at the manor house. He walked with outer confidence and a mind free of care, but inside he was very scared of being confronted by officials on the way. It was madness to take such a risk but his livelihood depended on the good relations he had with the aristocrats and he could not afford to offend the Countess after she had personally come to his house to repeat her invitation.

Surprisingly he got to the farm without any problems at all and when he entered the barn he found a little table with food and wine next to an improvised bed in the hay. You could say what you wanted about Johanna, he thought, but she had an amazing ability to surprise with kindness. She had also left him a few books, which he guessed Greta had left behind when leaving the farm. He started to read one of them, "Life of a Good for Nothing" by Eichendorff, Greta's declared favourite with the happy ending. He was quite taken in by the book and had almost forgotten the time when the maid Sarah came in to the barn just at the right moment to remind him that he had to leave. He put the book into his pocket and thanked the kind servant girl.

"I hope Johanna and Benedikt are treating you kindly here. You must understand that underneath her rough exterior Johanna has a good heart," he advised her.

"Thank you. I must not complain," was the curt reply.

"I know your family has lost the farm. It must be hard," Jonah tried to show his sympathy.

"Yes it is hard. Not that you would know. You still have your business and your house," she replied.

"We all have our difficulties," he said, confused by this unexpected attacking remark.

"You have no idea how hard it is to work for someone else just like a slave, being told you are lucky not to be deported and allowed a living," Sarah protested. "To be tolerated on your own farm and being bossed around by arrogant outsiders. I don't care whether she has a heart of gold or not. She stole our farm and she keeps me busy morning through to evening. The difference to a labour camp is not as great as you might think."

"You're right," Jonah said apologetically. "I know nothing of your problems, but neither do you know anything of mine. I live in constant fear that they take everything from me, come and take me, my children, my business, my life. If you think I am enjoying myself you are wrong. Every time someone we haven't seen before comes into our house we panic that they may be an informer, spy or officer. I hate looking at my mail. Whenever there is an official looking letter my heart sinks and I break into a sweat. You live in constant anger, I live in constant fear. Who can say what is worse?"

"I would choose fear," Sarah declared. "We too live in fear that our luck has run out. We could be deported any day too but the difference is we are kept so busy that we can hardly think about it."

"I am sorry I offended you young lady," he said, realising that there was no reasoning with this angry young girl. "I meant no harm. I will take my leave now. Thank you for your help all the same."

Jonah was rather surprised at her strong reaction to his remarks. Maybe she was right and he had spoken a little out of turn. He had not considered her situation as much as he probably should have done before speaking to her but there was no reason for her to be so nasty to him either. After all it was hardly his fault that her family had lost their farm and he had not yet lost his business. He had just been a lucky guy, but the future was uncertain for any of them. What was more disconcerting was that Sarah knew he was a Jew. He had assumed Johanna had been discreet about it and not blurted it out to her servants, but then again why wouldn't she mention it to another Jew. She was no longer related to them and had nothing to lose.

One thing was clear though, Johanna had gone out of her way

to keep Benedikt in the dark about his visit and he wondered why. Was it just that Benedikt did not want to be bothered with them? Had he joined the Hlinka party? Was he involved with the politics to further his status? Jonah had to admit that it was all too likely.

The manor house was like a completely different world to the one he was accustomed to. Despite the on-going food shortages there was a huge buffet and free flowing champagne. Nobody in their right mind could have guessed that this was a party during war times. The Countess greeted him with enthusiasm and introduced him to several fellow Hungarian noble men as well as the Dutch painter of the Madonna. In his honour the party had been held on this day because it was the day when the Germans and the Dutch celebrated the Saint Day of Saint Nikolaus. In their tradition, every guest would receive stockings filled with sweets and other food.

Another tradition was to have a man dress up as the lovely Saint Nikolaus and another one as his grumpy and nasty assistant who was called Krampus. They together would read out the good and bad deeds of everyone at the party and decide who would be rewarded with a stocking and who would receive a 'beating'. The assistant was wearing a dark costume, had wild dark hair and his face was covered in dirt. He was shaking his whip and a broom made of wood and would look at the guests with an intense stare. Occasionally he would make threatening noises and run after some guest or the other. While this was amusing to most people, some of the female guests were seriously scared and one woman in particular almost fainted in shock.

"He looks like a Jewish devil!" she screamed. "He is going to kill me. Please keep him away!"

"Oh darling!" intervened the hostess. "He is harmless. I personally have employed him. Believe me he is not Jewish. He works in my stables and he is a good lad. Andres!" she said addressing Saint Nikolaus's assistant. "Don't get carried away please. Don't scare the guests. Keep it light!"

"Of course my lady." came the reply and the assistant disappeared from the area.

The Countess made all her guests stand in a circle in her big drawing room, where Saint Nikolaus and his helper Krampus had taken up position. Saint Nikolaus was holding a huge golden scroll, from which he started to call out the names of some of the guests present and he told a few tales or anecdotes about them, giving them either good or bad character references. Whenever something was mentioned that the Countess had considered a bad thing Krampus would make his noise and shake the broom but all speeches ended with a good deed and Krampus would take a stocking and bring it to the guest.

"Jonah Weissensteiner, are you here or are you hiding somewhere?" said Saint Nikolaus.

Jonah was frozen in shock. He had not expected to be put in the spotlight and was worried that this would draw unnecessary attention to him.

Before he could say anything the Countess called out: "There he is. Looks like he is hiding!" and pointed at him.

"I hear you have been a bad weaver. You have tried to neglect your biggest beneficiary and tonight's hostess because you claim you have other clients to satisfy. You have turned down many of her generous invitations including this audience with my holy self so that you could work some more. You have forced the Countess to come to your workshop in person to persuade you!"

At that point Krampus was running up to Jonah and cracked his whip in the air. Jonah knew he should laugh but he was all tensed up and could not move.

"Is that so, my Jonah?" Saint Nikolaus called out.

"I am afraid it is," he managed to say. "I am sorry, Saint Nikolaus. Please have mercy!"

The people in the audience took his fearful tone for good acting and laughed heartily. The Countess walked up to him and hugged him gently.

"Oh you are such a wit, Jonah," she said.

"You have redeemed yourself, my humble servant Jonah," Saint Nikolaus continued. "I have heard from a reliable source that you have brought the Countess huge pleasure with your craft and have created beauty of the highest order with the most pious of biblical themes."

A huge round of applause went through the room.

"For this we forgive you your minor transgressions and order you in the next year to make many more artefacts for the benefit of our Christian children on earth," Saint Nikolaus decreed and ordered Krampus to bring another stocking.

Jonah was shaking. If anyone in this room here knew that he was a Jew they would also know that he had broken the law by manufacturing a carpet with Christian themes. In the eyes of the Christian anti-Semites this would be a bigger sin than just going to the cinema.

"Nice going!" said someone next to him. It was the Dutch painter.

"Thank you. Your painting is phenomenal," he complemented his fellow artist. It was an amazing feeling to regard himself as an artist for once. His day to day running of the business made him feel much more like part of a production line, even though the truth was probably somewhere in the middle.

"How kind of you to say. Now tell me Weissensteiner, how are you getting away with it?" the Dutch man asked him.

Jonah's jaw dropped. "Getting away with what?" he asked.

"Where I come from Weissensteiner is not a gentile name, is it, and yet here you are mingling with society as if it was the most natural thing in the fascist Slovak society. I admire your guts," the painter said.

"I don't know what you are talking about," Jonah said, eager to get away from the conversation before he might say something unwise.

"It's fine, Weissensteiner. Don't be such a putz. If I wanted to denounce you I would not have come to you directly. Don't you recognize one of your own people?" the painter added.

"I would never have guessed," Jonah admitted. "Your name sounds so Dutch."

"Visser is the Dutch equivalent of Fisher and it has Jewish roots. I have been fortunate in that I have been working in Hungary and Austria most of my life, so nobody has made the connection. If I was still in Holland my life would be quite different now I imagine. So we better keep it shtum. Tell me, how do you do it?"

"My dear friend, I have no idea," Jonah said. "My family has either got a secret friend in the right place or somehow we have slipped through the net. I am scared to death here. Both of us could be hanged for using Christian symbols in our work."

"That is a rather dark point of view," said Visser dismissively. "You have nothing to fear, Weissensteiner. The Countess has probably a good idea about you and might be the driving force

136

behind your safety. She is well connected with some of the party members and their wives. You were very wise to attend."

"That is what I thought, even though it has been a big risk to travel during the curfew," Jonah replied.

"Half of life is a confidence trick, my dear friend," Visser said. "Convince yourself you are a goy, dress and walk like one, full of confidence and the air of entitlement. Nobody is going to look at you twice. Jews have been doing it for centuries and the gentiles have been none the wiser."

"That is what I thought too!" agreed Jonah. "But I am not enjoying the thrill."

"It will get easier with time," Visser reassured him.

"I hope you are right. You are an exotic foreigner in these circles but I am well established and one of many; the trap could snap shut at any moment. I don't think I will ever relax," Jonah admitted.

"You must!" insisted the painter. "I hear the Countess has big plans for you. She wants you to keep designing carpets and even wants to make an exhibition of your work. She has told me that she wants to be your patron and you could become very rich."

"Rich and famous for sure - and dead as well," Jonah said with a laugh. "I am glad you warned me, I need to find a way out of this predicament."

"Well, best to wait and see what she has to say," advised Visser. "I am sure she has a plan already in place. She would not want to be embarrassed by supporting a Jewish artist."

"How come you know all this?" Jonah asked.

"The Countess and I are very close, Visser told him. "We don't have many secrets from each other. Behind the aristocratic and Christian exterior is a frivolous and rather modern woman. She always has had the wisdom to hide the more controversial sides of her lifestyle from the public eye."

"Controversial side? You do intrigue me Visser. Tell me more," Jonah demanded.

"Not tonight but you can expect a personal invitation soon. Next time the Countess calls for you make sure you come in person and do not send your aide Alma again. The Countess took serious offence when that happened, even though it was clear to me why you resorted to that measure," he advised the weaver.

"Oh I don't know," said Jonah. "I am not sure I am up for

such a dangerous life. I feel more comfortable living in my little corner of the world and hoping I will be alright."

"Weissensteiner, with the Countess behind you, you will always be alright," Visser assured him. "With a talent like yours you cannot hide in a corner. That ship has sailed my friend."

"What exactly is your relationship with the Countess?" Jonah asked.

"Over dinner, my friend. Over dinner. Relax and enjoy the party. I bet you have not celebrated much of late. Here, have some more champagne and try to be happy. The future looks good for you."

Jonah stayed at the party for several more hours, exchanging pleasantries with some of the guests, being complemented on his craft but generally being bored and wishing he could leave and go home to his Alma. He was nervous about travelling in the dark and after curfew, about the Jewish servant at the farm, who did not seem to like him much, about Benedikt finding out about him staying at the farm and about the future of the country as a whole. He found it easy to talk to customers and make small talk during any sales or design meeting, but social chit chat with people who must not find out about his background was much more of an effort for him.

He had expected the Countess to take him aside at some point but she was always busy and never got round to talk to him. In his fear, he started to worry that Visser was an undercover official who had just tried to sound him out, that the whole evening was a trap and set up purely to get him and his family. Part of him knew how ridiculous that thought was but with work camps and all the anti-Jewish legislation, even the most irrational of his fears seemed justified. The way and the reasons why people were being deported meant there was not much that could surprise him anymore.

He finally left the manor house and made his way through the cold and the darkness to the barn on Benedikt's farm. As he opened the barn door he saw Sarah, the Jewish servant sitting in the hay by the table.

"Were you waiting for me?" he asked.

"I was, Jonah," she admitted. "I needed to apologise to you. I had no right to confront you like I did. I guess I am just not used to hearing a sympathetic word these days. Everyone tells us how lucky we are and seems to think we should be grateful and happy for not being in a ghetto or a labour camp. I know things could be harder, but that is no consolation. I am young. I want to be happy, dance, sing, and fall in love. I am reduced to nothing and the future has little prospects for me. You were the only person I could safely rant to, so that is why I flared up like that. I am truly sorry. Will you accept my apology? Please."

"Of course I will but there is nothing to apologise for. I must admit that my comments were not the most sensitive ones. I'm afraid that I often speak before thinking. As long as I mean well, I think I can afford to do that but today was a good reminder that sometimes that too fails. "

"Thank you for seeing it my way too," she said.

"I was so surprised at Johanna, letting me stay here in the barn. It overwhelmed me for a while and made me see everything in an optimistic way. When my daughter lived here she had a hard time with Johanna at first but gradually the two of them got on. I just wanted to give you hope that one day she will warm to you the way she warms to most people. Eventually," he explained.

"She is very concerned for you," Sarah pointed out. "She often asks me how life is for the Jews in Slovakia, what has changed with the new laws and if I think you would be in danger of being discovered. For me, that is her one redeeming feature."

"Well, be sure to thank her for me tomorrow," Jonah instructed.

"I will. Good night now. And good luck!"

"Good luck to you too, Sarah."

At precisely this moment, the government secretly negotiated with Germany for the deportation of 20,000 Jews to concentration camps in Poland. The German government declared it would charge the Slovaks 500 Reichsmark a head for transportation and settlement costs; this was a lot of money that the state did not currently have to spare and was why the administration asked for more time before their commencement. The Hlinka guard and the Jewish administration immediately started drawing up lists of citizens suitable for deportation. The lists of 'eligible' candidates was then divided into men and women and then into age groups. The labour camps needed strong men and so the first ones to be sent to Poland would be men in their physical prime. Jonah's name was listed but a friendly, corrupt and heavily bribed pen crossed the Weissensteiners off all lists.

Chapter 7: Bratislava 1942

The New Year's Eve party at the manor house was once again the social event of the year. It was one of the few occasions where time seemed to have reverted to the 'good old days of the monarchy' during which so many of the guests had enjoyed privileges they were no longer accustomed to in the new and independent Slovakia. Many rich Hungarians had opted to stay here after the Great War hoping that it would be easier to keep their properties and money. They were concerned about the political instability of a republican Hungary where old enemies might seek retribution for the abuse of power and position but more so they feared a Bolshevik revolution. In the Czechoslovak state they had seen a tumbling of their influence at first due to the dominance of the Czech aristocracy followed by the German military leaders and their emerging Slovak 'puppet' politicians. The Hungarians were equally unpopular with the emerging intelligentsia and players of the Slovak society who still had their reservations against their former Magyar oppressors. To some it seemed a high price to pay for evading the threat of Communism.

At the manor house ball however, all of these problems seemed forgotten or unimportant. The Countess did not tolerate heated debate or disagreement in her house. As a charitable and generous woman she was a shining example of a respectable modern Hungarian and a role model to her countrymen.

The players in the current Slovak high society who had taken a shine to her also felt more positive to her countrymen. With her gift for diplomacy she calmed any tension that might arise. Almost everyone in Bratislava wanted to be invited to her festivities.

She welcomed the German army officers and generals in the same way as Slovak Party leaders, nobility and her beloved artist friends. Having been wined and dined in separate groups by the Countess during the year, they were all too obliged to her to dare stir up any trouble. Catholic party leaders spoke to their Lutheran rivals amicably about the goals they had in common, the army officials refrained from provoking the artists whose appearance they so detested, and the 'new aristocrats' of society pretended to be best of friends with the established and former noble men. To see such a convincing and unusual display of pretence and falsehood was in itself a sight that most people didn't want to miss out on. Jonah, however, would have loved to miss out on such a charade and would have done so if had it not been for his dependency on the good will of his patron.

His new friend Visser took him under his wing and introduced him to a few more of the artists at the party. There was a Polish piano player, a Lithuanian tenor, an apparently well-known French author and an Austrian poet. It was amazing how the Countess managed to keep all of these bohemian looking and politically left leaning people near her without raising the suspicion or worse, interference from the authorities. A string quartet played music for the first part of the evening but when the reception hall had filled up the Countess had the doors to the ballroom hall opened where a small orchestra started to play dance tunes and continued to do so well into the early morning hours.

Jonah and his group of artist protégés were not tempted to dance and decided to stay in the reception hall where they could talk. They managed to secure themselves chairs in a little seating area where they continued drinking champagne and listened to each other's life stories.

The Lithuanian tenor had been a star at the Hungarian Opera but had fled after the Communist Coup in 1919. Since then he had spent long periods at opera houses in Munich, Vienna and Paris, but still took smaller professional engagements, especially those that had been initiated by his dear friend the Countess. Because of their strong bond, he always accepted her social invitations and the presence of intriguing characters at her gatherings.

The Austrian poet had only recently been introduced to the Countess and was a novice to the circle. A close friend and admirer of his poems had insisted that the Countess meet this talented man.

The rest of the group all owed part of their success to the Countess, her connections and her sponsorship but what they all had in common – apart from some artistic talent – was a politeness and a distinct lack of competitiveness they employed in their conduct with each other. Jonah was surprised by the genuine support and admiration the members of the group displayed towards one another.

"The Countess has a good eye for congenial people it seems," Jonah confessed to his friend Visser. "I have not enjoyed myself like this in a long time."

"You are right. She would never take someone under her wing if she thought them socially inept for her little circle of friends," Visser replied. "No matter how talented they are."

"Is she as devout a Christian as they say?" Jonah wanted to know.

"Far from it," Visser replied. "She has some humanitarian idealistic notions which I am sure she will relate to you one day."

"I can't wait to hear about it. I am intrigued and flattered," Jonah said.

"So you should be. The Countess enjoys a philosophical debate about the human condition and loves nothing more than hearing a new perspective and a fresh reflection on her own thoughts on the matter. She said she thought she had noted a spirited soul in you that she wants to get acquainted with. For that reason she has chosen you and your art as her next big project, so that she can spend time with you in direct and indirect observation."

"Indirect observation? What am I to understand by that?" Jonah asked.

"To hear you discuss your own philosophy and see you implementing it in your daily work and life; to see if the two are coherent," Visser said with a hint of a smile.

"That sounds more like a court investigation than a social contact," Jonah said.

"I guess you could call it both," Visser admitted. "Only the Countess never judges. She merely wants to learn from you and your ideas. She will remain your friend even if she does not agree with you. She only abandons the people who hurt her."

"May I ask if the Countess has any special protégées, ones she cares for in more ways than the ones we just described?" Jonah wondered.

"My dear Weissensteiner, I like your directness, but I am not at liberty to tell such secrets," Visser replied. "However, I have been instructed to persuade you to stay in one of the guest rooms in the house tonight and stay for another day. Tomorrow evening there will be a small intimate dinner party for the closest friends of the Countess. In the more intimate setting of tomorrow's gathering you may find the answer to your questions."

"Visser, why do you waste your time painting? You should write plays with your sense of drama and suspense," Jonah teased the

Dutch man. "I shall not sleep a wink tonight but wonder about your riddles and allusions."

A few hours after midnight, Jonah was escorted to one of the guest rooms by a servant. Never in his life had he spent a night in a larger or more luxurious room. He wondered if this was part of the special treatment the Countess had intended for him in order to entice him into her little circle or whether all of the guest rooms had such remarkable size and décor. If this was part of a strategy it was certainly working, he could think of many things worse than coming here for intellectual conversations and a little bit of comfort. Only it would be difficult to satisfy the demands for increased weaving production while spending time away from the workshop.

As he was visualising a sheltered future for himself and his family in the safety of this brilliant new world and wondering how he could address the issue of the needed increased productivity, a few voices on the corridor brought him back to reality. A very loud and drunken man laughed in hysterics and sometimes speaking in German and sometimes in poor Czech to two muffled deep voices, who were probably servants or friends taking him to bed.

"Oh Nein, ha ha, nein, I am ticklish, let go of me ha ha."

"Please Herr Kommandant, please try to be quiet. We are in the sleeping quarters now."

"Jawohl, Herr Judengeneral, jawohl. All is quiet. Shh. Ha ha."

"Hold him while I open the door."

"Genau, aufgemacht. All go in and then lock the door," the drunkard giggled.

"Please be quiet!"

"You Czechs know how to party, oh I beg your pardon. You Slovaks. Tell her illustrious Highness I have had an excellent time tonight."

"Thank you Herr Kommandant, I will let her know."

"Tell her though that she must not invite such low life scum next time. These long haired communists and artists of the lower races. We must have none of that, ist das klar?"

"Jawohl Herr Kommandant, I shall advise the Countess of your sentiments. Now please enter the guest room."

"You will see, my friend, my dear Hungarian friend, all this is going to end. We are not just going to send them away any more, we are going to get rid of them once and for all. Too many, too filthy,

144

too dangerous. Stop tickling me ha ha."

With that the voices retreated to the room and even though Jonah could hear that the voices were still arguing and laughing, he could understand nothing more of their dialogue.

For the rest of the night he found it difficult to settle down and sleep. He kept waking up, dreaming of a dinner table with the Countess and his family, surrounded by soldiers with their rifles aimed at each of the dinner guests. His brief period of feeling safe had ended as abruptly as it had begun earlier in the evening.

At the farm Sarah was waiting up for Jonah who had asked Johanna to be allowed to sleep in the barn after the festivities. Sarah had found a good listener in Jonah who never asked her for anything in return and who never tried to influence her in any way. With him she was able to let herself go, to complain about the abuse the two girls in the house exposed her to, about the coldness with which Johanna treated her and how lonely and isolated she was since she started working on the farm. She was rarely allowed to spend the night with her family and when she did, they paid little attention to her. Her mother in particular seemed insensitive to the young girl's needs and treated her with contempt as if it had been Sarah's own idea and fault that she was ordered to help out at the German's family home. Instead of receiving sympathy for her isolation and hard lot, she was bossed around and made to feel guilty for not contributing enough in her own home and for preferring the 'easy' work with Johanna compared to doing the 'hard' work for her own flesh and blood.

No protest could placate the mother and no argument could convince her. Sarah's father and her brothers were too exhausted in the evenings to be good company and so the poor girl was starved of benign and decent human contact.

While she was waiting for Jonah in the hay she fell asleep exhausted from the long hours she had worked and she did not wake up until the morning, when her absence was already noticed in the cow shed by Benedikt. He sent Maria to look for the lazy scoundrel and mumbled swear words under his breath, suggesting the Jewess had been drinking and partying if not whoring with her folks over the New Year celebrations, unaware that the Jews celebrated New Year on a different day.

145

Nobody could find Sarah at first. Johanna was informed about the missing servant and she immediately panicked that someone would discover a sleeping and hung-over Jonah in the barn. She sent Maria off in the opposite direction so that she herself could enter the barn on her own. When she saw Sarah lying on the make shift bed instead of Jonah she assumed that something improper had taken place between her servant and the guest.

"You piece of filth, have you got no shame?" she shouted at Sarah. "Seducing an old man? Right in front of our noses? Where is he? Has he left?"

"No, he has not been here at all. I fell asleep waiting for him," Sarah defended herself.

"What business do you have waiting for him?" Johanna demanded to know.

"No business at all," Sarah said quietly. "Sometimes we talk. He listens to me like someone who cares. I am sorry if I did something wrong."

Johanna found her initial anger and ire inexplicably disappear. She almost felt sorry for the servant girl. Well, Sarah would get enough of an ear full from Benedikt when she confessed to oversleeping. There was no need to give her any more grief on top of what was bound to come.

"Go on then. Hurry to the stables. Benedikt is looking for you. Say nothing about the barn and Jonah if you know what's good for you, do you understand me?"

"Yes, thank you!" Sarah said relieved and hurried away.

So Sarah was seeking comfort on the shoulders of Jonah, Johanna thought to herself; probably not bad judgement on her behalf. He was more intelligent and realistic than any other Jew she knew and if her servant was associating with him then there was hope for her after all. Maybe the young Jewess had more potential than she had been given credit for. Johanna sighed deeply. She hated to admit it but once more in comparison with outsiders her own daughters were a disappointment, morally as well as in terms of productivity. This girl was a hard worker and never complained. The farmer's wife found herself annoyed at this realisation but in comparison, some of the Jews Benedict had employed were much more reliable and successful than she would have imagined.

Egon's career as radio engineer was far more prestigious in her eyes than Gunter's promotion in the infantry. Maria had always been socially inadequate but since she had lost her virginity to a married Jew and had brought so much shame to the family, Johanna would have happily traded her for the obnoxious ugly Wilma who at least was no trouble on that account. Roswitha was functioning well but was so desperate for love and attention that both Sarah and Greta were preferable to her too.

Johanna felt almost ashamed that she could feel such coldness for her own children, yet feel warm affection for complete strangers and, for all of that, Jews. She could not allow herself such kind feelings just because her own Aryan offspring was such a disappointment to her. Had not life been so much easier before Wilhelm had married Greta? The Jews were then only abstract strangers and oddly dressed figures on the street that she could hate along with everyone else. Now she found herself compromised in her feelings.

Benedikt had joined the Hlinka Party and was well respected thanks to his reputation amongst the farming community. His German background was no longer a hindrance in the party ranks but a welcome quality. There was even talk of him becoming an advisor to the agricultural secretary. Bound by strict party policy, he would not have much sympathy or understanding for his wife's conflicting emotions and for the occasional help she gave Jonah and his family.

Unaware of the worry he was causing his family by not returning to the farm or to the workshop the following day, Jonah had a lovely day at the manor house. When he came downstairs in the morning the house was already almost completely tidy and it was not even lunch time. He admired the Countess for such great organisational skills. The servants were still busy in the ballroom but the big reception hall was already prepared to seat and feed the many overnight guests. Jonah was one of the last ones to appear. His friend Visser was already seated and was playing cards with two ladies whom Jonah had not seen at all the night before.

Still shaken by the incident with the German Kommandant on the corridor during the night and by what he had heard the drunkard say, Jonah only reluctantly joined them at their table. He could have done with a little more solitude to digest the vicious threats voiced so casually by the drunken officer. It might have been helpful to talk

147

about this experience with Visser but not knowing the two ladies it wasn't an option.

"Weissensteiner, my friend. Come and join me and these two beautiful friends of mine. I hope you had pleasant dreams?" the painter asked.

"Good morning, good morning. May I introduce myself?" Jonah asked politely. "I am Jonah Weissensteiner, the weaver. I am afraid it seems our Dutch friend has forgotten all etiquette of introductions."

"Get over yourself you putz," Visser exclaimed. "This is Edith and this is Esther, two of the more elitist friends of her illustrious Highness."

"How do you do?" Jonah said formally and kissed their hands in old Habsburger style. "I don't think I saw you at the party last night. I should have mingled more and not wasted my time on this good for nothing," he joked.

"We did not attend the party," said Edith. On closer observation she did not look too much like a lady at all, even though she had a modern and fashionable dress on, no doubt an expensive design from Prague or Vienna. She had a dark skin complexion and thick bushy black eyebrows but her head hair was convincingly dyed straw blonde. Her hair was short and curled tight to her head, as a lot of modern women did these days with hot irons. She was petite but far from fragile or gentle. Jonah sensed a strength and assertiveness that he knew more from farmer's women such as Johanna or Maria than from aristocracy.

"Oh, did you just arrive this morning?" he asked to keep the conversation going, "I never thought the Countess would permit such a neglect of her invitation," he said with a wink in his eye.

"Far from it!" called out the other woman, Esther, who was equally well dressed but who too had a less noble air about her. She had dark hair, her nose was half way between Jewish and Slavic, and she appeared bigger and stronger than her friend and continued in a sober and matter of fact manner:

"We were staying upstairs, holding our own private soiree. We don't hold much for dancing and the high society of Bratislava. Or rather, they do not hold much for us."

Jonah was intrigued by this hinting at secrets but did not know how to find out more without sounding rude and impertinent. Visser came to his aid.

"I guess it is safe to tell you this since you too are an outsider in the current Slovak society, Edith and Esther are confirmed spinsters and hate pretending otherwise to officers and wannabe male suitors. The Countess is an eccentric and even though she is not of that persuasion she loves to surround herself with wild characters. I hope you are not offended."

"I can't say I am offended," Jonah said. "I don't know the first thing about it to be honest. May I ask you ladies why do you not want a husband? Why do you choose to live like that? Ach, as if life was not complicated enough," Jonah mused.

"I am sorry for my ignorant friend!" Visser apologized to the ladies.

"That's fine," Esther assured Visser. "I like directness and honesty in a man and I shall reward it with honesty and directness myself. Herr Weissensteiner, I for one did not choose it, even so, I am not sure I would blame or credit a God for it. A folly of nature maybe? I am not sad about it, so I don't want your pity. Did you choose to be a Jew? You did not I guess from your looks but others consciously have. Let us not try to solve that mystery. I would much rather discuss a delicate commission I have in mind for you. It is no coincidence that you should meet us here. We have come especially to seek you out. We would like to order one of your beautiful wall carpets and we would like it to have an Eve and Eve theme if you catch my drift. Would you at all consider designing and making one for us?"

"My dear lady, thank you so very much for considering me, but I must refuse," Jonah replied. "I am sure you can guess that I am in enough danger already. Just imagine what would happen if the Catholic Hlinka Guard discovered a Jew manufacturing indecent art. With a Christian biblical theme! It is too dangerous, as much as I would love to oblige you."

"Are you not designing biblical themes for others already?" asked Edith.

"Yes and as a Jew, my situation is dangerous enough as it is. I am already breaking the law by accepting such commissions, by coming here to socialise with gentile people and even just by travelling here. I must not tempt fate any more," Jonah explained.

"Our commission would not be dangerous my friend," Esther

149

promised. "We understand your situation perfectly well and we had in mind to offer you a safe place where you could carry out this work in complete safety from the Hlinka devils. The Countess suggested you may do it here in the manor house."

"The Countess knows about your plans and she approves?" Jonah asked surprised.

"Jonah, the arts have always been a bit more liberal and free," Visser said. "In the current fascist climate, the Countess plays along with the powerful people but her heart has remained as open and as daring as it always has been. If she enjoys the finished product she said she might well order one of those frivolous artefacts herself."

"What a strange idea to have a hanging carpet of such themes. Why not have a painting or a sculpture?" Jonah asked the ladies.

"I was impressed with your detail and your precision," Edith explained. "Stunning, I thought, that man is pure genius and so I wanted one of your carpets for myself. Only in the Garden of Eden I don't want an Adam with my Eve, and that is how the whole idea was born,"

"We could not stop thinking about it ever since," Esther added. "We simply must have one. Please say yes!"

"How would that even be possible?" Jonah asked. "Move my workshop here to the manor house? I have a family and the two big looms take up a lot of space. Where would we be able to fit all that?"

"The Countess is a patron of the arts and I trust she has not only seen your weaving workshop but several others in her life," Visser dismissed Jonah's doubts. "She is confident that there will be enough room for you to work and live in the grounds."

"What if you don't like my designs?" Jonah worried. "Ladies, it is a lot you are asking me to do, a lot to risk. Is this some kind of whim or have you thought it through thoroughly? I would need to speak to the Countess."

"Of course we have thought it through," Edith assured him. "The Countess is very excited about you being here. There are a few outbuildings that could be used as your studio as well as for your living quarters. Your life may also be much safer in the confinements of the Estate."

"Maybe you are right but so far I have been very lucky," Jonah said hesitatingly. "I would be tempting fate by changing any of my circumstances now."

"With a name like that you can't seriously believe in luck and coincidence?" Esther said, shaking her head in disbelief. "Don't tell me you thought you were saved by your God or Lady Luck? You are far too intelligent to be so superstitious. You must have at least suspected, if not known, that it is the Countess who bribes your name off all the lists?"

Jonah's heart sank. So the authorities did have their eye on him. His hopes that somehow in the complex administration his name had failed to register were smashed into pieces.

"It may sound foolish now but I did believe in my luck," Jonah admitted. "The Habsburg Empire was a complex multi-national melting pot. I always thought it very conceivable that administrative errors might occur. How naïve of me indeed," Jonah said disillusioned.

"Now don't despair my dear friend!" Visser tried to reassure him. "So far it has saved you and your family. You should be happy. If the bureaucrats accept her money today, they will also take it tomorrow. Had it only been luck, then it could have run out at any moment. The Jews here are safe compared to other places in Europe but the Countess has excellent connections that make bribing and protection much less complicated. Without those you would have to find a trustworthy go between who approaches the civil servants in question. You would have to pay him before you can even pay the bribe itself. You are as safe here as you can be."

"Is the Countess not risking her own life and fortune by doing this?" asked Jonah worriedly.

"I don't think so," Visser assured him. "All of the nobility have their own 'pet-Jews' as you might call the phenomenon. The leader of the Hlinka party has a Jewish tailor, another party official is protecting his chess partner and that is just the tip of the iceberg. When it comes to party politics they are hard liners but in their private life they bend the rules and turn a blind eye. If the schemes of the Countess were ever to become known, she would be in good company. She would be reprimanded at the most."

"Just think how safe you all would be here!" said Esther. "No Hlinka guard, no house searches or whatever might be considered as the next step in the anti-Semitic policies."

"It sounds tempting, but as you can imagine I will need a little bit more time to reflect on this and I will need to discuss it with my children. "

"It is your children that will benefit the most from it," Visser said. "There will be more protection here than anywhere else."

"Don't take too long," warned Esther. "This current quiet in Slovakia feels much more like the calm before a storm."

Soon after this conversation, Jonah took his leave and made his way to the farm. He had hoped to speak to the Countess herself that morning, but Visser informed him that she had left the manor house early on urgent business in Vienna and the dinner plans had been postponed until her return. She seemed an interesting character the Countess, always full of ideas and plans, and never standing still in one place.

Only just before he arrived at the barn did he remember that he had said he would be back after midnight and by failing to appear he might have worried Sarah or Johanna. As he entered the barn he saw that the make-shift bed had been taken down and there was no sign that anyone ever had expected him to stay the night.

Jonah approached the farm building carefully, looking for signs of Benedikt and the other workers. He seemed to be lucky and managed to sneak into the building unobserved. His luck stayed with him and he managed to find Sarah in the laundry room without alerting Maria or Roswitha to his presence.

"Thank God you are here," Sarah sighed. "I was so worried about you when you did not show up last night. Are you all right? What happened?"

"Oh I am fine," he assured her. "Of course I am fine. The Countess invited me to stay at the house to meet some of her guests in the morning. I couldn't deny her."

"What a relief!" Sarah exclaimed. "Johanna came to visit you in the barn as well and she was not impressed to find me there. She thought I was there to seduce you. So she does not know about Alma does she?"

"It never came up." said Jonah with a wink. "My girls believe that Johanna has a suspicion about Alma and me but I don't want to say anything and implicate Alma any more than necessary. She is risking her life for this foolish thing between us."

"Johanna is implicated enough herself by putting you up here in the barn and bringing you food, I would not worry about her.

How was the party?" she asked.

"Grand as you can imagine. A lot of people I would not normally feel comfortable with. I would say the Countess has a very varied spectrum of friends. Fortunately I was accepted into the circle of artists and eccentrics and that felt more relaxed. She must have spent a small fortune on the festivities; there was even a small orchestra. I can't believe she managed to keep that much of her fortune to afford all this," Jonah told her.

"I don't think I would feel very comfortable at such a big party," Sarah confessed.

"I was far from comfortable," Jonah protested. "Maybe something good will come of it. I may be moving my workshop to the manor house."

"To the manor house? How?" said Sarah, amazed.

"I am meant to stay in an outhouse to fulfil a private commission. I would be removed from the public eye and solely employed by the Countess and her rich art lover friends."

"You would be nearer us." Sarah said excitedly.

"It would solve a lot of my problems but I will have to talk to my children about it and to Alma," Jonah said. "I found out that my name is on the lists of Jews the Hlinka Guard have compiled. The Countess is paying to keep me safe. I am not sure I can refuse her anything now that I know."

"You would be safer here than in town," Sarah reflected. "Most attacks on Jews happen in bigger places. Apart from our co-workers, we rarely see any these days; nobody wants to travel unless they have to. We have not seen our relatives for a long time. Roswitha has been to town more often and she says she has seen some ugly scenes. I can't believe everything she tells me of course. She hates me and likes to make me feel bad."

"I have heard of a few incidents myself, but like you and your family we hardly ever leave the house. Alma is too protective of our feelings to tell us if she had witnessed any attacks on Jews herself. Listen, I better go, I just stopped to let you know that I am fine. They will be waiting for me and worried at home too. Give my regards and thanks to Johanna."

"I will. You be careful!"

Greta and Wilma had spent New Year's Eve with Alma, whom they welcomed as an unofficial stepmother with open arms. They had never seen their father happier than he had been the last few months.

The daughters had been most amused when they had caught the love birds holding hands for the first time. There could not have been a better timing for this romance. It made the whole business of the Jewish Code a little bit more bearable, since the family's focus was on the new lovers instead of the political climate outside. New commissions kept coming their way and the girls were so busy that they never would have known a week had gone by without either of them setting a foot outside the door. Ernst was a remarkable child who would happily play with his toys next to his mother and aunt or use some wooden building blocks to build a house. Wilma had found an old song book and Greta had taught him new tunes, which they sang during their long hours of labour in the workshop. It was all the distraction and attention the boy needed.

However, when Jonah did not appear back at the workshop the next morning all three women started to become agitated and worried. Wilma imagined the worst and would not rest. She could not concentrate, was hopeless with the weaving and useless in the kitchen. She followed Alma's advice to go upstairs and lie down but she could not keep still and soon came back down again, pacing through the house in a complete state of hysteria. Alma shook her, shouted at her and even slapped her lightly on the cheek but nothing seemed to bring Wilma to her senses. Greta tried to calm her by talking to her but could not persuade the distressed sister that their missing father was alive and well.

"We knew it was going to happen. How could he have been so stupid and walk outside without the Yellow Star?" Wilma lamented. "I bet they were just waiting for him. I told him to be careful. We must go to the police and find out what has happened to him."

"You are insane!" exclaimed Greta. "Not a word to the police. There is probably a simple explanation to the whole affair. Maybe he got drunk and slept in at the farm or maybe he is hiding somewhere by the road."

"What if he has been arrested?" Wilma worried.

"If he has been arrested there is nothing we can do for him right now. Come on, think. It is New Year. There won't be many soldiers and policemen on the road. They all have been partying themselves, they always do."

"We must look for him. Maybe he needs help," Wilma urged

her sister.

"Yes, more Jews on the road, that will help him if he is hiding," Greta ridiculed her. "Go on, you know we cannot do anything. We just need to be calm and patient and wait."

"I wish I could be calm!" Wilma exclaimed. "How do you do it? Father is missing. He may be already half way to the camp in Terezin!"

"Oh Wilma, of course I worry too but I won't allow myself to think that way. Not until I know anything for sure. Maybe his host has invited him to stay or maybe he is still drinking with his new friends. There are many good things that could have happened as well as bad ones."

All of her efforts were in vain. Wilma cried and paced madly around the house all day long. When it got darker outside and Jonah had still not returned she became quieter and began rocking back and forth in her chair. Greta and Alma decided to take shifts to stay with her and to make sure she was not going to run off and look for her father. In her state anything seemed possible and the last thing they wanted was another missing person to worry about.

Ernst kept waking up because of the noise Wilma was creating and it was his intervention that signified a turning point. He came downstairs from his afternoon nap crying looking for his mother and when he saw the state Wilma was in he stopped and hugged her legs hard with his arms. It was this action that brought Wilma back to normality. She wiped her tears away with her sleeve, picked Ernst up and said to him:

"Young man, we can't have you up all day. Let's go to bed. I'll read you another story."

"Max und Moritz," Ernst shouted, the name of his favourite story.

"Max and Moritz it is." Wilma said gently and calmly and the two of them disappeared up the stairs.

The three women were hugely relieved when Jonah arrived safe and sound back at the workshop later. Once they had scolded him for worrying the entire family he told them about the offer he had received and asked them for their opinion. They were very excited about the prospect of moving into the manor house.

"I can't wait!" exclaimed Wilma, as if all her hysterics earlier had never taken place. "It is such a beautiful house, I can't believe we could be living on those fantastic grounds. Even a broom cupboard there is better than here. Have you seen the gardens there? They are huge!"

"Calm down, Wilma!" objected Greta. "We won't be there for a holiday. We will be working and not be mingling with the Countess and her friends."

"It will be much better all the same," insisted Wilma. "We see nothing but grey houses and smoke from our windows here and we never go outside. On her estate we must have some kind of view and a little bit of beauty around us."

"We will be hiding there just as much as we do here," Greta warned.

"We will have a little bit more freedom," Jonah contradicted. "We will be on private grounds under the protection of the owner."

"We should go as soon as we can," Alma said.

"I don't see any reason to rush anything. We are already kept safe by bribes," Wilma said confidently.

"Whoever is taking the money could change their mind. We cannot take our luck for granted!" Greta warned.

Jonah took her point and informed the Countess of their decision to accept her generous offer. Preparations for the move started immediately. At the same time as the Wannsee Conference in Berlin decided on the total extermination of all Jews in Germany, in sharp contrast, the Weissensteiners felt more protected than they had in a long time.

The Countess assigned Jonah and his family a small cottage-like guest house to live in. The house was situated away from the manor house in the middle of the extensive forests on the grounds, next to a very small lake. The cottage had been erected by the previous owners who had a passion for fishing and who liked to retreat here for days at a time. The kitchen was small and basic but the family was invited to eat with the house servants whenever they wanted. The Countess emphasised that this was purely for practical reasons and did not mean that the artist and his family should feel reduced to the ranks of mere employees. There were only two bedrooms in the cottage. The sisters shared their room with the child while Alma and Jonah shared the other.

The weaving workshop was installed in a former farm building. There had not been any animals on the estate for years and the building had been derelict for a long time and needed some work done to it. It was very spacious and it was possible for the family to start working there right away at the end of January. Two carpenters were employed to furnish the place according to Jonah's needs and specifications.

The Weissensteiners felt like small Gods in their new life. Wilma was hugely relieved to be away from the streets of Bratislava and those ugly memories. The haunting incident on the bridge had left deep scars on her soul and she had never been able to properly relax since. She was hopeful to return to her non-traumatised previous self. Being surrounded by woodlands the cottage felt like a secret hideaway, which helped the anxious young woman to settle in. No one would find them here.

Jonah did not miss Bratislava and its dangers either but he did feel bad for letting his other customers down by becoming exclusively employed by the Countess. Apart from occasional trips to get artistic supplies, there was no need to stray from the premises which left them all plenty of time to focus on their work. The servants from the main house were reserved but polite towards the newcomers and there was so much work to do for the family that – were it not for Egon's occasional letters from Russia - they almost could have forgotten that there was a war going on.

March, at last, saw the first of many planned mass deportations of Jews from Bratislava to Poland. Like everywhere under German influence, most Jews had lost their jobs due to the discriminating laws. According to the Codex Judaicus in Slovakia they had a duty to work and were rounded up in labour camps in Novaky, Vyhne and Sered. The government had been slow to organise the promised deportations but gradually succumbed to the heavy pressure from Germany. First selected were men between 16 and 35 which meant that families that had previously been kept together were now in danger of being broken up. The Christian wing of the Hlinka Party was opposed to these measures and only the reassurance of the Reichsprotektor Heydrich that prisoners would be humanely treated in the camps and families would be reunited, enabled the government to proceed. So the first transports commenced.

The Weissensteiners were unaware of this situation for several months. They enjoyed themselves in their new safe haven at the manor house. They were very much left to their own devices and could do as they pleased in their spare time. Wilma took Ernst for long walks around the lake and through the forest, never seriously worried about their safety. The other employees were not interested in them and left them alone.

Greta, Alma and Jonah spent most of their days together in the workshop, occasionally interrupted by visits from the Countess or her lady friends. Jonah had been looking forward to the frequent contact and the philosophical discussions with her Highness that Visser had promised him at the New Year's Eve Party, but those scenes never materialised. The Countess was far too busy to make it regularly to the house and it occurred to Jonah that she was not only busy but also a little flaky and easily bored, a privilege of the rich he had heard about many times.

Esther took a particular liking to Ernst and spent a lot of time playing with him, seemingly unconcerned about her dress getting dirty during hide and seek and other games. She appeared to be a child herself, an untamed wild one at heart who refused to grow up and become a respectable member of society. Edith was a little more business like when they paid visits to the workshop and kept her focus on the progress of the carpet but when Esther went outside with Ernst she let her guard down a little more. It was noticeable that she had taken a fancy to Greta.

When she asked Jonah questions her eyes would wander over to where Greta was working and she was always paying a little more attention to her than to the others. Alma could see the struggle in Edith to start up a conversation with Greta amateurishly concealed under her restrained manner. Jonah was aware of the infatuation as well but felt it safer not to draw any attention to it and possibly offend their generous benefactors. In their isolation in the woods these visits were welcome diversions.

Sarah also managed to visit the family occasionally and she struck up a great friendship with Wilma. Unfortunately it was the blossoming of their friendship that one day in September brought back Wilma's anxiety when – without considering the impact of the information on the anxious woman - Sarah told the family about the continuous deportation of Jews from the camps in Slovakia to Poland.

"My brother says that even Jews who were previously not

interned in a camp have been picked up from their homes without warning and are being transported to train stations. The Germans want all the young and strong men they can get their hands on," she told Alma.

"Does that mean that they will round your brother up too?" asked Alma.

"That is what we are not sure about," Sarah replied. "He and the other men in my family should have been taken to the camps a long time ago but we think because Benedikt is in the party we are his 'pet Jews' and are exempt from the draft. The Germans are so desperate for men of working age now that they are putting more pressure on the government to deliver the numbers that were promised. I have no idea if Benedikt's influence can hold under such conditions."

"What about fleeing to Hungary?" Alma suggested.

"Father mentioned it," Sarah said. "He wants everyone to leave but then the next moment he wants to stay. He is so desperate to stay near his land that he knows no rhyme or reason anymore."

"Will you try to escape?" Alma asked.

"I don't think so," Sarah said. "I would like to but my family seems to believe because we have been exempt this far our luck will hold. It is sheer madness if you ask me. Who knows how long Hungary remains an option as a gateway to freedom."

"Is it safe in Hungary?" Alma asked.

"I don't know. People go there because it is easy to cross the border and are hoping to make it further to Palestine from there," Sarah explained.

"What about you Sarah, why are you staying?"

"Where would I go by myself? If father stays behind I can't leave him," she replied.

"Judging from what you say about his iron will that seems unlikely then," Alma pointed out.

"Without all of us Benedikt could not run the farm and feed the Germans, he says," Sarah told her.

"I am not sure that is enough of a safety net," Alma warned her.

"I am counting on the corruption within the Slovak administration," Sarah replied.

"Now, that is a God worth praying to," Alma said with a laugh.

"Father has heard that the Catholic Church are pulling strings within the Hlinka Party and are granting help to those who are willing to convert," Sarah told them. "He is considering it."

"I am not sure I would trust them," said Greta. "Jews are a race and not a confessional group. There is no safety in help from the Church anymore!"

"Those who are going through the conversion process will be spared, they are saying. The administration will turn a blind eye," Sarah insisted. "It is not an official policy but a secret deal between party members. Despite everything, the Christians amongst the Hlinka Party are trying to do what they can to escape their damnation in the afterlife."

"That sounds too good to be true," Alma sighed.

"Maybe, but it seems worth a try. There are so many Jews who would never consider going through that, maybe it would be small enough a number to slip through the system. I am considering it myself. After all, I can still be a Jew in my heart," Sarah argued.

"You must let us know if you decide to go through with it. We might consider doing it ourselves," Jonah said.

"It won't be easy," said Greta. "I converted before the war. I had to go to evening and weekend classes for a few months, had to do homework and learn prayers. Ask Johanna, she and Benedikt did the same thing. They used to be Lutherans but decided it would be more advantageous to blend in with the majority. The priest who converted us was not very keen to do it. Johanna had to persuade him."

"What a dark horse that woman is," Sarah said. "I will speak to her about it and let you know what I learn from father's sources.

Johanna was excited to hear that the Jews around her were sensible enough to think about converting but when she approached Father Haslinger about it he was outraged at the suggestion. She really should have known better. He had made their own conversion hard work then and had always emphasized how redemption and salvation could only be achieved if you really believed.

The conversion of opportunistic Jews who just wanted to escape the prosecution – which they deserved in his eyes - was out of the question. He resented Johanna for even suggesting it and told her in no uncertain terms how despicable her plan was to him.

Fortunately once she had put her mind to something Johanna

did not give up easily and through her friend Marika she got a contact name at a monastery that was open to the cause. Once again her connections proved the useful ones. Father Johannes at the monastery agreed, for some donations and a minor fee, to convert them. The monks were not willing to attract public attention to their activities and so they did not require a lengthy course in preparation for the conversion. One evening was enough; the rest should be done through Bible study at home and frequent church attendance whenever possible.

Father Johannes also resented the whole process. He was happy to help people in need and to welcome any true new believer into the Church but to help Jews, who did not really believe in his God by baptising them, was against anything he felt he stood for. His superiors had given him no option about this and ordered him not to turn any willing Jew away. Effectual conversions of Jews to Catholicism had been carried out ever since the new legislation had been passed.

This was part of a complex political trade-off within the Christian wing of the Hlinka Party. Pro-war members in the wing were willing to vote for an exemption for all clergymen and monks to military service as the anti-war members demanded. In return, these anti-war members voted for more general support to the war effort in other areas. This united support from the religious wing allowed for further troops to be sent to Russia, which was well received with the fascist wing of the party, and they, in turn, turned a blind eye to the exemptions for the freshly converted Jews.

As things improved between the party factions, the Christians of the party dropped their resistance to the establishment of work camps for Jews and Gypsies as long as the fascist group promised to go slow with the deportations to Poland. At 500 Deutschmark per Jew, which the Germans charged in transport fees, the government was very happy to accommodate that request and save money. Through pure chance several hundred Jews managed to slip through the system that way.

Johanna was never one to wait until the last minute and was so worried that the situation might change at any moment that she arranged for a group conversion of the two families at the Monastery for the week after her meeting with Father Johannes.

At that precise moment, the Slovak Parliament passed further

161

legislation, one that surprisingly limited the planned deportations of Jews to Poland for different reasons. Inspectors who had been sent to the camps in the neighbouring country had brought back gruesome reports about the appalling conditions there and that had changed the political climate. Christians, budget weary members and secret liberals amongst the Hlinka Party united. These new laws brought the deportations to a complete standstill.

Individual Jews could be given special identification papers that stated that they were not required to be evacuated. These exemption papers were of a personal nature and could officially only be granted by the President himself to specific individuals. President Tiso however delegated this responsibility and once word had spread what a deportation to Poland meant, the new process was widely used. Johanna's friend Marika was one of the first to hear about the possibility of exemption from deportation and negotiated with Father Johannes to dispense such papers for the group of converts. Unwilling to see anyone deported to their almost certain death, he reluctantly agreed to recommend all of them to receive such papers even before the conversion happened.

On the arranged day Father Johannes took the group of Jews through the vestry of the Monastery church down into the basement. Johanna had come to accompany them and amongst the ones who had decided to convert were Sarah, her two brothers, her mother and her father, Wilma and Jonah.

"We can't do anything up there," the monk explained in the main church. "It would attract too much attention. We have to be discreet."

"I really appreciate what you are doing for us," Johanna said nervously to keep good relations.

Father Johannes turned to face her for a brief moment and with clear disregard said: "It wouldn't have been my choice to do this. The Jews killed Jesus Christ, no baptism or confession can ever take that guilt away from them."

"Isn't your God about forgiveness?" Wilma asked. "That is what I have always been told."

"Killing the Messiah – that is where I draw the line for forgiveness," he said angrily. "Never mind, it is not my decision. I have been ordered to christen you and that I will do. I am not to question orders from above, even though I really cannot understand it. May the Lord forgive me for my sins."

"Aren't you against killing? Does your God ask you not to kill another human being? Because ours does," Wilma carried on.

"Be quiet Wilma!" Jonah hissed. "I am sorry, Father Johannes, we are all very nervous. We appreciate what you are doing."

"Oh I am sure you appreciate it," Father Johannes answered. "It will help you escape sure death in this life but let me tell you that I can only wish you luck in the hereafter. I cannot see how what I am doing is going to help you there."

"We heard that you have exemption documents for us?" Jonah asked politely.

"Oh yes, I have those," Johannes replied grumpily. "You will need to keep them with you at all times. We have had a lot of help from the administration of the President in the matter. You are lucky that he is a priest himself. He is kinder hearted than I would be in his place. We have to tread very carefully. It wouldn't cost the Nazis anything to take full control of the country and punish us all for that we are doing here. All this for a pack of Jews. I wouldn't risk it, let me tell you."

"It is not our new faith that will keep us safe in the future, is it? It is these exemption documents," Wilma blurted out.

"Shut up Wilma. We are lucky they are helping us," Jonah scolded his daughter.

"No need to beat around the bush. Yes it is the documents that will save your life. Conversion to the true Catholic faith has been helpful to many of your people in the past. Now you are being helped twice. A waste if you ask me. I only act on strict orders that I must obey. I will warn you again, if you do not believe in Jesus Christ in your heart you won't receive salvation in the afterlife!"

"Yes, thank you Father Johannes. You are very kind and we are very grateful," Jonah said to reassure the Father of their gratefulness.

"Maybe you are grateful," Johannes said. "The others seem a little less convinced. All we ask from you is to renounce the devil and accept Christ as your saviour. That is not too much of a favour is it? If it was the other way round you would mutilate the men and their sex as a sacrifice to your God. We are much more humane, we just splash a little holy water onto you."

"But how can we renounce the devil when we never believed in him in the first place?" asked Wilma rationally.

"Wilma just shut up. You promised," Jonah hissed.

"Oh the devil is with all the Jews," declared Father Johannes. "Renounce him!"

"We do!" Jonah said humbly and then the others all did the same.

The whole process was utterly humiliating and degrading in Wilma's eyes. Father Johannes kept insulting the Jews and their inferiority while telling them the story of Christ, his self-sacrifice, his forgiveness and his kind love. He recited the Lord's Prayer and the Hail Mary, which he recommended they learn by heart, and repeat several times a day to atone for their sins. He explained the principles of the original sin, confession, redemption and salvation and then he gave each one of the assembled group the holy sacraments. When he had finished he once again impressed upon them the importance of practising and keeping their new faith, handed them the documents and let them go.

Wilma had been furious when she got to the church but over the course of the evening a paralysing sense of being powerless had come over her and taken all spirit and fight out of her. Everyone else accepted the miserable monk's attitude as necessary evil on their way to (earthly) salvation and endured it without the upset it had caused her. For weeks after she was introverted and depressed and even Ernst could not cheer her up the same way as he used to.

In the manor house, Sarah was still their main connection to the outside world and one day she came to the studio and reported that for a whole month there had been no trains leaving for Polish concentration camps from Slovakia. She had heard a rumour that thousands and thousands of these exemption papers had been given out and the Hlinka Guard could not fill a whole train of Jewish men unless they were prepared to give up all of the workers in their own work camps - which apparently they were not willing to do. The news received a huge cheer in the studio, but Wilma was becoming very resentful that she had had to undergo the humiliating conversion for these papers that had been given to others without the need to degrade themselves.

After Jonah had completed not one but two erotic carpets for Esther and Edith as well as one for the Countess, there were suddenly no new projects or commissions. Even though many friends and acquaintances of the ladies had expressed an interest in ordering some carpets, nobody seemed to be coming forward and the Countess decided to commission more herself as an investment, to keep her promise and to keep Jonah and his family in business.

She was without inspiration as to what theme the new carpets should have though and so it was up to Jonah to draw up some designs for her. In this rather quiet period Greta and Wilma took Ernst for long walks into the forest with its astonishingly coloured leaves. To Greta this was an amazing time of the year and she adored the changing colours around her. Wilma in contrast only noticed the shortening of the days, the early darkness and the cold temperatures that were coming to stay. She became even more depressed than before and could not understand how her sister could be so cheerful and happy when all of their lives were dependent on the good will of the President and the Church. On top of that their brother was somewhere in Russia fighting for the very people that may destroy his family, Jewish people were being murdered in Poland and there was no work for the family right now to distract themselves with.

Greta replied to these complaints that she was happy just to be with her family, for being relatively safe and that she thought that the extreme resistance that the German army was currently experiencing in Stalingrad was a reason to be hopeful. Radio propaganda by the Allies painted a less glorious picture for the Axis states than the German and Slovak newspapers and broadcasts. Optimists said there was hope for a peace treaty soon. However, the Allies also gave voice to the Czechoslovak Government in exile, which was threatening the Slovak 'traitors' and spoke of the restoration of the Czechoslovak state after the war. Slovak Nationalists knew now that their only future as an independent nation was through the continued success of the Germans and that in the case of a defeat for the Axis states, the current government would find themselves prosecuted by a returning Czech one.

Greta spent a great deal of time explaining the complexities of the political situation to her sister but Wilma had lost interest in politics. Quiet and withdrawn she endured the lectures without really paying attention to them and whenever she could she now tried to go for walks alone – with or without Ernst.

It was on one of those lonely outings that she encountered a steward from the manor house. She mumbled a quick hello and continued on her way but he called after her and when she did not respond he followed her and made her stop.

"Hey! I was calling you. Won't you talk to me?" he said angrily.

"I am in a hurry and I don't want to talk!" she said curtly and tried to hurry on her way.

"You think you are something special? An artist way above us common workers," he shouted, continuing his rant.

"I don't know what you mean," she said anxiously. "I don't think anything like that. I don't trust strangers and prefer my own company. Please respect that and accept my apology for any offence I have caused you."

"Not so hasty. I am no stranger. We both work for the Countess. We are colleagues, both proletarians. We should be friendly to each other," he said and came closer.

"Be that as it may I am not a communist, I am just a woman who tries to mind her own business," she said and quickened her step. She was shaken by fear and worry. Would anybody hear her if she screamed? What did that guy want from her?

"You don't like communists?" he sneered. "Do you prefer the Nazis? I find that hard to believe, they'd shoot you on the spot. We communists give everyone a fair chance. Even you Jews!"

"Why are you talking to me like that? I have done nothing to you. Can you please, please let me go? You are scaring me!" Wilma said, hoping that her honesty would make a difference to this irate young man.

"I thought you and I were the same," said the rejected steward with sadness in his voice. "Both oppressed by politics. I liked you. I have seen you on the grounds many times and you have always been so much fun with the little boy. I am sorry I scared you but you have hurt me by turning me down without even talking to me."

"Sorry, but I have got to go," she called out to him and ran away.

"Go to hell!" he said and threw a conker he held in his hand at her.

The incident pushed Wilma into further states of anxiety. She refused to leave the house or the studio on her own. Greta knew that something was wrong but it took her a lot of persuasion before Wilma was ready to tell her about the steward and his unwelcome

166

advances.

Apart from the fear, she also felt guilty for hurting his feelings. The incident had gnawed on her mind. She hoped that by ignoring the matter it would all go away but it didn't. Since the incident on the bridge with the Hitler Youth it took little for Wilma to feel threatened.

Greta told Edith and Esther about it, who offered to have the steward fired but the Countess said it was wiser to let it go. A disgruntled and unstable employee like this one could easily try and get his revenge on the Jews with help from the Hlinka Guard. There were always other ways of making him pay for his outrageous behaviour. Patience was of the essence. A few weeks later the insensitive man found himself locked in his sleeping quarters with a hungry rat family, an action of revenge that Edith had thought of so he could experience himself what it felt like to be scared.

Chapter 8: Bratislava 1943

Jonah had drawn up several new designs of carpets for the Countess but it took her a long time before she decided to go ahead with at least a few of them. Last year she had been confident she would be able to sell or help to sell many carpets without any difficulties, now she was no longer sure she could. The main problem was not finding buyers but choosing the right designs that prospective customers would be able to put on a wall freely and without controversy.

Almost exactly a year ago, when Jonah arrived at the manor house she knew that his Christian and heroic motifs would be easy to find a market for, but now that the war could be at a turning point, it seemed unwise to manufacture carpets that may be prohibited, destroyed or confiscated by the Soviet Army or a communist government. Historical themes were controversial in a country that had been called Upper Hungary, Czechoslovakia, Czecho-Slovakia and which was in danger of becoming controlled by either German or Russian in the near future.

Should the Axis powers win she guessed anything liberal and frivolous would have to be hidden or destroyed. Even those of her friends who had originally expressed a definite interest were now holding back until the outcome of the war was clearer to everyone. The compromise for the new designs was therefore a series of nature themes that the Countess felt were admittedly a little dull but which she could always give to the more conservative of her acquaintances. Production had to be delayed further because there were increasing supply problems caused by the army which needed more blankets and clothes for the winter. Textile materials were hard to come by.

The Allied air raids had not yet spread to Slovakia and its factories and so German interest in the country seemed to be focused on the productivity of the industry and its food production rather than the complete deportation of Jews to Poland. The sea blockade by the British and American forces had brought hunger to large parts of the population in the Reich, which demanded and took more than its fair share from the produce in Slovakia to compensate for its own shortcomings.

The Countess hoped that the war would come to an end soon

now that the Red Army was expected to sweep in from the East and the US was rumoured to land in the West. Peace seemed to be so close and yet, at the same time, still so incredibly far out of reach.

She was glad however that she had brought Jonah and his family to her Estate. He had such an incredible talent and after the war it might well be possible for him to achieve worldwide fame for his art. It was all down to her to make sure he survived, to do everything in her power to keep the man out of reach of the Jew haters in the country. So far her schemes of bribes and personal favours had worked very well.

The administration of the country was young and impressionable and for the first time in its history only answerable to its own people, not to Hungarian or Czech superiors. German requests were dealt with favourably but there were few of those as the super power was busy with the more rebellious of its recent territorial acquisitions.

The Countess knew when and how to address the egotism of the new officials she was working with and when to appeal to their greed. It seemed almost too easy to be true at times. In Jonah's case another party was intervening to keep the names off lists, the Countess found out from one particularly talkative civil servant, someone related to the military. After investigating further - at her request - the official told her that this intervention was carried out by an old war veteran, a recruitment officer who was covering up for Jonah's son Egon. Apparently the young soldier was very successful in the army and was regarded as indispensable. The civil servant of course was quick to point out that the weaver was only secondary to the army's goal of protecting Egon and the Countess would be well advised to 'carry on with her own safeguarding measures'.

Getting the family out of Bratislava and on to her Estate had been the most important part of her plan. Her connections were powerful, even at higher levels of the administration, but it was violence and unprovoked attacks on the streets that she worried about. Politicians could be controlled much more easily than the thugs in this country, even though she had her doubts how much longer it would be before the evil forces of Germany would put their foot down and demand the same measures against Jews as they were implementing everywhere else.

169

Jonah was not only a gifted artist, he was also a lovely character whom she wanted to introduce to her own circles of friends. He had a disarming laughter and his outlook on life was very philosophical and a welcome alternative to the other Jews she knew. The ones she was friendly with often tended to be of the mystical branch of Judaism, free thinking and spiritually open one minute and then dogmatic about the teachings of the Kabbalah the next; something which was hard for her rational nature to accept.

Jonah appeared to possess a more practical and pragmatic approach in his views of the world but – when queried in discussion - he confessed to having views that occasionally changed, very much in the Jewish tradition of questioning and searching oneself for the concepts of God and ethics. She used to host a series of discussions with her philosophically inclined friends but so many of the regular attendees had left the country that this would prove a rather dull affair now. Instead of such structured gatherings she tried to bring regular conversations away from mundane topics onto more spiritual subjects but it proved difficult with Jonah who tried so hard to keep his focus on the work tasks ahead of him. He remembered how Visser had predicted her interest in his philosophical views but Jonah no longer felt comfortable wasting time just talking to her when he knew how indebted he was to her financially. He wanted to pay his way and not be seen to be taking advantage.

Greta wanted to make herself useful during this time of no work in the weaving workshop. She had mentioned her love of books to Edith who had suggested to the Countess that this knowledgeable young woman should be allowed to spend time in the Estate library to take advantage of the great treasures it held. When Greta visited the library for the first time she found it difficult to locate specific books and authors on the many shelves that held the collection. Frustrated and also challenged she offered to sort and organise the books in her spare time. The Countess welcomed the suggestion with huge enthusiasm. Not only had she been aware of how neglected the collection had been since the departure of her bibliophile former steward to Palestine.

Greta's interest also reassured the Countess that Jonah and his family were not planning to leave the Estate just because there was temporarily nothing for them to do until the new materials were delivered. Greta was delighted by the vast amount and the quality of the books on the shelves. There had to be at least 20,000 volumes, if her estimates were correct. The chaos that prevailed however was appalling. It seemed as if no one had given the order of the books any consistent thought for years. Works by one author were often found in separate places, translated texts were sometimes next to the originals in the French or Latin section and sometimes together with other books by the same writer, the history books were not shelved together either and for anyone to find a particular book would prove difficult if not impossible.

Greta was delighted to be able to help their beneficiary and together with Wilma and Ernst she went to the library almost every day. While Ernst was playing on the floor or at a little table, Greta was going through the shelves one by one and handed Wilma books that she thought needed relocating. Later they would go through these and decide how to classify the collection. For Wilma this work was calming and almost cathartic. It gave her a sense of restoration and order in this period of suspension and lack of structure. With every tidy shelf she felt a little closer to the inner peace and stability that she was missing. For Greta, the reorganisation of the library was an equally emotionally charged experience but for quite different reasons. She came across a lot of books by her favourite German romantic authors, who she had not thought about for a very long time and she started to re-read them in the evenings.

She could not help but feel a little cynical about the big dreams and fairy tale happy endings in these books and the sharp contrast that the sound of the German language in those stories had to her these days, now associated with orders, war propaganda and Hitler's voice on the wireless. This spoiled many of her favourite novels for her for good. She found the same to be true for her Russian writers who had romanticised a Tsarist society, which had since turned into another heartless fascist state.

Edith offered to teach her some French, but Jonah advised his daughter to be aware of the potential implication of an intimate friendship with one of the two lovers and reminded her of the dangers a jealous Esther might bring to the family. Greta took this advice and ensured that she did not spend too much time alone with either of the two courting ladies.

It was hard to shake off the two women completely since they were also living under voluntary house arrest on the Estate. Greta was still raw and hurt from the loss of her first born son and her husband, and her stomach turned whenever she saw books that Wilhelm had liked.

She would have liked to know how he and Karl were getting on in Berlin. Had Karl successfully become an Aryan in the eyes of the authorities or had he been found out and deported? The thought of it made her feel nauseous. She tried hard not to think of him at all. When the thoughts came back to haunt her she persuaded herself to believe that Wilhelm and his family connections in Berlin must have been successful in preventing such a fate. Wilhelm would have been drafted to the war by now or had he been exempt? Who would be looking after their son Karl if he was at the front? Did her boy have enough to eat? Did he still think about her, even remember her or had he forgotten his mother and been adopted into a new family?

Wilhelm had probably re-married by now and produced more children for the Fuhrer. There was so much on her mind and so many questions might never be answered. She was too proud to ask Johanna and if anyone knew, they did not tell her. The books in the library had initially been a welcome distraction and an escape from her reality but the handling of some of those books brought back many memories she would have preferred to keep out of her mind.

Wilma was upset just as easily by the tainted memories that the treasures of this library represented. To her, they were symbols of an easier and happier time, when her sister had been happy and the flow of interesting books brought back by her brother-in-law had seemed never ending. Nowadays she could not make herself read much at all, she was too afraid that a story might not end well and add to her melancholic mood.

Children's books for Ernst would have been useful but there were very few of those in the manor house Library. The ones that she found were not in great condition and naturally most of them were written in Hungarian, which Ernst had not learned to speak. Wilma had not only lost her interest in books and reading but also the drive to sing one of the many folk songs which she had so loved to perform dramatically for Ernst in the past. She preferred to play with building blocks these days, or to build houses out of playing cards or fold papers into planes or boats – all activities that did not demand too much conversation or interaction with the child. He was the last person on earth she would have wanted to take her sad mood out on.

172

There had been no word from Egon for several months now and Wilma was very nervous about that too. Mail deliveries during the war had always been irregular and Jonah had maintained for some time that there was no need to become worried. Alma added that no news was also always good news. While there was no confirmation that he was well at least they had no proof that he was missing or wounded either. Wilma suffered terrible nightmares and could not stop herself from imagining him lying wounded in a battle field, in a hospital or captured by the enemy.

It was hard to argue with Alma and Jonah about it. Their optimism was unbreakable, yet even in her most pessimistic of moments Wilma never once thought of him as being dead. That possibility was completely banned from her imagination.

In that regard Jonah was actually much less optimistic than her. He knew that the death of his son was a very likely possibility but he kept up an outward cheerfulness and said that he guessed that Egon had never received their notice of the new address and so all of his letters would not have been delivered. Besides, the military had to keep the location of their soldiers a secret and given Egon's deployment in classified work, it was even less likely for them to hear from him.

Wilma took a little comfort in this possibility. She knew that at least Alma might have tried to find out if any letters had been delivered to the address on Gajova.

After they had left Bratislava, the workshop had been empty for a few weeks but then new tenants had moved in and turned it into a furniture shop. Since the confiscation of Jewish property in Slovakia and even more so in the Protectorate of Bohemia and Moravia, there were a lot more goods available on the market.

Owners of new shops often had the right party connections and also important free access to the warehouses of confiscated goods. It seemed advisable to Jonah not to draw the attention of such potential party members to himself and his new location. Even though his entire family had been issued with exemption papers he did not blindly trust their effectiveness and he certainly did not feel he could afford to trust the new occupants of his workshop by leaving a forwarding address. Jonah forced himself to believe that there were good reasons why they had not heard from his son and took comfort in the fact that there had never been much news from him before their move out of Bratislava either, but a small doubt remained miserably at the back of his mind.

It was only when the German army was defeated in Stalingrad in February that Jonah seriously started to worry. He was not sure which division of the German army the Slovak units had been assisting but he felt a sad certainty that the spy or radio work that Egon was involved in simply must have been part of this enormous battle of all battles. He could only hope that his son had been fortunate enough to be taken prisoner by the Soviets rather than being amongst the huge number of casualties. Alma on the other hand was not so sure that being a prisoner of war during winter was preferable to an immediate death or to a lengthy stay in a hospital. She tried to keep the family from talking about it as much as she could. In the absence of concrete news it seemed futile to speculate and Wilma in particular was already on the verge of losing her calm.

Spring came and the awaited reprisals from the Soviet army or the predicted push from Allied troops against the Western front still had not materialised. Newsreels at the picture houses and radio broadcasts painted the usual optimistic picture of the course of the war for the Axis powers, while the BBC broadcasts said the exact opposite. Since the defeat at Stalingrad, Germany seemed too busy with its own problems to interfere with Slovak politics. Life in Bratislava was full of unfulfilled expectations and everything seemed to hang idly in a state of suspension, waiting for the big unknown. There were still no further deportations of Jews, only hard work in the labour camps for the ones already arrested, continued high productivity at factories and mines, food shortages and black market activity.

Benedikt had risen even further within the party hierarchy and was elected as one of the agricultural advisers to the government. This meant that he had to spend several days a week in Bratislava to attend meetings and he had to delegate more of his own farm duties to someone else, especially the supervision. He had obtained exemption papers for all of his farm workers but kept a reign of terror by making it quite clear to them that these could be withdrawn on his wish at any given moment.

Of course there was no need for such threats. His employees were all aware of the advantages that they were enjoying by working for such a big fish. Senior labourers had already warned the more recent arrivals of the fate Marius and his family had met when the married servant had been caught with the farmer's daughter Maria. That was enough of a deterrent for them to toe the line. Benedikt had chosen two workers as supervisors in his absence. One was Sarah's brother Elias, the other was a slightly older Gypsy by the name of Hanzi.

The two of them had been chosen because they represented opposing groups within the work force, making it difficult for anybody to steal or to be lazy without being reported to Benedikt by a member of the opposing group. This divide and conquer method had worked well for Benedikt in the past and even though the tensions amongst his labourers grew the farm seemed to do well in his absence.

Hanzi had not been very pleased when he was appointed to his new position; life had been difficult enough for him already. The Jews on this farm were a closed group and seemed to look out only for each other. Gypsies were fewer in number and had less support behind them to help them to survive. Hanzi's family members were eager for him to get his hands on some of the farm produce to feed their hungry mouths and he had difficulties to stop them from helping themselves. If he got caught he risked denunciation and would probably be made responsible for any thefts committed by his own community. Because there was no solidarity between the two groups the set up was toxic for the relations between them and both sides eyed each other with suspicion and kept double checking everything the other side did. Elias had suggested a truce or a deal between himself and Hanzi but the Gypsy elders warned him off. They were certain such a deal with the 'untrustworthy' Jews would only short change them.

During Benedikt's absences from the farm Johanna was free to visit the Weissensteiners at the manor house. There was no longer a need to bring them free food as the cook was willing to buy it off her at exorbitant black market prices and Jonah and his family would still have access to it later in the staff kitchen. Of late her trips to the Estate had become an escapism for her. At the farm she felt increasingly frustrated and unwanted. She had never known a loving atmosphere at her own family home when she was a child and had certainly not sought to create anything like it with her own children and husband. Then the Berlin relatives had arrived and turned their life upside down by bringing with them a sense of familiarity and closeness. This was the first time in her life that she had encountered such a way of living. Having observed it suspiciously and having at first rejected it she gradually had come to like the new atmosphere on the farm without even realising it herself. She had fought against it and made it hard for her guests to feel welcome and at home. Now that they were all gone she found she missed those days, yet she lacked the ability to connect to her own children in this way and to establish warm and friendly relationships with them.

The Jewish maid Sarah had become her new best friend instead of her children who were equally unsure how to bridge the gap between them and their own mother. The bond between the mistress and her servant did not help with this situation at all and caused further problems with Johanna's children. They had grown understandably jealous first of Wilhelm and Greta, then Karl, then Ernst and now of the Jewish maid. When Johanna naively tried to reach out to her daughters they withdrew from her. It was not just jealousy. They were uncomfortable with this unprecedented kindness and were fearful of hidden ulterior motives. Sarah was unable to mediate because Maria and Roswitha were stonewalling her attempts to break the ice too. It was astonishing how much could be said without any words being exchanged between the women on the farm.

At the Weissensteiners all these politics, tactics and mind games were absent. Jonah and Alma were living in a friendly and peaceful manner and it was easier for Johanna to follow their lead of exchanging pleasantries than having to create such harmony herself. Maybe one day she might be able to apply what she was observing here in her own life but for now she was only here to enjoy and to rest from the harsh climate at home.

Whenever possible she took Sarah with her as well, knowing how much Sarah needed such a diversion and how helpful the maid's presence was for Wilma and her peace of mind. It was probably another nail in the coffin of her family relations but Johanna was gradually giving up her hopes for success in that endeavour.

If Greta and her sister were busy in the library at the manor house, Sarah would go there directly without spending any time with Jonah. She would help the sisters by taking care of Ernst or assist them with the library project and rejoice in the all-female company,

176

something she did not know from her own life. Her siblings were all boys and since his promotion at the farm Elias had become very bossy – as if she did not have enough people breathing down her neck.

Greta always welcomed it when Sarah came to see them because it meant either extra attention for Ernst or it speeded up their progress with the preliminary sorting of books. She was so involved in the process that she often forgot to talk about anything else but the library. By letting herself be absorbed in the project and the search for a logical and easy solution to the sorting problems she seemed to be able to push any other worry out of her mind.

The effect was sadly that she had become an obsessed woman quite out of touch with the real world. Wilma shared her enthusiasm but found it hard to deal with her sister's seriousness and single minded focus. With Sarah, at long last, came the diversion and the youthful influence that both sisters at times needed. The lack of word from Egon had seriously damaged all of their spirits.

At the house by the lake Alma would usually ask Johanna about her life and listen patiently to all the news and worries on her visitor's troubled mind. Jonah tried to make time from his work to sit down with the women whenever he could but he welcomed that Alma should have a female friend her own age and so he tried to strike a balance between attentiveness to his visitor and giving space to the developing new friendship. The bond that was forming between them was against all odds. Alma stood for so many things that the otherwise hard minded Johanna was opposed to: being with a Jewish man, living with him in sin, not supporting Hitler and the war, not supporting the Christian or any faith for that matter, being so soft on the younger generation and being so god-damned happy despite her modest income and simple life.

In turn Johanna's ambition, her coldness, her abrupt manners, her judgemental character and her belief in a Christian and conservative world order were so alien to Alma that she could watch them in bemusement as an observer, but she could also see the vulnerable woman underneath the harshness, the woman who did not always behave as heartlessly as she preached, the fearful woman who hid behind big words but who had a soft core and a little child who just needed reassurance, attention and love.

Alma made Johanna forget about the loveless world she lived

in. For a few hours she could enjoy the presence of someone who tried to see life from her perspective, who understood how difficult her two daughters were, how her husband had moved out of reach and was only thinking about his career and the party and never paid her any attention any more, how her son was somewhere in that war and with his weak constitution was probably in grave danger right now, how she still missed little Karl and her beloved Wilhelm, how dull life had become since everyone had left her on the farm and how lonely she was when Sarah went back to her home every evening.

Alma understood her very well and she felt sorry for the farmer's wife, even though she knew that Johanna really only had herself to blame for the state her life was in. Personally, she found Johanna's abrupt and rude manners endearing and knew that the insults and harsh remarks were not meant to hurt but she could see how other people would take offence and try to cut that mean spirited woman out of their lives. Underneath that edgy and bitter exterior there was someone capable of loving and giving, who just needed to be handled with a little bit of care. By ignoring the criticism and the judgement and encouraging the nicer sides of Johanna's character, Alma was able to bring out the best in the rigid German and became a close friend.

Alma on the other hand was flattered that Johanna would open up to her and seek out her company. Even though the farmer's wife was desperate for love and companionship she had singled her out and valued Alma's opinion. Alma had quite a lot of needs herself, some of which were perfectly met by Johanna's interest in her. At the age of 14 Alma had been sent to Budapest to live with relatives and to learn a trade. Her father died of pneumonia and when her mother remarried it was made clear to Alma that there would be no room for her in the new family home, especially since her mother wanted to have more children as soon as possible. Alma stayed in Budapest until the foundation of the Slovak state. She had always felt as an outsider in Hungary, unwanted by her own family and since her first love died in the Great War she had also given up on love.

She had hoped to find some kind of solidarity and kindred spirit in the new state of Slovakia, where her nationality would bind her to an entire country but the reality of a new nation fell short of these romantic ideas. No one had been waiting for expatriates to come home and join them, no one was welcoming her with open arms. The only good thing in her life had been Jonah and his family and so she felt very reassured and pleased that Johanna, this Jew hating harsh German farmer, had not only gone out of her way to help this kind man of hers to survive with the food supplies, but she also had started to trust in Alma and confide in her.

Alma desperately needed to believe in a world where kindness existed, where solidarity and charity were exchanged even between people on opposing sides of the political and sociological conflicts, otherwise her Jonah would have no chance of survival in the long run. Seeing the good in Johanna's character was therefore a necessity in Alma's war survival strategy and her trust in the good in the other woman became a self-fulfilling prophecy that encouraged Johanna to better herself and to want to become a nicer person.

It was a relief for Johanna to be able to confide in her new friend and at long last be allowed to talk about her husband in a way that she would have previously described as disloyal. She disliked his new party involvement, the time he spent away from the farm and the image consciousness he had recently begun to display. Her husband was a proud man and he had never wasted time on what other people thought about him. He used to look in the mirror for approval, not into other people's faces. Johanna had a hard time catching up with what had become important in his new philosophy now.

Jews had been a minor topic in his life, now the issue was political and could not just be laughed off or brushed away any more. Johanna was not cut out for the life of a party official, she longed for simplicity and she felt threatened by his new ambitions. In their times alone at the weaving workshop the two ladies practised imitating the way Benedikt was talking at those party meetings and laughed about how ridiculous it must sound to his fellow statesmen. They were both astonished at his rise within the party when his mannerisms were so boorish and unsophisticated. Was that really what the new regime was all about?

Jonah observed the change in Johanna with amazement and happiness. Not only did she seem less hostile, she was becoming more content in herself and was almost on the verge of developing a sense of humour and irony. Once again the Weissensteiner family seemed favoured by a lucky star which had delivered them to this safe place right next to their benefactor and new friend Johanna.

Jonah's main worry now was work. The Countess had assured him of her belief in him and his art but she had failed to secure the commissions she had so optimistically predicted and the remote location of his workshop had effectively cut him off from some of his suppliers. Just how strong were her connections? Could she grow tired and bored of him and drop him from one day to the next for a new and less controversial protégé?

Might Lady Edith demand some personal favours of his daughter to whom she had taken such a fancy or was that thought just an absurd product of his over-active worrying mind? He found it difficult to count his blessings every day and be grateful for the obviously rather pleasant circumstances he found himself in at present. Fear and even resentment against the people that had put him into this golden cage were rising within him and he had a hard time fighting them efficiently.

He could not understand why the Countess was wasting so much money on him and his family when she probably could have relocated him to Palestine for far less than it cost to manufacture all his art work for her. Little did he know that this had been her original plan until she had learned of the sinking of the Struma, a boat full of Jewish refugees that had been blocked from the shores of Palestine by the British. The Romanian Captain had tried to disembark his passengers in Istanbul but the Turkish authorities had also turned them away and towed the vessel into open waters where it was sunk by a Russian torpedo. She had never had the heart to tell him about such incidents and so he remained under the impression that the Countess had not exhausted all of her options in order to have him near her, while in reality her options were limited and the gamble that she was taking with his life was, under the unpredictable circumstances, the best educated guess she could venture.

In April the Countess finally got hold of the promised weaving materials and life for the Weissensteiners could at last return to a state of normality.

Greta and Wilma had completely reorganised and improved the entire library and all that remained was to compile an itemised index of the books, which was a task neither of them had ever looked forward to with any sort of enthusiasm. Going back to weaving was not only a welcome excuse to abort the dull exercise of classifying the book collection, it symbolised a break from the melancholic mood they had lived in during their library work over the past few months. Resuming their craft was the beginning of a new chapter for both sisters and they were suddenly full of energy and optimism again.

From time to time Wilma still experienced what Jonah had come to term as 'funny turns': short and usually completely unprovoked bouts of anxiety and hysteria. Alma seemed to handle these situations the best by holding Wilma's hand or shoulders and sitting with her until the attack was over.

In the time the women spent working together, Alma would talk about her life in Budapest before and after the Great War and they would speculate what would happen to the pieces of the former Empire when this current war finally came to an end. Alma believed that the Soviet Army was likely to get to Slovakia first and that there would be a big influence from the Bolsheviks but in the end that phase would fade not only here but also in Russia.

"I am not sure about that," contradicted Greta. "The Bolsheviks have been in power for a very long time now and people say that all their important opponents have been eliminated. A counter revolution is increasingly unlikely. Our government in exile has relocated to Moscow. They will follow right behind the Red Army all the way to Prague. In that I agree with you, but they won't be much more than a puppet government for the Reds."

"I am not sure that Stalin would bother with such a farce," Alma guessed. "My guess is he will install his own communist government right away. We have communists in the Resistance and allegedly there are a lot of army deserters fighting with the Red Army against our own troops and the Germans. He won't need the exile government."

"I wonder what the Countess is going to do?" contemplated Wilma. "Will they confiscate all of her property or leave her some?"

"They will take it all," Greta supposed. "It is too big a house for her, it will become a barracks or hospital or a party building. Everything for the people. Maybe they will allow us to stay, but I am not sure where they stand on the issue of art. It may be regarded as a bourgeois luxury that we manufacture here and we might be told to go back to producing practical goods instead."

"Would you rather everything stayed the way it is now?" asked Wilma provocatively.

"I don't know," Greta replied.

"Our situation really is quite bearable," Alma contributed to the conversation. "You must agree with that. The question is can we carry on like this? If there was a truce would the current government and the Hlinka Guard stop sending the Jews to Poland or Berlin? Will we be hiding here for ever? We can't do that. Something is going to happen and it will change the way we live."

"Wouldn't you want to flee the country if the Bolsheviks take over?" Wilma asked her. "You could have stayed in Hungary if you had wanted to live under communist rule.

"No Wilma. I love it here, I am happy with your father, I cannot give that up. I don't want to run any more. The Reds are lesser enemies of the Jews than the Nazis. I would try my luck with them if they come here," she replied.

"Whatever happens we will stick together," Greta said.

Wilma nodded but as usual those type of discussions and speculations only made her more nervous and anxious.

Jonah had used his 'idle' time of waiting for the materials wisely and had improved upon the original designs for the new carpets drastically. He had added beautiful details to the depicted scenes, had worked on the colour schemes and experimented with dyes to give the carpets a more intense and lively feel. The Countess was in awe and so were Esther and Edith. That man clearly was a genius if they ever had used that word for a weaver. Jonah had needed to keep himself busy to keep the reoccurring thoughts about Egon and his possible death at Stalingrad from his mind. They had heard nothing from the military or from his son. So many soldiers had been reported as missing since the battle had begun but if you believed Allied propaganda on the wireless that could mean not just death but also captivity or desertion.

Egon's fate could be many things. For all they knew he might well be one of the soldiers liberating Slovakia from Hitler. Anything was possible. The not knowing was the hard part. He had asked the Countess if she could try and find out any news about his son's location for him and she had promised him to look into the matter but so far her enquiries had produced no results one way or the other. The Slovak army was not as organised as the families of fallen soldiers would have liked it to be and information was hard to come by in the prevailing chaos. Jonah frequently woke up in the middle of the night with a stabbing pain in his chest and he was convinced it was a sign that his Egon had been killed by a bayonet, but Alma told him that his imagination was getting the better of him. He admitted freely to that possibility but in his heart of hearts he was certain it was the connection from father to son that made him feel this pain and that his worst fears had already come true.

For the sake of peace and Wilma's sanity he kept these thoughts to himself and if he ever needed distraction from his gloomy mind he would take his grandson Ernst into the workshop and teach him the basics of weaving. Ernst proved surprisingly dexterous and capable for a five year old but he preferred it when his grandfather told him stories or read to him from a book. The two had a great relationship but Jonah was getting on in years and realised that his grandson really preferred the company of the younger adults.

When production resumed at the workshop there was less time available for the adults to play with Ernst, who had grown accustomed to the increased attention. He now lived for the visits of the ladies Esther and Edith, who would take him almost daily for walks around the lake and read to him from brand new books they had delivered to the manor house especially for him.

Esther was his favourite new aunt, always full of sparks and laughter and a complete natural with children it seemed. Strangely enough Esther confessed to Greta that she had always hated children. In Ernst, she had for the first time found a boy with such pleasant and unspoilt manners that she could just take him with her and never bring him back.

On hearing this Jonah felt sorry for her and her unfortunate inclination that meant she would always be deprived of the pleasure of having children of her own. He wondered quietly if a desire to have children could ever be enough for her to change her mind about the whole Edith thing. Esther was much better looking and would find it easy to land a good catch – even in war times when men were becoming a minority outside the battlefields. Alma scolded him for thinking so low of their love, just because he did not understand it but when she was honest with herself she had to confess she did not understand that strange relationship either. She had never desired another woman and while she had to believe the two ladies when they assured her that they were really happy in their life together, she still secretly doubted that this could be true.

Wilma had told her father that the couple's money was all Edith's and that Esther was completely dependent on her 'friend' to survive. Edith had been disinherited by her Viennese father when he opened a incriminating letter sent to her by a former lover. Edith found shelter with a more understanding, liberally minded and conveniently childless sister of her mother who took Edith under her wing and – after her death in 1928 - left her all her belongings. Since then Edith had toured Europe and searched for a place to settle down. In Paris she had met and fallen madly in love with the then cabaret artist Esther, daughter of a Spanish mother and a French father. Even though Esther could prove her gentile bloodline for many generations, she looked and often was treated as a Jew wherever she went. The two ladies in love faced a similar dilemma to that which Greta and Wilhelm had to battle when they were still married. Very few places in Europe were safe for them as a couple and no country outside the Axis powers would issue a visa for the Austrian-German Edith. The Germans in the Allied countries had been rounded up in concentration camps to prevent spy activities and that was a life definitely not suitable for two lesbians.

So they had decided to bet on the protection of the Countess and her idyllic country estate. The friendship between the lovers and the Countess was based on a shared appreciation of the classic and modern arts but had recently taken on a new dimension. Edith had ventured to make the odd remark and the occasional very polite suggestion on how to improve the way the Countess was running the Estate. Being a wealthy and childless widow with few obligations her Highness had been able to overlook wastage and inefficiency but with the arrival of war rationing and food shortages Edith and her talents were much needed indeed. Her efforts in that department relieved the Countess of the mundane worries she hated to waste her precious time on. It enabled her to focus harder on the increasingly complex tasks of diplomacy and public relations. Wining and dining army officials, party leaders and the local aristocracy were more important than ever and the Countess wanted to remain in everyone's good books. Edith in the meantime acted as the new estate manager with Esther being her right hand and advisor. The three of them combined the business of the material world with the pleasure of their trust and friendship.

Deprived of a more prominent, glamorous and aristocratic social life like the one they had enjoyed in Paris and Vienna before the war, the ladies had to look for company in more secluded provincial circles and under less exciting circumstances.

Jonah, with his gentleness and philosophical simplicity, appealed to them and ever since that New Year's Day when they had shared a breakfast table with him they had deliberately sought him out for company. Even when there were visitors to the manor house they never neglected the Weissensteiner family and kept appearing regularly. Jonah was the one who would come up with the right proverbs, the one to disarm them with humour and charm when the sisters had disagreements with each other and he provided them with a father figure that both of them could accept without feeling patronised. His advice was always sound and his judgement always impartial.

Since March the Countess had also given shelter to the Dutch painter Visser but the ladies were not really interested in him and when he came to visit Jonah at the same time they usually took their leave soon afterwards.

Visser's arrival at the Estate had been very sudden. He had recently run into some serious trouble. First his name had appeared on a list of Jewish artists in the Netherlands and a warrant for his arrest had been issued. However, all of this had happened about two years ago and nothing serious had ever come of it. Only much more recently an artist from that very list had been captured in Belgium and had tried to bargain with his captors by offering to reveal the location of other Jewish or communist artists in hiding - in exchange for his escape. The Gestapo in Amsterdam agreed to the deal and after he had told them where he thought his fellow Jews were currently placed they started their hunt and shot the traitor anyway.

The Nazis didn't know exactly where Visser was hiding but they were able to narrow their search down to the former Austro-Hungarian Empire and asked for his name to be on search lists in these areas. Some Hlinka officials had come to the manor house and had enquired about Visser's whereabouts. The Countess declared that she believed that he had left a few months ago to relocate to Palestine and was unfortunately very likely to have been on the sunken ship Struma last winter. Shortly after that visit she had

185

'renewed her friendship' with the local police officer who - after another demonstration of the value she put on his kindness – could report that her version of events had been accepted as the confirmed official result of the investigation into the fate of Visser.

After an appropriate period of waiting to see if the search for Visser had indeed stopped she contacted him and offered him to come and stay with her and use her attic as his studio. The Dutch painter was not as grateful to the Countess as she had dared to assume he would be. He was prone to bad mood swings and excessive drinking and seemed to resent everyone at the manor house for keeping him under house arrest. He kept himself only just under control when the Countess was present but took out his rage on pretty much everyone else without guard.

Edith had taken him aside a few times and had tried to make him see sense in a series of not so gentle 'heart to hearts' but to no avail. Visser also refused to paint while he was 'in exile' but in the absence of his usual occupation he was bored out of his mind and upset everyone by pacing through the corridors, talking to himself and swearing loudly. The Countess had scolded him several times about his attitude and tried to anger him into painting again but her efforts remained fruitless.

Jonah, too, had unsuccessfully attempted to calm down his friend and feared the man would become a liability to the Countess and a danger to everyone on the Estate by drawing attention to himself.

Visser's attitude was in crass contrast with Jonah's who was very grateful for the risks her Highness was taking for them. He was not informed or well-connected enough to appreciate how big these risks were but he felt humbled and guilty for accepting her hospitality. Visser on his downward spiral irritated him and Jonah tried to avoid him wherever he could.

In the summer at last there was good news on the Allied radio broadcasts. In one single week the Russians had smashed a campaign by Hitler and were now launching a well-equipped counter offensive. On top of that the Allied troops had landed on Sicily. The long awaited road to liberation seemed to have begun. No one doubted that this was going to be the end of Hitler and his Germany but it was a matter of time before the fruits of these proceedings could be enjoyed and everyone in hiding had to be patient and wait for the liberation to happen. How soon could the Allied troops bring the Axis Powers to their knees? Would there be a treaty or a total war as Hitler had announced? A revolution in Germany? A rebellion? Surrender? Everyone had a different opinion and everything still seemed possible.

The Countess frequently invited Jonah and the ladies to her drawing room where she tried to continue her tradition of philosophical discussions. Together with her guests she regularly listened to broadcasts from both military leaders before discussing and analysing them. Visser often occupied the room next to them at this hour when he played depressing and mad sounding piano pieces without ever honouring them with his presence.

"Visser is a pure genius!" the Countess stated matter of factly one day while listening to his masterful playing. "Madness and genius are usually linked closely together. I so wish he would paint again and use all the anger he has inside of him and bring it onto the canvass. Can you imagine what kind of creations could come of his rage? This hammering on the piano is probably good for his moods too but when he is finished we have nothing to show for it. You and I are enjoying it but when the last note has died away it only remains in our memories. A painting would last for generations."

"Oh, your illustrious Highness!" said Jonah. "You are always so practical in your observations. I must say I don't care so much about that. I just want my friend to be happy again. He should be pleased to be in this safe place amongst friends and decent company. Instead he gives in to madness and misery and self-destructive habits."

"People are all different," injected Esther. "Not everyone has strength and discipline. Do you really have those qualities yourself? Because I suspect that you have chosen to be passive and you are trying to make your fortune by the way of avoidance and escapism. That suits your peaceful character and that is why your art is so pleasing and not very controversial. Your genius is reined in by self-preservation and the responsibility of caring for your family. It is a miracle that you ever let your genius out enough to come up with your creative ideas that we so admire. Visser is different. He is a complete slave to his muses. He has no choice and no say in the matter. Painting consumes him and now that his physical body experiences boundaries and feels he lives in a golden cage his talent is rebelling or out to destroy him from the inside. You should not

187

condemn him you should feel sorry for him."

"You are a little melodramatic my love!" said Edith. "He is still a human with a rational mind. We all have to be able to limit the damage our primitive urges are capable of bringing to our lives. He is out of control and if no one can stop him he will drink himself to death or be found by the Hlinka Guard."

"You are right Edith," agreed the Countess. "He should reign in his madness. I can reassure you that the Hlinka Guard are instructed not to come near the manor house and they swore to turn a blind eye on us as long as we don't provoke them or draw attention to us in a way that cannot be ignored. Visser is on the brink of ruining that for us. However, he has promised me that he will not leave the Estate and with that in mind we can be relaxed about his current behaviour. Be assured my darling, he has a little bit of sanity left. Hopefully he will have exhausted himself with all the drama before it becomes too much or too dangerous."

"I hope so. I really hope so!" Jonah said.

"If the Allies start making progress Visser will improve, I am sure of it. He must. Then we can all sigh with relief," added Esther.

"I am not entirely sure of that," said the Countess. "If the Bolsheviks take over the country I am going to lose everything and we all have to reconsider our options. Their way of running the country is far from free and liberated."

"We don't know for sure if they will take over the government as well. They are harbouring our exile government in Moscow now. We could be back under Czech rule. That would mean no confiscations and comrade business but retaliation for the deserters," Jonah predicted.

"That I could live with," said the Countess. "The Czechs don't like the Hungarians much but I am not planning to run for office, so they should leave me alone. Apart from their taxes of course but I prefer the taxes to the confiscation."

"A woman of your intelligence, such foresight and your many connections you must have planned ahead and taken precautions for all possible outcomes I presume?" Jonah asked.

"Of course I have," admitted the Countess. "A lot of my money is in Switzerland, but I needed to keep a large part of it here too. I will lose a lot either way I assume. It is always good to be prepared for all eventualities. I will leave the country ahead of the

Allied troops to avoid looting or violence from the Red Army. I am in the possession of a French passport and Edith and Esther will try and escape with me to a hopefully liberated France. What plans do you have Jonah?"

"I am afraid I have not made any plans," replied the weaver. "How could I? The Russian have killed so many Jews, I find it hard to believe that communist ideology has changed that culture of hatred. I would find it hard to live under their rule. They can't take much money from us but we could fall from one pogrom into the next. Would you believe the languages we speak best are Russian and German – both countries firmly in the hands of our enemies."

"You are widely believed to be a German Jew, is that not true?" asked Edith.

"Officially I am only known as a German. Not many people know that I and my family are Jewish. We are in fact from the Ukraine. We came before the big wave and might have gone unnoticed. However, our names are on those lists at the administration, so somebody must know we are Jewish – how I do not know," Jonah contemplated.

"Don't ever worry about those lists, dear Jonah. I keep wiping them clean," the Countess reassured him.

"I know and I feel humbled and eternally indebted to you for it. How will I ever be able to repay your kindness?" said Jonah woefully.

"You already have. Good friends are hard to come by and I know I can always rely on you, even though I have no need to call in favours from you yet."

By September the Allied forces landed on mainland Italy and according to their radio transmissions made steady progress. The Czechoslovak government in exile was calling its citizens to armed resistance and partisan activities against the 'illegal' government of Slovakia. To arrive at the perception of a change of luck in the war was however very difficult in the quiet and peaceful life of Slovakia. Hunger and food shortages increased, mainly due to the uncompromising demands of the German army and civilians, but the war still seemed thousands of miles away and for the people at the manor house it was natural to question if the propaganda of the Allies might not be an exaggeration after all.

The only thing that had a direct impact on the little community was the rumour that Hitler had increased pressure on President Tiso to deliver the Jews to Poland as he had promised for so long. The administration was again busy compiling lists and taking bribes. According to the sources the President had no intention of fulfilling his promise to Hitler and was still using his presidential exemptions generously. The Countess however warned Jonah that her influence might soon not be enough to save his family anymore and she proposed that she would get him and his family new passports.

"I appreciate the offer your illustrious Highness, but this seems incredibly risky. I cannot believe for one moment that we could fool a border patrol or police officer with forged documents. There must be so many dodgy passports in circulation these days that the proper ones are too easy to distinguish from the fake ones," he said, refusing her offer.

"You are always such a pessimist when it comes to thinking about your future prospects," the Countess gently scolded him. "Remember I am moving in artistic circles and the trade we are talking about is full of artists. I am only buying from the best and I would bet you that even Himmler himself could not tell the difference between these artefacts and the real thing."

"I could never repay you in any case," continued Jonah in his refusal. "There are five of us in this family now, some of whom look suspiciously Jewish. The Gestapo are locking up suspects and hold them behind bars until they have confirmed passport details from their respective registry offices. You are having naïve notions about the efficiency of the German administration. Even in war times they are never neglectful and their systems work like clockwork." Jonah protested.

"As far as the money is concerned, my dear Jonah, you can repay me with your art. I want to see more of that in any case and I must make sure that it will be continued. It is the privilege of my status as wealthy muse of the arts. It has always vexed me to be an admirer but never a maker of art myself. To save gifted artists is the closest I will ever come to the miracle of its creation," the Countess assured him. "As for the registry offices, I am not in the least naïve my dear Weissensteiner. The Allied bombings have destroyed several of these during the last two years.

The Gestapo may have other means of checking your data but it would never be as straightforward and easy as you fear. My contacts have been in the business for some time and they know which registry offices are the best ones to use on a passport. Leave it to those professionals and worry about the colour of your next carpet instead. That is much more suitable."

"All the money it must cost you, just for a putz like me," he called out in despair.

"You must never call yourself that, Jonah," Esther burst out "It sounds to me as if you already believe all the negative things the Nazis are saying about you and the Jews, as if you agree with them yourself. Your humble demeanour usually does you credit but you must not take it so far and think that you are less worth than anyone else."

"Do you have any preference for your new name dear Jonah?" asked the Countess.

"What about Weber?" suggested Jonah.

"A weaver called Weber. Oh that does not sound great," said Edith dismissively.

"Well, we will have to think of a good German name soon," concluded the Countess.

Chapter 9: Bratislava 1944

The New Year started with a terrible shock for everyone on the Estate. Early on New Year's Eve Jonah had left home to invite his melancholic friend Visser to party with them in the cottage. Nobody should be on their own on such a big night and the Dutchman's silly sulking behaviour had to be challenged. Jonah knew that Esther and Edith had decided to have an intimate dinner to bring in the New Year and so it was likely that the Dutch painter would be drinking alone in his rooms, indulging in self-pity and misery. Jonah found Visser's door locked and was informed by the service men that he had not been seen since breakfast – something not unusual for the recently so withdrawn odd resident of the Estate. Jonah made a lot of noise banging at the door and shouting but the stubborn man seemed to ignore him.

"I am getting tired of his attitude!" admitted Edith who had arrived at the scene to investigate the sudden noise. "He is surrounded by people he can trust and who want to help him but he keeps us locked out."

"If only life was that black and white," contradicted Jonah. "It can take a lot of strength to accept help. Once someone lets in the devil of depression it is hard to escape. It is just like an addiction. I have seen my share of capable people succumbing to it. I fear that Visser has done something stupid."

"What do you mean by that?" Edith asked alarmed.

"I think he might have decided to leave us. Find a partisan group and join the resistance," Jonah guessed. "He hated being so powerless."

"He told me himself that he was a big coward and too afraid to fight," Edith said.

"We should get that door unlocked and see," Jonah suggested. "Maybe he is just drunk and asleep on the sofa. In any case he should not be on his own when the clock strikes twelve. It is time he came out of that ditch he has driven himself into."

"You are right. I will get the housekeeper to open up for us," Edith agreed.

After a short while the correct key was found. Jonah entered the living quarters of his fellow Jew and called out his name but found both living room and bed chamber empty. Edith found Visser hanging by a rope from an attic beam in his studio. The body was already cold.

Immediately, all sense of festivity was gone. Jonah sent for the Countess who was the only one who cried at the sight of the dead painter. Edith and the housekeeper helped the weaver to cut the man down.

"Let's not waste any time," said the Countess, who had quickly overcome her shock and was the first to think practically. "We better bury him right away. Now that he is dead it is better to get rid of all evidence that he ever stayed here. I will have a service man dig a hole in the woods and send for you once we are ready to say goodbye to our dear and foolish friend."

"What an idiot!" Edith hissed. "Our liberators are coming. They are so close - it can only be a matter of time. Why would he do this now?"

"He probably didn't believe it was really going to happen," Jonah guessed. "It has been almost a year since the big victory of Stalingrad and the Germans are still holding their own."

"The Soviets are on their way," Edith contradicted.

"The Red Army has not really come that far yet. According to reports the Germans have pushed them back a few times and nobody knows how much reinforcement Stalin really can pull out of his hat. I can appreciate that Visser got frustrated and doubtful," said Jonah. "I am getting a little impatient and worried myself. If a giant like Russia has not got the means to crush Germany then who has?"

"Fear is no reason to end it all," said the Countess adamantly. "Maybe a few years ago one could have understood it when there was no movement at all but now is simply a ridiculous time for this, when there is so much more hope than there ever was for liberation. I could slap him. I really could. How could he do this to us?"

"Maybe he just had enough of living like this," Jonah said, still trying to get into the mind-set of the painter. "Having to run and hide for no other reason than for being a Jew. He has done it for years. Perhaps it is not so much a surprise that he did it now but that he has not done it long before."

"We are so close to the end!" cried Edith in frustration. "So incredibly close. We all know that Hitler can't win this war. I can't pretend that I liked the man but it is such a stupid waste of a life."

"We will have to go through his papers tomorrow morning to see if he has left a will or any instructions for his paintings and his estate," suggested the Countess. "Jonah would you like to help me with this? I think he would have wanted you to do him that honour."

"Of course your Highness," replied Jonah. "He may have left us a note to explain his behaviour. For now I would like to retreat and join Alma and my children for their celebrations. They must be worried where I have been. I left them quite a while ago. I will be back here tomorrow morning. Would you be able to wait for the funeral until then? I will send for someone who can recite the Jewish prayers for the occasion."

"Thank you, Jonah. Please send everyone my regards and best wishes. I shall be waiting for you tomorrow morning."

Back at their little house by the lake Wilma naturally had the strongest emotional response of the Weissensteiner family to the sad news even though she hardly knew the painter. Even Alma's calming embraces and soothing words could not cheer her up. Wilma had not even liked Visser, a pretentious and egotistic fake of a person she thought, who at best was stimulating in conversations but at worst was incredibly irritating and toxic for a pleasant atmosphere. It was the abrupt, inappropriate and senseless timing of his suicide that upset her and stirred up her feelings of anxiety once again.

The recent news about the progress of the war and its likely near end had helped a little for her to get over her sad state and her constant fears for Egon. She had only just started to feel a surge of optimism. The sudden death of Visser brought back the issues of mortality and the unpredictability of war. Everyone of course was worried about Egon, not just Wilma, but it had become an unspoken rule that nobody would talk about him until there was any concrete news.

Greta dressed Ernst and took him over to the manor house to get him away from her sister's hysterics. She hoped that Edith and Esther would be kind enough to let her join them for the evening, now that their plans for a quiet celebration had been ruined, and indeed the two lovers were delighted to have Greta's company as a distraction from the seriousness that had befallen them. Esther ran towards Ernst and embraced him for a long time, flung him up in the air, sat him down on the top of the piano and then sat down herself

194

to play and sing his favourite tunes.

Edith ordered a bottle of champagne to be opened for the occasion.

"You only live once. Enjoy!"

"Thank you Edith but I must not get drunk. I am not used to alcohol you see and I have to keep it together for my little boy here," Greta explained.

"Of course," agreed an already tipsy Lady Edith. "Drunken people can be so vulgar, we shall try and avoid that at any cost. It would be too unbecoming for someone as elegant and beautiful as you. "

"Thank you, thank you. You are such a flirt," said Greta laughing, already feeling a little better.

"Yes I am," admitted Edith. "I shall tell you another thing. We will not give in to that miserable Dutch man and his attempt to spoil the evening. What was he thinking making such a dramatic exit! We must not talk about him any more tonight. After all, it is New Year's Eve and the New Year can only be an improvement upon the last. Despite Visser's stupid fears and anxiety we have reason to be optimistic. Let us rejoice in that feeling and let's not get melancholic over this."

"I appreciate that," Greta agreed. "I had to get Ernst away from all the crying at our house. He is already growing up in such sad times. We try to stay positive but we are a family of melancholic and worried people. I wish I could spare him all this grief. I remember being a young girl. I was always cheerful and carefree. We had our share of problems but my sister and I, we managed to smile. I wanted life for him to be like that, to be able to be a child and a happy one at that. Our circumstances have kept us alive and well fed but I could not protect him from the sadness. It is a miracle he has kept his cheery outlook this much."

"For such a young mother you seem very mature, my dear Greta," said Edith.

"I guess the times have made me so. You use the word mature, I would call it less naïve and more pessimistic," Greta said full of thought.

"The times have made most people miserable and depressed. Few have the spirit that you show every day," Edith contradicted her. "Maybe you have lost some of your childlike qualities and grown up

195

into someone more realistic. Your attitude is still admirable and a credit to your character. The man who left you was a complete idiot."

"I am not sure about that," Greta admited. "Maybe he was an idiot or maybe a complete genius. I don't know what has become of him and if he did the right thing or not in the end. I don't even know if he is still alive."

"What was he like?" asked Edith. "Why did he leave you?"

"To cut a long story short, he was a principled German but he could not cope with having a Jewish wife under the Fuhrer's rule," Greta summed up.

"If what he saw in you was only a Jewish wife than he missed a lot of other strings to your bow," declared Edith.

"Thank you for your kindness. My guess is the main problem between him and me was that we were both very young and naïve when we got married. We met in his book shop and we had this common interest in literature and philosophy that drew us together. Reality is different from fiction and theory. In the outside world we had to earn a living and bring up a child. We had little time for our hobbies and interests. We could have been a great couple if we had been allowed to live in a world where labels like Jew and Aryan don't have any meaning or consequences and where what attracts you to your sweetheart will always stay at the centre of your relationship," pondered Greta.

"My dear girl, I can see how those labels have complicated your life but they must not mean everything. Look at me and Esther," replied Edith. "She is no Jew but she might as well be one for all the abuse she gets. She is so beautiful but everybody sees – let me use your phrase – the label Jew on her. Now I am indisputably Aryan, and yet that does not stop us from being together. We both wear the label of homosexuals. As long as we cover up the labels that does not matter either. There are always ways to at least try and make the fairy tale become a reality. Your husband could have tried to keep the spark alive, to keep literature and discussion at the heart of your life together. Did he try? Did you?"

"I don't know," Greta admitted. "Maybe we both could have tried harder. When I married him I thought it would be for the rest of our lives. I would have tried harder if I knew that time was running out for us. I saw the situation only as temporary. There would be time to rekindle the spark of our philosophical and intellectual connection once the children were older or when we would be living back in town."

"He must have said how he felt at least?" suggested Edith.

"We never spoke about our situation that much. When he left he did not tell me the truth. He claimed we would reunite as soon as possible but then divorced me through the German courts. I only found out much later from his relatives that he had done so. I have not seen or heard from him in years. I can guess why he did what he did but I might never know the truth. I am just grateful that I have my family around me. The past is the past and there is no use in dwelling on it. I need to remain happy and composed for the sake of my little boy."

"I admire you for your resolve." said Edith. "Let us look to the future! I for one feel very happy about the progress the war is making. I am rather hopeful that there will be more reinforcements for the Allies who will force Hitler to his knees before long. They say there are partisans against the Germans in all the occupied territories now. Maybe the Red Army does not even need to come here at all. It is not beyond the means of possibility that the German Reich will collapse and surrender before it comes to an invasion."

"You are taking an extremely optimistic viewpoint dear Edith," Greta replied. "I wish I could share your sentiments but I think we will be seeing a struggle for some time to come. I am just praying that everything stays the same and as stable as it has been for us."

"We have been very lucky," Edith said thoughtfully.

"Do you think when the Reds come that we will be able to continue our lives as we are now?" Greta wondered. "You and Esther, us Jewish weavers on the Estate of a Hungarian Aristocrat. How do you think it will all turn out for us?"

"The Russians are a deeply anti-Semitic people," Edith started to explain. "Very intolerant. If I was you I would not trust their slogans of everyone being equal. They always hated Jews and they will not change from one day to the other. The same goes for us. There has never been a tradition of tolerance for same sex couples in Russia and I doubt their new ideas of equality will ever go this far. I intend to escape to a liberated France as soon as I possibly can, preferably as far ahead of the Soviet troops as I can muster. Soldiers of any nation can be savages and women can never be sure that they will be left alone. The Soviets have a dreadful reputation in that regard and I am not going to take my chances. You can imagine my disgust at the mere thought of that."

"I can imagine but I am not sure it is any better for us 'normal' women," Greta said. "We were spared all this in 1939 because the Germans took over peacefully."

"Now imagine these Bolsheviks coming and seeing us living here in this enormous house. We will be a prime target on their list to kill and rape, all with the comfortable ideological excuse of bringing down the bourgeoisie in the name of Communism. As if the average soldier really cared about all that," Edith said enraged.

"You certainly seem to have no optimism or false illusions on that account," stated Greta, in reply to her friend's grim outlook. "What do you think we should be doing? Flee to France with you? Will they even let us in?"

"I am not sure what the best option would be for you Jews," Edith replied. "Even Palestine has closed its borders. I have no idea. You and your family could try and come with us, leave before the Red Army comes. You are a pretty girl and you won't be safe from those soldiers."

"Fleeing into Germany seems rather dangerous in itself. There must be other options," Greta said with despair.

"There are lots of options and possibilities," agreed Edith. "In the end we are all gambling with our lives in this war: Killed by the Germans, raped by the Russians or shot by friendly fire. All of this could happen and none of it. There is a huge element of luck involved. I wish I could give you sound and reliable advice, but in fact I can only tell you why I chose to gamble with my own life in the way that I am, what my game plan is. You will need to make your own choices and hope for the best."

"My father desperately wants to stay," Greta told her friend. "We have not heard from my brother for a long time. If we move away he won't be able to find us."

"Couldn't you leave word with your former in-laws?" Edith suggested. "They don't live far from the city and he is bound to contact them if he can't find you."

"You are right Edith." Greta admitted. "We could ask them, but we must never forget that they are Germans and we don't know what might happen to their farm if the Soviets arrive. Benedikt has become a party member and his future is less than certain after the war. Father would prefer to stay and wait for Egon himself. His other reason for staying is of course the weaving looms, his precious possession."

"I will have to talk to him about that," Edith said with resolve. "You all must know that those looms are already very outdated. It won't be long before they are worth nothing at all. He may have a sentimental notion of them but he only got them so cheaply because most factories are already using different ones. If he continues to produce fabrics he will need more modern equipment. The Countess will help him with that if he lets her. The manual weaving you do does not depend on those looms and that is where your artistic future and your future fortune is, mark my words!"

"Good luck with that conversation. My father is very stubborn," Greta warned her.

"I have noticed that but so am I. More important than your craft is staying safe. Then you can think about contacting Egon. You won't be any use to your brother if you are dead," said Edith with as much gravity in her voice as she could bear using.

"I told my father as much. He said that he has survived this long under Nazi rule, he will survive even longer under communist rule," Greta informed her friend.

"Do you know that the Countess is getting false passports for you all so that you can flee with us?" Edith asked the young mother.

"I did not know that but I am sure father will never leave without Egon. I am certain of that," Greta promised.

"Not even if Alma begs him to?" Edith wondered.

"For nothing in the world. He may not hold much on Judaism but he knows about the importance of the tribe and that is seared into his very essence. He will get us all to flee and stay behind for Egon. That is his idea of being the head of the family."

"That will split his tribe," Edith pointed out.

"He will risk his life for the possibility of a complete family reunion. No one gets left behind," explained Greta.

"What an admirable spirit. If only his presence here would make any difference to Egon but I seriously doubt that this is the case," said Edith sarcastically.

"Well, he just wants to find Egon and then the two of them can set out to find us. He won't let us take the same risk," added Greta.

"Oh, dear Lord! What if Egon never comes home? He could be dead or held in a prison in Siberia? Is Jonah ever going to give up?" asked Edith.

"I doubt he will ever give up," admitted Greta. "There is hope for Egon if you think about it. We have not heard from him so the news is neither good nor bad. Of all the casualties and missing soldiers, a lot of their families have been informed by now. We have not received anything. No news could be good news."

"What if the letters are waiting at the workshop? Have you been there lately to find out?" asked Edith.

"I am sure Alma has been there a few times. Father could not bear not to know," guessed Greta.

"The Slovak soldiers are only posted in Poland and in the Ukraine," stated Edith. "I was under the impression that they were not fighting at the front at all. Someone told me that the army is too young and inexperienced for that."

"There have been some exceptions," explained Greta. "Egon and his unit were assigned to assist the German army. The Slovak Infantry stayed behind to secure the occupied territories but some of the specialist teams are active at the front. One of my in-laws, Gunter, he turned out to be a talented shot and the Germans demanded his services as a sniper right away. I have also heard that all the pilots have been sent to Germany for training."

"If Egon is fighting with the Germans then it should not be difficult for you to hear about him," stated Edith. "Has the Countess not tried to enquire on your behalf?"

"She has but we have not been able to find out anything as yet," Greta said. "Of course she has to be discreet and I doubt that Egon would be one of her priorities. She has to protect herself."

"If the Russians have captured him he might not be coming home for years," Edith warned. "Jonah must be aware that he might be waiting for some time, and it is extremely questionable that he would be safe here on his own. There won't be a Countess bribing on his behalf. He should really consider coming along with her."

"Please, you go ahead and try and tell him that. You have my blessing, in fact you have the blessing of the entire family but it is doubtful that it will amount to anything," Greta said disillusioned.

"I will at least try to make him see sense," said Edith with resolve. "There have been enough unnecessary deaths already."

Johanna had spent her New Year's Eve at home with Sarah. Benedikt was out with his party friends at some gala ball or other. Naturally he had told her about it some time ago and had asked her to come along but when she declined he had been relieved about her decision to stay at home. She was not very presentable in his new circles where even he himself had trouble fitting in. Johanna was still breathtakingly beautiful in his eyes but her social skills with the party members were poor. He wished she had more elegance and could be more feminine in the style of film stars. Her beauty was raw and her manners unsophisticated. He had never looked for such qualities in a wife but since he himself was a farmer, and was obvious as such to everyone in the government, he could have done with a wife that could compensate for his short comings in this area. Many of his colleagues had presentable women at their side and he envied them for it.

Johanna was too worried about their son Gunter at the front to sound patriotic about the war and its course. Most party members were concerned about the recent turn of events in the war but it was impossible to talk about it publicly with honesty. Benedikt did not mind pretending that everything was going well and to toast the Fuhrer regardless but his wife would have certainly given away her true feelings about the war without having to say anything at all. It was much easier to attend a party without having to worry about her.

Their daughters Roswitha and Maria were celebrating the New Year at a barn dance organised by the Hlinka Youth. The parents hated for their daughters to be out at night with local adolescent boys and no effective supervision but the pressure from the Hlinka party was too great for the Winkelmeiers to forbid their daughters to go out and celebrate the New Year that would bring victory to the Axis Powers.

The Hlinka Youth Organisation had links with the Catholic Church and all the chastity ideals that came with the territory. Benedikt however did not think for one second that it would make any difference to the control of male hormones.

Sarah had been kind enough to keep Johanna company and used the opportunity to inform her mistress of the tensions that were rising between the opposing camps of workers on the farm. The Gypsies had secretly started to make lists of everything that their

Jewish co-workers did and quite often there were inconsistencies between their reports and those of the Jewish workers. Her brother Elias said that this was part of an organised campaign by the Gypsies to discredit him and his colleagues. He claimed to have been very generous to the Gypsy community and that he had turned a blind eye to some minor discrepancies that had occurred at their end of the production line in order to save them punishment. The Gypsies had started reporting alleged thefts and claimed false book keeping by Elias. The previous cover-ups - which Elias had committed in good faith for them to keep the peace - now appeared to expose even further fraud by the Jews.

Benedikt had been informed but had not given his verdict yet, adding fuel to the tension between the warring communities. Sarah hated the guts of her cold and arrogant brother Elias but he did not deserve to be cheated like that. She was worried that her family might lose their privileged position and she hoped that Johanna might be able to help her.

"Benedikt does not listen much to me anymore," was Johanna's disappointing answer. "He will say that your brother told you to influence me in his favour. If anything, it might damage Elias's chances for a ruling to his advantage."

"All of this is a matter of trust and belief," Sarah insisted. "It is one word against the other. It depends entirely upon whom Benedikt chooses to believe. There is no evidence, just accusations on either side. The Gypsies have been very clever. All they are doing is undermining your confidence in my family. Elias says it is part of their plan. If Benedikt believes them we will be sent away to a camp and our successors will always be worried that they will suffer the same fate. Whoever takes over from us will be scared, leaving Hanzi and his friends to have free reign for their own fraud. We don't steal anything, we never have. They steal. Everyone knows that about the Gypsies. Just imagine them in charge. You'd be stripped of your last shirt."

"I have to say that all sounds very far-fetched," said Johanna in disbelief. She did love her friend but did not want to be drawn into the running of the farm. Benedikt had never welcomed her involvement and rarely valued her opinion. On a night like this she wasn't in the mood for heavy talk.

"Such a scheme by the Gypsies would be extremely risky," she insisted.

"That is exactly what they are doing and why it works," Sarah claimed.

"In that case I would tell Benedikt to get rid of both parties. If everyone loses, then no one will try to pull such a stunt again," Johanna replied. "That is how we have always dealt with such matters."

"If he does that we will all end up in the camps," cried Sarah.

"You wouldn't be sent to a camp my darling. Elias might, but then he should have been more careful. He was trusted with a lot of responsibility. He has to answer for such mistakes. We are at war. We don't have the resources to let control of our farm slip. "

"How can you say that?" exclaimed Sarah. "He has been so proud of his responsibilities, he would never have taken anything. If he let the Gypsies have anything it was for the greater good. It is too hard to find any workers at all now, you would suffer yourselves from losing them to the camps. Our entire family are all so very grateful to be able to work on the farm and live like this. It is almost like it used to be. Please don't take it away from us. You must believe us. We really are innocent."

"Sarah I am completely sure that you are innocent and I am inclined to believe you more than I do those Gypsies but it all comes down to what Benedikt believes and what he thinks he needs to do. Since he has become a politician it is not possible to rely on his common sense any more either," warned Johanna.

"That is why you have to help us! Please!" begged Sarah.

"I promise I will try but my influence on him is not very powerful, I warn you. He has his head high in the clouds and he will do as he pleases or as the party doctrine tells him," Johanna said.

"Please try. The labour camps are a very hard punishment for something we did not do."

Johanna was glad when the pleading and begging finally stopped. What a cheek that slave girl had to ask her to get involved. How should she know who was stealing and who wasn't? Johanna had overcome some of her ideas against Jewish people over the last few years but she was far from being fond of them as a group and still thought them untrustworthy. They and the Gypsies were almost as bad as each other. Sarah had often mentioned that Elias had not been the kindest of brothers to her, so why should Johanna risk an argument with her husband over such a trivial thing? She had good mind to get them both fired as she had mentioned to Sarah before but in the end it was New Year's Eve, a sentimental day and her feelings for Sarah mellowed. For the sake of their friendship Johanna decided to go ahead and talk with Benedikt about the matter once he was back from Bratislava.

When Benedikt did eventually return to the farm on New Year's Day however she never got a chance to intervene on her friends behalf. He called all the parties concerned into the barn and listened to their accounts of events one more time and without any further delay declared that Hanzi's account of events showed inconsistencies with the original report from a few days earlier and therefore had to be a lie.

Benedikt took the exemption papers off all the Gypsies and told them they would be sent to a labour camp outside of Bratislava later this afternoon.

He appointed Elias as the sole supervisor for the time being but warned him that he would watch him closely. With that he stood up and left the congregation. Johanna was relieved that her friend had been saved and Sarah thanked him enthusiastically for his fair ruling of the matter, which Benedikt shrugged off with utter disinterest. She also thanked Johanna for helping, which she was sure was the reason for this ruling in Elias's favour.

In reality Benedikt was very hung over and was not in the least interested in small dramas amongst his work force. He could not stand either of the two warring camps but he knew Elias a little better and thought him more capable to run the farm in the absence of the politician. The argument came in handy as he had recently been pressured by party colleagues to give up some of his generous allocation of slave workers to please the German demands.

Elias – in Benedikt's eyes - was scum just like the Gypsies were and there was no way of finding out the truth from either of them; they were all liars and cheats when it came to it. Benedikt could honestly not remember what Hanzi had told him when they had discussed the matter for the first time. The statement about the alleged inconsistencies was totally made up and he would have said the same thing to Elias if he had wanted Hanzi to stay on.

His main concern was whether the Germans would be able to win the war or negotiate a truce. Benedikt had done so well in the

Slovak government in such a short time, it would be a pity if he would lose his privileges and influence all because a Czechoslovak government of cowards and escapists in exile was returning to power. In his view only those who had stayed had a right to govern. Unfortunately his own future was now more than ever linked to that of the Fuhrer and his allies in Slovakia. There was no way back from here for Benedikt.

Sarah fell into the arms of her absolved brother full of happiness, but instead of the relief she expected to see in his face she recognised a twitchy smirk she knew well from her childhood, something he usually displayed when he had tricked someone successfully or got away with something. It took her a little while to realise the trap her brother had laid out for Hanzi and how everyone had fallen for his act.

"You devil! You made all of this up to get rid of Hanzi and the Gypsies, didn't you?" she hissed at her brother, almost paralysed and numb by the shock.

"Of course I did and I could not have done it without your help," he replied teasingly.

"You destroyed his life!" she shouted at her brother.

"It is not as if I had not warned him. He had it coming," said Elias coldly.

"How could you? What has he ever done to you?" Sarah cried.

"He could have cooperated with us. You mustn't be naïve," Elias started to explain to his sister. "Our people don't get much food in the labour camps from the government. If we don't help them nobody will and they will all die. How else are we going to get the food to keep them alive if not by stealing it from the farms? There is not even enough for the Slovaks in the country any more. It all goes to the krauts and the soldiers. I had to get Hanzi out of the way. I had no choice. If he had helped us we could have helped him. Since he would not cooperate with us there was always a danger that he and his people might have crossed us. A danger to me and to everyone really."

"You amaze me. You would kill to get what you want, wouldn't you? You are cold blooded," she cried.

"Better we survive than them!" was the curt reply.

"How could you be so sure Benedikt was going to rule in your favour?" Sarah wondered.

"I worked with him before. He thinks he is so subtle and clever but I can read that man like a book. If he and I were playing cards, I would strip him of his last possession before he knew what had hit him. I could always tell when he was planning another raid. I always knew when he was going to check up on me, so I made sure that everything he ever checked was better than good. He was always going to believe my word over Hanzi's. We are all pretty low in Benedikt's eyes but Jews are still a little higher up than the Gypsies."

Sarah was disgusted and she had good mind to go and tell on him but she found it impossible to expose her brother despite the injustice he had committed. If Elias was not lying then he was doing it for a good cause but he had sacrificed an innocent man for it.

"I risked my own life for this too you know," Elias justified his actions. "Benedikt could have believed Hanzi and chosen to execute me and my friends," he said. "This is war and we are lucky to survive."

"It is because of people with your dog eats dog behaviour that we are at war in the first place. You are no better than any of them. If you weren't a Jew you would get on great with Benedikt. Shame on you!" Sarah cried and ran away.

At the manor house Jonah and the Countess were going through the drawers of the late Visser to see if there was any information on relatives or friends they should inform of his passing. Now that he himself was dead and buried it would of course be foolish to keep any of his belongings that, if discovered, might incriminate her Highness. Jonah hated to intrude on the dead man's privacy, especially reading the letters, but he realised they had no other choice. Fortunately there was little in the way of indiscriminating information to be found. Jonah had not known that Visser had been a homosexual as well and had had a love affair with a much younger student in Rome. The letters were carefully worded so as not to endanger either of them if found or censored but reading all of the letters together there was no doubt about the nature of their relationship. The exchange of letters had stopped quite some time ago and Jonah wondered if there had been a falling out or another reason for this long silence. He found no indications in the letters in that regard. Jonah sat down and wrote a letter to inform the young student of the sad news. The Countess had her secretary write brief notes to Visser's business contacts but she said it was too dangerous to post them from here. She would have to send them from Vienna where she was expected next week for a concert and a business meeting.

"Did you know about the student?" Jonah asked the Countess.

"I had no idea at all. It is funny, because Visser always talked so scientifically and was distant about Edith and Esther's inclination, I would never have guessed he was of the same persuasion. How silly of him to withhold this from us when he already knew where we all stood on the matter. What a foolish, foolish man he was," she said and burst into tears again. "I am sorry," she apologised. "I just didn't understand him at all."

"Indeed, it seems rather unnecessary," said Jonah. "No, no, don't cry your Highness. He made his choice and we have to accept it and live with it. There are much more important things to worry about. It seems there is a lot we did not know about our friend, maybe he had very good reasons to choose his premature exit from this life. He was very, very troubled of late. Maybe the young man broke things off or was drafted? Arrested? The fact that he was in love opens a huge array of reasons for his actions. Let us not judge him without knowing."

"What can be so difficult that one would chose to end it all?" she shouted. "Pretty boys are fickle and a new one can be found on any street corner. Visser was under my full protection, there really was no need for despair, no need at all. His people struggle to survive in labour camps all over Europe every day, holding on to dear life without food, and he who has it so good throws it away. Over house arrest? Over a broken heart? Then he was an ungrateful idiot who did not know how good he had it."

"If you think he was an idiot then don't cry. Countess, I am sad too about him but we should not worry about the lives of those who did not want theirs. There is no shortage of people who want to live and who are in need of your attention and protection. Let's focus on them. They are more worthy of it."

"Now you are one to talk about that" the Countess said with rage. "I heard just this morning that you are planning to stay behind to wait for your son Egon, despite what it might mean for your own safety."

"Who told you that?" asked Jonah, hoping to distract the

Countess by straying from the subject.

"Edith, who learned about it from your daughter last night," the Countess said. "I don't doubt for a second that you are going through with this suicidal and foolish plan. So don't talk about people not putting value on their own life!"

"Countess I love my life, more than you think," Jonah assured her. "I am willing to risk it for my son. He might need help when he comes back. If I ran away from here now my entire future life would be spent in painful wondering if he is alive and whether he knows where we are. It is no use, I need to stay."

"You are being silly, Jonah!" the Countess declared. "Are you saying that you seriously believe your son needs your help? That son who comes home from a brutal war which he managed to survive? You think that man needs your help? The help of an old man?" she laughed. "You are flattering yourself and your powers my dear Jonah, you amuse me!"

"I hear you," laughed Jonah, taking her criticism calm and kindly, "but the heart wants what it wants. I know my children are grown up now but I can't help feeling that I still need to look after them. It is my duty as their father."

"What about Wilma? Won't she need you much more than your son?" asked the Countess.

"Wilma needs her sister Greta and her nephew Ernst," replied Jonah matter of factly. "I play a very minor role in her life. Don't think for one minute I have not thought this through. I would love it if I could go with them as well as stay here but I have had to make this decision and I trust my daughters will be fine together. I have to find out about Egon, not just up and leave."

"I can appreciate your desire but I think you are very ill advised!" the Countess said disapprovingly.

"Then of course there is the issue of my new flame Alma," Jonah added. "She also wants to stay. I hope we will find Egon and maybe then we can all reunite in some place that will take a bunch of Eastern Jews without shooting us on site. Perhaps even here?" he said provocatively.

"Now there is some optimism," was the cold reply.

What an intolerable man, the Countess thought. So stubborn and unreasonable. She hated herself for continuously choosing artists as friends who were so difficult to convince with rational arguments.

This man was ruining his life and she could not bear to let him do this; could not bear to watch him doing it.

"I have ordered your papers," she said in another attempt to persuade him to reconsider. "Think about it. They will be at your disposal in any case, so you can always change your mind. Please promise me you will think about it. Your son won't thank you if you die in your attempt to help him."

"Thank you, your Highness. I will think about it. Now did you find out anything more about Visser's will or next of kin?" he said to change the subject.

"I am afraid I did not. There is no diary or anything else that would give us a clue. It is strange, I always thought I knew him so well, now I realise how little I really knew about him." the Countess pondered.

"It takes extreme measures and circumstances before people even know themselves," replied Jonah. "He left no note and no will, so I don't think he cared what we are going to do with his belongings, or he trusted your judgement."

"I have a few ideas about what to do with his art, the rest is all pretty useless to me I am afraid."

When Jonah got back home he saw that Wilma had still not calmed down. Alma was completely lost, wondering what to do since her usual remedies had all failed to help. The hysteria was persistent and nothing seemed to be able to soothe the troubled woman. Calling a doctor was too risky in case they would recommend locking her up in a mental institution or removing her ovaries to balance her hormones.

The family had to stay together but somehow they had to avoid that other people got wind of Wilma's fragile state. Unexpected help came from the ladies Edith and Esther who, on the black market, were able to get some sedatives from the local hospital at rather exuberant prices.

Jonah was mortified to think just how much he owed to her Highness and her friends by now, it was already more than he would be able to pay her back in his lifetime. Edith told him not to bore him with his constant whining about the costs and playfully demanded in exchange for the medication more play time with Ernst for her lover Esther.

In consequence, the little boy spent entire days in the manor house and in the bargain it freed time for Alma and Greta to get busy on the carpet production. With Edith spending so much time running the Estate, Esther found herself very bored and so she sent one of the maids on frequent trips into town to find presents for Ernst. Her joy in spoiling the young boy was so great that she even had her maid make him new clothes from some of her own and older clothes. Greta watched this development with mixed feelings. On the one hand she was pleased at the attention and the riches her son suddenly could enjoy – especially at a time when the entire continent was struggling - but on the other hand she felt quite jealous and worried that her son was drifting away from her and into the arms of a much richer woman.

She had lost one child to Wilhelm and his Fuhrer, one unborn and she did not want to lose Ernst too. Fortunately Greta was usually so occupied with Wilma and her recovery that she did not have enough time to dwell on the matter. She had to inject her sister once a day and the entire family struggled to hold down the hysterical woman who suffered from a strong fear of needles. Her arm had several bruises from the tourniquet and unsuccessful attempts to insert the needle. For hours afterwards Wilma would be calm but also drowsy, unresponsive and looking right through the people around her.

The entire family found it hard to watch her but didn't dare to lower the dose without the advice of a doctor. Edith assured them that this was all very normal and nothing to worry about. She had visited some of her friends in mental institutions over the years – proof in her eyes that living on the verge of madness made a person much more interesting than the average normal person – and they had all been in such sedated vegetative states for periods of time. There was no cause for alarm about it.

In the afternoon Wilma would usually become more lively and communicative, sometimes even smile, but after her dinner she would take a tablet to help her sleep. The nurse who had smuggled most of the medication from the hospital and had sold it to Edith had advised them to continue for at least two or three months with this treatment and then gradually lower the dose. She had not mentioned the addictive nature of the drugs nor that they would soon become less effective. Ernst was being kept away from his sick aunt to spare him the shock.

Greta was surprised that her father insisted they all worked so hard on the completion of those silly wall carpets; there were no buyers lined up for them. It was obvious the Countess was keeping them busy with these commissions only so that the family would not leave the manor house. In her eyes it was ridiculous to keep up the pretence of urgency. To dedicate so much time on the business when Wilma needed care and attention seemed very wrong. Jonah endured her criticism stoically without pointing out just how much the family was indebted to the Countess. In his book, putting all the effort they could muster into her orders was the least they could do and while Wilma was kept calm by the medication and proved so unresponsive it seemed a waste to try and talk to her. The thought of his daughter not making a full recovery was so painful that he had to occupy his mind with other things.

In March, Johanna received a letter from the military informing her that Gunter now was officially missing. He had been part of a reconnaissance unit trying to hold up the Russian advance in the Leningrad region and had not been seen for a couple of days. Of course there was hope that he had been able to hide and would attempt to break through the enemy lines back to his squadron but for now one had to be prepared for the worst. The Fuhrer thanked her for the sacrifice she had made for the Reich and the Axis Powers.

She read the letter several times, unable to take the information in, then she had to laugh. It was so like her son to mess things up at the worst possible time. Gunter had lasted almost five years in this war.

First he seemed safe because he was spared the dangers of the infantry. When all of the Slovak army was spared the further combats he was amongst the few that had been selected to assist the Germans against Russia. He survived Stalingrad and other fatal battles and now he got himself captured or killed when a German defeat was almost a certainty.

She knew she should be more upset about the scary news but in her mind she had worried about her son so much before, she refused to believe he would be caught out by the war at this late stage. She had never been proud of her son and only during the years of his army service had she created a little room in her cold heart for him. Absence makes the heart grow fonder she thought, and now with this sad and upsetting news he had returned to her life and reminded her of all the little things about him that she found so annoying and disappointing. She cried at night but she was not really sure she was crying for her missing son. She cried for all the sadness that she had carried around for her entire life. She cried and cried but her thoughts were not so much about her son than about herself and the overwhelming self-pity she felt all of a sudden, a feeling that she simply could not explain.

Benedikt was genuinely subdued about the news. Not because of profound parental concern and a deep love for his son either. He was alarmed by the rapid progress of the Red Army which he had known about in theory but which had only hit home when he received the letter. His feelings for Gunter had always been even colder than those of Johanna and he had never believed that his son would last this long in the war anyway. When Gunter had been drafted, that was the moment that to Benedikt his son had died. The actual event was only a matter of time, he had come to terms with it right there and then.

Radio reports from the front line had been almost absurd, it was hard to place it in the context of the peaceful reality at home. With the letter, the conflict and the threat of losing the war had become real and personal to Benedikt. This meant that his time in the spotlight was nearing an end, too.

Sarah found it hard to see Johanna so unaffected during these days, especially when she realised that the letter had arrived a week before Johanna even mentioned it to her maid. It was at this point that she realised how cold her mistress was – despite their growing friendship – and how careful she had to be around her. From here on Sarah decided to repair the relations with her brother Elias and the rest of the family who had come to shun her as Johanna's pet Jew. Friendships were fickle but family might stick.

Elias had done well in Benedikt's eyes and the irregular controls of his work confirmed his immaculate running of the business. Benedikt had congratulated himself for his wisdom and his people skills and had no idea that he was cheated out of a large portion of his fortune and was keeping hundreds of Jews alive against his will.

Wilma's period of medication came to an end after a few more months. She appeared to have made a good recovery. She was very tired and dozy for most of the day and was not very productive but her subdued calmness was very welcome to the family after her hysterical former self.

On Jonah's request Johanna never mentioned Gunter and his status as missing in action when she came to visit, which suited the not too grief struck woman just fine. She only brought Sarah with her once but the maid was visibly uncomfortable with a sedated or subdued Wilma and was ordered to stay at home from there on.

News from the war alternated between good and bad. The Red Army was coming closer, but then it was unexpectedly held up and pushed back by German forces. There were big time gaps between campaigns, a fact that some interpreted as a sign that the tables were yet again to be turned, whereas others believed this was temporary until further reinforcements had been mobilised. Success of the Japanese in East Asia brought hope to Benedikt but it was soon smashed to pieces when the Allied troops landed on the French coast in June. Resistance fighters and opportunistic opposition leaders in Slovakia had been communicating with each other since the end of the last year and were planning to stage an uprising to oust the pro-German government and to assist the Red Army in its approach to the Reich.

At the end of August an armed uprising began with focus on east and central Slovakia but it suffered from a lack of coordination between the participating forces and from the small scale of outside support.

Benedikt was at the party headquarters when a telephone call came through announcing the first wave of riot activities. The party secretary mobilised the local branch of the Hlinka Guard to protect the governmental buildings and the party office but without any major attacks Bratislava remained firmly in the hands of the Tiso government, probably due to its proximity to the Protectorate. In the north-east part of the country the pro-government Slovak army managed to secure some territory but many soldiers defected, some of which were able to get through 'enemy' lines and join the rebel forces, while others were disarmed and arrested by the Germans. Soviet partisans and weapons had been brought in to support the uprising but in lesser numbers than had been expected.

Initial success of the rebellion was confined to central Slovakia.

213

Germany sent in troops from the north and from Hungary in the south to prevent a meeting of the Slovak soldiers with the Red Army, which had been expected to push into the east part of Slovakia shortly after the beginning of the uprising. However Stalin redirected his military focus suddenly onto Poland while other parts of his troops were held back by unexpected delays in their campaign progress themselves and this left the Slovak guerrilla fighters, now proudly called the 1st Czechoslovak Army in Slovakia, in the lurch, struggling against six German divisions and one pro-Nazi Slovak unit.

Benedikt and his fellow party members had been surprised and shocked by the conflict and had to endure rage and ridicule by the German officers who came to Slovakia's rescue against its own people. The rebels managed to hold on to their territories for a surprisingly long time. The support they received from the population was greater than expected.

As the rebel forces were all linked to the Czechoslovak government in exile, supporting the uprising meant that their nation could join the winning side at the last minute and could escape the consequences of losing alongside the Axis powers. It was an opportunity for collaborators with the Slovak government – which had been declared illegal by the Allies – to switch sides and wash themselves free of treason charges.

Benedikt secretly cursed his luck to be in the wrong part of the country during this crisis. Because of its distance from the fighting, Bratislava would be last to fall into rebel hands and without connections to the opposition he was once again stuck on the Tiso side under German influence. He would sink with this ship while in the east of the country politicians and party members had a chance to repent their sins and switch sides in time before their 'judgement' day.

The little community at the manor house was not enthusiastic about these developments either. Everything seemed to be happening really quickly but reliable information was hard to come by and decisions had to be made on hunches rather than knowledge. The Countess knew she had to act soon but she did not feel quite ready to leave the country and her estate just yet. She had no certain idea how far the Americans had advanced on the continent and which would be the best route for her and the ladies to take to get to Paris. The arrival of the Red Army seemed to be halted for the time being but with the increased presence of German soldiers in the country there was not much safety. She scolded herself for taking the absence of Nazi control in Slovakia for granted.

She wanted to make it at least to Switzerland but was too afraid to start the journey. She decided to wait a little longer in the hope that the continuously changing political map of Europe and its moving borders would become more transparent.

Jonah had made up his mind and unsurprisingly he insisted on staying behind in Bratislava with Alma. The two of them were confident that their 'new passports' would be of help. The real difficulty had come to lie in persuading Wilma and Greta to join the ladies Edith and Esther on their journey to the west and to ensure that they got enough medication for Wilma to take with them on the trip - in case her nerves should suffer from the stress.

Greta lived under the impression that it would be easier for them to live as Jews in a Soviet occupied country than travelling through Nazi Germany with a false passport. The way she presented her argument was sound and difficult to argue with – even for the Countess. The rumours of vandalism, looting and rape by the Soviet army worried her of course but she was hopeful that this could be averted. After all they were Jews and had been oppressed by the Germans, the soldiers would pick on someone else. She was much more concerned for the mental stability of her sister and somehow she felt inclined to take her chances by staying rather than leaving. Travelling with Wilma in her fragile state might not be a realistic option she claimed. Alma tried hard to convince her to go, pointing out that seeing Wilma medicated had alarmed anyone beyond reason. The poor girl had recovered well and there was now enough medication to ensure that any hysterics on the journey could be suppressed.

By the end of October and before anyone on the estate had made up their mind about their plans the Slovak uprising was crushed by the German troops and while partisan fighting continued on a much smaller scale in the mountains the Germans started to retaliate for the uprising by arresting, deporting and killing all Slovaks that they suspected of helping the rebels or of harbouring Jews.

In an official ceremony President Tiso decorated German soldiers who had killed the Slovak partisans and he finally lifted all resistance to the deportation of the Jews in his labour camps to the death camps in Poland. With the extensive presence of German troops in the country Slovakia had more or less the status of an occupied country, even though Tiso was still officially the reigning President.

Under the immediate and immense pressure by the German security forces not only all Jews from the camps were deported but also the so called pet Jews and other ones that had been exempted by powerful patrons. The Slovak administration was now 'assisted' by German officers and the name Weissensteiner found its way back on all the lists. The Countess received a warning from her contacts and for a further gesture of approval bought the silence of the messenger with regards to her interest in Jonah and his family. Travelling was far too dangerous and with the advantage of the warning the family was considered safest on the estate as long as they went into one of the secret hiding places. The wine cellar in the basement of the manor house had been slightly altered a few years ago so that it concealed a spacious chamber where the Countess had planned to hide during a search or a surprise raid by German or Soviet troops.

Edith and Esther were furious because they felt that they had missed their chance of escaping. With the current level of Nazi presence in town it seemed too dangerous to leave the estate. The hunt for collaborators and Jews was in full swing despite the urgent need for men at the Russian front. The ladies now had to occupy separate guest rooms in the house and according to Edith's new papers she was the wife of a French collaborator in Lyons.

Jonah and his family were moved into the secret room in the wine cellar and were not allowed to leave the basement during daylight, which didn't do Wilma's nerves any good. The month of November was the longest the family had ever experienced. The Countess had supplied them with plenty of candles and books and blankets and there was at least a little food but the days dragged on endlessly. All of them were so used to hard work and continuous activity that they found it hard to switch to the long days of reading and waiting for news. Wilma did not have the peace of mind to read for long anyway and after a few days she started to have nervous twitches. Worried that their location would attract attention Jonah decided to give her injections again. The fighting in the south was very close to Budapest now and they all hoped they would not have to last much longer in hiding.

Benedikt's farm staff including Sarah were all rounded up and deported without prior notice and without any exceptions. The party officials protested to the German officers that Slovakia still needed some of its Jews but to no avail. The official party line was now that even the existence of those subversive and undesired elements of society was no longer tolerable to the future of a healthy Europe.

Benedikt was very disappointed by this foolish and blind dogmatism, especially right now when nobody could possibly believe in a full German victory any more. If there was even the slightest chance of a victory it had to be by using all the manpower that was available. Sending perfectly healthy and workable slaves to their death was against any sound logic.

Johanna found it incredible that the uprising and the closeness of the Red Army did not cause a loosening of the strict Nazi morale. Quite to the contrary it had led to a much more forceful drive in deportations and clinging to the racial ideology. Losing her servant and friend was an odd experience. She had witnessed the soldiers arriving on their truck and loading up the entire family. Elias and a friend of his had been smart enough to get away before the truck arrived but they had been found and shot only hours later. Johanna was sad that she could not be there for her friend Sarah and console her in her grief over her brother – if she even knew about his death that was. Many Jews were willing to cooperate and went with the Germans without trying to escape. These optimists thought they would not stay in the camps for long, so they might as well avoid being shot on the run. Their liberators were on the way now and the sad example of Elias and his failed attempt to flee proved to those who had heard about it that they had made the right choice.

"Won't Germany surrender soon, Benedikt?" she asked her husband. "Surely they must see sense, their actions are desperate now. There can't be any hope left for a victory!"

"Don't ever say that out loud, do you hear me?" he shouted. "Never! There is a lot we do not know. The Russians are slowing down, they might be running out of steam. The landing of the Allies in France cost the Americans dearly. The Japanese are still doing well in Asia. Romania might switch back to our side and everywhere the Red Army has been there are now partisans fighting against them. The Ukrainians want their freedom back. They helped Hitler when he arrived. This is far from over yet. Maybe, and I mean just maybe, there will be a treaty but it won't make any difference for your

217

beloved Jews. You should be ashamed of yourself to doubt the Fuhrer and his decisions. Anybody who heard you just now could turn you in and see you deported yourself for treason. Be warned and don't do anything stupid. My position won't be able to save you. The Germans are not in the mood for negotiations any more. The uprising has disappointed them and their opinion of us Slovaks is much lower."

Johanna saw that her husband would not tolerate any discussion on the matter and so she did not dare ask him what he thought might become of Sarah and her family. She was surprisingly calm about her friend's deportation, accepting the fate she had known was always a clear possibility for the Jewish maid. It was more a feeling of emptiness rather than grief and since she could not get any information out of Benedikt she put the matter to rest and devoted her energies to the upkeep of the farm.

Her daughters Roswitha and Maria could no longer get away with idleness and cosy days inside. Now it was all hands on preparing the farm for the winter. Both girls had been lacking enthusiasm ever since they heard the bad news about their brother Gunter being missing. Now was the time to get them back on track and to stop all their silly girlie sensitivity for which there was no place any more. Johanna realised the times now called for hardened souls and strict discipline and she was going to give this mission her all and make her daughters do the same.

She wondered what had happened to Alma and Jonah but the best she could do for them was not to draw attention to them by investigating their luck or by making a visit to their workshop on the estate. The way the tide had turned it was obvious that nobody would tell her the truth.

She had her marriage to party official Benedikt to thank for that. In her efforts to keep everything together and not to let weak emotions get the better of her, she pushed those thoughts aside as well and decided to let other people worry about this kind of thing.

Unfortunately this new resolve did not seem to work anymore. She was deeply grieved to see herself increasingly thinking and missing her friends and worrying about her son and the future. What irony, she thought, that she had been content with herself and her life without any closeness all these years and the stone wall around her heart had broken down just as all these tragedies were occurring. A few years ago she would never have been affected by this in the same way.

Benedikt, whose record of commitment to the party was officially spotless was promoted to the post of minister. His predecessor had been volunteered for army service like most party loyal Slovaks of a suitable age were. Benedikt was exempt because he was the oldest in his circle of agricultural functionaries. In his new capacity he found it easier to ignore the obvious signs of the nearing end and like his wife sought escape in relentless dedication to his work, making illusory plans for the next planting season.

In December, the fighting reached the Southern borders of Slovakia and the Romanian army under Soviet guidance pushed the German troops out of the southern provinces. As so often happened throughout the whole campaign, this advance was followed by a period of consolidation and a re-grouping of armies, fostering the idea in those who wanted to believe in it that this was where the fighting would come to a halt. After the initial shock that the enemy had entered Slovak soil receded, a sense of calm and acceptance settled in the minds of the population and politicians. It took another three weeks before a further push by the Red Army from the east drove onto eastern Slovakia.

The community at the manor house in the meantime carried on as usual. The lack of daylight and the absence of a daily routine were hard for everyone who lived in hiding. The situation improved a little when Edith and Esther started to bring them some materials for embroidery work and clothes from their wardrobe that needed to be mended. The Countess had rejected such proposals in the past, demanding more respect for the family in hiding than to create the impression that they were made to pay for their keep by doing such minor work. However, when Esther mentioned her plans to Jonah she was surprised at how keen Jonah appeared to be permitted to do the work. In fact, all the Weissensteiners were very grateful for the chance to do something and threw themselves into their new projects. Jonah warned the women not to rush, it might be some time before they all could leave the basement and so it was probably best to make the little work they had to occupy themselves with last for as long as possible. The most important thing in their situation was to keep up a positive spirit and a sense of purpose. They had begged the Countess to let them bring in the looms or at least some of the equipment to the manor house but as much as she would have liked to oblige them they all knew that it was far too risky.

Should there be any enquiries related to the Weissensteiner family directed at the manor house the official answer was going to be that no one had seen them ever since the beginning of the uprising. In early December a Gestapo officer had come to the door with a woman from the Hlinka Youth and enquired if they knew of any Jews that were in hiding. The Countess meant to tell them about the 'missing' weavers but could not make herself say anything to this horrible man. By naming Jonah and his family as Jews or possible Rebels she would start a manhunt that could easily include a thorough search of her property and lead to the end for everybody involved. By her failure to mention the 'escapees' on the other hand she had just destroyed her alibi should a specific search for Jonah begin anyway and her link to them become exposed.

The Weissensteiners had become a big part of her life and she had to come to a decision whether to stay behind and hide and feed them or to save her own skin ahead of the next Russian advance. It was unbelievable that anybody able to fight was still wasting their time on Jews and rebels. In her master plan, she had been certain it would be easy for all of them to travel to France but she did not feel it was safe yet and kept postponing her departure. Wilma was the only one who was not adjusting to their new life in hiding at all. The medication kept her calm but Edith had not been able to secure much more of it and they were running low. She spoke about this with Greta and the two women decided to lower the dose to make their stock last longer. The ladies and the Countess tried to get some more medication but the hospital had stricter controls and the nurse they had approached before was so scared of being exposed for her illegal activities that she refused to even meet with her Highness, insisting that there was a misunderstanding and the Countess must mean a different nurse. At the beginning of March the Red Army had taken over the north west of Slovakia and was coming very close to Bratislava. German civilians left the city with everything they could carry, yet even in this chaos there were searches for rebels, deserters and Jews. The Countess decided that they would leave ahead of a Soviet invasion and told the ladies Esther and Edith to pack their belongings. She told Jonah that this was now the last chance for him and Alma as well.

"Jonah, I have thought about it and I think you are making a huge mistake if you are going to stay here. Your Egon will take a long time to come back from a prisoner of war camp. In the mean time you would be safer with us in France. You can always come back here once the war is over and things have settled down. What you are attempting is madness at best and suicide at worst."

"What if Egon is coming back fighting against the Germans with the Red Army? I would never forgive myself if I missed him. If he came to see us and thought we were dead ourselves? He needs to know we are alive so he will be looking for us. I need to stay and wait for him, I just have to."

"But we will need your help to get away, Jonah. Wilma can't stay here with you, we will need you to carry her when she is drugged. None of us is strong enough," the Countess insisted.

"Didn't you say it was too dangerous to leave the estate and be seen in public?" he replied.

"It still is dangerous but our priorities have changed now," she explained. "We risk more by staying here than by leaving. I have a shotgun, we can defend ourselves if necessary and anyway our papers should get us through. Wilma being ill might even help. If they see we have someone sick with us they won't want to examine us too closely for fear they might catch whatever it is she has."

"I will have to speak to Johanna and leave word with her," he said. "When Egon comes he won't leave the area without asking her what she knows about us."

"I will go and tell her. It is safer for me. What do you want me to tell her to tell him?" she asked.

"Tell her I plan to come back to Bratislava after the fighting has stopped and that he should stay in Bratislava or leave a message for you with Johanna."

"Good, I will do that. Now while I am gone I need you to get everyone ready."

Chapter 10: Brno and Pilsen November 1944

Jonah and his family had only taken the bare essentials with them to their hiding place in the basement and so their packing was a matter of minutes rather than hours. Edith and Esther on the other hand had rather large amounts of clothing, jewellery and some artefacts and took a long time deciding what to leave behind.

The Countess had organised two horse drawn carriages, one which was a very old fashioned closed cabin carriage with little space for luggage as it was designed for luxurious but short term travel. The layout was similar to the fiacres of Vienna, the horse drawn cabs named after Saint Fiacre, although it lacked the ostentatious style and glamour that those were famous for. Its appearance however did imply wealth and so valuables were not to be carried in it, the Countess insisted.

The other vehicle was a rather large cart, a telega, simple and wooden. It was normally used to carry heavy loads. Jonah, Alma and Wilma travelled in this one with most of the luggage. There was just enough space for Wilma to lie down if she needed to be sedated. Her Highness shared her carriage with Esther, Edith, Greta and Ernst. Edith and Greta both had experience at how to direct and control the horses of the carriage and would take turns at holding the reigns.

It was a shame that they could not use the motor car but petrol was too scarce to rely on and there would have been space for only two passengers. The plan was to blend in with the stream of Germans making for the Protectorate and not to stand out.

Most people on the roads tried to move into a north-westerly direction where they hoped to fall into American rather than Russian hands. Due to the late time of their departure, there was no hope for the two carriages to make it to Brno in one day but they should reach the border to the Protectorate soon. The Countess hoped the huge volume of travellers might make the patrols less attentive.

The group reached the border during daylight and Greta, who had been holding the reigns since they left the Estate, was disheartened by the scene that presented itself: a long line of vehicles and foot passengers who waited for inspection and clearance. The fiacre and the telega both had to wait an hour before it was their turn to show their documents. Greta wondered how the German army could waste manpower resources like this on a border patrol between two territories which it either occupied or controlled by other means. Several uniformed soldiers covered the post and apparently were taking their task seriously. One older soldier, limping and heavily leaning on a walking stick, was walking along the lines, inspecting the refugees carefully. He had obviously been wounded and no longer fit for fighting duty. He brought with him much needed experience, because the other officers seemed very young in comparison, and frankly, not old enough to have a passport themselves. The limping officer opened the door to the landau coach and asked the ladies to step out onto the road.

When he saw the confident and ladylike demeanour of the Countess he was visibly impressed and after only a cursory glance at her papers, which he evaluated with an admiring whistling sound. He looked at the rest of the passengers, held his glance on Esther and asked to see her papers as well but when he saw her produce a fresh looking German passport he already seemed to have lost interest, gave the document little attention and told them to step back into the coach and carry on with their journey.

Jonah's cart had deliberately fallen behind in the queue, so that they would have time to reconsider their plan in case the Countess and the ladies were encountering any difficulties with their passports. Now he had to wait another twenty minutes before it was his turn. The older officer had already looked at them suspiciously and when they came to the front of the queue he ordered them to wait at the side of the border post to be inspected in more detail by one of the younger officers, who currently were still busy examining other refugees and their papers.

Jonah had expected this and told Alma not to worry and not to show any fear towards the officers but instead to treat them with welcoming arms as equals and helpers. As he said this he realised that all the luggage for the Countess and the ladies was on his cart and he would be held accountable for it. Not only was he clueless as to what they might have taken with them but it was going to be difficult to justify why he had those possessions in his care. He might even be taken for a thief.

Greta and her fellow passengers could hardly believe their luck of getting across the border without a lengthy and painful examination. Then they came to realise that the second part of their party was still on the other side of the control post, receiving more attention by the border police.

"We have to go back and help them!" exclaimed Greta in panic.

"We can't help them, my dear. It is now in God's hands," said the Countess.

"Then let's stop and wait here. I want to be able to see what happens," the distressed daughter suggested.

"No, we have to carry on as if nothing has happened," explained her Highness. "If we stop here waiting we might arouse suspicion. Jonah knows the way to Brno, we will wait along the road as soon as we find an opportune place for it."

The fiacre carried on for another half an hour and then stopped by the side of the road.

On the other side of the border it was finally Jonah's turn to be inspected.

The young officer dealing with them appeared to be the nicest one of the bunch and when he saw the medicated and slow responding Wilma he assumed that she was sick, offered her a little drink of water and only then asked for their papers.

"You must forgive my colleague," the young officer said rolling his eyes. "He is in a lot of pain and he likes to take out his misery on other people. I guess he picked you out of spite because you are travelling with an invalid. He hates to see physical illness because it reminds him of his own handicap. Let me just have a look at your papers so he doesn't think I am not doing my job properly."

"Thank you, you are very kind," said Alma with a motherly smile.

"You have a Hungarian accent!" the officer said with excitement in his voice. "How exotic. Were you born there?"

"I was born in Slovakia. I moved to Budapest with my family but I fled to Bratislava during the communist revolution in 1919. This is where I met my husband here," Alma replied cautiously.

"You got married in Germany?" the young man asked her. "Your documents are stamped in Prussia. How did that happen?"

"We went there to marry because it is where my husband's family lives. They had offered to pay for the reception, who would say no to that! We are headed there now to join them."

"You mustn't go there," the border patrol warned them and whispered to them quietly. "If you take my advice, stay in the south.

The Americans are coming north from Bavaria up from the Rhine towards Berlin, the Bolsheviks are moving towards Berlin from the east." He looked over his shoulder to see where his limping colleague was and then continue. "You don't want to be taken by them." Then he straightened up and said loudly. "The roads to Prussia are in excellent condition, it won't take you long to get there. A perfect place to witness the German victory."

"Thank you, we will take that advice," said Jonah. "You have been very helpful, officer."

"It is all credit to your pretty wife," he said, leaning towards Jonah in a familiar manner. "I really would not want to see her getting hurt. My father fought in the Balkans in the last war and he always talked highly of the beautiful women of the east. Now I know what he meant."

"Thank you officer," said Alma and laughed.

At this moment the older officer came limping towards them and shouted at the young one: "What are you doing here laughing with these suspects? Have you checked their papers? "

"Yes I have," said the young officer rolling his eyes. "They are all in order."

"I presume you have asked them where they are going and why?" barked the older one, continuing his inquisition.

"To the north of Germany to stay with their family. Everyone here is running away from the Soviets. What other story have we heard for the last few weeks? There is no need to ask. We are all wasting our time. We should be at the front fighting," the young man replied.

"I picked these people out because they don't look kosher, understand, my young colleague?" the old soldier said suggestively.

"Yes, I understand. I know why we are here. Now, look at their passports yourself." He handed them over the documents and read out: "Joseph and Anna Finsterwalder, with his daughter from a previous marriage. Married in Stettin, Prussia, coming from Slovakia ahead of the Red Army to meet with his family in the north. Sometimes I wonder why you insist on doing all this. There must be better ways for you to be useful? "

The older one's face was getting red with anger at this provocation and he only just managed to control his rage by responding very slowly, emphasising every syllable with fisted hand movements.

"Passports can be forged. Did they not teach you anything? Am I the only one here who has training and experience?"

"Oh shut up will you," the young man exploded. "They have transferred you from post to post since nobody could stand you longer than a week. We are stuck with you because nobody else will have you. If you were so experienced and clever you would probably still be walking like a normal person."

"Keep talking big mouth," said the older one calmly. "You would not last a minute at the front. They would shoot you sooner than you could look at your watch to see what time it is. So shut up. This is important work we are doing here. We are here to protect the Reich from communists, rebels and especially, the last existing Jews. They have to be brought to justice. We can't allow them to infiltrate our country and spy on us. If you continue with your attitude I will have to report you for being a traitor yourself."

The young one still smiled sarcastically at the speech given to him and said with a bored tone in his voice: "The few Jews that are still free are running the opposite way to us, you fool. They are waiting for the Soviets. They think they will be equals with the Russians now. Which Jew with any kind of sense left would be running towards us? You really are out of your mind."

Jonah and Alma found it hard to keep their calm and appear nonchalant during this exchange. They had to pretend to be in agreement with the wounded soldier but their fear was growing the longer the argument went on.

"I will tell you why a Jew might be coming running towards us," the older one replied with intense and almost mad looking eyes: "Because a Jew is fooling you by doing the opposite of what you expect him to. One Jew may want to return to his old residence in Germany to take back what he thinks belongs to him, and another one is going to cowardly stab you in your sleep. There is no evil thought that the Jew has not thought of and no deed that he is not capable of."

"If you say so. I tell you all Jews are already back in Galicia and the Ukraine where they came from. You won't find any here," said the young officer, looking away dismissively.

"Now look at that man and his face," the older one continued. "It is classically shaped like that of a Jew. Calls himself Joseph

Finsterwalder. He would not be the first one to try such a trick."

The young officer looked apologetically at Jonah, implying with his body language that it was best to wait and just endure this charade.

"You are not the first one to mention this," Jonah said. "I am used to it by now. I can't tell you how I hate to look like this myself. To think I always have to have my papers on me so I can prove that I am not a dirty Jew."

"I don't think I have asked you to speak," was the rude reply. "You would say that. Jews can be very good actors, in fact most actors were before we got them. Now, look you know-it-all: The best way to find a forgery is to examine the stamp on it really carefully. It is the hardest part to falsify successfully."

"You tell me that several times a day," said the young one, stamping his foot impatiently. "I have looked very closely. Please check again and tell me what I missed."

To Jonah's relief there was not the triumphant reply that he had expected, but a rather shy and quiet: "Hmmn, it actually seems fine to me. But the girl: I am not convinced. What exactly is wrong with her?"

"She has a fever, we don't know what it is. Maybe the travelling and the hunger," replied Alma.

"How long has she been like this? Could it be Typhus?" asked the old soldier.

"I don't know. Are you familiar with diseases? Would you mind having a look for us and tell me what you think?" suggested Alma, playing on the fear of a contagious disease that she thought she might have detected in his voice.

"Hem, no I don't. Let's have a look at the luggage. That is quite a huge collection of suitcases that you are travelling with, not as shabby as I would have expected judging from your clothes. I wonder what we can find in here."

"I am sure you understand that we would have been ill advised to dress up nicely for the journey, officer," replied Alma. "We don't want to be robbed of the little that we have left. I am a seamstress and I have been able to save a few of the valuable dresses from my shop."

Jonah was proud of his 'wife' and her clever answer, which would explain the beautiful and fancy costumes in the suitcases.

At this moment there was a sudden shouting from a different

227

part of the queue. One of the officers had opened a trunk and found a man hiding in it. The soldier called for reinforcements and so the old border patrol turned away from Jonah and their luggage, grabbed his gun and limped over to deal with his colleague's find.

"Just go!" hissed the young officer to Jonah. "If you really are Jews you are going in the wrong direction, trust me. Anyway, good luck! Hurry!" and he waived them on past the barricade.

"Well that was a bit of your famous Weissensteiner luck!" exclaimed Alma.

"Don't jinx it! Anyway, from now on we will have to call it the Finsterwalder luck. Look in your passport, wife. The old soldier would have had us if they had not found the man in the trunk over there. What luck is it that relies on someone else's misfortune! God help him."

"The papers must be very good if he could not see anything wrong with them. We have to thank her Highness for that," said Alma.

"We do indeed," agreed Jonah.

"How lucky was it that Wilma was not even asked one question? That has been my biggest worry," Alma confessed. "I always knew that you and I would get through but I thought that it would be difficult with Wilma. You know what the Germans are meant to be doing with mentally ill people? If they had made her talk there wouldn't have been much hope for her."

The two carriages met soon after. The Countess had spoken to other refugees on the road and had found out that the Americans were believed to be well advanced in the west. She wanted to avoid the Russians at all cost and decided not to risk their luck by going too far north. She suggested changing direction to a southwesterly route where the front line should be. As expected Jonah refused to come all the way to France and insisted on staying in the vicinity so he could return to Bratislava at the earliest opportunity.

"This is where our ways part," he said decisively.

"I knew you were going to do this," said the Countess disappointedly. "My dear Jonah, it is no use. I will not watch you getting yourself killed. This is why I told that farmer woman Johanna to tell your son that you would come to Paris with us. "

"You did what?" asked Jonah in disbelief.

"You heard me. I told her you were coming with us. You have

228

to join us now. Egon will not be staying in Bratislava once he has spoken to Johanna but he will set out and try and find you in Paris. He has my address there, he will know where to go and who to look for. All is taken care of," she said triumphantly.

"Your Highness, what on earth have you done!" Jonah shouted. "Forgive me but that was a foolish thing to do. Just how do you think he will be able to find us? You don't know if your apartment in Paris is still yours! The building might have been bombed, your contacts could be dead or living in America by now. It was always going to be difficult for the two of us to find you but for him who has never spoken to you and has not even met the ladies, it will be impossible. Now I could not come with you if I wanted to. I have to go back and tell Johanna. The only way to make sure I meet my son is by staying here."

"You ignorant, ungrateful putz!" Edith cried out before the Countess could answer. "You can't abandon everyone here for your son. Are we nothing to you? Do you not realise that we all need you to protect us? A group is always safer if there is a man with them, even if it is an old and stubborn one like you. What about your own girls? Do you want to endanger your daughters' lives as well?"

"Nothing of the sort," Jonah said, not rising to the bait. "If I could do both I would. Believe me! But I can only be in one place at any given time. Judging from your glorious performance by the border you ladies will be fine by yourself. Remember how easy that was for you. If anything I am going to be a hindrance and a burden to you when it comes to contact with officials, as we just have seen for ourselves. As for robbers: I am not strong enough to deter anyone, we know that. Alma and I are going to walk from here to Brno, so you can keep the vehicles. We have talked about this on our journey and have decided on it. We will wait until the war is over and things have settled. I have friends where I can hide if necessary. Greta can steer one cart, Edith the other. I am so very grateful for everything you three have done for us. Please don't think I am abandoning you! It is just that my conscience forbids me any other course of action. I sincerely hope we will reunite after the war. Goodbye my ladies."

"Are you going to let your father leave you just like that?" Esther asked Greta, hoping that family pressure might change Jonah's mind.

"Of course," Greta replied calmly. "If you knew him as well as I do you would realise that there is nothing in the world that will stop him from going through with his plan. We are safe so now he can try and save Egon."

Jonah hugged his daughters goodbye. Wilma reacted with surprising calm, undoubtedly due to her medication. He kissed his grandson, wished them luck and without any further ado he took his one suitcase and hand in hand with Alma he walked north in the direction of Brno, not once looking back at the friends and family he just had left behind so as not to lose his strength and resolve.

The shock and sadness over the sudden separation fortunately passed quickly amongst the remaining members of the party. It had not come as a huge surprise and after a while a fresh sense of direction emerged.

"Fine!" said the Countess eventually. "We better get going then."

Without saying anything Greta got on the telega with her son Ernst and waited for the ladies and the Countess to get into the fiacre cabin. The two carts headed west to reach Bavaria via the Austrian roads north of Vienna. They saw more Germans and Austrians fleeing from the south and from the east. The positions of the Americans and the Soviets given to them by those refugees joining the convoy were vague, unclear and often contradicted each other. After lengthy consideration and weighing up of the likeliness of each new story they had heard, the Countess and Edith decided to head for Budweis in the north, abandoning the original plans to travel towards Linz and Passau in the south, which in their calculations of which tales could be trusted, was deemed to be still too close to the advance of the Red Army.

Wilma luckily was doing rather well. Being in the open air and travelling with her sister and her nephew on the telega made for a welcome change from the stuffy sunless existence in the basement and she was too dazed and confused to fully grasp the nature of their journey.

Esther occasionally joined the remaining Weissensteiners on the cart and they would all sing together and play road games with Ernst. Greta was amazed at just how much strength she found in herself to cheer her sister on and to ban all the worries and grief she was feeling about her father from her mind. She could not afford to let her sadness get the better of her and so she carried on as if this trip was really just a long awaited holiday for everyone.

The delay at the border and their change of direction forced them to spend the night by the side of the road. Edith and Esther stayed awake during this first night of their journey to protect the group.

Despite being exhausted from the travelling nobody really slept very well. The blankets were not thick enough for the cold temperatures and there was too much noise on the road. Everyone was slightly worried about thieves or a surprise visit from a control unit of the Gestapo. Someone had lit a fire not far from the road and was roasting some strange smelling meat. Several refugees decided to camp where the fire was.

People exchanged stories about the houses and the wealth they had left behind, about the family members they had lost in the war or who were still fighting for the Fatherland somewhere in the world, about their hunger and about their unbroken spirit to defeat the communists and those arrogant Americans. Edith and Esther heard the talk but tried to keep out of it. It was easy to fool a soldier at the border but to keep up your assumed identity amongst regular folks and Nazi supporters over a period of time was much more difficult.

Talking to these travellers was risky. They were likely to know villages and towns in the east and might ask them for the names, professions and addresses of alleged relatives. It could be tricky not to give away the lack of substance to their new assumed life stories. Better to keep quiet and not attract attention.

During the next day Edith and Esther took turns to catch up with their sleep on the telega and the Countess had to learn fast how to steer a cart herself. Luckily she was good with horses and soon got the hang of it. The roads were packed with refugees most of whom acted subdued.

During the second night they repeated the same routine. Edith and Esther stayed awake again as the carts were pulled off the road for a rest. Greta had offered to take one shift of the vigil but Edith was the only one who could effectively fire the gun and Esther insisted on staying with her lover.

Greta was also needed during the day to keep Wilma and Ernst company.

The group had taken shelter by the ruins of an abandoned farm building close to the road. It was surprising that nobody else had spotted it and taken up residence there. The Countess took this as a sign that they had to be close to a city and she was tempted to continue on their journey a little longer to see if they could reach Budweis. Edith however welcomed the solitude. Not having to mingle with the fleeing Germans had the advantage of not having to lie.

The people on the roads were all too concerned with their own misfortune to really listen to each other's life stories but Edith felt one could do without the risk. Halfway through the day, the road had split and a surprisingly large number of people took a turn towards the south. When the Countess questioned some of them as to why they were heading towards an advancing Russian army many replied they were returning to places in Austria where their ancestors had come from, whereas others did not want to be trapped in Czech territory under any circumstances.

The next day they arrived in Budweis and found shelter on a farm that was run by a mother and her four daughters. Rooms were available for a small sum and the Countess paid for three of those, so that the entire group could get a good rest. There was also hay for the horses. The women thought it would be wise to give the poor animals a day to recover. During their stay at the shelter fellow travellers told them that the Red Army had begun a siege of Vienna. Enemy troops were now likely to be moving towards Prague from both the east and from the south.

Edith and the Countess decided to head further towards the west as quickly as possible, hoping to reach Pilsen, a city south west of Prague and close to Bavaria, as their next stop. The entire group was delighted with the progress Wilma was making. They had run out of serum for her injections on the day they had arrived in Budweis and had not many of the tablets left either and so were forced to split the night time tablets, administering one half during the day and one half during the night. Edith had used their day of rest in Budweis to investigate the possibilities of buying more but had to return without success. The hospital was crowded with wounded soldiers from the front and Edith felt she could not risk trying to bribe anyone. Wilma however seemed stable. Too dazed to interact with the other travellers but looking content.

Esther stayed in her room the entire day finally catching up with her sleep. The nights on the road had taken their toll and now that she was sleeping in a real bed nothing and nobody could wake her.

Ernst was as well behaved and as easy to handle as he ever was. Greta kept practising with him the new names they had assumed by way of their new passports.

"What is your name?"

"Edwin Finsterwalder."

"What is my name?"

"Margarethe Finsterwalder!"

"What is the name of your aunt?"

"Wilhelmina Finsterwalder!"

"And my name?"

"Margarethe Finsterwalder."

"And your grandfather's name?"

"Joseph Finsterwalder!"

"And his wife is?"

"Anna Finsterwalder."

Ernst loved this 'game' and repeatedly asked to play it again. The Countess had complimented Greta on his behaviour and said it was a credit to her loving and careful upbringing that the boy had not caused any problems on their journey at all. He had been very patient and fitted in amazingly, nothing compared to some of the crying and screaming toddlers and children that they had witnessed on the road.

The Countess had become the most worried of their travelling party, especially since they had learnt about the siege of Vienna, where she also used to have a house. Travelling under these chaotic circumstances was different from what she had expected and she was beginning to lose her confidence, realising that her money and position no longer were any protection. Her bravery and fearlessness had been the product of complete naivety.

She had imagined the journey would be much quicker and had secretly expected to be shaking hands with American soldiers by now and to be staying in luxurious guest houses on her way to Switzerland or Paris, depending on the movement of the liberating armies. To find that German and Austrian troops seemed to be able to withstand their enemies still so fiercely around some of the big cities and that the advance of the Red Army was so difficult to predict, all of this ate away at her sense of security.

All of her life she had felt protected in one way or another, now she was suddenly confronted with her own mortality and the clear and present danger of the approaching fronts. She had never given it any thought that they might die in enemy fire or be hit by a shell. The war and its atrocities had happened so far away from Bratislava that they had never seemed real. In her silly optimism she had seen herself hiding in the barn of a farm while German troops were retreating and Americans in turn were progressing. A friendly American would shout into the barn for all people inside to come out, he would inspect their papers and congratulate them all on their new freedom, the ladies would thank them for liberating them and then the road would lead them to Paris in complete safety and peace. Crossing the line of fire was not so easy if you listened to the reports of those people whom they had met on the road.

According to these tales people were killed completely by mistake. Not only the German soldiers but also German civilians had been known for shooting at deserters and refugees who were heading in the direction of the Allies. Enemy troops were suspicious of traps and snipers and they did not welcome or trust anyone coming towards them with a white flag either. She had tried to talk about her fears with Edith when they were alone on the coach but her tough companion did not want to hear her hysteric notions.

"It is a bit late to worry about it now, don't you think? You need to pull yourself together and stop dwelling on it!" was her advice.

"I know but I feel responsible for putting everyone in danger. Maybe we should have stayed in Bratislava in the manor house. If we are taking such a huge risk here we might as well have stayed and taken it there. It was me who persuaded everyone to make a move," the Countess carried on.

"You were not the only one who wanted to get going and no one was forced to leave – well maybe apart from Jonah. But he can't complain. He got across the border safely thanks to your documents," she consoled her friend.

"You have been a fantastic friend and helper to all of us, you must never blame yourself if anything happens in the future. We are all taking chances here and no one could possibly predict what will be. We are all alive and if it was not for everything that you have done

234

for us who knows if any of us would still be? Stop worrying and enjoy the scenery. Look, it is April and it is getting warmer, the flowers are coming out everywhere. If we are going to die here it is still better than in a labour camp or in the basement of your manor house."

"Thanks Edith. You are being very generous in your view of me," the Countess said. "Whatever I have done, it feels so little compared to what I should have done. My father and my husband always told me how lucky and privileged I am and that this role comes with an obligation towards the less fortunate. I feel a little guilty for the advantages I have enjoyed in my life. I never had to work or sacrifice anything to be in such a lucky position. Life has been so very generous to me and I have managed to do so little for others in return. God, I tried, but those last years were so difficult, I feel I have failed too many people whom I probably could have helped."

"Who are you talking about dear Countess? I hope it is not the ungrateful and disturbed painter Visser?" snipped Edith.

"Oh yes, him first and foremost. I also should have taken more of my staff from Hungary with me. Many wanted to come but I was selfish and did not want to be pestered with too many responsibilities at the time," the Countess confessed with tears in her eyes.

"What is done is done," said Edith, trying to stop this wailing. "I am sure you would have taken all of them with if you had you known what history had in store for them. How could you have known? The politicians in Europe did not know, otherwise they would have been ready to crush Hitler in his infancy. Stop blaming yourself, you are starting to get boring."

"Maybe I could have employed and saved more Jews in Bratislava and in Hungary," the Countess went on. "I should have tried to have more Jews exempted from deportation, hidden some more in my house. I have wasted so many opportunities to do good. I only saved a few because I loved their art. If I had been more careful I could have seen what was on Visser's mind and saved his life, prevented his suicide. Now you are all on the road with me so I would not have to travel on my own. You see now how selfish and horrible a person I am? You are all in danger because of me and my selfish pursuits."

"Countess, these thoughts are a credit to you and your good

natured heart but none of this is going to help. Even if you have done good deeds for the wrong reasons, they were still good deeds. We are more than grateful for them. If you had done more, maybe your name would have come up on one of those lists and you would have been deported. Don't you see that all of this is mere speculation? What if this? What if that? You have done more than most, be happy with that. If you still feel this urge to make up for your past mistakes and neglects, I would advise you to pull yourself together and be strong for everyone's sake. We are lucky that Wilma is doing so well. We rely on her good spirit. If you break down it will only worsen her recovery. Ernst is six years old, he understands more than he should and we need to be careful not to frighten him."

"You are right my dear Edith. Thank you for making me see sense. I am so glad we are friends."

On the road to Brno, Alma and Jonah made slow progress. The road was narrow and busy with coaches and cars so that pedestrians had to walk by the side the road. Alma had slipped in the mud once and sprained her ankle, which slowed her down and made it unlikely that they would reach Brno today or even tomorrow. They had a good 30km to go Jonah guessed. Alma suggested they try to get a lift from someone with a bit of space on their cart but Jonah pointed out to her that they had not seen anyone offering to help their fellow refugees.

Every vehicle was loaded to their full capacity and those who had space were usually in a hurry to get away and did not want to be slowed down by extra weight. They probably had left possessions behind so that they could gain speed.

Jonah and Alma had decided to keep to themselves anyway. The mood amongst the crowd on the roads was fearful and subdued and they did not want to absorb any more of it than was absolutely necessary. Some of the people did have encouraging words for each other, helped each other with food and with travel advice but there were also many who were desperate to get away and who drove recklessly and shouted at anyone who seemed to be vaguely in their way. Among those rushing vehicles was an army truck which they had seen driving south to the border earlier. Now it was moving back north, accompanied with a lot of swearing and tooting of the horn.

The aggressive driver had over done it with the horn and a

horse had gone mad ahead of the truck, overturning the cart it had been pulling. The truck had to stop. Shouting at the poor owner, the soldiers pushed the belongings that were spread out on the road on to the field at the side of the road. Jonah recognised one of the soldiers as the old patrol officer from the border. It transpired that they had arrested the man who had hidden in the trunk and all the people who had helped him to hide. There were about ten prisoners on the truck.

"Get your shit off the road," shouted the crippled officer to the intimidated owner of the wild horse. "Don't just stand there watching us, get busy or we are going to take you with us, too, you lazy pig!"

Some people came to his aid but most just tried to carry on their way. Jonah whispered to Alma that they better move away from the scene to avoid being recognised and questioned again. While the road was being cleared by soldiers and volunteers the officer paced up and down by the scene of the accident as fast as his cane allowed him to move. He was staring angrily at the refugees as well and started to shout at them now:

"You should all be ashamed of yourself, running away from the enemy. You should have stayed behind and helped with fighting our enemies. You disgust me you stinky little rats. The Fuhrer doesn't need you. You can go to hell. We will win this war without you and you will live with your shame forever!"

Nobody replied to his ranting. Those who were sad to see the fall of Hitler's Reich were indeed ashamed of themselves running for their lives; even the old and fragile ones who had no means of fighting. Those who were glad to see the end of the Nazi regime would have risked their life by speaking their mind.

"I thought that's what you would say," the old soldier commented on the deadly silence that was encompassing the place. "None of you deserve to survive. Cowards!" he hissed.

By now the road had been cleared, mainly by soldiers recklessly throwing everything onto the side of the road. A few shards of glass were still right in the middle of the road but in the absence of a brush someone just put an old newspaper over it. The truck manoeuvred carefully around the broken glass and the limping soldier struggled to get back on. He lost his grip and fell on the floor, much to the amusement and silent satisfaction of his onlookers. Then he spotted Jonah and something in his mind clicked.

"Stop! We have got another passenger I think," he shouted to the driver and stormed towards his victim as quickly as he could.

"I don't remember letting you through at the border," he said to Jonah and Alma. "What are you doing here then?"

"Your colleague let us go," replied Alma. "He said our papers were in order."

"My colleague! That little boy has not even learned to tell left from right. How could he have assessed your papers. That is laughable," fumed the irate cripple. "We have a couple on the run here and I wonder why."

"Please look at our papers again. I remember you saying that they seemed all right to you, too," Jonah said calmly, while almost fainting from fear.

"I don't remember anything like that!"

"Your exact words were that the stamp was the most difficult part to forge. Then you looked at it closely and let us go," added Alma.

The soldier stopped for a split second as if he just now remembered the encounter, obviously wondering what to do next. He had drawn a lot of attention to himself and he might lose face now if he left the scene without an arrest but he also seemed to have lost his momentum in his attempt to uncover another runaway. His memory had clearly let him down and now that it had returned he could not just admit that he was wrong before. At that moment the driver of the truck used his horn and shouted to his colleague to get on the truck with or without his new prey.

"I'm coming!" was the reply and the soldier turned away and got on the truck.

When the truck was out of sight Alma suggested they take a different route to make sure they did not run into this maniac of a Nazi officer again. They got off the main road and took a turn towards the west. By evening they came to a little lake where someone had made a fire and was grilling fish. Jonah and Alma tried to keep a distance from these strangers by changing direction but someone called to them in German and invited them to join the group. The two of them were so hungry that they could not resist and so they complied. Their host was an old man named Reinhard with his two teenage granddaughters, Lisbeth and Margot. They were from Vienna and like everyone else were trying to escape the Red

238

Army.

Reinhard's hobby was fishing and this skill had paid off on their journey several times already. They had so many fish it would have been a waste not to share it they said, and they loved to have some company.

"You must have a dreadful time with that nose of yours my dear Joseph," the old man said to Jonah. "I had a friend who committed suicide because of one of those. Everyone thought of him as a Jew. A terrible thing to happen to someone."

"Yes I had my struggles with it, I must admit," Jonah humoured him. "I always took my passport with me wherever I went. Complete Arier Nachweis, Ahnenbuch, the lot. Not one drop of Jewish blood in my veins and still looking like one. Not even as much as a Spanish or Italian ancestor as far as we could trace it."

"What incredibly bad luck," Reinhard said. "Do you mind if I have a look at your papers? I am sorry to be so forward."

Jonah was shocked. This man who had seemed so nice turned out to be just another Nazi. He had not anticipated this from a civilian and found it hard to hide his feelings but his survival depended upon a good acting performance.

"Of course not. I would do the same. You can't be too careful with those cheating Jews," Jonah laughed and handed his papers to the old man. "I got beaten up twice on the street since Hitler took over the Protectorate but in the course of six years for someone with a face like me that is not really too bad. What do you think?"

"How often did the street police check up on you?" asked Reinhard while carefully studying the documents.

"Maybe twice a month," Jonah said smiling. His legs started shaking. "I hated leaving the house but then the neighbours would have thought I had something to hide."

"Bad luck. One of these days someone is going to kill you by mistake."

The old man seemed to have no idea he was being lied to. Instead he sounded rather full of sympathy for Jonah.

"How far back can you prove you are an Aryan?" he asked Jonah.

"More than six generations as you can see, so how I came to have this nose I don't know. As I said, not as much as a Slav or a Spaniard in the mix."

"What a hard lot to draw," said Reinhard and returned the papers to Jonah.

"Oh, you don't have to tell me," Jonah said with a little sigh of relief escaping him.

"Where are you going from here?" asked his camp companion. "Are you heading for Linz or Passau?"

"We are planning to go to Brno," Jonah volunteered, wondering if it had been wise to disclose his destination to this Nazi. The words had just come out and it was too late to take them back now. "You see, we lived in Bratislava and we hope to go back there once the war is over."

What is the matter with me, Jonah asked himself. He knew the guy was not a friend of the Jews yet he kept telling him about his plans and past.

"At this moment going to Brno is not going to be any different than staying in Bratislava, my dear friend," Reinhard informed him. "I assume you want to get away from the Russians. For that you will have to go much further west. You could come with us if you like, we are going to Budweis."

"You don't seem to be on the right road to get to Budweis if I am not mistaken," Jonah noticed.

"The main roads are busy and it is difficult to find food there. We are going the back way. It is safer as well. There are a lot of pick pockets and thieves amongst the refugees. Some of the people who have lost everything have lost their morals as well. I heard terrible stories of travellers being robbed in their sleep and some even stabbed. "

"Dreadful. People are turning into wolves," Jonah said.

"Exactly!" agreed Reinhard, "So let's stick together."

"Thank you very much for your offer Reinhard but we are going to keep going with our own plan," said Alma, coming to Jonah's aid.

"You know they are still looking for Jews everywhere, send them away or kill them. You are in big danger everywhere with your looks, but in Brno you will have both the Nazis and the Russians after you. You better believe me," Reinhard assured him.

"Why are you taking such an interest in us?" asked Alma.

"I don't like what is going on in this war," the old man explained. "I have seen too many people dying for nothing. My son

240

went missing in Stalingrad, his wife died of pneumonia. Now I see you making a stupid and fatal decision, I feel I have to warn you. Ultimately it is your life but pains me to watch you throw it away. I like you, despite your big nose!" He smiled at Jonah.

"All we need to worry about are the Russians. We have papers to prove we are not Jews," Jonah replied.

"Let me tell you Joseph: You have been one lucky schmuck to get away with it so far. Sooner or later some Nazi soldier is going to rip that passport of yours in half and kill you anyway. He will say: If you look like a Jew you probably are a Jew. You are not fooling me!"

Did Reinhard mean to say the last sentence to Jonah or was that part of that theoretical scene with a soldier? Had Reinhard caught on? Why had he called him schmuck? They should have stayed on their own, how foolish to risk their life for a little grilled fish.

"Don't be so shocked!" said Reinhard to the silent pair. "I am only trying to help. Your passports are excellent, I have no idea how you did this. The Russians are savages. Your pretty wife is going to be popular with their soldiers. I am taking my girls to safety. I know the roads and I can help you if you let me. You survived this long, don't throw it away now."

"Sorry Reinhard, you got it all wrong. The papers are no forgeries, we really are not Jewish!" said Alma, not trusting the old man.

"Come off it," Reinhard said dismissively. "I believe that you might not be a Jewess, princess. Your husband is. I have a nose for these things." He giggled at his own wit.

"What are you saying?" asked Alma.

"I am not saying anything," he said calmly. "I am going to lie down. You think about my offer and let me know in the morning. We will start our journey as soon as we get up. As I said, no time to lose."

Jonah felt trapped. Could they trust this man? Was he trying to sound them out or was he genuine? He could not discuss it with Alma, their voices would carry far in the quiet of the night. Jonah decided it was better to run right here and now. His instinct told him he could trust the man but is was a risk he did not want to take. The teenage girls had been asleep for some time. Once Reinhard was snoring regularly, Jonah signalled to Alma to get her things and follow him. The moon gave enough light for them to get away from the lake but the escape through the woods was difficult and Alma fell a few times, hurting her strained ankle again.

"We have to give up!" she said in resignation. "I can hardly walk as it is. We will have to wait for sunrise before we can carry on."

"You are right. I don't think I could even find the way back to the lake in this darkness," admitted Jonah. "We are stuck here now or we are just going to get lost completely."

"Should we go back to Reinhard and his daughters? I don't know what to think about him. He seemed genuine to me," Alma confessed. "He could have just shot us if he had wanted to."

"We can't afford to trust him," Jonah said. "All his talk was so ambiguous and we still don't know if he is our friend or enemy. We better stick with our plan. Besides, you would never reach Budweis with a foot like that."

They cuddled up to each other and slept leaning against a large tree; their dreams were both anxious and nervous. They were on their way as soon as it was light enough to see the tree roots and rabbit holes in the ground. Alma's ankle had swollen considerably and hurt in her shoes even before she put weight on it. Knowing that she had no choice she put on a brave face and pushed herself to go on. They made good progress considering her handicap and once they were back on the road they blended in with the crowd of refugees. Alma was worried that they might come across the nasty border patrol again on the main road but with her ankle being so weak they could no longer use the longer and more clandestine route as they had planned.

By noon they had made good progress and Jonah guessed they would have to sleep one more night on the road before reaching Brno. An old woman came up to Alma and told her to take her shoes off. She had some ointment she wanted to rub into the flesh around the ankle to help with the swelling. Alma protested, worrying that if she took off her shoes she would never get them on again but the old woman insisted and Alma gave in. The ointment stung and burnt for a while but when the pain receded the ankle felt warm and comfortable. Jonah and Alma thanked the woman overwhelmingly but she just shrugged her shoulders and made the sign of the cross to bless the two. Getting the shoe back on proved too difficult and eventually they gave up and just put a few extra pairs of socks on the swollen foot instead.

They continued their journey for a few more hours, Alma feeling much better than she had in the morning. The army truck with the old border patrol passed them twice, once driving towards Brno and then coming back shortly after. Fortunately this time it did not stop or push anyone off the road. The horn had been pushed almost constantly and everyone managed to get off the road before the truck passed. Jonah took the short interval between the sightings of the truck as a good sign. Surely they had to be close to the city now if the truck had taken so little time to off load its passengers and return in the other direction towards the border to Slovakia.

Soon after the second passing of the army truck a young girl on a cart stopped and offered Alma a ride which she gladly accepted. Jonah and his suitcase were allowed on as well. The young girl did not speak to them during the journey and Jonah wondered why she was being so kind when she almost seemed to resent the two. Jonah and Alma were grateful all the same and since the girl was also on her way to Brno they asked her to drop them somewhere in the east of the city, where Jonah was hoping to find his friend Kolya.

Kolya had been a civil servant from the Czech part of Czechoslovakia and had been expelled from Slovakia after the declaration of Independence in 1938. He had lived in the same area of Bratislava where Jonah had his workshop and the two men enjoyed the occasional game of chess and a glass of wine. When Kolya left Slovakia, he had come to say goodbye to the family and had written them a letter with his new address inviting them to visit.

With the German occupation only a few months later and with the outbreak of the war in the summer nothing had ever come of these plans. Jonah looked forward to seeing his old friend again. They reached Brno in the late afternoon and stood in front of Kolya's house before dusk. Alma had tried to warn her lover that the chances of finding his old friend at the same address after so many years were slim but they were in luck and a slightly aged and silver haired Kolya opened the door to them.

"Holy Mary and Joseph! Jonah, my friend. What are you doing here?" he exclaimed and opened his arms for a warm embrace. "Come in, come in. Who is this pretty lady? Not one of your daughters I hope? They couldn't have aged this much."

"This is my wife, Alma," he replied.

"She would not have a sister to keep me company, would she?" Kolya said with a wink. "Come on in!"

Jonah was too tired for all this banter and cut right to the chase.

"Listen Kolya, it is good to see you but I won't lie to you. We are in trouble and we need your help."

"I guessed as much," Kolya replied. "You don't see many Jews in the Protectorate these days that don't need help. What exactly did you have in mind?"

"We need somewhere to hide. We left Bratislava a few days ago to help my daughters across the border but my son is still missing in the war. I want to go back to Bratislava once the fighting has gone past here and meet him when he gets home. Do you think there is anywhere where we can stay?" asked Jonah.

"You will stay here with me of course. We will play chess until you learn how to beat me," said Kolya teasingly.

"I hoped to stay longer than that. I already know how to beat you at chess. I will give you lessons in it. Maybe you will stop losing your queen even after my opening moves if I stay here long enough to teach you," Jonah replied. "But seriously, we don't want to put you in danger!"

"There is not much risk. There are informers around of course but not as many as before. The Germans are only looking for resistance fighters and communists now. There is no hunt for Jews, they believe that they got them all. I can hide you in my wine cellar. I can put a rug over the trap door in the floor, so no visitors will know. I work in a factory during the day so you will be on your own. You can't make any noise of course."

"Still no wife?" asked Jonah.

"Still all alone. If your wife has no sister, maybe you can spare one of your daughters after the war?" he said and roared with laughter.

"They would be lucky to have you." Jonah replied.

The wine cellar was very small compared to the space they had used as a hideaway on the estate of the Countess. There was no wine left in the cellar and it dawned on the pair that they would probably have to wait hungry as well as in the dark.

"I am afraid I had to sell all my wine to buy food. Everything we grow or make gets taken away by the Germans. I can get you probably just enough food so that you won't starve. I have two blankets and a lamp but please try and use this only when you need to. I have so little oil left for it."

"Of course," promised Alma.

"When I got back from Slovakia I had to move in here with my parents." Kolya told them. "There were so many of us Czech civil servants coming home – all at the same time - and no work for any of us. I was lucky to find a job at the factory. When the Germans took over they sent all unemployed men west to work in their own factories like slaves. From those who managed to come back we heard how appalling the conditions there were."

"That is terrible. Where are your parents now?" Alma asked.

"My parents died of typhus in a German labour camp right at the beginning of the occupation. Somehow their names were on a list of communists and a lorry picked them up one evening. I can't imagine how they could have been politically involved at all. I never knew anything about it. Well, at least they were old and did not have to wait long for their death."

"I am so sorry to hear that," Alma said.

"Well, that is all in the past now," Kolya said quickly. "Jonah, I want a game of chess right now and trust me, I won't show you any mercy!"

Jonah beat Kolya in three successive games and every time the loser complained about foul play. The three of them had a great evening, despite only having a little watery soup to share between them. Jonah told in great detail the events of the last seven years, about his new grandson and about his time on the estate, the hiding and their escape from Bratislava. Kolya was impressed with their survival story and said that having them in his house was like having a lucky charm. With a Weissensteiner present, he was bound to get through this last part of the war.

The next day Kolya had already left when Jonah woke up. The cellar was completely dark and it was hard to figure out what time it was. It was only now that he realised how hard it was going to be to sit in the dark without any distraction and with the premise to make no noise. The hours dragged endlessly without any light but they had agreed to save the oil for emergencies only. Kolya did not return until late. When he opened the trap door it had almost been an entire day since they had last eaten. "Sorry, I had to make a detour on my way home. I went to see my cousin Bogdan. He might be able to help us with the food situation," explained Kolya.

"How?" asked Alma.

"Well, the black market I guess. Some people claim food rations for their dead relatives and then sell them on. Highly illegal and punished by death but some people are desperate. The resistance is pinching food from farms and food transports and are willing to trade it for weapons and information. There are lots of deals going on and it is better for me to know as little as possible," Kolya said. "I have a little ham. It isn't much but it's better than that disgusting soup."

Jonah and Alma took the ham he gave them greedily and were finished with it in no time.

"Sorry, that is all there is," Kolya apologised. "I have some news you might like to hear: The Red Army captured Bratislava yesterday. You got out of there just in time. It won't be long before they get here. We are expecting air raids at the factory but you should be safe here in the cellar."

"Thank you," Alma said.

"I need to get up even earlier tomorrow," Kolya told them. "I will turn in now. The windows are blacked out so you can stay in the living room a little if you like. Good night."

"Good night and thank you," said Jonah.

After Kolya had left the two of them found some old papers in the living room and read them. All of course absurd propaganda and not in the least the distraction they had hoped for. The couple also turned in soon for the night but their sleep was soon interrupted by the sound of aircraft engines and bombs dropping. Only after the attack had almost finished did the air raid alarm go off and the sirens started to sound. With the constant expectation of repeat alarms there was not much sleep to be had for the rest of the night. The couple were still awake when Kolya left for work.

The next three nights were quiet but naturally no one slept soundly, half expecting another air raid. Kolya told them that the last air raid had been the fiercest the city had ever seen and people were so scared that many had stopped going to work. The fighting had come closer and in parts of the city it was possible to hear artillery noise. It was only a matter of time now.

Kolya had also decided to stay home from the factory, since

246

there were such shortages that production had become something of a farce anyway. Nobody believed that management would be able to pay them soon either. Their Czech friend had not been able to buy any bread for them, only some potatoes. Alma found some ingredients in the larder to make a vegetable broth which Kolya said was worse than no food at all.

That night there was another heavy air raid and the following morning a huge mass exodus of German civilians headed towards the west. Kolya reported that the train station was hopelessly overcrowded.

After two weeks of constant air raids and battle noise the Red Army finally rolled into the city. Nobody could believe it had taken them so long. Kolya told his guests to keep staying in the cellar to avoid confrontation. The soldiers were running through the streets, looting all houses and looking for Germans. The locals used white flags to signal to the Soviets where the Germans were but the looting and raping was not entirely limited to those premises.

Kolya reported in the evening that it had been not as gruesome as could have been expected. The Czechoslovak government in exile had set up residence in Kosice in the eastern part of Slovakia. Because it had advised and assisted the Red Army in the war effort, they had, in exchange, received certain guarantees of humanitarian conduct by the troops against their people.

The Germans who had been stupid enough not to flee the country were violently abused by both the liberators and the Czechs, whose life the Nazis had made so miserable over the last seven years. There was no distinction between Austrians, Germans, Nazis and neutrals. Anyone with a German name or accent was a target.

Alma and Jonah remained in hiding. After all, their papers were now German. Nobody but Kolya could speak for them. Proving their story might be difficult. They had been lucky enough to survive the first days of house searches and looting. That danger was still very present.

Over the next weeks Germans were rounded up and brought together in camps and stories of cruelty and revenge made their way through the streets of Brno. Kolya had contacted his cousin Bogdan and asked what to do about Jonah and Alma. Bogdan came to the house with a few of his men and they took the old couple and

247

brought them to a farm outside of Brno where there was a community of Ukrainian refuges and forced labourers. He explained that the Soviets were keen to bring home all the displaced people after the war and gathered them in camps. This farm was under the protection of the Red Army.

No harm could come to Jonah and Alma here from anyone thinking that they were Germans. He burned their forged passports by the names of Finsterwalder and left them to their fate amongst the other liberated refugees.

The last few weeks had been quite different for the other part of the Weissensteiner family. After a day of rest the women had left Budweis and had travelled successfully to Pilsen in the space of only a few days. The city was heaving with people pushing west. They had to sleep in an open field outside the city limits that the administration had assigned for the passing refugees. Greta was worried that the excitement and chaos of this place might have a negative effect on Wilma but fortunately this was not the case. The sister spoke calmly about missing her father and Egon.

Someone had organised a field kitchen and refugees were being fed for free. Children were playing everywhere and at times the atmosphere was more like a fun fair than that of a country at war. In this colourful place people traded their possessions and Edith was able to use some of her jewellery to buy more of the serum for Wilma. The tablets would have been more useful because of their less dramatic effect but beggars could not be choosers. Wilma was almost back to her old self, not as communicative and playful as she once had been, but certainly able to hold a conversation and laugh.

Two teenage girls whose cart was right next to Greta's were playing 'old maid' and asked Ernst to join them. After a few animated games and a lot of laughter they adopted Ernst for the rest of the day and took him with them on their tour round the field camp. Greta was pleased as it gave her the opportunity to spend some time alone with Wilma.

"You are looking very well," she said to her ill sister. "How are you feeling?"

"I am so pleased we are in the fresh air now," was her reply.

"This is like a little adventure!" Greta said cheerfully. "I am looking forward to Paris. They are meant to have food there that we never even heard of. Edith said the women all dress in the most amazing fashion."

"I don't care about clothes," Wilma replied. "They are such a waste of money."

"I am sure that Esther and Edith are going to dress us up like dolls before they even think about being seen with us in their circles. We will have to do our best to fit in," said Greta.

"I hope we won't be there for long. I want to go back home," said Wilma.

"I don't want to go back to Slovakia," Greta replied. "We have been living in hiding for long enough. I would like to live somewhere where we can be ourselves. Paris might just be the place."

"I want to go back," Wilma insisted. "Our life is there!"

"Wilma, we need to move on. Our workshop is gone and our rich customers have probably all fled like us. I don't think we will ever be able to go back, and even if we did, it will not be the same. There will be a new home for us somewhere else," Greta said hopefully. "I think that prospect is rather exciting and thrilling."

"Where?" Wilma asked, not very impressed.

"France, maybe America. Now that these countries are crushing Hitler's army and his ideology they will look out for us and find a solution. They simply must. Why else would they have come and fought him?

"Let's hope so. I can't shake the feeling that it will always be like it was for us. They liberated the Poles and the Czechs, even the Slovaks but they won't change anything for the Jews," said Wilma, disillusioned.

"You mustn't think like that. You and I will either have great adventures or we will settle down somewhere comfortably with the help of the Countess and the ladies," promised Greta.

"You want to be careful about that," Wilma warned her. "Edith is still very fond of you."

"Nonsense. I think Esther is sweet for you. It will be you who is breaking their hearts," Greta said with a wink.

Ernst, in the meantime, had been out exploring with the two girls. Their grandfather had left them alone while trying to find some provisions in the city and even though they had promised him to stay with their belongings and make sure nothing was being stolen the boredom had got the better of them and so they had asked complete strangers next to them to watch out for any thieves.

"What is your name?" Ernst suddenly asked them.

"We already told you. I am Lisbeth and this is Margot. Have you forgotten already? Or is this some game? What is yours?"

"My name is Edwin Finsterwalder!" he said. "My mother is Margarethe Finsterwalder and my aunt is Wilhelmina Finsterwalder."

"Finsterwalder?"

"Yes, my name is Ernst, ehm, Edwin Finsterwalder. Edwin Finsterwalder!"

"How funny," said Lisbeth, who was the older sister and always the one talking for the two of them. "We met an elderly couple by that name on the road. That was only a few days ago. We have to tell grandfather. They left us in the middle of the night and we never got to say goodbye to them. Grandfather was very angry at them for it. You wouldn't know any Finsterwalders who were on their way to Brno?"

"My Grandfather went to Brno. His name is Joseph Finsterwalder and Alma is Anna Finsterwalder," Ernst said, thinking this was still part of the game.

"What do you mean: Alma is Anna Finsterwalder and why did you say earlier that you are Ernst Finsterwalder? Which one is it? Ernst or Edwin? Alma or Anna?" asked Margot.

"My name is Edwin Finsterwalder and my grandmother is Anna Finsterwalder." Ernst said now, realising his mistake and remembering how his mother had made him swear never to use the old names again. "There is no Ernst and no Alma."

The sisters exchanged a meaningful look and whispered into each other's ears. Ernst tried hard but could not understand what they were saying.

"Let us go back to our place. Our grandfather must not know that we left the cart. We promised," said Lisbeth.

Finding the way back was not as easy as they had imagined. The place was full of people who were moving around and it took a while before they saw Greta and Wilma sitting on the grass between the two carriages.

Lisbeth and Margot disappeared to go back to their space behind another cart. Ernst told his mother about slipping up in the name 'game'. Greta was mortified but could not risk worrying Wilma or her poor little boy who was too young to be forced into lying and

250

being good at it.

"Don't worry. Just make sure you don't make the same mistake again," she said in a calming tone. Wilma didn't seem to have taken notice of the news. She was busy pulling petals of daisies.

When the Countess and the ladies got back Greta took them to one side and told them about their cover being compromised.

"We probably have to think about leaving as soon as we can," said Edith." I heard that we are still too close to the Soviets here. We need to go further west really quickly."

"It is too late in the day to leave now," the Countess said. "It will be dark soon."

"It does not matter, even a few hours ahead of someone who suspects our identity is fake is better than staying another night next to them," Edith said decidedly.

"I feel the same," agreed Greta.

"It will be a drain on the horses," the Countess argued. "Without proper rest the poor animals will be slower tomorrow."

"We need to take that risk. I'll get everything ready," Edith stated and walked towards the fiacre.

As Greta turned around the corner she saw Ernst talking animatedly with Lisbeth and Margot and her heart sank. Had they left it too late already? She stormed to the scene to find out.

"Someone stole one of our bags," Lisbeth explained to her. "We left our neighbour in the camp in charge of our stuff while taking a stroll but now one suitcase is missing. Grandfather will be furious with us."

"Do you know what was in it?" asked Greta.

"I don't. He will be so angry, I should never have disobeyed his orders," she sobbed, falling into her also tearful sister's arms. "We let him down again. We let him down."

"Can you be there when we tell him?" asked Margot now. "Maybe he won't get so mad with us if you are there."

"I would love to but we decided to be on our way now. Your grandfather won't be angry. He will be happy that nothing has happened to you. The camp is a dangerous place. He should never have left you two alone without protection. Tell him that from me when you see him," she told the young girls in distress and left them to their own devices, not without feeling guilt for abandoning them.

If only she had a choice in the matter, she would have looked out for these two as well but it was just too risky now. Who could tell if they were friends or enemies? As soon as Lisbeth and Margot had gone, the fiacre and the telega were on their way towards Pilsen. Getting through the narrow path that the dwellers had left on the field took some time and many of the ones they had to pass shouted abuse at them, asking them why they had to leave now and disturb everyone.

"I shouldn't be saying this but we were lucky the girls have been robbed. They forgot all about us and our names," observed Edith.

"I hope there was nothing important in the bag," said Greta. "I don't think they would have reported us."

"Greta you are still so lovely and naïve!" said the Countess, entering the discussion. "You always have to stay a little suspicious of the ones who appear to be nice. Quite often they turn out to be a wolf in sheepskin. You need to see behind the exterior and always remember that everyone on the road here has lost everything and is desperate for anything that can better their own fortune. Selling us to the Gestapo might bring them another meal, praise from their grandfather or a piece of bread."

"I guess you are right," admitted Greta with a sad tone in her voice.

The horses were slow, just as the Countess had predicted, and they didn't make it very far from Budweis. Defeated by the facts Edith suggested that they stop for the night.

"As long as we are far enough from the main road we will be safe. No one is going to look for us in the dark," she assured everyone.

Their luck continued for the next few days, the grandfather and his teenage girls never caught up with them and the women made steady progress towards Carlsbad. Ernst had been a little subdued because he worried that he had endangered their group but Greta kept reassuring him that everything was fine and thanks to Esther's habit of singing with him and playing children's games, such as 'I spy with my little eye', he soon forgot all about it.

A few days later their party arrived at Carlsbad. During their journey they had learned some horrific news from other travellers. According to these rumours the front line was not coming any closer at all. The Allies seemed to have refocused their attention to the north and the south of the country. Instead of pushing east into Bohemia and Moravia they had turned south towards Bavaria and Austria. North of the Protectorate the troops continued to advance towards Berlin without coming any further towards Prague or Carlsbad. Ironically, the army they were chasing was running away from them.

To avoid further slip ups from Ernst and to make sure that they would not run into the old man and his granddaughters, they decided to stay away from their fellow refugees in Carlsbad as much as they could. After some searching they found a farmer who agreed to let them stay. Greta and Wilma offered to help with the cows but he said that he had enough help and would rather have their money.

The Czechs were increasingly confident and cocky with the German civilians and this farmer was no exception. He had agreed to take them for purely commercial reasons, not out of the goodness of his heart or out of compassion. The German refugees were part of the nation that had brought suffering to his people, the Jews and the rest of Europe. Now that the German star was falling it was possible to show his hate openly without fear of punishment.

Not every German of course had committed crimes but few Czechs had the patience to differentiate, too great were their pain and anger.

Greta did not blame them. She had seen and experienced enough first hand to understand these sentiments and couldn't wait for the moment when she could tell everyone that she was not a German, not an oppressor or a murderer, but as much as a victim of the Nazis as the Czechs.

For now of course they had to continue playing their roles until the Gestapo was disarmed and powerless, which was far from being the case. Instead of supporting the troops at the front, armed officers still performed random checks of the refugees, searched houses and killed Jews who were in hiding. Their efforts were no longer as organised and thorough as they once were but it was enough to assure the population that the end of the war was not here yet.

A Ukrainian woman who worked on the farm told Esther that she had seen some people coming back from the west where they had tried to get behind the enemies lines towards peace. Gestapo officers had stopped these refugees from escaping and had shot those 'traitors' without ever even knowing if they were Germans, Czechs, Poles, Ukrainians or Jews.

The border was shut and according to this woman Esther and her comrades would have to bide their time here until either the Americans or the Russians came. The local industry was considered important enough to attract air raids, so the waiting was anything from comfortable. Bombers seemed to miss their target most of the time. The farm was situated considerably far from the industrial areas, yet it had seen some minor bombing in the area.

Esther developed quite a close friendship with Ilina, the Ukrainian woman. Ilina was isolated amongst the workforce as the only non-Polish worker. For some reason the Poles had not let her into their circle of trust and treated her with contempt or ignorance, leaving her to fight for herself. The arrivals on the farm were a welcome relief from the loneliness she had been suffering, especially as some of these guests were able to speak to her in Russian.

The farmer and Ilina had an unspoken understanding by which he would come to her bed when he felt the urge to do so and, in turn, he would give her extra rations or let her listen to the enemy radio with him in the loft. As a result of this, one day she informed Esther that Nuremberg had fallen into the hands of the Allies, as had been rumoured amongst the refugees. Yet once again the American army was now heading slightly south towards Regensburg and not towards the Czech regions as had been hoped.

Edith and the Countess had made the occasional excursion into Carlsbad, where they had heard similar reports about the state of the war from other refugees. Parts of the local population were fearful of excessive air raids and bombings whereas others were furious with the Allies for 'not bothering' with the liberation of Czechoslovakia anymore and leaving them under the dictatorship of the Germans unnecessarily. The resulting impatience and fear did not make the life of the refugees any easier. Ilina even told Esther she had heard that it was planned to put all Germans into concentration camps the minute the war was over. Edith dismissed such rumours as ridiculous, refusing to believe that revenge on the Germans would be this harsh and cruel. The Countess was less sure of this.

"You, Wilma and Ernst should try and get across the border. Maybe the Gestapo won't bother so much with two women and a child," she suggested. "If you are caught by Czechs with German papers you could be sent to a camp with the lot of them and pay for their crimes against you and your people. Can you imagine?"

"I won't risk being shot by the border," Greta insisted. "I am sure there will be a way for us to prove we are not meant to be in a concentration camp. Wilma and Ernst are easily believable as Jews and a concentration camp run by the Americans can never be as bad. I want to survive, your Highness. I won't run."

A week later Regensburg had fallen and American troops had pushed towards the border of Czechoslovakia but stopped there. By now it had become transparent that the Allies were not interested in the Czechs and an escape into American occupied territory was even more dangerous according to the few brave ones who had attempted such a mission, had failed but were still alive to tell the tale.

The desperation of the remaining Germans who were losing ground very quickly, expressed itself in ever harder and more irrational killings and punishment of traitors and collaborators. Instead of letting go of the reigns to incite some goodwill amongst the Czechs, which might be needed in the future when the tables were turned, they followed their orders from above with precision, determined to take everything and everyone down with them.

The Countess wasted entire days tormenting herself for the choices she had made that had led them into this worrisome situation, creating one theory after another about how they would be safe now if they had gone to Vienna, Linz, Passau or even Budapest. Edith did her best to distract her Highness from these unproductive thoughts but it seemed a hard habit to break.

Wilma's sedation had proven very helpful through the noise of bombing and the strange and sometimes hostile atmosphere on the farm. It seemed the time in hiding on the estate in Bratislava had affected her in a way that being out in the open was all she cared about. She hated the dark and the only time she appeared slightly hysterical was when she woke up at night and could not immediately recognise her surroundings and her room partners. Once this pattern had transpired Greta took to sleeping with her sister in the barn outside, while little Ernst was allowed to share the free room with Esther.

The relationship between Esther and Edith had become a little strained of late but not for the reasons everyone had been expecting. Esther was oblivious to Edith's crush on Greta and, even if she had been aware of it, she fortunately wasn't the jealous type and would never have felt seriously threatened by it. The tension between them came from Edith, who herself could not explain why she felt so increasingly irritated by her lover. She too had no sense of rivalry in the relationship and had no problem with the fact that Esther was spending so much time with Ilina or Ernst. On the contrary, such contacts pleased her and she was happy for Esther to have a meaningful and rewarding social life and an occupation to take her mind off the war. What Edith really started to get tired off was that she alone always had to be in charge, that it was her who had to make the important decisions continuously without her lover's input.

Esther had become so passive and naïve. Instead of taking part in any discussion about the future she obviously preferred to stick her head in the sand and wait for any difficulty to be sorted out by someone else. Yet, Edith could not explain why this character trait had come to annoy her now, when it had been present right from the beginning of their romance.

She had probably encouraged this in the past, proud to be in control and to take on the role of the provider. Now it was wearing her down and her frustration was becoming an additional burden around her neck.

Almost every day the Countess wondered out loud if they should leave and try a different escape route rather than waiting in the unknown, with no idea which army would eventually bother to liberate the remains of the Czech territories.

There had been persistent rumours that the American army would wait by the borders and leave the country entirely to the Soviets. Many people believed that the Allies had drawn up a map of the future Europe already and that Czechoslovakia – just like the Ukraine and the Baltic states before the war – would become part of the Soviet Union. There were also rumours that a whole tank division of the Germans had surrendered to the Americans and still they were not entering Czech territories.

Discussions about the best course of action went around and around in circles. Greta wanted to stay for Wilma's sake but the Countess was eager to press on. Edith would have preferred if her partner had some thoughts on the matter as well but to no avail. Edith sided with Greta because she felt unable to refuse her anything but she was not sure if her affection was blinding her or whether her

256

trust in the pretty Jewess was deserved. Staying might be just as dangerous as leaving. The days here were spent in search of food and in waiting for any news that would announce the final days of the war but no one could predict what would happen next.

Finally, the Americans crossed the border and were reported to be coming towards Carlsbad. The Czechs in Pilsen staged an uprising in the city but were unsuccessful in disarming the occupying forces, while in turn the Germans could not bring down the Czechs either. Greta and her travel companions were lucky to be away from the fighting and in the relatively peaceful city of Carlsbad. Worries over what would happen to everyone once the fighting was over were still frightening. The Americans finally arrived in Carlsbad and a day later the German soldiers in Pilsen surrendered to them as well. The Czech people greeted their liberators with enormous enthusiasm.

Chapter 11: Spring 1945: Peace

After the Germans had been disarmed the situation became dangerous for Greta and her friends. The Czechoslovak nation had been encouraged by their president in exile to seek revenge and those who followed his call were looking for Germans everywhere, looting their property, beating up men and women and putting those who were considered fit for work into labour camps. In other parts of the country the last of the fighting was coming to an end but for the previously protected Sudetenlanders the atrocities had only just begun. As soon as the first reports of violence reached their farm, the Countess suggested they head for France immediately.

"We won't get through!" warned Esther. "Ilina says there are road blocks everywhere. The army needs the roads and won't let any civilians use them until their manoeuvres are over.

"I am sorry but I can't wait. Call me a coward but I won't sit here and wait for some mob to roughen us up," the Countess admitted.

"I am afraid we don't have an option," Edith stated calmly.

"Oh yes we do," the Countess replied and mounted one of the horses. "I wish I had it in me to stick with you, my friends, but I can't. I am leaving you everything I have brought with me but I will take this horse and try to get out on my own. Please forgive me!" and with that she galloped onto the road, without a single glance back.

Her sudden and abrupt departure left the four women speechless. The remaining horses were insufficient to travel on in the same luxurious manner they had gotten accustomed to. Shocked by the Countess and her solo lead, suddenly they too considered leaving – now of course on foot and without much luggage.

They repacked parts of their clothes into bed linen and carried them over their shoulders. Three people at a time could sit on the horses while the others would walk beside them. Eager to leave before a wave of hate crimes could reach them they left immediately.

Greta found herself a little unsettled by the cowardly actions of the Countess who had always been so strong and confident. After all, they were in the American zone and relatively safe from the feared violence by the Soviet liberators. Vengeance by the Czechs could not be as bad as it was made out to be. The Americans were there to intervene. Seeing her Highness abandoning everyone so hastily infected her with fear.

They did not get far. After a few miles of walking in the fields beside the road that led west to Bavaria they met with a group of armed Czech men who were demanding to see their papers. Greta answered in her Slovak dialect that they did not have any. She had burnt the Finsterwalder papers as soon as they had heard that the Americans were coming and buried the remains in the soil near their farmhouse. Being a German was no longer of use. Unfortunately many Germans in the Sudetenland and the former Protectorate had done exactly the same and the men on the control post were already no longer satisfied with dialect as the only proof of nationality.

"Why are you heading west? Don't you want to go home to Slovakia?" asked one of them. "What have you got to hide?"

"We have nothing to hide!" Greta replied quickly. "We prefer not to be come in contact with Russian soldiers. We will go back home to Slovakia when they have gone."

"What about you two?" the man asked Edith and Esther.

"German Jews," Greta lied. "They want to go back home and meet with their family."

"I guess I should have seen that," admitted the Czech man. "Good luck and be careful. You are in Sudetenland territory with still a lot of Nazi rats at large!" he warned them and sent them on their way.

After only a few more miles they were held up by another Czech patrol.

"Why are you heading west and not home to Slovakia?" they were asked again. "If you leave the country to the Bolsheviks you won't have any place to go home to."

"We are scared of the soldiers. They don't have much respect for women," Greta answered. "And they don't like Jews either," she added. "Especially if they are Germans."

"All the Germans are being rounded up in camps," said the Czech now in a militant tone. "Have you not heard the orders? You shouldn't be leaving. You must report to the authorities."

"But they are Jews. It is obvious, why waste time?" asked Greta persuasively.

"Let the camp commanders decide who is a Jew and who is pretending to be one. No one must be allowed to escape their justice.

Who of you are Germans?" he asked.

"This is absurd. Look at us," Greta pleaded. "Can't you see we are all Jewish? It doesn't take a bureaucrat or expert to see that. Please let us continue on our way. We still have a long journey ahead of us."

The man hesitated, and conferred with one of his colleagues in a whisper. At that moment a group of women approached the check point, trying to get around it without acknowledging the guards. The Czech men stopped them and quickly had identified them as Germans. During a quick search it was found that one of them had a swastika painted on her forehead which she had tried to hide under a head shawl.

The patrol men threatened the women with their rifles and opened their suitcases stripping them of money, food and jewellery. The men demanded all rings and watches, took the shoes off their victims and then surprisingly let them go without arresting them.

"Consider yourselves lucky," one of the men shouted at them. "This is nothing compared to what you did to us. Get out of our sight before we change our mind."

The women started to run but it was remarkable how they had managed to remain so stoic throughout the ordeal. Greta wondered where they had found the strength to endure the humiliation so easily. Was it a guilty conscious or was this nothing compared to what they already had been through? Had they committed crimes or were they innocent? If they had been guilty, what exactly could they have done? Greta had been unable to guess from their demeanour. She had expected some pleading of innocence or begging for forgiveness, but the women had given nothing away.

"You can go too," the guard told Greta and her entourage. "I believe you, but be careful. Others are stricter than I am. President Benes asked us to take revenge on all Germans. I personally just want them to be gone as fast as they can run but some of my colleagues want to enjoy the punishment. Good luck and shalom!"

Greta thanked him and they went on their way.

"We better not waste any more time," Edith said. "That was a narrow escape."

Greta looked at her scornfully, nodding at Ernst and Wilma, as if to say: 'Don't make this any harder on these two than we have to.'

Wilma stiffened when she witnessed how the women had been

260

treated by the patrol. Esther had held her tight and squeezed her hand, managing to keep her fragile friend under control. The hysteria however got to Wilma soon after they had passed the control point and she was quietly sobbing and shaking. When they decided to take shelter in a nearby forest for the night Wilma's nerves finally gave up and she entered into a state of mad frenzy, calling for her father and her brother.

Edith and Greta decided to use one of the few injections they had left to keep her calm for the night but the medication didn't work as well as they would have hoped. Wilma was restless, plagued by nightmares and woke everyone with her whimpering.

The next morning their party was shattered from lack of sleep; Ernst was the only one who seemed to not be affected. Wilma at least had exhausted herself and had entered into a lethargic state. She sat on one of the horses during the morning. Ernst suddenly wanted to know where they were going and why.

"We are going to meet the Countess in Paris," said Esther with an excited tone in her voice that sounded a little too strained to fool even the young boy.

"Why?" he asked unimpressed.

"She has a lovely place there and she has invited us to visit. It would be impolite to turn down such a request," Edith chipped in. If her lover had to try to cheer up the boy she had to do a bit better than that she thought and she decided to take over the task.

"I am absolutely sure that you will love it. It is a beautiful place right in the city of Paris. Have you ever heard about the Eiffel Tower and the big Cathedral of Notre Dame? They are fine sights to be seen. There is no city just like Paris," she promised him. The poor little boy was going through so much at such a young age. They all had a responsibility to make this as smooth for him as possible.

"I have seen a book with pictures of Paris in the library," Ernst replied casually. "But why has the Countess left us?" he wanted to know undeterred.

"She went ahead so she can get the place tidy for us. There will be a huge party when we get there," Esther promised her little prince, having composed herself and up for the task of lightening the mood.

"The French make excellent bread and sweets. There are streets with nothing but shops for chocolate and pastries. You will love them," Esther assured him.

261

"Where is grandfather?" Ernst asked suddenly. "And Alma?"

"Oh, they are waiting for Egon. The minute your uncle is back from the war they will join us in Paris and then we will all be together," said Esther.

"Will my father be there too?" asked Ernst.

"Maybe not in Paris but once he comes back from the war you can meet him. I think you will most likely see him in Berlin," answered Greta. "He is always busy and he told me that he can hardly leave his house there, he has so much work to do."

"What does he do there?" asked the boy.

"He works in a big bookshop. You remember the big library at the manor house that Wilma and I often worked in?" asked Greta.

"Yes."

"It is a place just like that, only he sells the books from the shelves. They have even more books than the Countess has collected in her library. Do you remember how long it took your aunt and me to get those shelves into order? Then you can imagine how much he has to do. He has got to do it all by himself. He couldn't just leave and travel to Paris but one day I hope you can go and visit him," Greta promised.

Ernst's curiosity was satisfied.

It was a beautiful sunny day but for travellers it was almost too hot. Whenever possible they made short stops to cool down in the shade of trees. They had advanced only a small fragment of their way but were already exhausted. There were much fewer people on the road than there had been between Budweis, Pilsen and Carlsbad. Edith put this down to the fact that there was no longer the danger from the Red Army but it felt a little strange to see so few refugees.

The road blocks meant that many people were unable to move, especially those unwilling to leave luggage and means of transport behind but there had to be more Germans on the run concerned about the violent acts of retribution by the Czechs. Greta was very troubled by what the last road patrol had said to her about his colleagues. Sooner or later they could run into some unreasonable Czechs or militia and be mistaken for Germans.

She found it hard to understand why Germans should be interned when the goal of the nation was to rid itself of them as soon as possible. While she was still trying to see the reason behind this illogical policy a large truck approached on the road ahead of them. It was a German army truck with the Czechoslovak flag hanging out of one window. Greta prepared herself for the next patrol and its questioning but the truck drove past them. Greta saw that the back of the truck was heaving with civilians and she guessed that these were Germans being transported into the next internment camp. If there had been any more space the driver would have probably stopped and frisked them. That was one more escape she thought, hoping that their luck would hold out just a little bit longer until they had passed the border into Germany. Once there they hopefully would be free from worries about controls and misunderstandings, even though there might be other issues which they had not anticipated.

Obviously their group had chosen the right route to avoid the American road blocks, which were affecting traffic running south or north rather than west or east. Greta and her friends were running low on food provisions but decided not to try and buy anything until they were across the border. The Countess had told them how in Pilsen, even during the last few weeks of the war, Czech shopkeepers were already refusing to sell food to Germans and entering a local shop as a stranger could easily lead to complications that they could do without.

In the early afternoon the truck they had seen in the morning came back empty and promptly stopped next to them by the side of the road.

"Papers!" an armed Czech officer shouted in German.

Greta answered in Slovak that they were not in possession of passports. Before she got to explain any further the officer aimed his rifle at her and shouted at her to shut up. His colleagues stormed from the truck and searched their luggage.

Esther said "Jewish", but one officer only laughed and hit her in the face. "Shut up!" he shouted and continued his search of their luggage. The soldiers took all of their jewellery and stuffed them into their own pockets. Wilma panicked completely, grabbed Ernst and tried to run away to a nearby little forest but one of the armed men chased after her and pushed her to the floor, pulled her up by her hair and dragged her back to the side of the road. "Ugly woman," he said to his friends and laughed dirtily.

Then one soldier held up an old Austrian passport. Edith's face froze. She had forgotten that she had sown her old passport from the times before the Anschluss into one of her coats. Back then she had wanted to preserve it in case it might prove useful at a later date. Now it proved to be her ruin.

"Nemecky" he shouted. German.

"That's not a German passport, it is Austrian," Edith tried to explain, but the guard again just threatened her with his rifle. None of them were allowed to speak. They were ordered on to the truck with gestures instead of words. One officer stayed behind with the horses, presumably to sell them in the next village. Their luggage and clothes were left behind on the road.

The truck drove further east and on the way picked up more people from the side of the road as it had done with Greta and her entourage. The patrol rarely let people go, only those with Czech papers it seemed and even from that group some were ordered on the truck. According to their stories the fellow prisoners were Czech but had German sounding names. Many Jewish names sounded German to the Czechs and regardless of their nationality they were usually arrested as well. They were particularly upset to come out of their hiding places and now find themselves arrested by their alleged liberators.

By the afternoon the truck was bursting with people, many of which were Germans from Austria-Hungary, pleading that they had nothing to do with the Nazis and that their families had lived in the area for centuries. The guards were not in the least interested, only in the riches they had been able to appropriate for themselves. No response or remorse could be read in their faces, only disgust and hate.

The truck took them back to Pilsen. Everywhere in town hung red posters informing the Germans of something which Greta could not decipher from the moving vehicle. The car finally stopped in a suburban road and unloaded its human cargo at an underground cinema building. Greta expected there to be a reception of some kind where they could clear up the obvious mistake that had been made and where there would be apologies to the Jewish people that had been arrested by mistake. Nothing of the sort occurred. The same guards that had been ignoring them throughout the whole journey were now pushing them down the stairs into the big auditorium which was already almost full of people.

Then the doors were locked from the outside and only a small light from the projector room was visible. Children were screaming, voices were whispering but for the first few minutes the prisoners in the cinema were waiting for something to happen. There were arguments over seats between newcomers and those who had already been here longer.

In the semi darkness it was difficult to make out people and seat rows but many men and women gave up seats for the elderly, children and pregnant women. Others insisted on staying in their seat, fighting off even those who only tried to get past them to find a space somewhere else.

Wilma's sedatives were still on the road where the truck had picked them up and the darkness combined with the slightly volatile aura in the auditorium threatened to set her off again. Ernst held on tight to Esther who had started to stay by his side all the time now so that Greta could take care of her sister. They had not seen any spare seats and sat down at the bottom of the theatre between the first few seat rows near the screen.

"Find the light switch!" someone shouted in German.

"The switches don't work!" an answer came back.

"Let me through I am going to be sick!" a voice shouted in panic not far from their group. "Let me through, let me through!"

A series of swear words and apologies followed and from their growing distance Greta estimated that the voice had made it halfway to the top before it was too late. It smelled awful.

The new prisoners started to get more animated and loud as the waiting continued, while established ones had resigned themselves to their fate.

"We have got to get out of here. They are going to kill us," shouted one woman.

"Calm down, we have been here all day. Nothing is going to happen to us," someone called back. "Shut up!"

"How would you know?" the woman's voice asked.

"One guard told me we will be here until the trains are ready to bring us to Germany," another woman answered.

"They can tell you anything. They beat me up. Me, a helpless woman!" shouted the first one back. "Those animals! I lost a tooth from his rifle."

"Let's find the projector-room and get some light in here," someone else shouted in the dark.

"Save yourself the bother. It is locked. We tried that already," came a reply from right next to Greta.

"Do you know what those red posters in town were for?" she asked in the general direction of where that last voice had come from. Her eyes had still not adjusted to the darkness enough to see anything but vague shapes.

"All German men had to report to the main square this morning. They were brought to the factories to do the hard work or to camps like this," someone answered.

"How do you know what happened to them?" Greta asked.

"I don't know," came the answer. "It is all just rumours but there are some guards here who feel sorry for us and who know that most of us have done nothing wrong. Occasionally one of them will bring in some food, let us have a cigarette or speak to us."

"How long have you been in here?" she asked the voice, whom she believed to be an elderly German woman.

"Since yesterday morning. We came here from Silesia with what was left of our family. We spent a week in a refugee camp set up by the German Army somewhere near Carlsbad. When we heard about the capitulation we took off but we didn't get far. At first we were in a heavily guarded open air camp just outside of Carlsbad but yesterday that was taken over to intern more dangerous prisoners from Prague. We all got transferred in the morning and ended up here. It is not too bad once you get used to the dark. In the other camp some of us got beaten. Here we seem to be left alone."

"Is there a doctor or a nurse?" asked Greta, thinking of Wilma who may not last long before having another fit.

"Not that I know of," the woman replied. "Maybe one of the newcomers is. It won't be long before someone takes charge. Yesterday there was a fight between two grumpy old men who both had a Fuhrer complex. They wanted to hold an election. An election in the dark! We asked them what they wanted to be leaders for and they said to be a spokesman for the group. To negotiate with the Czechs, as if there was any bargaining power for us here. If it was not so sad it would be really funny."

"Maybe if there was someone in charge they could make sure that the ones in need get to sit down and not the ones who shout the loudest," suggested Greta.

"You try and do that. Good luck to you," came the cynical response.

"What happened with those two old men yesterday? How did the situation get resolved?" Greta asked.

"It ended with a fist fight. One of them held quite a speech about the future. He said he was sure that we were all innocent in here and that none of us were party members but in the dark there were several remarks to the contrary. One woman hit another who she thought had made a nasty comment but the other claimed it was not her. It is difficult in the dark. Even after two days I still can't adjust to it."

"My sister is not very well. She gets attacks when she is in the dark for too long. Is there anywhere with more light? What about the toilets?" Greta wondered.

"The toilets are right by the entrance. There is light in there but in a way it's not very good because it takes a long time to adjust your eyes back to the darkness. We ran out of newspapers yesterday by the way. I would not want to go there. Why does your sister not like the darkness? Were you hiding? Are you Jews?" the woman asked with an increased interest in her voice.

Greta did not want to answer that question at all. On the truck here most people had sworn to their prison guards that they were innocent, resistance fighters really, Czechs or Jews, hoping to be released on those grounds. In here - without the guards - the situation was entirely different. What would she risk if she said she was Jewish? That woman had not let on whether she had sympathy for the Jews or not. Her entire story had been told in a matter of fact way and so it was difficult to judge what consequences the revelation of the truth would cause.

"No, of course not. She has always disliked the dark since she was a child," Greta quickly lied.

"Good," came the answer from the dark. "I hate the Jews. They got us into this mess."

Edith had heard the entire conversation but decided not to partake. She felt responsible for the group being captured. If only she had chosen a different coat to take with her on the journey they might have got away from the patrol. Greta had tried to calm her and insisted that they would have been captured anyway. Those soldiers had not been particularly friendly and seemed keener to fill up the lorry than to hold a fair trial. To them any person on the road was presumed guilty and just their suspicion was enough to prove them guilty.

Regardless of such reasoning Edith felt awful and when she heard the woman in the dark blame the Jews for her misfortune she had to control herself not to respond. She turned back towards Esther and Ernst who were telling each other fairy tales, making use of the dark by tickling each other at appropriate moments in the stories and by using exaggerated voices for the characters.

"No wonder you were an actress once," said Edith to her lover. "You are very good at telling these stories. I am glad you are here with us."

"I am glad you are here too," replied Esther. "Don't blame yourself. Without your help we might have even made it this far. Let's hope that this nightmare comes to an end soon."

The group was sitting huddled close together but Wilma at least had managed to position herself so that she could lean against the bottom of the screen and drift off to sleep. The first night seemed to be never ending. There was no more attention from the guards and there were no more new arrivals. A few voices still emerged every so often predicting death and spreading panic but usually somebody around them grew tired of it and made them to be quiet by one way or another.

Then suddenly and without warning the lights in the auditorium came on bright. Czech soldiers with machine guns walked in and started to pick out all the men from the auditorium. Greta looked around her to see if she could find the woman she had the conversation with last night but they secmed all too young to fit the image she had formed of that woman.

There were only little boys and elderly men in the cinema and it depended on the mood of the soldiers which ones were asked to leave and which were allowed to stay. Greta estimated that less than 5% had been spared, the rest were hurried towards the exit, regardless of how fragile some of them were. Wives and daughters screamed and begged for mercy and some mothers had to say goodbye to what appeared to be boys of only ten years of age. The guards threw in a few sacks of bread, then they left and turned off the lights. The darkness did not encourage honesty amongst some of the inmates and even though, as far as Greta could tell, the distribution of the bread was done in an almost orderly fashion soon there were loud complaints and calls that there had been foul play and some had missed out completely.

Wilma was unsettled by the hostile shouting and tried to get up and out. Esther and Greta tried to hold her down but Wilma pulled away and fell over some of her fellow prisoners, one of whom hit her hard in the face.

"You stupid cow!" the woman shouted. "You stepped on my hand. Are you completely mad?"

Greta tried to intervene but Wilma was too far away and in the dark she could not get close enough to her sister. More people got involved.

At last a few rows up a woman seemed to get hold of her and with some help pinned her to the floor.

"Take this!" Greta heard being shouted and then the landing of a few heavy blows. She finally managed to get to her sister and wanted to shout: "You beasts!", but before she could say anything she heard a nasty voice next to her.

"Keep her under control or else. We can't have that kind of madness in here. It brings everyone down. Next time I will finish her off."

For the rest of the day Wilma was quiet and made no sound. Esther and Greta took turns to hold her but the poor soul was completely unresponsive until the next morning, which fortunately, at last, saw the end of their ordeal in the dark.

The lights in the cinema came on very early and this time everyone was ordered to march out of the stuffy auditorium. The prisoners were loaded onto a series of trucks and then driven to a big open field outside of town that had been secured by barbed wire. Everyone was given a white arm band that identified them as Germans and prisoners were warned that taking it off would be punished severely. Greta tried to protest that none of her party was German, but she was not alone in trying to change their captors' mind. The large number of people claiming not to belong in here rendered her efforts unconvincing and useless.

There was no further interrogation or examination, all prisoners were treated equally and two officers with machine guns separated out the few remaining men amongst them and led them into their own part of the camp. At the far end of the field stood several small barracks that Greta had not seen initially and she wondered if this was one of the camps the Germans had built.

"At least we are safe from the beatings and the raping!" she heard a women nearby say. "My neighbour was a very pretty girl and she got raped by at least four different soldiers in one day and then beaten to a pulp by the mob that put us behind bars. Whatever work they are going to make us do I feel almost safe in here."

Another woman disagreed. "I have seen a group of male prisoners on the road. They had to carry rocks and debris from bombed out buildings and looked as if they were already close to collapsing. I fear we are in for a nasty surprise. They want to show that the shoe is on the other foot now!"

When their little group got to the barracks the best beds had already been taken and there were not enough spaces left for all of them in one and the same barrack. Edith and Esther joined a hut that had several children in it and invited Ernst to stay with them. Wilma and Greta found two beds in a larger wood building which appeared to house other infirm and ill detainees. Greta explained her sister's condition to the fellow inmates who refused to put up with such an inconvenience. After the beating in the cinema she was determined to find a safe space for her sister.

Only after a further lengthy search did the two secure bunks in a barrack where the inhabitants were willing to take them in. Or rather, one of the women was happy to have them and invited them in, the others had admittedly been much less forthcoming, but did not try to intervene. After the humiliating march from door to door, looking for a place to stay, the sisters were willing to settle for being tolerated, as the absence of resistance was probably as good as it would get for them in here.

The situation in Brno meanwhile was equally volatile for the Germans. The rage of the Czech people here easily surpassed that of the Russian liberators, who by now had exhausted most of their thirst for violence and retribution on their way through the Ukraine and the Baltics. The Red Army moved on towards Prague, which still had not surrendered and the remaining units in Brno only rarely interfered with the revenge activities performed by civilians.

270

The Russian soldiers searched German houses for valuables and pretty girls but by and large that was the extent of their cruelty. Russians and Czechs had both been called to orderly behaviour by the army leadership and government officials after first reports about their conduct reached the authorities and the foreign press, but there were no effective processes in place to punish those who transgressed those directives.

Every time someone new arrived at the farm where Jonah and Alma were staying they had further stories to tell about the on-going looting, beatings, humiliations and rapes. People had been thrown into rivers from bridges, tortured, beaten to death and even hanged - many just because they were or appeared to be German - without a trial or as much as the tiniest proof of committed crimes. Even amongst the Ukrainians in the camp – many of whom had been forced to work on German farms - there was some sympathy for the victims of this blind revenge.

Not every one of the exiled workers from the east had been mistreated by their German bosses and many had seen the difficulties which non-conformist German families had suffered since Hitler's invasion. Many Sudetenlanders had been living in Brno for generations and had wanted nothing to do with Hitler and his plans for Europe but were intimidated by the German military force. In the aftermath of the war, such differentiations and considerations did not matter to people whose lives had been ruined by the Nazis. To Russian soldiers – many of whom had liberated concentration camps on their way - such actions were certainly understandable and did not tempt them to interfere.

Once the fighting had stopped, the German Reich had completely surrendered and even the last partisan units had laid down their weapons, the Allies were beginning to address the issue of the displaced people in Europe, but seemed to be taking their time to come to agreements.

The Czechoslovak president, Benes, who had led the government in exile during the war, immediately called for a rapid expulsion of all Germans from his country but the Allies were reluctant to agree to that policy. Czech and Slovak citizens therefore started their own initiatives and many cities in the Soviet occupied parts of the country confiscated all German property and forced the inhabitants towards the border.

Three weeks after the end of the war all Germans were expelled from Brno and brought to the Austrian border in the south. Russian soldiers refused them entry on orders to await a joint decision by the Allied forces about the fate of all displaced people in Europe. The Germans had to walk back to Brno, by now so weakened that many died of dysentery on the way. Because of the high number of casualties the survivors named the event the Brno Death March. Czechs who did not agree with the violence and had sympathy for these civilians had to be careful not to become objects of hate themselves.

In the absence of a clear decision by the politicians, some Ukrainians and Poles considered returning to their countries by themselves, either by rail or by foot. They were disheartened to find out that rail traffic for civilians had been suspended and those desperate to go home had to do so on foot. Some of these started their journey immediately; many others however were quite reluctant to go home to a Soviet satellite state. Some Ukrainians had seen the Germans as liberators from Bolshevik rule and even though they soon realised that they had merely exchanged one dictatorship for another, they were still unhappy to go back to what they perceived as their old oppressors back in control. A large number of the inhabitants on the farm – which had turned into something more resembling a big camp by now - were happy to stay in Czechoslovakia, if only the Allies and the locals would let them.

Alma and Jonah were almost enjoying their time in the camp. After twice hiding in dark basements for long periods of time they were pleased to be out in the fresh air and not having to hide any more. The place was guarded by soldiers and there was no forced labour or hunger – as there was in the camps for the German prisoners.

Alma befriended a young woman, Halyna, the mother of two children who had been taken away from her by the Germans. She was desperate to find out what had happened to them but neither Czechs nor Russians were particularly forthcoming with help. Halyna had worked herself into a state of hysteria in the year since her children had gone missing, trying to convince herself that they were living happily with a German family somewhere as had been rumoured to have happened at the later stages of the war in an attempt to repopulate the country with Aryan looking children. As disgusting as this thought was to her, it was preferable to the idea of her children being experimented on in one of the death camps like Terezin.

People on the farm had started to avoid her because of her uncontrolled and continuous whining. Jonah and Alma, with their experience in dealing with Wilma, were perfectly suited to her as friends.

With her gentle and loving manner Alma was able to help Halyna sit out her panic attacks and anxiety. Once calmed, the Ukrainian woman was able to talk sensibly about her fears and become more pragmatic about her situation. Halyna was grateful for the attention and Alma, in turn, was happy to have a project to take her mind off her own uncertain future.

Jonah and Alma cherished the blossoming friendship because they too had been isolated from the rest of the community on the farm. Even though Jonah's family had come from the Ukraine he was quite visibly Jewish, which for many of them was a good enough reason to avoid him. Tsarist Russia had seen several violent waves of anti-Semitism and the sentiment had not dramatically changed since. The farm camp held a lot of workers who had welcomed the German forces and had volunteered to leave their home and work in the west. The Nazis had been stopped but it was not the end of troubles for the Jews, as Jonah and his lover experienced regularly.

One day several military trucks arrived at the farm and Russian soldiers gestured for the residents of the camp to pack their belongings and get on the vehicles. Not trusting men in uniforms the people were scared to follow the orders as they associated such transports with deportation to death camps and once again being at the mercy of an unpredictable military power.

The hesitation irritated the soldiers and made them appear more brutal than they had been to begin with. Screams and panic spread across the crowd and one officer fired a warning shot into the air.

In the silence that followed he ordered the people around him onto the trucks and - resigned to their fate - the first few did as they had been told. Soon the transports were full and disappeared, leaving Jonah, Alma and Halyna behind with about thirty others.

"We will have to get away soon," Alma said in panic. "If we get sent to the Ukraine we will never get back to Bratislava and find Egon."

"If we could get past the guards we could walk to Bratislava. Maybe we can bribe someone to let us go," Jonah said hopefully.

"We are taking Halyna with us, aren't we?" asked Alma.

"Naturally. If only this place had a proper commander we could explain that we are Slovaks from Bratislava. It is ridiculous that we can't argue with anyone about this but have to accept whatever is decided on our behalf. Do we have anything we can use as a bribe? Maybe our wedding rings?" suggested Jonah. He had given Alma his late wife's wedding ring when they left the estate and it seemed a huge but probably necessary sacrifice for their freedom.

"Yes, I am afraid that is the only thing we have left that is worth anything. Let me try tonight. My Russian is better than yours and I think they always find women more difficult to refuse," Alma suggested.

"I am not sure about that. Please don't do anything silly. We don't even know where the trucks took them. Maybe there is some proper camp where all refugees are being kept," Jonah said.

That evening Alma approached the guard she considered the softest. He offered her a cigarette and showed her a picture of his young baby boy. Slowly she started to tell him about their situation and that they had no business in the Ukraine. The officer seemed to feel for their predicament but when Alma suggested he should let them out of the camp he refused her, saying he would not risk being reprimanded and possibly not seeing his son for her. Nothing could persuade him, no begging and no wedding rings. Defeated she returned to Jonah and Halyna, who suggested they should try to get away over the fence in the dark. The camp was not very well secured and she had seen some people escape before, even though they had been younger and quicker than Jonah.

While they were discussing this option another soldier came over to the three of them, ordered them to take their belongings and led them to the gate. Scared that they would now be punished for their attempt to bribe a Soviet soldier they followed his orders fearfully and prepared themselves to be taken away to an unknown fate. Instead of some cruel sadistic retribution however the guard offered them their freedom in exchange for the wedding rings. Apparently the first guard Alma had approached had told this other one about the incident and he did not possess the same scruples as his colleague. Shortly after midnight they were free and on their way to Bratislava. Jonah was so happy he kept jumping for joy during the walk; his mind had been fixated on the task of finding out about Egon and how to go about it.

They chose a route away from the main road to avoid being picked up by 'helpful' soldiers who might try and off-load them later into just another camp. Halyna's documents and her accent identified her as Ukrainian and Jonah and Alma would be considered the same by association. The couple had no passports on them and although they could prove their nationalities by local knowledge and language, this might not be of any use with foreign soldiers. Halyna would not part with her documents because she needed them to find and fight for her children. Jonah was very frustrated. Because of the detour the journey would take much longer. Both women warned him however never to become complacent in this chaos and always to err on the side of caution.

After a few days they reached Bratislava without any incidents and headed directly for Benedikt and Johanna's farm, which luckily was on their way into town anyway.

Jonah almost did not recognise the building when they got to it. Presumably in an act of revenge the family house had been set on fire and only its stone parts were still intact. The animals seemed to have been taken away as the huge stalls were completely empty. There were people out in the fields working, of whom some seemed to use German army trucks to bring in the harvest. Clearly Benedikt and Johanna were no longer living here but Jonah wondered if they had been kept on to work or if they had fled.

Alma approached two of the workers who she thought were speaking in Polish and asked them in German and in Russian if they knew what had happened to the owners of the farm. Assuming she was a relative trying to lay claim to the property they gestured for her to go away and shouted "confiscated". Scared that she might be mistaken for a German or a collaborator she left the scene. The three decided to try the workshop on Gajova to see if Egon had reappeared or if anyone there had heard from him.

The furniture shop that had once housed the old weaving home had also been vandalised. Jonah remembered that the new owners of the shop had been members of the Hlinka party and must have felt the wrath of retribution. As they were standing helpless and confused outside their old residence a neighbour came out on the street and walked up to Jonah.

"Aren't you the weaver?" he asked right out.

"Yes, I am," Jonah replied.

"Big mess that house," he said. "It is even worse inside. Everything has been broken. The husband has been executed on the main square on Benes's orders, the wife and children were made to watch, then they were taken away to a camp. Are you thinking of living here again?"

"No. It isn't mine and without my tools it would be a bit big just for me and my wife. I am trying to find out about my son. His name was Egon. Do you remember him?" Jonah asked. "Have you heard anything about him? Has he been here?"

"I sure remember him," said the neighbour pointedly. "He was a soldier wasn't he? Real proud!"

"Yes, he was with the army," Jonah said reluctantly. "I have not heard from him for a while. You wouldn't have seen him?"

The man leaned close into Jonah's shoulder and whispered:

"Sorry my friend, I know nothing about him. But let me warn you: Be very careful who you speak to. Benes and his men are running a retribution campaign against the Hlinka party and what they call the collaborators. He says the government was illegal and needs to be prosecuted. That is why the owner of the furniture shop was killed. If you mention that your son was a soldier you may not get any help from those who associate the Slovak army with the Hlinka guards. Your son looked particularly proud when he wore his uniform."

"It is funny," said Alma. "You had to join the Hlinka party to survive the war without problems - even if you didn't want anything to do with them - and now that very party affiliation can cost you everything if you are unlucky."

"Yes!" agreed the old man. "It is a real witch hunt out there, so be careful. Fortunately Benes has unknowingly chosen many of the old guards to execute his plans for him. Some examples had to be set to satisfy his thirst for revenge – but now if you keep your head down you will be fine," he said with a wink. "I bet you must be proud of your son. I heard he was amongst the few who were selected to fight with the Germans."

"Oh I am! Very proud. I just wish I could find out what has happened to him!" said Jonah quickly, hating to play up to this fascist in order to keep his trust.

"I am sure the family who lived here would have told us if a letter had come from your son. They were very patriotic which is why the house is such a mess. I guess the survivors of that family are now in a labour camp in the north along with the Germans. God help them," the old man said. "You could ask the Svoboda's opposite. Maybe they know something. Just be careful: They were hiding a Jew in their loft, I think their dentist or something like that. They walk around all high and mighty now. Ask, but be careful what you say."

"I could always claim to be a Jew myself!" said Jonah in a joking tone.

The old man burst into laughter. "Good one! Best of luck. Now do you want me to tell your son anything if I do see him?"

"Yes, tell him I am looking for him. Tell him to leave word with you where he is. Once I have found a place to stay I will let you know where he can find me. Maybe I will try and stay at the workshop while I am waiting. I will let you know if I do. Thank you. You are a life saver," Jonah said.

"Don't mention it. Hard times ahead for us good people, we need to stick together," said the old man and disappeared back into his house.

Jonah went over to the Svobodas and knocked on their door. A young woman with a baby on her arm came to the door. She looked him up and down and then at the two women with him before she even greeted him and then she asked him abruptly what he wanted. He explained about his son being missing and asked her if she had heard anything.

"Wasn't your son a soldier?" she asked.

"Yes he was. Drafted," Jonah replied.

"We were against the war and the Germans. Why would I help you find someone who murdered innocent people?" she said, but she didn't slam the door in his face as he would have expected from her tone.

Jonah pointed at his face and said: "I heard you were hiding people from the Nazis. Well look at me closely and have a think if I am really a collaborator with the Hitler regime. I am a Jew and so is

277

my son. His joining the army saved us from certain death. His being a soldier was our alibi. I beg you to tell me if you have heard anything about him."

"I am afraid I can't help you. We had to keep to ourselves during the war and not attract any attention. We avoided you because of your son and we did the same to the people that came after you. We would not have heard anything and we certainly would not have thought it noticeable if a soldier came to their door. I am very sorry for you, but I have to go inside and feed this little bastard. Best of luck."

With that she closed the door.

"Well we better go back to the farm now and see if we can find out anything about Johanna," said Jonah. "Now that we came this far I can't just stop."

"You need to rest, and so do we!" said Alma in disagreement.

"We can sleep some other time. We can find a new place some other time. Everything can wait, but not this. I am not wasting a single moment more," said Jonah with determination.

"If it is bad news it certainly could wait another day!" Halyna added to the discussion. "I think we better wait."

There was no holding back Jonah and reluctantly the two women followed his lead back out of town. Alma's ankle had started to play up again over the last couple of days but she saw how desperate Jonah was in his quest and so she kept it to herself. He was too obsessed to notice her slight limp and hopefully after today there would be no more long journeys.

When they were near the burnt out farm building Alma went to speak to the people on the neighbouring farms to see if she could at least find Sarah and her family. Once she had discovered what had become of her Jewish friend she could investigate the rest of the farm more easily. She left Jonah and Halyna behind in a small forest at the edge of grazing fields and limped away, cursing her swollen ankle. Halyna was exhausted and fell asleep on the soft moss, while Jonah paced nervously up and down the entire time his lover was gone.

Several hours later Alma returned, not smiling but bringing some potatoes and bread with her, which Halyna immediately grabbed and devoured.

Alma had not found out much at all. One Slovak farmer had told her to go to hell when she mentioned Benedikt and Johanna but she had spoken to a servant girl on a different farm, who had seen the mob that had gone to Benedikt's farm, set the farm on fire and had hanged the former minister from a tree outside the house.

Only after a few days when the body started to smell did someone cut the rope. It had been rumoured that the body had been fed to the pigs but nobody had actually seen it happen. The farm animals had been split between the other farms, as had all equipment. Johanna had been spared because one of the slave workers on the farm had stood up for her and praised her for the way she had helped the Jews before they had been deported. He spoke animatedly how Johanna had taken her maid Sarah under her wings and how she had settled a dispute amongst the workers in favour of the Jewish people. Johanna had come under the protection of a former rivalling neighbour and now worked in his kitchen but the girl had not been able to tell Alma where exactly that farm was.

Jonah was too excited that night to sleep but Alma was exhausted from all the walking and emotionally drained. With the first beams of sunlight he woke up Alma and Halyna and urged them to hurry. The women were now really feeling the strain they had been under since leaving the camp in Brno and found it hard to order their bodies to obey. Together, slowly, they made their way from farm to farm until they finally found Johanna. Her new Slovak boss was clearly besotted with his new cook – despite her obvious lack of expertise in this area of house work – and he was happy for her to receive visitors.

"I can't tell you how much I have missed you!" Johanna said to Alma. "Since you disappeared I have felt completely alone. They killed my Benedikt. Hanged him outside our house. Can you believe it? Before you left the Gestapo took Sarah to Poland. After that I couldn't risk visiting you anymore and then the Countess came and said you were all leaving the manor house for France. I prayed that you would be safe. I am so glad you are alive! What brought you back so quickly?"

"We never made it to France!" Alma told her. "It was a close call a couple of times but here we are. Back home. Thank God you are alive."

"What about your girls?" Jonah asked her.

"Maria was shot," Johanna told him without much emotion. "Do you remember when the Germans brought in the army to deal with the rebels during the uprising last year? Well, the little floozy went with one of those Nazi officers. She was head over heels in love with him apparently. A stunning looking man I must admit but he had a reputation for cruelty. People on the street said that he was an utterly sadistic pig. His unit retreated when the Red Army approached Brno and we haven't seen him since, of course. The locals never forgave her for the connection with him. She died the night they came to our house and burnt it down. First they hung Benedikt, simple and quick, but when it came to her they took their time. Someone ripped her clothes off, they cut off her hair and then they beat her mercilessly. They spat on her, shouted at her. Then one man took out his gun and shot her in the head."

"Oh that is terrible, Johanna." said Alma.

"Oh she was still lucky," came the outrageous reply. "They have done much worse to women who went with Germans and they could have gone on for longer if the guy had not ended it for her with his gun."

"I am not sure lucky is the right word," Halyna disagreed.

"How about Roswitha?" Alma asked quickly.

"Roswitha was in the field when the army pushed north and came past our area. We have not seen her since. I don't know whether I should hope for her sake that she is dead or still alive. Skirts and gold is all they can think of. Not very good communists are they! Very greedy."

Alma was sorry to hear all this bad news but was amazed how easy Johanna seemed to take all of it. These events had only taken place several weeks ago and already it sounded as if her friend had accepted the new circumstances and had made her peace with it.

"You seem to be coping well," she said, voicing here thoughts.

"I have to, Alma. I survived and I have fallen on my feet. I am safe here. I might even become another farmer's wife but not with a miserable face and red eyes from crying. I mustn't dwell on what has happened but doesn't mean I don't have feelings," said Johanna.

"It seems a little quick to have come to terms with so much death and uncertainty around you," said Jonah.

"Well that is the way it is," Johanna said defiantly.

"We are just concerned for you, that's all!" Alma tried to clarify.

"What about you?" asked Johanna, turning the focus away from herself.

"We took Wilma, Greta and Ernst across the border on their way to Paris but decided to separate from them and wait in Brno for the end of the war. Now we have come back to find Egon. Tell us, have you heard from him at all?" Jonah finally got to ask.

"I am afraid I haven't," was the disappointing answer. "I am so sorry but don't worry. It is going to take some time before everyone in the world gets home from where they are now. I am not going anywhere and if you have been able to find me, then so will he. My own children Roswitha and Gunter could come back any day. We just have to wait. Where are you going to live?"

"We don't know," replied Jonah. "I am not sure I will be able to make a living with my carpets. I have to find some other occupation." Jonah said. "My looms are still somewhere in the manor house anyway," he added.

"The manor house is now a quarter for the Soviet army," Johanna informed him. "You could go there and ask for your belongings back."

"Oh I would not want to draw any attention to my former connections with the Countess, especially not where the Communist Army is concerned. That will have to wait until they are leaving and our society is back to normal," Jonah said.

"Could you return to the workshop in town?" Johanna asked.

"I doubt it," Anna replied. "The place is totally devastated. We went there yesterday and it is completely inhospitable."

"Did it get hit by the bombs?" Johanna asked.

"No, by vandalism. The new owner ran a furniture shop there, but there is not a single piece left now. He was a Hlinka politician according to the neighbours and was executed in the main square," Alma said.

"Oh I think Benedikt knew him," Johanna said. "We bought a dining table from him. Well, I always warned Benedikt about this party business but he didn't want to listen."

"Have you ever heard from Karl and Wilhelm again?" asked Jonah.

"Not for some time. Wilhelm was drafted and sent to Norway. He should still be alive but we have not had any letters from that side of the family for a few months. Berlin has been bombed into the ground I expect. It would be a miracle if they survived," Johanna said coldly, as if she was talking about a novel rather than real people.

"Whatever happened to Karl?" Jonah reluctantly enquired.

"If I read the code in their letters correctly he was adopted by another Winkelmeier family who claimed it was their neighbour's orphaned son. He was sent to the countryside along with most of Berlin's children," she said.

"So he might be orphaned again and living with strangers?" Jonah suggested.

"Yes, that is possible," Johanna admitted.

"In that case we have to find him, too," Jonah said excitedly.

"Yes we do. I will write to Berlin as soon as there is a postal service again. Jaro, my new boss here, has already said he will help me," Johanna said.

"You seem more concerned for Karl than for your own children," observed Halyna cynically but Johanna seemed to take no offence.

"My children were hard work. I hated being their mother," she admitted. "Karl was like a grandchild to me, I absolutely adored him. I guess I am better use as a grandmother than a mother. It takes all sorts."

Johanna asked her boss and admirer to let the three of them stay at the farm. Jaro was happy to fulfil any wish of his attractive new kitchen maid and said he could do with some extra help on the farm if she wanted them to stay, at least until the end of the harvest season in autumn.

The Russians had already begun to return displaced people from the east to their original home in the Soviet satellite states. This was bound to start in Slovakia soon as well. All Germans – with the exception of some indispensable ones – would be sent away too. There could be a shortage of labour before long.

Alma was relieved about Jaro's generous offer. At Jonah's advanced age it would have been difficult to find someone willing to employ him. Now they would have Jaro testifying that they were neither Germans nor Ukrainians who had to be deported. Only Halyna would have to be hidden in case of a search.

Jonah was delighted to have found a safe place so near Bratislava. He decided to go back to Gajova right away and leave word with his former neighbours for Egon. Alma urged him to have a rest today but once again there was no stopping him. "The heart wants what the heart wants!" he told her.

On the way to Bratislava he started to feel very short of breath and suffered a dizzy spell that almost made him faint. He briefly sat down but the fatherly duty he felt towards his son urged him soon again on his way. He arrived at the former workshop late in the afternoon and went straight to the old neighbour to inform him of his new circumstances. Nobody answered to his knocking but the door was ajar and so Jonah went inside, making his arrival known by shouting "Hello!" and "I am coming in!"

He could only see one open door in the hallway, carefully approached it and glanced into the unlocked room. The neighbour who had only yesterday congratulated himself for having been spared by the retribution activities was hanging by a rope from the ceiling. Someone had painted a swastika on his forehead. Jonah's heart sank. Not because of the shock – he had seen many dead people in Brno and on the way to Bratislava. Almost bereft of sympathy for the executed fascist he was sad that the one person who was most likely to pass on a message to his son had been killed. He felt a short spasm in his chest and had to double over to ease the pain but as quickly as the pain had begun it also disappeared.

Jonah went over to the Svoboda house and knocked. This time a different woman opened the door, presumably the grandmother of the little child from yesterday. He explained his situation to her and told her where Egon could find him should he show up.

The woman nodded without indicating that she had understood or was willing to help. Just as she was about to close the door Jonah told her about the body in the house next door.

"Thank you. I will make sure they take him down before it smells," she said and then shut the door quickly.

Somewhat dissatisfied with his mission and worried that his son might not get the information he stepped into the workshop and deposited a letter he had written for Egon. On the way home he kept feeling faint and dizzy and had to stop several times. Tomorrow he would take Alma's advice and have a day of rest – assuming Jaro would allow him to.

Johanna and Alma were very relieved when he returned unharmed and served him some dinner.

"You look pale," Johanna commented. "You must eat. Jaro has big plans for you this week. Since you worked with mechanical looms he thinks you will be an engineering genius."

"Do you think he will grant me a rest day? I feel rather exhausted after all the walking," he asked.

"Now don't be ungrateful. You have no papers, you speak Slovak with an accent, and you would be wild game on the streets of Bratislava. He took you in regardless. Now don't disappoint him," Johanna scolded him.

"Of course, you are right. I am being silly," Jonah replied.

That night he dreamt about his son. Egon had both hands tied up behind his back and was led through a dark underground labyrinth by a German and a Russian soldier. The march seemed never to end and was following a narrow path between two stony walls. Jonah felt his heart tighten in panic as he followed them at a safe distance. Suddenly the German soldier opened a door ahead of him and the three of them stepped onto a sunlit market square where a group of enraged onlookers waited for them. To the left side of the door was a pyre, on the right side stood a scaffold with a rope. Egon was positioned exactly between those two while the German officer walked towards the pyre and the Russian towards the hanging beams. Suddenly he saw the Countess approaching the shouting and threatening crowd, addressing them in Czech:

"My dear citizen, I am in a pickle here. My left arm wants to burn this creature for the Jew that he is. My right arm wants to hang him for the war crimes he committed. I am miserable because I can only do one or the other. I ask you citizens, which one shall it be?"

The people shouted back at her "The rope!", "The pyre!", "Hang him!", "Burn him!"

"You are of no help to me today. We have to find a compromise. I am going to stab him for being a liar," she said calmly, pulling out a knife. She apologised to the blood thirsty soldiers and walked towards Egon.

"No!" shouted Jonah and charged towards his son. He got there in time to step between Egon and the Countess and just before the blade could pierce his heart he woke up covered in sweat.

He could not go back to sleep, trying to make sense of his dream. His late wife Barbara had always told him to take dreams seriously and to search for their meanings. Seeing the almost death of his son was too much to even imagine. Egon had to be alive. This dream could not be about his son, it was about the Countess.

Why had she appeared as a murderess when she was the one

who had helped Jonah all through the war? Where was all this coming from? As he tossed and turned Johanna woke up several times and feeling guilty for disrupting her sleep he left the barn and went for a walk.

After he had walked a short distance away from the building he felt another dizzy spell and tumbled to the floor. His heart felt as if it was being held and crushed by iron pliers. Panic ridden he tried to crawl back to the barn and call for Alma but his strength left him and as the life ebbed out of him he realised how weak he really was. His determination to find Egon had kept him going beyond the capabilities of his fragile old body and now that he had done everything he could to make contact with his missing son, it was time to pay the price. Before his mind's eye he saw his late wife standing in front of him and heard her say: "Come along now. You have done enough. Now let the others finish what you have started. Come here. We have been waiting for you! You are free to go!" Only then did he notice another two figures standing next to his wife: The Countess and Egon. He turned around one more time towards the barn where Alma was still fast asleep, then he stood up and ran towards his family in the hereafter.

By the time Alma found her lover in the morning the body was already cold. Halyna held her friend and let her shed her silent tears. After only a short while Alma pulled herself together, covered Jonah with a blanket and went to the main house to tell Johanna.

"Oh my God!" exclaimed her friend when she heard the news. "My poor darling. Come here!" and she hugged Alma for a little while, then she broke free and said: "Well, he reached a good age all things considered. It is almost a miracle he made it this long."

"He was fine. If only he hadn't set his mind on rushing back and forth between Bratislava and here in this heat and all in one day. No wonder his heart gave up," Alma complained.

"Maybe it was for the better," Johanna commented. "If something has happened to Egon – and we must assume that it has – he was spared finding out about it. Losing your child is horrible. When they killed my Maria it was worse than I could ever have imagined. If only I had not seen it. It was worse than when they killed Benedikt. I am glad I don't know what has happened to my other children. If they are dead I would prefer not to know. At least I

285

can cling to the hope that they have found happiness somewhere else and I am a strong and cool headed person. Imagine Jonah going through the same ordeal."

"You are certainly right there. He could not have taken it," Alma agreed.

"Then there are Greta and Wilma, on their way to Paris. He doesn't have to worry about them any more either. I think it was a blessing dying quickly in the middle of the night. I hope that is the way I go eventually," Johanna continued her insensitive evaluation of the death.

Alma realised that when it came to talking about loss, Johanna was not the best person to choose as a partner. She went back outside and sat with Jonah for a while, until Jaro joined her with one of his helpers and put the body in a grave behind the pear trees.

"I wish we had some Jewish people here to say the Kaddish for him!" said Alma with regret. "He did not believe in it all that much but it was his culture if nothing else. It feels wrong to just bury him like this."

"There are a few more Jews in the ground next to him already!" Jaro told her. "We hid seventeen of them under the cow shed. They are gone now but two of them died of natural causes. I am sure they will sing the Kaddish for him," he said. "Don't worry about that."

"Did you know a girl called Sarah?" she asked the Slovak farmer.

"Yes, I knew the family. Her father and I argued all the time about the boundaries and stupid things but then we made up and celebrated the harvest together. They should have gone into hiding when they could but they were desperate to hold on to their farm so they missed their chance."

"Do you know what happened to them after their arrest? Have you heard anything?" Alma dared to ask even though she did not expect to hear good news.

"I am afraid not. After the uprising President Tiso sent most of our Jews to Poland to be killed. I have always thought that since all of them arrived there so late in the war, most of them must have survived. The more time passes since the liberation the more I doubt that the Russians came quickly enough to save them. Nobody knows. It has been a few weeks and nobody has come back. I hope they are amongst the survivors. Some never return to their homes but go on to Palestine or New York."

"I wish I knew. She was a great woman." Alma said.

"Johanna thinks so too. You and my cook were good friends I hear. What would you suggest I do to make her my wife? She is so beautiful, it kills me. She knows farm work, she is perfect. I know I am not much to look at and not the youngest either but I have a good heart. She seems to like me but then I am not sure. What do you say?"

"It is a bit too soon to think about these things. Her husband and daughter only died a little while ago, she will need time," Alma suggested.

"I know. It is just that I am so smitten with her. She certainly has her charms despite her grief," Jaro said laughingly. "Do you think she will take me at all?"

"You better move slowly and carefully with her!" Alma advised him, "I can let you in on a little secret: She already thinks of your farm as her new home. She is not the romantic type, so don't expect a miracle. In time I am certain she will accept your proposal and it won't come as a surprise; a blind man can tell that you are in love with her."

"Oh God!" Jaro laughed relieved. "I guess subtlety is not my strength."

"Will you allow me to plant another tree on top of the grave as a secret memorial?" Alma asked.

"Anything you like, my dear. I am so sorry for you. I hope you will stay with us on the farm to keep my Johanna company." he said with a wink.

"I would love to."

The first few days after Jonah's death seemed never ending and Alma was glad that there was a lot of hard work to be done in the fields. It tired her physically so much that she managed to forget about her grief at least a few times each day. Halyna with her own worries and sadness was a godsend because it allowed Alma to direct her mental energy on to other things instead of just stewing in self-pity.

Jonah would never have wanted her to break down over this and would have told her to keep the focus on her own life and the present. Finding Halyna's children would be difficult if not impossible.

287

Neither the army nor the authorities were in a position yet to reunite separated families or even to gather the relevant information. They would have to hold out here for a little bit longer before their search could begin and be successful. On the other hand the Soviets were rushing the re-homing of the displaced people from the east, a workforce on which the local farmers like Jaro had relied upon of late.

The thought of losing Halyna as well was simply too painful for Alma to address at all and they failed to take precautions. There was a sense of false security amongst the workers who knew how important they were for the farmers, factories and the economy, especially once all Germans would be expelled. They were mentally not prepared for the rigid and dogmatic way in which the deportations were going to be carried out.

Only two days after Jonah had died military trucks arrived at the farm and Soviet soldiers rounded up everyone they thought to be of eastern European nationality. Jaro tried to intervene and save some of his workforce but the officers were following orders and whoever could not produce satisfactory papers or had aroused the suspicion of the soldiers was loaded onto the trucks. Halyna and Alma both were taken away and brought to an old school building near the station in Bratislava.

One high ranking officer sat on a table in the middle of the school yard with three interpreters and one by one the prisoners were interviewed about their origins, their place of birth, names of local politicians and landmarks. Most people trying to hide their nationality failed quickly but others had been better prepared and they managed to fool their interrogators. According to the findings by the four examiners everyone was escorted to a different part of the school building.

Halyna failed the test to pass herself off as a local and she was ushered towards a group of women right by the end of the courtyard, without the chance to say goodbye to her friend. Worried about what may become of Halyna in her mental state if left alone, Alma decided that she had nothing left to lose and tried to get on the same transport as Halyna, claiming to be from the same village in the Ukraine as her friend.

The examining officers knew that she was lying but wanted to know why. Instead of being sent to join her friend Alma was kept

288

behind with other prisoners who had escaped the deportation. She had to spend the night in a small sports hall, sleeping on the naked floor. From her fellow inmates she learned that she was amongst the women suspected to be enemies of the state and that her situation was very serious. Alma would be re-examined by a specialist inspector who got to decide if she would be sent to a gulag or somewhere else.

When she asked if anyone knew what would happen to the people that were kept in the yard corner she was informed that these prisoners had been selected for the first train home. By the time it was her turn to meet the next inspector she had already missed the train Halyna was on. So she told the truth, hoping to be released and to be allowed to return to Jaro and Johanna. Sadly this time no one believed her either and fed up with what appeared to be a waste of his time the special agent dealing with her decided to transfer her to a camp in Siberia. No pleading and arguing helped her cause and she found herself on an eastbound train the very next day.

Even on the train, crowded in and surrounded by people already resigned to their fate, she could not believe her misfortune after all the trials and dramas that she had survived. Prisoners on the train related horrific tales about the gulag life ahead of her, yet her main worry was with Halyna. Not only was the poor woman alone under people who might not be sympathetic to her mental condition but she might never be able to return and look for her kidnapped children.

Had Alma told the truth at the tribunal from the beginning she might have had at least a chance to stay behind and execute that task for her friend. Her own life did not matter much to her any more now that Jonah had passed. She would never meet her friend Johanna again and she had let down her Ukrainian friend - and all in vain. For the first time since the beginning of her life in Slovakia she felt completely powerless and drained of all energy. She spent her time in the train compartment in withdrawn isolation and sleep - as much as that was possible.

Chapter 12: Summer 1945 - The Camp

Edith and Esther's roommates were a difficult bunch. Directly next to the two ladies on their left a German woman had settled in with her two young children and she frequently looked at Esther with suspicion. There were rumours amongst the Germans that Czech and Jewish spies had infiltrated the camp to pick out who were regarded as the worst offenders and war criminals. How else could one explain that nobody had been questioned and no distinction had been made between the prisoners so far? There was deep mistrust between everyone.

Ernst spoke German with an accent, so the trio must have seemed a little dubious to their roommates. The suspicious woman's name was Gerlinde and she had a hard time keeping her sons, Heinrich and Adolf, away from Ernst. The three boys were of a similar age and immediately took a liking to each other. Despite all circumstances they saw the camp more like a summer holiday than an imprisonment.

Ernst was very happy to finally have playmates his own age while the two German boys were relieved simply to get away from their mother, who was constantly telling them off. Gerlinde seemed a lot more bitter than anyone else. During the first few days in the camp, whenever she had to go somewhere, she ordered her sons specifically not to speak to anyone and to wait quietly for her return; the second she was gone however they rushed over to play with Ernst.

Edith found out from the little boys that Gerlinde had been the wife of a high ranking SS officer from Dresden who had been 'killed by the hands of some dirty Bolshevik pig' in Russia. After the air raids had set the city on fire, Gerlinde was homeless and decided to take to the road. Once the widow realised that her story was known she allowed the children to play together but she still kept a distance from everyone. Within the hut community she seemed to trust only one other person, a young woman called Irmingard, who had been engaged to a soldier named Ralph who was missing since 1943.

Irmingard was much friendlier towards her inmates than her confidante but Edith and Esther found it hard to establish warm relations with her. Having given her heart to a proud and elegant soldier true to the Reich, Irmingard refused to accept the end of what she had naively considered the golden age of Germany. She was not educated enough to have a proper grasp of the Nazi ideology and all its implications, but she had been drawn towards the imagery and the rhetoric and refused to believe any of the 'evil and hateful propaganda' that was now directed against the Nazis.

Six years ago she had made a commitment to Ralph and the Fuhrer and had patiently waited for the best part of her youth: For victory, for the occasional home visits of her lover from the front or for the birth of a child, which would be her ultimate gift to the only two worthwhile men in her life. She too had heard rumours about spies within the camp and had sworn to Gerlinde to be careful with whom she discussed politics but in her loneliness and pain she easily got carried away and voiced, or rather repeated, the party slogans about races and the European war without noticeable inhibitions. The two Nazi women had soon made such a name for themselves that even those who agreed with them kept their distance for fear that undercover officers were listening in.

Irmingard and Gerlinde often whispered to each other even when they were alone, the former always hopeful and naïve, the latter usually in a foul mood and in need of a little cheering up.

"You must not despair, Gerlinde. Your husband died for a good cause. He was a hero who died with honour," Irmingard once tried to reassure her ally.

"I know all that," was the abrupt reply. "That is no good to me now. I have two children to feed and I will have to start from square one. We don't even know where we will end up after this prison. God knows what they have in mind for us!"

"No, you must not give in to fear. This is all just a temporary setback. I believe that the Fuhrer is not really dead," Irmingard continued. "He is still alive and is forming another German army as we speak, to liberate us from the shame of occupation. Do you know how many of us in the Sudetenland voted for Henlein? Two thirds! Can you imagine! There have to be many more potential soldiers in this country, just waiting to hit back. They call them the German Werewolves, and the Czechs are scared of them. It is only a matter of time! The German prisoners in Russia will overpower their guards and march to Moscow. We are a strong nation and we will not be beaten. You must not believe what we are being told over here. Just remember how far the Reich has stretched across Europe. It can't just shrivel to the size of a peanut and stay that way. It is not in the nature of our race to give in. We are a huge nation and we need all that space, we deserve it. We will overcome our enemies in the end."

"Oh you make me laugh with your ideas," Gerlinde said cynically. "For crying out loud, Irmingard, we are detained in a camp by Czechs and Russians. The Reich is over."

"No it is not!" Irmingard insisted. "You must not believe what they are telling us. Maybe this is a setback but our Fuhrer has planned everything through to the end, of that, I am as certain as I can be. Just think of all the Russians, Poles and Jews that your husband has killed. How many children these men and women might have had? This is far from over, believe me."

"They killed my husband too, I don't know what I should be hoping for now!" Gerlinde said with bitterness in her voice.

"Thank your lucky stars that he already gave you two amazing boys who will take his place. They will help repopulate this country and make it once again a force to be reckoned with. That is why Hitler encouraged us to have children. If only I had been so lucky myself. Not that we didn't try," Irmingard carried on.

"I don't know about what is coming for us Germans but I sure as hell do not regret a single shot my husband fired," said Gerlinde with a sinister tone in her voice. "I despise the Jews and the Slavs and I cannot bear to see their faces all smug and superior. It is quite disgusting to think that those evil and inferior bastards have triumphed and are allowed to rule the world. If it was not for them there would not have even been a war."

"They will get what they deserve." Irmingard said.

"My husband came here once after the Czechs assassinated their German leader Heydrich, who used to be a good friend of our family, a great man, and a credit to our race. My husband Wolfgang asked to be transferred to participate in the revenge, until they needed him in Russia. May the bastard who shot him rot in hell."

"I hope so too," Irmingard agreed.

Edith had coincidentally overheard this conversation. Esther had taken Ernst for a walk but Edith felt too depressed to join them, still convinced that all of her friends could be free if only she had been more careful. As she was wallowing in her guilt, she had fallen asleep and woke up to the whispers of the malicious women. She was chilled to her bone that even after the fall of the evil Reich, people could be so hateful and ignorant. Even if one believed only half the stories that were told about the concentration camps, it was enough for any decent human being to distance themselves from the system that had allowed such atrocities. How these two women could hold on to their hateful ideology was beyond her comprehension but then again so was most that she had witnessed during the war years.

Maybe it was naïve to expect those convictions to vanish altogether along with the leadership and on hearing Gerlinde and Irmingard she could somehow understand the Czechs and their blind rage a little better. Most of the inmates here, fortunately, seemed pleased that the war was over and with it the terrors that the Nazi regime had brought to their country.

Another concern for some ethnic Germans was the sudden rift from the Czechs whom they had considered their fellow citizens. Unlike those prisoners who had been born in the Reich itself, the Sudetenlanders in Czechoslovakia had been part of the Austro-Hungarian Empire for centuries, and had not defined themselves by their language or culture alone but also to a large extent by a shared history and affiliation to first, the crown in Vienna, and later, to the government in Prague. They might not have been the same race or people by ideology but they shared a love for the same country in which they had lived peacefully together. Edith felt their pain but when she heard hateful opinions like the ones Gerlinde and Irmingard had just exchanged she could better appreciate why the government wanted to get rid of any Germans regardless.

She wanted to confront these horrible women but then thought better of it. She did not want to be a target for angry Nazi women in a camp where she had few friends. But she felt ashamed for keeping quiet. She knew that her desire for survival in this camp was poor justification for her lack of action but the war had made her feel powerless against trigger happy Nazis.

"One woman cornered me yesterday and told me that I would have to rename my sons," Gerlinde continued with rage in her voice. "She said it was a disgrace to run around the camp and shout Adolf or Heinrich. I could not believe my ears."

"What did you say?" asked Irmingard.

"I said that my children were used to those names now and that would have to be the end of it. She gave me a long speech about the shame of our Nation and our duty to make amends. I pretended to agree only to get her off my back. Think of all the people that named their children after Hitler and Himmler. Should we call them all Anton and Herbert instead? That is absurd!" Gerlinde exclaimed.

"You should have told her where to go," suggested her friend.

"I would have but then I thought: If that cow informs on me, she would have won and I would have sacrificed myself for nothing; only for an argument. I won't do her that favour. That is all she wants. She couldn't possibly care what my sons are called."

After that conversation, Edith and Esther were even more on guard with Gerlinde but fortunately they had very little interaction with her and tended to meet up with Greta and Wilma.

The Weissensteiner sisters were a little luckier with the company in their hut. The woman who had so generously invited them in was one of many who claimed to have been selected for this camp by a complete mistake. Her name was Evka; she was Czech and accused of being a collaborator. She told the two sisters in lengthy detail about the ordeal of her arrest and its background.

Her problems had begun when she had fallen out with her best friend over a man. Evka and her friend Ludmila were in their thirties and had been considered old spinsters. They shared a small flat in Pilsen and worked together at the same factory. Both women fell for the same man, a middle aged Latvian, who at first, flirted with both women at the factory but then focused his attentions on Ludmila. Soon after that the man moved in and Evka was told by her friend to look for her own place to give the love birds some privacy.

Their friendship had never recovered from this episode but Evka swore she had no ill feelings towards the couple. When the Soviets came to collect the Latvian man to return him to his now Soviet home state, Ludmila was convinced it had been Evka who informed on them, in revenge for being rejected. Evka's effort to reassure Ludmila of her innocence was fruitless and one night, shortly after their last argument about the lover's deportation, someone painted a red swastika on Evka's door. She could not wash it off easily and a dark shadow remained on the door where the symbol had been. Later that day she was collected at the factory by two Czech soldiers and put into prison, together with other Czechs who were under suspicion of being collaborators. With not even the remotest of connections to the Nazis, Evka was sure the misunderstanding would be cleared up in no time but there never was a trial. One of the prison guards told her that there would never be a trial. There was a reliable witness report and she would be expelled with the Germans as soon as a time for it had been agreed by the politicians. She broke into tears and pleaded repeatedly that this was a lie. The guard told her to thank her lucky stars for being in prison rather than on the street.

Evka hated being in the same boat as Germans and Czechs who had helped the Nazis. She did not want to be associated with any of them. When Greta and Wilma asked to take up the spare bunks, Evka took a shine to these women and invited them in. It was a welcome change to have people staying who had a problem beyond the political situation. She hoped it would help her to shift her focus from the injustice that was being done to her and to distance herself from the collaborators and Nazis.

The sisters were mainly interested in keeping a low profile and had little to do with her. Other Czech women in the camp often winked at Evka when they heard her accent, implying co-conspiracy and solidarity, which upset her tremendously. She had hoped an association with two outsiders would free her of such attentions but neither she nor the Weissensteiners were so lucky. There was more interest in Greta and Wilma than one would have thought. A variety of women entered their hut during the first week, some to assure themselves that what Wilma was suffering from was not contagious, whereas others came to ask probing questions about their background.

Greta did not volunteer any more information than was absolutely necessary. In some cases it was obvious that the aim of the social calls was to find out whether Wilma was Jewish or not, but it was not necessarily clear why the visitors wanted to know. They could be Nazis or Jews themselves, who were merely looking for other members of the 'tribe'.

On the truck many had claimed to be mistaken for Germans because of their names. If those people really were Jewish they had reason to be careful. They had to find their kind without attracting too much attention from Germans who might be part of a Nazi resistance group. On the other hand, those women asking questions could easily be Nazis still looking for the Jews amongst them.

Evka was resourceful and stepped in whenever Greta was not at ease with the nosy and intrusive visitors. She would quickly turn the questions around at the ones who had asked them, putting them into the spotlight and interrogating them instead, something which seemed more difficult for Greta, who tried not to arouse suspicion. Evka would often tell her own story and disrupt the inquisitions that way.

Her interference kept the nosy people at bay, enemies and the three women became a bit of an island within their compound. Wilma took very much to Evka and liked the sound of her Czech accent, which she said reminded her of Bratislava and the good old days.

Edith and Esther had tried to trade places with some women in Greta's hut but to no avail. None of the women in either hut wanted to move.

Contrary to expectations, there was no forced labour in this camp. According to the rumours all detainees here were awaiting immediate deportation which still had to be cleared with the liberating armies. In many places, the civilians had enough of waiting and took matters in their own hands and marched their undesirable Germans to the borders themselves, using any force necessary to achieve compliance. Greta and her inmates could consider themselves lucky to have escaped those violent scenes which often occurred without even the slightest interference from police and militia.

After a week the mood had turned into doom and worry. Lack of distraction seemed to magnify all fears. One day, a large number of women, among them Irmingard and Gerlinde, were selected and escorted out of the camp, which seemed to confirm the rumours about spies and informers and added fuel to the fear and paranoia in the camp. None of the women that were arrested ever came back. As the current guardians for Ernst, Edith and Esther took on that role for Adolf and Heinrich as well. Quite naturally the poor boys were very distressed about their mother's unknown fate and easily came to the ladies for comfort.

Shortly after those unexpected arrests, a large number of armed civilians stormed the camp and informed the inmates that they were leaving Czechoslovakia within the hour. There was no interference

296

from the guards. In the ensuing panic and chaos of packing, Edith and Esther were unable to reach Greta and Wilma and ended up marching separately from their friends on their long way to a different refugee camp for Germans located just across the border in Bavaria.

Ernst was a little distressed to be going without his mother and aunt but the two ladies managed to calm him and the two other boys in their charge and distracted them by giving the departure a sense of adventure. Those efforts however were fruitless when the refugees had to pass a pile of corpses on their way. The bodies belonged to Jewish people and had been found in a shallow grave in the forest. German prisoners had been made to dig them back up and the Czech guards forced everyone to look at them while walking past the spot to remind them of the crimes that the Nazis had committed.

A crowd of onlookers shouted insults as the march progressed and even the more loud mouthed women from the camp fell into a heavy silence. Only after the procession had left the area did people start to talk again. Edith and Esther struggled to cheer up the children. Adolf wanted to know why those people by the road had been dead. Heinrich did not understand why people were shouting at them. Weren't they German, better than anyone else and supposed to be applauded rather than booed? Edith shushed them; this was not to be discussed in public. She knew better than to hold a moral lecture surrounded by such an unknown group of people. It would take a while to explain the facts of life to those boys and wash out the absurd ideology of their parents.

Esther asked Adolf and Heinrich for their favourite songs and, once they found some that were cheerful and sure not to offend anyone else on the march, they started to sing until the boys were exhausted and were happy to walk in silence.

Wilma was visibly shaking when they passed the corpses. Czechs had gathered to hurl their abuse at them. Tightly squeezed between Evka and Greta, she managed to keep herself together. Evka chanted Catholic prayers in Czech, which Wilma understood only little but the sound of the language and the rhythmic repetition soothed her enough to get through the ordeal. At that moment, Greta would not have been able to do this for her sister as her own fears were too great. Worries about Ernst and a possible panic attack of Wilma made her almost frozen.

She felt an immense relief after they had passed that scene without further problems and realised what a gem they had found in the resourceful Evka who was strong enough to support both sisters single-handedly. Since Evka had joined them, Greta noticed a return of her sister's more feisty and confident character traits and began to think of the problems as beatable. Passing those bodies without major difficulties with Wilma was a good sign.

As the march slowly progressed towards the border, some of the elderly and frail amongst the prisoners began to collapse by the road and some had to be left behind. A former German army lorry collected them and drove them across the border where they were quickly offloaded and left under supervision of soldiers whose purpose was only to make sure that nobody could slip back into the country. If someone died during the march their body was also thrown on the truck and dumped on the other side of the border.

The prisoners were attacked twice by groups of armed bandits who searched them for valuables but apart from shoes and minor items there was not much left to be taken. No one interfered on their behalf.

On the evening of the second day, the group finally reached the German border. The subdued quiet of the tired march was disturbed when one woman threw herself at the feet of the Czech guards and screamed, shouting she was a Jew and that she could not live with all these Germans. She begged to be allowed to stay and swore that a mistake had been made. The guards seemed surprised by the sudden outburst and were clearly considering what to do but as more people raised their hands to say they were Jewish too the wave of compassion ebbed away again and the guards just shook their heads.

An American soldier at the other side of the border gently helped the Jewish woman up and tried to speak to her in English but she obviously did not understand him. She clung to him as for dear life and the other refugees who had claimed to be Jewish joined them. The soldier had become the guardian for the Jews and those who pretended to be Jewish to be allowed to return to their country.

The American army had been informed that the Czechs from Pilsen were bringing a large number of prisoners across the border and waited to escort them to temporary accommodation at a former labour camp.

Greta heard many voices trying to persuade the guards as the prisoners passed the border but only one of the Czech guards was even bothered enough to reply to these pleadings. "If you were selected for expulsion then you can't be kosher," he called out to them. "Good riddance the lot of you!"

At their new 'home', the buildings were much larger than in the last camp and the barracks were equipped with more bunks per hut, but there was much less space between the beds. Greta thanked her faithful lucky star for Evka, who stayed with Wilma while she herself went to search for Ernst. She knew it would have been more sensible to wait until all the refugees had settled in but she could not stop herself.

During the march she had kept an eye out for him and his travel companions but her attempts had been futile. The guards had reprimanded her several times when she had tried to fall behind and join the next unit of the march. The camp was huge and the refugees tried to take advantage of this fact by spreading themselves out amongst the huts.

However, some buildings in their section were locked and guards had blocked off entire parts, allegedly to accommodate further arrivals that were expected soon. Fortunately Greta spotted Edith outside one of the huts, stormed past her without a word of hello and once inside she flew into her son's arms. There were still some bunks here for Greta, Evka and Wilma. At last the group was reunited.

Next to Evka was a Czech couple. The man had obviously been beaten, his face was bloody and one of his eyes was badly black and swollen. His wife was just lying on her bed staring quietly at the wall. Every so often, Greta could hear a little whimper and wondered what was making the woman so sad. The man tried to soothe her but it seemed unclear if his wife even heard him. When he noticed Evka's accent he started talking to her in Czech, which she stubbornly ignored. To be here in the camp he had to be a collaborator and Evka wanted nothing to do with him until she could be sure that he wasn't.

In the morning the wife seemed in a better state and Evka heard snippets of their conversation. From what she could gather the woman had been a piano teacher in Prague and her husband a civil servant. Both of them were lamenting the injustice they had suffered after the war. He kept saying that it had not been his fault and the wife seemed to agree. Evka was intrigued to find out more but still could not make herself talk to them.

Next to Edith at the other end was a proud and harsh looking woman with her younger sister. They were speaking German to each other. Hildegard, the older of the two, was frequently ranting about the jubilant Czechs to the impressionable Gudrun, who seemed not to mind that her sister kept repeating the same old monologue.

"I think they are despicable for calling themselves victims. They never had it better in their lives than under Hitler. None of them cowards had to fight, their economy was good, I don't know what they complain about," she told her sister. "For twenty years we were no longer part of a glorious Austrian Empire but lived as a minority and immigrants in their filthy inefficient republic. The fools turned their country into a mess. They have forgotten what it was like when they first became independent. What they did to us then was despicable. The land reform that advantaged the Czechs over the hard working and successful Austrian land owners. You don't hear them mention that. Now we Austrians count as Germans and are treated in the same way. Remember how in 1919 the Czech soldiers shot civilians who dared protest against the foundation of a Czechoslovak state? I hope the Russians swallow the country whole. That will teach them!"

"Exactly!" agreed Gudrun. "You are right, no one ever took revenge for what was done to us then. Only Hitler cared for us."

"He was too forgiving and generous!" Hildegard claimed. "He didn't harm one Czech civilian unless they were a criminal."

"Precisely. And what have we ever done to the Czechs that they get so aggressive now?" asked Gudrun. "We only fought against our enemies. The ones that behaved were left alone, weren't they?"

"I guess we showed them how useless they were. They are not achieving people. You will see, they won't know what to do with all our land and the property they have stolen from us. Give it a year and the country will be crying for us to come back and help them out. I never employed Czechs in my bakery because they were so lazy and inefficient. God knows what they will do to it now." Hildegard lamented. "Mark my words! We will be back."

Esther and Edith did not know whether to laugh at the woman or to be scared of her. On one hand she sounded deluded and confused, but on the other, her speech demonstrated a nastiness that the lovers would rather not provoke. It was a shame to be so close to the openly Nazi sympathisers. By and large most Germans or 'Austrians' in the camp seemed genuinely relieved that the Nazi regime had fallen and they had shed no tears about the end of the war.

Whether it was sincere or not, at least they were acknowledging the injustices that had happened during the occupation and refrained from talking up the Hitler regime. Their sorrow came from losing their home where some of them had lived for generations. They had no natural loyalty to Germany. By political affiliation most of them had been Austrian for decades and only over the last twenty years they had been citizens of the newly formed state of Czechoslovakia. They would not necessarily have been sad to return to the pre-war status quo and were disappointed that their former neighbours and friends had kicked them out without discussion. They were enraged when they learned from the Americans that the Allies had not even officially agreed on an expulsion policy. Many Germans were still on Czechoslovakian soil, awaiting a political solution to the situation, which made some hopeful that they might be allowed to return to their homes one day while others considered themselves unlucky to be here, angry that they had been victims of an unauthorized expulsion that now might not be reversible.

Hildegard and Gudrun seemed to believe that they would return to the same privileged positions they had before. Nobody in the hut wanted to challenge the two deluded women.

Edith wondered how many people here secretly agreed with those comments. Could the Austrian or German leopard ever change its spots? Both lesbians were painfully aware that they were on German soil where Hitler's rise had begun and were hoping to get out soon.

Evka's Czech neighbour one day decided that it was time to break down the barrier between them and managed to corner her outside the hut.

"My name is Gregor Czerny. I know you can understand me and I know what you think of me. I need to tell you that I had nothing to do with the Germans. I am not a collaborator! I don't know why I am here."

Evka looked away but her body language gave away that she

was listening and so Gregor Czerny continued. "I was promoted when Hitler invaded us. It was not my fault that some of my superiors were removed from office by his people. I was next in line, my promotion was nothing personal. As a civil servant you need to be loyal to your government and I carried on with my duties as I was told. I was working for the housing office and had to assign houses and apartments that were cleared for new occupants. I took nothing away from the Jews, it was the Germans who did that. I just did my job by allocating the space."

Evka rolled her eyes at his last statement but he continued undeterred.

"All of my colleagues are still in their position but I was singled out and made an example of. I swear I did the Germans no favour. I hated the Sudetenlander people. They always felt so superior to us and treated me as second class citizen. When I had a choice I would assign the good flats to Czechs rather than to Germans, but none of that is being acknowledged. My career improved after the Germans came and now my jealous colleagues have taken advantage by denouncing me. That is why I am here. I am no more guilty than a housekeeper or a chauffeur who worked for a German. You must believe me," he said.

Evka did not respond and he went inside and sat back down on his bed next to his wife, who was still unresponsive and lethargic.

Evka did not like the man. Admittedly his story sounded credible but she could see how his sub-servient mannerisms could have appeared to his colleagues as crawling to the Germans. She had no doubt that he was convinced of his innocence but whether he was being honest to himself was a different question altogether. It certainly raised a question in her mind about what was collaboration and what wasn't. Was his lack of resistance a silent agreement? Was only a complete general strike proof enough of disagreement with the regime? She was not sure how she felt about Gregor now but she preferred to be left alone. Becoming friends with him and his wife on grounds of their language was out of the question and she didn't think she had much else in common with him. She had Greta and Wilma and that was all she needed.

The following days saw a few more arrivals, mostly individuals and smaller groups who had fled on their own accord and who had been directed to the camp by soldiers at the border or by locals on

302

the road. There was no further group as large as the march Greta and Wilma had been part of for another few weeks. The Allied powers had set up food relief programmes which supplied the camp with small but very well received rations. It was a minor miracle they received food at all, since international charities preferred to feed the victims rather than Germans. Politics and animosities between inmates of the camp were on-going but the presence of American soldiers made most people feel safe and secure.

After a few days rest, many of the refugees decided to move on to other camps and those who had them set out to find friends or relatives who lived somewhere else in Germany. First efforts were made to record the names of the inmates to help the process of reuniting families but only much later did these lists become comprehensive and useful.

Ordered by the Allied powers to do so, the Czechoslovak president Benes called his citizens to refrain from further un-sanctified expulsions of Germans. Regardless of those efforts large groups of them continued to arrive after being forced across the border with nothing more than the clothes they were wearing. These new arrivals were the source of much sought-after information about developments in the former home. They were asked questions about how the Germans were being treated in this village or in that town and if by chance they had heard of this person or that relative. Hope usually gave way to frustration when the newcomers could not relay anything useful.

The most important news however was that the government had drawn up rules for expulsion and that people who were useful to the state, former resistance workers and those married to Czech nationals were allowed to stay in Czechoslovakia. Committees had been set up to establish eligibility for such exceptions. By and large there was little consistency in the findings of those committees, just as the state of internment and labour camps for Germans varied widely from harmless to violent. New hope surged amongst the inmates that a return to their home might be possible under the new rules and they might be listened to by a more objective and sympathetic judge - if only they could get past the border patrols and back into Czechoslovakia.

Every wave of arrivals at the camp was followed by a series of

303

departures. The Czech couple, Czerny, had tried several times to get back into their country but had always failed. They considered crossing over illegally as too dangerous and so they kept coming back after every refusal at the border.

The sisters Hildegard and Gudrun stayed put, obviously still convinced that they would soon return to their bakery by official means. Other refugees decided to try and make a new start outside the compound, workers from larger companies were hoping to secure a new living at other branches or factories of their former employers.

Edith and Esther were eager to push on towards France but knew they could not leave Greta and Wilma with three children to look after. The two orphaned boys Adolf and Heinrich had stopped asking after their mother and had completely adopted the ladies as surrogate mothers, a responsibility that neither of the lovers really wanted to give up. Jokingly, the lovers had often spoken about founding a family together but lived too much in the moment ever to make concrete plans and look for a potential father for such a future to become a reality.

Edith thought this might be an opportunity to make those dreams come true, albeit in a slightly different way, and hoped they could take the boys with them. Esther was not sure she wanted to give up her freedom just yet and never spoke of the boys as part of their future. She just wanted to return to Paris as soon as possible.

Greta was reluctant to leave the safety of the camp and to force another long journey on her sister. Any chance for at least a temporary stability was worth clinging to for Wilma's sake.

At the same time they had all made a commitment to their father to meet in Paris. What if Jonah had already met with Egon and was on his way there? It had seemed so simple when they had drawn up the plans to meet after the war. Now there were new circumstances, more facts and many more possibilities to consider. Travelling to France seemed an awfully long way while there was so much uncertainty. They didn't even know what had happened to the Countess since she had left them so suddenly in Carlsbad. All these thoughts went around in Greta's head and she kept changing her mind about what might be the best course of action.

While there was at least a little food and shelter, it was easy to postpone the decision and to stay and wait for further international political developments. There was hope that the lists that were regularly compiled with the names of camp inmates might lead to their father more quickly and safely than the journey to France. After lengthy discussions, Edith and Esther decided to stay and wait a little longer. Edith assumed complete responsibility for Adolf and Heinrich until blood relatives could be found via a Red Cross tracing programme. Edith was not too keen on that possibility. She thought it would be better for the children to grow up under her warm and tolerant influence instead of being drilled by yet another cold German family, which their mother's behaviour had suggested such relatives might be. Esther however refused to kidnap the children on such ideological grounds.

At the end of the summer, the Nazi women Hildegard and Gudrun left the camp to try and make it on their own. Hildegard had long voiced that she hated living at the expense of the Americans who had destroyed her life.

She did not need any charity and would rather die on the road than taking any more of this life in a cage. It was a brave statement given that she had neither friends nor family to go to, nor did the small rations in the camp inspire too much confidence that there was plentiful food outside the camp. Gudrun seemed much less optimistic and less convinced of success in this endeavour but, as usual, she was unable to contradict her sister and went away with her. Ten days later they returned to the camp, much to the amusement and ridicule of their bunk mates.

"We Austrians have no future in Germany!" said Hildegard matter of factly. "They don't want us refugees, that is quite clear. I don't really blame them. The Americans have practically destroyed their country and have given them nothing in return. The Germans can hardly cope with their own problems. How could they care for us people as well? Why should they? Looks like the only thing we can do is take the charity from the Americans and hope it will exhaust their funds rather than inconvenience our German friends. That is now our last patriotic task."

Edith had to control her anger at this self-righteous and ignorant woman while everyone else just laughed at the blind delusion and arrogance Hildegard was so proud to display against the hand that was feeding her.

In the outside world and the political arena there was still no sign of a solution to their situation. Just like Hildegard and Gudrun had experienced on their short quest for independence, many refugees found that life outside the camp was difficult. There was not enough housing due to the air raids during the war and there was not enough food to go around either. Of course there was food distribution outside of the camp but it was less organised and unreliable since donors were less charitably inclined towards the Germans and gave mainly to the victims of the war.

Evka had learned that there were other camps for so-called displaced people, who did not just consist of Germans. Some contained the slave labourers brought to Germany from eastern Europe during the war, other political refugees and survivors of the German labour and concentration camps. She suggested that it would be better for the group to live in an environment with other victims of the Nazi regimes and less Germans and collaborators, but Greta urged them to endure the unpleasant circumstances for Wilma's sake. Greta had become very concerned for her father and the Countess of late and felt it was essential to remain in the vicinity of the border. There was no doubt that her Highness had not made it to France and had been quickly caught by the Czech patrols; there had been too many road blocks to assume anything else. It had become set in her mind that Jonah and Alma would soon appear in the camp themselves, either with a group of refugees from Slovakia or on their own, looking for the rest of their family. Greta had heard about the forceful expulsion of Germans from Brno, exactly where her father and his mistress had been headed when the family parted ways two months previously.

She was convinced that without any papers, and as an unknown in the city, the authorities would have ordered him to leave the country. According to the little that was known about other camps in the region, Jonah and Alma probably had been taken to Passau. After asserting that Greta and Wilma were not living there, Jonah would try to reach the other camps near the border to find his daughters and continue the search for Egon at the same time. Maybe their father had even seen their names on a list.

Time and time again she weighed her options and asked for reassurance from the ladies Esther and Edith.

"None of us know enough to give you advice. If we stay in one place he has a better chance of finding us," said Esther at last, taking part of the responsibility of her troubled friend's mind.

Other Jewish inmates were leaving for less German dominated camps. The committee who eventually interviewed all inmates to collect demographic statistics for future political decision making was very critical of Greta's claim to be Jewish. In light of the voluntary departures of so many other Jews her desire to remain in here was taken as evidence that she was lying. The primary task of these investigators was to establish statistics for relief organisations, which wanted to establish the strength of the various refugee groups, in order to prepare re-homing and repatriation.

An American woman volunteer who spoke to Greta and Wilma had done the same work at a different camp near Munich but had asked to be transferred because she could not cope with the poor physical conditions of the inmates there; most of them had been in the Dachau concentration camp. The experience had left her scared and haunted by nightmares. On a different level her work had been frustrating because of the naked fear and the lack of cooperation that people in the old camp had displayed towards her and to anyone else who was wearing a uniform. She was grateful for her transfer to a place where the inmates were comparatively unharmed. At the same time, having seen the worst cases near Munich, she lacked pity for the German 'monsters' and their petty demands and was less inclined to believe their stories. Greta explained her predicament in as much detail as the woman let her but in the statistics Greta and her friends were noted down as Sudetenlander refugees.

The following months saw large groups of Latvians, Ukrainians and Lithuanians joining the compound, all of whom had fled the systematic deportations from Czechoslovakia organised by the Soviets. The newcomers were eventually given their own separate section by the American soldiers and they soon established their own communities with improvised schools and churches.

They kept a safe distance from the Germans and they were wary of members from other nations, all of whom they suspected to have been collaborators. Anyone not part of their community was an enemy, including the soldiers feeding them. Now that the place had been divided into opposing sections, the army had the additional task of keeping the peace.

The Czech couple Czerny finally moved out of the hut into a different building that was full of Czech speaking refugees. Evka had continued to ignore the couple despite their desperate pleas of their innocence. Her consistency hardened Gregor's own heart, he gave up his plans for the rehabilitation of his character and joined his fellow landsmen, although he had genuine reservations regarding their political past.

For a few days the bunks remained empty until a young couple, Freddie and Luise, chose them as their new residence. The boy was Jewish and had worked at the girl's family toy store in Prague before the war. His employers were kind people and when his family was taken to Terezin Luise managed to hide him in their loft, where he survived the entire war. He and Luise fell in love very quickly during his long years in hiding.

Luise had felt terribly sorry for him for being confined to the dark and kept him company whenever she could. To make him feel less of a burden, Luise would engage him in conversations and asked him questions about what it meant to be a Jew, what he believed and why so many people hated them so much. He taught her everything he knew about the Jewish faith, its history and rituals, and she was deeply fascinated by the new world he showed her. Her parents had been Catholics but not very religious in their daily lives and when religion became less popular under Hitler, it served them as an excuse to abandon their half-hearted efforts altogether.

To meet a man with such strong philosophical and religious convictions and with so much other knowledge impressed her; inspired by his passion she felt strongly attracted to the world of Judaism. It was difficult to understand why the Jews had been persecuted and victimized through the centuries when there was so much wisdom and spiritual goodness in the scriptures. Luise started to think of herself as a Jewess and planned to convert at the first given opportunity.

The young couple were proud and provocatively openly Jewish. Thanks to the presence of the Militia, they felt sure of themselves and were not in the least worried about displaying their faith. They got on well with Greta and her group and represented a welcome challenge to the otherwise grim and moody atmosphere of the hut. Freddie, in particular, was a big optimist and felt very hopeful for the future. He assured everyone he knew that not all Germans were bad people or were against the Jews, always arguing that he himself had been saved by ethnic Germans.

Luise of course had seen her share of crimes against Jews in Prague and not only regarded her partner's ideas as naïve but she also feared for more anti-Semitism in Germany in the future. Right now, it might be rare to hear a word against the Jews in public but she knew better than to expect the country to change overnight. Hildegard and Gudrun were less vocal in their hateful rants since Freddie had arrived but it did not take a psychic to read their thoughts.

Luise's hopes were to get to New York or Palestine where they could be completely themselves. She planned to convert to Judaism and help repopulate the tribe. Since she had learned that Jewishness could only be obtained through conversion or by birth from a Jewish mother, it was doubly important that she did so.

When Luise found out that Greta and Wilma were Jewish too but were not practising their faith, she put the many lessons that Freddie had given her in the loft to use and went on a mission to convince the apostate women of the necessity to keep the Jewish way of life going. Like her father, Greta had no interest in that tradition and quoted a Jewish philosopher who had called their people to "be a Jew at home and a goy in the street".

"Being Jewish is so much more than just believing in the Talmud. It is all the traditions and customs that make us a distinct culture," Luise explained to her ignorant friend.

"All through my childhood and my adult life I have had very little contact with those traditions," Greta had to disappoint the self-declared rabbi in front of her. "It is impossible for me to identify with 'our tribe' because of it. If I could do it I would. It would suit me. My family have travelled from the Ukraine to Slovakia and now I am in Germany. I never felt completely welcome or at home in any of these places. If I felt part of a culture that could give me that feeling I would embrace it happily. "

"Even if you reject the traditions you are always part of the same tribe," Luise impressed upon her. "Your ancestors were Jewish and you share their blood. You cannot deny that."

"Maybe, unless of course one of them converted," Greta replied.

"Then their blood would also be Jewish. Don't split hairs. We need to stick together. Yes, maybe you can be a goy in the street but then please try to be a proper Jew in your heart. Don't be a traitor to your people," Luise pleaded.

"I could only be a traitor if I was part of it in the first place," Greta pointed out. "I don't fit in in the synagogues, I can't read a Kaddish, and so I am a traitor to you already. I have never been anything else than a Jew to others. Even my husband started to forget that I was the book loving girl he had fallen in love with and the mother of his children. He too started to think of me as a Jew even though I never practised my faith. If I were to go to Palestine with you I would remain the odd one out without the conviction of faith, don't you think?"

"No, because of your Jewish family you are part of the chosen people and Palestine will be the home for all of us," Luise promised. "Whether you are believers or not, the rabbis and I will bring you back on the right path. You can tell us to go away, but we will be the ones to accept you completely."

"All that preaching and persuading does not sound like I will be accepted unconditionally at all," said Greta stubbornly. "I do appreciate your good intentions but I am content with my family and happy to try and live in the world just the way I always have been."

"What I like most about the Jewish faith is that everyone is allowed to argue and try to find out the truth for themselves," Luise carried on regardless. "It is not as dogmatic as I always believed it to be when I saw groups of them coming out of the Synagogue with their hats and locks."

"Then you have not met many of them in person," Greta said jokingly. "The orthodox or traditional ones can easily be perceived as being dogmatic. Maybe you will enjoy that, you seem to like a good argument or debate yourself. I prefer to do without it."

Freddie adored the way Luise was fighting for the Jewish cause but tried not to be part of such discussions. His presence would have given these conversations a darker and heavier tone. He usually made a quick exit and often took the boys to an improvised playground behind one of the barracks. Ropes had been hung down from trees so that children could swing or climb. There was even a little slide made of old plastic tarpaulin. The boys took to Freddie with an enthusiasm that almost hurt the women who had tried to be everything for them and now felt they had failed the children. Ernst had never really had a father figure and had never seemed to miss it but Heinrich and Adolf had longed for more exciting and active fun than just singing and playing cards.

It was in this playground that Ernst saw the two teenage girls from Budweis again with whom he had played cards and who had seen his grandfather. He left Freddie and the two boys, who had joined a football team that was playing against young Latvians, and walked up to them.

"Hello Lisbeth, hello Margot!" he greeted them.

"Oh, look, it is our friend Edwin Ernst. Have you found out what your real name is yet?" Margot teased him.

"Yes, of course I know my real name. I was not supposed to tell anyone during the war, I don't really know why," Ernst apologised.

"Well never mind, Ernst. We knew and we don't mind," Margot replied.

"What did you know?" Ernst wondered.

"That you were Jews. You must tell your mother. She must not think we meant any harm," said Lisbeth.

Freddie joined them, looking to see if Ernst was troubling these sweet girls.

"Not at all!" Lisbeth assured him. "We are old acquaintances from Budweis. We met on the road. We also met his grandfather on a different occasion and apparently we scared all of them, unintentionally. I was just explaining to Ernst here that our father was very hurt about it. He was offering to help Ernst's grandfather and his wife but they did not trust him and left in the middle of the night."

"You wouldn't trust a stranger on the road those days as a Jew," Freddie said, defending Jonah. "Even now, I am not sure it is a good idea."

"We understood that, but grandfather was wondering for days what he had said that had upset or frightened any of you. He never meant any harm. We understood that Ernst and his mother were panicking because we knew about their fake names. With Jonah he really did not know why. Maybe it was because father had asked to see his papers. He only did that to help them," swore Margot.

"How would that have helped Jonah?" asked Freddie visibly confused.

"You see, my aunt married a Jew. She tried to escape on forged

311

papers that were not very good ones and got arrested at the border to Hungary. Father was devastated that he had not seen that the forgeries were poorly done. Since then he tried to help others avoid the same fate," explained Margot.

"What a nice man. I hope he got over his hurt," said Freddie diplomatically.

"Did you find your missing bag?" asked Ernst.

"Yes, we did get it back, thank God," said Lisbeth animatedly. "A man next to us looked after it, so that no one would steal it. When he returned it we didn't know if anything was missing. We didn't dare search it in front of him but I think he felt that we wanted to. He looked very angry over that. Everything was still there: Passports and money. We were so relieved but when we looked for the man to thank him properly he had gone."

"Where is your father now?" asked Freddie.

"We got separated in Budweis. The men were taken away. The soldiers here are saying that he is going to be released soon and sent here as well. I cannot wait," Lisbeth said excitedly.

"I hope so too!" Freddie assured her. "The Czechs want to start their own life now and won't need him. The politicians are all going to agree on that, don't worry."

Back at the barracks Edith and Esther were discussing their own future. Life as a same sex couple in Germany seemed unthinkable and they both longed for a more sophisticated and flamboyant surrounding than the dire camp. Since Adolf and Heinrich had taken so well to Freddie and Luise, the ladies had serious doubts that adopting the boys themselves was beneficial for any party. Would the young couple consider taking care of them?

If so, the ladies were free to go and seek the pleasures and amusements of gay Paris. Edith still had some of her fortune in Switzerland, so the two of them were not without means but it probably would not be enough to bring up two children and keep the lifestyle the two lovers had in mind to return to after all this.

Greta encouraged them to seek their own luck. Now that she had Evka with her, she was more than capable of looking after Wilma and Ernst. Freddie and Luise seemed very fond of the boys but if they were to decline the task of fostering them Greta would happily step in. Three was almost easier than one she said. They kept each other company and let her to do other things while only needing to keep one eye on them. The last thing she wanted was any of her friends to suffer any more hardship. The two ladies were free and could be themselves in France without the added burden.

Greta's own life was already defined by motherhood and being a carer for her sister, she might as well take on some more responsibility. Besides, she still remembered how horrible the German mother had been. It was a sweet irony to think that the children were not only safe from the mother's hateful influence but on top of that were going to be raised as Jewish.

Greta had been surprised how little they cried after their mother had gone and how quickly they adapted to their new situation. Adolf had suffered from nightmares for the first few days but neither of them ever dared ask what had happened to their mother. When Esther tried to reassure them that she would only be looking after them until their own mother returned, they were completely silent and tense. Only when Edith added that the boys would never have to be alone and could always stay with the two ladies did the grim young faces turn into shy smiles. This promise was the only obstacle on their path to Paris now.

Luise had spent the afternoon in the eastern European section of the camp, looking for a rabbi who would convert her and marry her to Freddie. Despite awkward language barriers and a fair deal of mistrust and disbelief on the part of the people she spoke to, she eventually succeeded in finding a man who promised he could help her. Arriving at the hut full of joy and excitement she ran up to Greta to tell her the good news. It was the opportunity Greta had waited for.

"I am so happy for you Luise," she said, genuinely pleased. The girl had waited for such an opportunity for so long, one had to rejoice with her. "Are you going to have babies right away?"

"I hope so. We haven't really spoken about it yet. Freddie is a little unsure if he can survive making and repairing toys but I keep telling him that he has a gift to sell things. He loves talking to people and he is always so happy and upbeat, I am sure he can find a position almost anywhere." Luise said full of excitement.

"You are right there," agreed Greta. "He has a gift. Have you noticed how the boys adore him? They have taken to him really well, don't you agree. I have to let you in on a little secret. Will you promise me to keep it?"

313

"I am not sure I can do that," Luise replied.

"Promise anyway," demanded Greta.

"Can I tell Freddie?" Luise asked, pleading like a little girl.

"That you can," agreed her friend.

"I am very curious now," Luise admitted.

"Edith and Esther....they are not just old friends. They.....they have been very, very close for a long time now. You see.....you could call them a couple if you wanted," said Greta hesitantly.

"You mean like......oh....oooh! I see. No, that can't be," Luise tried to grasp the news but found it hard to take it in. She had heard about such things before but had no idea what to make of it. Her mind was trying hard to make sense of what she had just heard. Lovers? Two women? Was that not a sin? She would have to tell Freddie and ask him about it. What did the Bible have to say to that?

"You approve?" she asked to be sure.

"There is not much to approve or disapprove," Greta said. "It is what it is. What matters to me is that they are good people, Luise. I hope you know that."

"Of course I do. Well I never....I guess there is no harm if they don't bother anyone else," Luise tried to process the information.

"Exactly, and there is the problem. You see, in France they are protected by the law and can be themselves. In Germany they can't, even if there will be laws to help them. They would not want to risk it after all that has happened during the war here."

"I see," Luise said.

"They have looked after Heinrich and Adolf as if they were their own ever since the boys lost their mother. They made promises never to leave the boys alone but they can hardly kidnap or legally adopt the two of them," Greta carried on.

"Of course, they must never go back on their word to those lovely boys," Luise agreed.

"Those promises should never have been made so easily. We were all concerned for these innocent children but now we are in a position where we have to be very resourceful if we want to make them true. I think we need to look for an alternative solution to the problem and I think that we just found the answer to our question this afternoon when you decided to get married," Greta said, happy to have come to the point in exactly the way she had planned to. "How would you feel about adopting the boys and raising them

314

Jewish? That would be two more strikes on your quest to make the world more Jewish."

"You must be completely mad!" shouted Luise. "Me, raising the offspring of some Nazis?"

"Exactly, that is the genius part of the plan," Greta said "You can erase what their parents have told them and tip the balance in favour of the tribe. The boys want to be loved and they need to be taken care of. Think about it. I know it is a lot to ask but it seems so little when you look at how they already hang on every word Freddie tells them. Yes they love the ladies too but it's plain to see that there is an age gap that is hard to bridge. In Paris, they will be raised by a maid, not by the ladies. They have not got it in them to raise two boys. They will try, but it will never be as good as if it was you."

"I don't know," Luise hesitated "The ladies have money and experience. I am young and have so much to learn myself."

"Then you will learn it together with them. There are always more mature mothers but who knows if they are better ones? It is of course all down to the boys themselves. We will not force any solution on them and the ladies will not go back on their word. That is why it would be better if you would offer to have them. If you two are not comfortable with this responsibility it is fine. Then I will offer, or rather, Ernst will."

"That is very honourable of you but how will you cope? A sister to look after and three boys?" Luise asked.

"It will be hard but I have Evka. She has agreed to stay with us. In Germany we are all that she has. Hopefully sometime soon my father will join us with his wife and then it will be a whole bunch of parents. Maybe even my brother Egon."

"What do you think the boys would want?" Luise asked.

"I am sure they will choose you two without the shadow of a doubt," Greta said. "But do not rush the decision. Speak to Freddie. Maybe he is not ready to become a father figure, maybe he can't wait."

Freddie was delighted by all the news Luise could share with him that evening. He was eager to marry Luise for more than one reason and the prospect of doing so within the near future was more than he had hoped for. The proximity of a rabbi also raised their hopes of finding intermediates with the right connections to arrange their journey to Palestine or advise them how to get a visa to New

York. All of this sounded promising already but his joy had no limits when he heard about the proposal regarding the boys.

He had loved them from day one and found his role as a surrogate father came naturally to him. What he had been asked to do was not a hardship at all but a great gift. He tried to persuade his future wife to see it the same way. Luise had more reservations about the feasibility of the idea but one by one Freddie managed to argue them away with his bright smile, his sparkling eyes and his enthusiasm for the future.

At last, Adolf and Heinrich were asked whom they would prefer to spend their time waiting for their mother with.

"Mother is not coming back, is she?" said Heinrich abruptly.

"We don't know," admitted Greta.

"We will do everything we can to find her," promised Esther.

"But you are right, she may never come back. We must be prepared for that possibility, which is why you should think carefully about your answer," Edith said with gravity.

"We all love you and we all want to have you," Freddie said smilingly. "We were going to fight over you, but then decided to let you make the choice."

Adolf looked helplessly around the room.

"You can choose whoever you want," Evka assured him. "Freddie is just joking. Nobody is upset if you don't choose them. Everyone wants you to be happy and to live with who you most want to be with."

"Adolf and Heinrich looked at each other, nodded as if they had already spoken about it, and then both said simultaneously: "Freddie."

"Yes, yes, yes, yes!" shouted Freddie, took the boys and Luise and danced around the room to the tune of a Jewish folk song he was humming.

"Are you sure?" asked Luise. "You know that we are Jewish and that we are thinking of going to live by the sea in the Mediterranean or America. Are you happy to come along?"

"Yes, we want to see the sea. Can we swim there or is it too dangerous?" asked Heinrich full of excitement.

"Yes, you can swim there, as long as you don't swim out too far. Can you swim yet?" asked Freddie.

"No," said Heinrich full of disappointment.

"Well then, we will have to teach you then how to do it. It is easy!" Freddie promised.

Two days later Edith and Esther decided to start their journey towards Paris and the following morning they said their farewells to the group. The fact that there were no fixed addresses they could exchange with each other was upsetting for everyone, because it meant that this could be their final goodbye. After such a long time together it seemed impossible for Greta and Wilma to let go of their two friends.

"Write to my lawyer in Zurich when you have settled somewhere," Edith told the sisters. "He should be able to forward your letters to us. Once we have found somewhere ourselves we will let him know. I promise: We will see each other again!"

"I hope so!" said Wilma tearfully.

"Now, now," said Esther and took her in her arms. Then she looked at Greta and smiled. "Thank you for everything."

Adolf was very quiet and subdued, thinking that he had done something bad to make the ladies leave. Evka had explained to him that this was not the case but it was obvious that he could not shake off the feeling. Heinrich was quiet too but more in a disinterested way, as if he had already written the leaving women off. It broke Esther's heart to see his cool attitude towards her but she understood that the little boy had to protect himself from yet another separation.

"Take good care of them for us," Esther whispered into Freddie's ears, then she pulled herself away and went outside to wait for Edith.

Wilma had sunk back on her bed and Evka sat down beside her, waving at Esther as she walked through the door. Luise, who had left her parents behind to be with Freddie, was herself close to tears and decided to help console Wilma.

"Let's walk them to the gate," suggested Freddie to the three boys and the four rushed out of the hut and joined Esther. Greta and Edith now stood alone in the corner near the door, out of everybody's sight.

"Greta you are an amazing woman!" Edith said quietly. "Tell that father of yours we want to see him and his wife as soon as possible. He still owes us a lot of his art. We will find him and demand our share of it!"

"Thank you Edith. I will tell him. Good luck and be careful,"

Greta replied, then she kissed her friend goodbye.

"Now you are kissing me!" Edith said jokingly. "Now that I am leaving."

She turned away and stepped outside, leaving her friend to take care of her sobbing sister.

The following few days the remaining members of Greta's circle of friends were subdued and unmotivated. As much as Freddie tried, he could not get the boys to shake off the sadness that had taken hold of them. Only Heinrich suggested playing football and other games but he was obviously just pretending to be strong.

The departure reminded everyone of their own future and the need to move on. Now that the war had come to an end they would soon be forced to live in the outside world again and try and make a living and feed themselves by their own means. Evka and Greta would probably both have to find employment to provide for Wilma and Ernst.

The more time passed, the more uncertain Greta became about her father's fate. Had he come to harm in Brno or was he stuck on the other side of the border? Was he stubbornly waiting for Egon for the rest of his life without ever giving up and trying to find herself and her sister? Wouldn't he find a way to send her a message, tell other refugees to look for them on their way?

Whenever new people arrived at the camp, they asked around for relatives or friends, or they had news from travellers they had encountered on their way to pass on to anyone who knew them. Most families, that were separated, had not managed to be reunited and information about their beloved was their main concern. Lucky were those who at least knew that their parents or children were still alive and had been seen; the rest had to fight fears and worries. Greta had listened to the stories of refugees from Brno and Bratislava, but nothing indicated that her father had been seen dead or alive.

Luise had, at last, made the arrangements for her conversion and marriage. The only rabbi she had been able to locate in the camp was from Estonia and lived in a different sector of the compound. He was not as Orthodox and strict as Luise would have liked him to be but he was willing to help. The extent of her knowledge and understanding impressed him and after only a few lessons in a communal room that he had to share with the Greek orthodox community he judged her ready to join his people. In an improvised bath, he symbolically performed her immersion in the mikveh and officially welcomed her to the Jewish faith. The wedding was performed the very next day in the same room. The small Jewish community participated at the event to make it as authentic and traditional as they could for the couple and in the evening they were allowed two hours of privacy in a room that had been especially prepared for them and the occasion.

For days, Luise and Freddie could not stop smiling, so happy were they to be finally married. Having loosely joined the Jewish community in the other part of the compound, they were also one step closer to their exodus to Palestine. A group of activists helped Jews to gather in Bad Reichenhall from where they would make their way to the Mediterranean ports. People traffickers there would smuggle them across the borders to Italy. Luise and Freddie could leave the following week and take Adolf and Heinrich with them.

Greta was sad that the departure was going to be so soon but understood that her friends were eager to leave and start their new life. Her main concern was really for Ernst, who would lose his two best friends and the father figure he had found in Freddie.

When the newly formed family left, Wilma and Ernst were both crying, something that was unusual for the otherwise relaxed and calm boy.

Chapter 13: Welcome to Germany

The run up to Christmas was a miserable time. Due to its vicinity to the border, the camp was the first point of rest for many refugees which, in turn, led to an acute shortage of space and related animosities between new and old residents. With the announcement of systematic and well organised deportations of all ethnic Germans from the Sudetenland in the New Year, there was an increased fear of being pushed further and further away from home soil and into an even harsher exile in the west. All communities in Germany had been given a quota of refugees to take in and the inmates feared being transferred further away to make space for the expected train loads of expelled Germans from Czechoslovakia.

The unknown caused anxiety at a time that was already overshadowed by grief for lost ones and worry about those who were still unaccounted for. The impending arrival of even more compatriots was another step in the wrong direction and put the Sudetenlander community further away from their goal of returning home. What had been viewed as a temporary measure and a mere tactical move on the political chess board of post-war Europe was now threatening to become a long term if not an irrevocable and permanent scenario that had to be avoided.

The inmates already knew too well that the people in Germany had no interest in welcoming them with open arms. Theirs was a country with its own shortages of habitable living space and food. Reports of violence against the unwelcome guests by local farmers and citizens increased and verbal abuse for those who took to the road was not unusual either.

The American soldiers were looking for inmates to be transferred towards other camps further west so that the authorities could accommodate the vast amounts of newcomers every day. Volunteers for these trains were mainly citizens of countries that were now occupied by the Soviet army. They were hoping that any move away from the border might better their chances of being able to stay here.

Ethnic Germans from Silesia and other former German or Austrian territories preferred to stay put, hoping to return to their homes as soon as this political madness had come to an end. The former group however could not be moved without upsetting the Soviets who had made it known that they wanted to relocate every one of their 'citizens' to their origins. The latter group simply refused to go; individual officers made guarantees to the refugees but few were willing to trust them.

Rivalry and animosities between the many different ethnic and religious groups within the camp were on the increase.

The Czech collaborators in the camp had managed to unite themselves in two of the huts within the part of the camp occupied by the Sudetenlanders and had their hands full with defending the safety of their members. In the absence of anyone else to blame, expelled ethnic Germans used them as scapegoats for their accumulated aggression and frustration. Exiled and beaten mercilessly by Czechs, it was now the turn of the Sudetenlanders to take counter revenge on any citizen of that hated nation wherever they could, egging on the nonsensical spiral of violence and conflict. That some of these Czechs had been on their side previously was of no concern to them.

The expelled Sudetengermans felt mistreated and claimed to be innocent victims but many of the Allies discounted such excuses; in their opinion, no one was without guilt. Those people crying foul now had let the crimes happen without interfering and so were just as bad as the ones committing the crimes. No use to get on a high moral horse at this late stage. If they were now fighting against the Czechs for the injustice done to them, why didn't they have that same courage or decency to fight during the Nazi regime?

Even though Luise and Freddie had made contact with the Jews from the eastern part of the camp and had put in a word for their Jewish friends, Greta and her extended family were not particularly welcome in their circles. Since she had only looked after her own interests during the war and had not been part of the tribe, why should they roll out the red carpet for her now? When was the last time she or her family had been to a synagogue? What kind of opportunists were they? If she wanted to be part of a group she would have to look elsewhere.

It was not as if Greta felt any more Jewish now than she had before the war or wanted to be included in their community. But she was a victim of the same fascist criminals and had somehow hoped for sympathy or solidarity. Sadly there was too much fear amongst the survivors to allow such openness to outsiders and the Weissensteiner clan was left isolated, surrounded by Germans they could not make themselves trust. Greta was grateful to have Evka to talk to.

Ernst was quite subdued since his friends had left for Palestine. At first, he visited the playground of the camp and approached another group of children without much hesitation. He was soon banned from their games because he spoke like a Czech and therefore did not fit in. One of the boys even hit him and said:

"That is for what your friends did to my mother!"

Another group refused him because of his aunt Wilma, whose previous hysterics had become known.

"We don't play with mad people like you. You need to get locked up in a hospital!" a little girl informed him in an almost kind and lecturing rather than a nasty and hateful manner.

Despite his young age, Ernst had the clarity of mind to guess that his mother would be upset if she found out how he was treated by the other children. To protect her from pain he continued to leave the hut frequently for the playground so Greta would not realise how much of an outsider he had become. Instead of looking for new acquaintances, he began to withdraw and played alone in an area of sand, constructing tall and large castles with extensive grounds and defence walls around them.

"You are quite an architect," said a skinny middle aged man with an accent that was unfamiliar to the little boy. "I am impressed by how much you understand about the safety precautions for the Royal family of your castle. You must have built many great houses to be able to do this!"

Ernst had been told not to speak to strangers but the flattery and unexpected attention worked like magic and he found himself drawn towards the kind and apparently also lonely man.

"My name is Joschka," said the man.

"I am Ernst."

"Nice to meet you Ernst. Tell me why are you in here and not on the other side of the barbed wire, constructing new buildings for us all to live in?"

"We are waiting for my grandfather and my uncle Egon," said the little boy.

"Always nice to see families looking out for each other,"

commented the older man. Looking at him more closely now Ernst was fascinated just how thin this man was. His cheeks were hollow and the skin across his face seemed stretched to its limit, it was almost horrifying were it not for the inviting and friendly green eyes.

"Don't you have any family?" Ernst asked his new companion.

"I do, but I haven't seen them in years. I have to admit that we do not get on so well with each other as your family does. I am not sure I could find them in this chaos. I am even less certain that I want to. I think I am going to find myself a brand new family of my own," he said, smiling bravely.

"Can you help me build a really tall tower?" Ernst asked.

"I can certainly try. If you are here tomorrow at the same time I will bring some tools. For an aspiring architect you don't seem to have the necessary equipment. "

"Yes, I will be here tomorrow," Ernst said excitedly and indeed they both were.

The next day, Joschka brought a few pieces of wood and made an upright standing square construction with them which Ernst then filled up with sand. The result was not great at the first attempt but as the two improved their technique and learnt from their mistakes, the towers they managed to create grew in size and stability.

Joschka had a numbered tattoo on his arm but refused to talk about it when Ernst asked. Instead Joschka distracted his little friend with questions about the blueprint of their current project. Ernst was too happy to have found a new male playmate to risk spoiling it with further enquiries. Joschka was particularly talented and patient in adding little details. With a little twig he carved lines into the defence walls, making it look as if they consisted of real bricks. Ernst, on the other hand, had an incredible imagination and every day he destroyed his previous creations and started a brand new and totally different building. One day it was a series of pyramids, the next it was a mosque, or a Greek temple. Soon the spectacular castles became an attraction on the playground and both children and parents came to watch the odd couple constructing them.

"Have you seen all these buildings in real life?" Joschka asked.

"No, but I have seen pictures in books!" Ernst said and explained about the library at the manor house.

After several consecutive days of playing with the strange Joschka, Ernst told Evka about him.

"You should marry him. He is very nice," the little match maker suggested.

Evak laughed at his forwardness. "I could have married many a nice man. When you grow up you will understand that there is a lot more to marrying someone than just being nice."

"But he is your age and he has no real family, just like you. If you marry him then he can become part of our new big family," Ernst insisted.

"I see you have it all planned out for me. How about that: I will come with you to the playground tomorrow and then I can make up my own mind if he is the right kind of nice for me," Evka suggested.

"Yes, yes, yes!" Ernst cheered her on. "You will love him. He is nice, nice, nice."

"I think you said that already," Evka smiled.

That evening, a German woman approached Greta and asked to speak to her in private.

"I have seen your little boy playing with an old man for the best part of a week now. Do you know that man?" she asked.

Greta was taken aback by this inquisition but was also intrigued as to why the woman had chosen to make this her business.

"I have not met him yet, no, but I plan to do so tomorrow," she admitted. "Why do you ask?"

"The man is one of the survivors of the death camps. He has got the number on his arm," the woman said with an implied expectation that this information was enough for Greta to grasp the nature of her warning.

"Are you worried that my son is playing with a Jew?" she asked with a slightly indignant tone to her voice.

"I am not sure he is Jewish," the woman replied. "That is not what is wrong with him. I have seen him for weeks now, lingering around the playground staring at our children. It is not normal for a man his age to seek out children to play with. Why does he not hang out with people of his own generation? "

"Maybe he has lost his own children in the war? I can't see anything wrong with it," Greta said angrily but the seeds of doubt had been planted and she was now eager to meet this man, more out of concern than out of curiosity.

"You are so naïve. You have a lot to learn as a mother. Has no one ever warned you of older men abducting little boys and doing unspeakable things to them?" the woman scolded her. "When the Russians came it was not just young girls who were raped by them. The boys are usually even more ashamed than the girls and don't speak of it. You need to be careful."

Greta was rather unsettled by what she had just heard but could not get herself to admit defeat in this conversation to the woman, who for all she knew might just be a malicious gossip monger.

"How can you tell that this man is after anything other than human contact?" she asked, trying to put her opponent on the spot.

"He is not one of us. He comes from the other section of the camp. By his accent I would guess he is from Hungary. They must have a playground there as well but he chooses to come to our part. Maybe over there they know something about him that we don't and he is not tolerated there," said the woman with much less hate and venom than Greta would have expected. Maybe this was not just a case of malicious bad mouthing.

"Oh, that is absurd," Greta said dismissively to distract from the fact that she was starting to get worried.

"Suit yourself! I am only trying to help. If it was my son I would like to be warned," said the woman and left.

"Don't worry!" said Evka calmly to Greta after hearing the accusations. "Don't let those hateful people get to you. I will meet him tomorrow and that will help clear the picture soon enough. Even if he were one of those - so what? We didn't mind Esther and Edith."

"That was different," Greta said. "Men are much more sexual. You don't see women raping boys or other girls. I want to have a good look at him."

"My brother loved men," revealed Evka. "He moved to France to have a better life than he could have had in Prague. I met quite a few of his kind before he left. They were all far too gentle and soft to do anything so horrendous. Don't let that woman poison your mind."

"She said Russian soldiers raped boys in her village, so there must be some homosexuals out there who aren't soft and gentle," Greta pointed out.

"Well, we will have to see tomorrow. I would not lose sleep over it. Ernst is besotted with the guy and I don't think he would be if something improper had taken place. If the guy were a pervert he would have done something by now, don't you think?"

"I hope you are right," Greta said.

The following day Joschka did not show up at the playground and Ernst and his three female escorts waited in vain. Had his absence anything to do with the women being present or was there a connection to the woman who had warned Greta about him the night before? Ernst waited impatiently and paced up and down, looking to see if his friend was hiding somewhere or was just approaching the grounds. The rain last night had destroyed the creation from the day before but the wetness of the sand would have been a huge advantage in the production of a new building. It seemed unthinkable that Joschka would miss this opportunity. When it became apparent that his friend would not show up today and the disappointment sank in, it weighed so heavily on Ernst's body that he had to sit down and stared wordlessly at the ground.

"Show us what you can do, Ernst!" Evka encouraged the boy. "You don't need anyone else for this, and if you do: We can help you."

"No, thank you but if I can't play with Joschka I would rather not play at all. Let's go back," Ernst said disappointedly.

"You must be very disappointed, Evka!" said Wilma cheekily. "You even washed yourself today and then the man does not show up."

Evka's face flushed. She had indeed put more effort in getting ready today but was not aware that she had been spotted doing so. Unable to respond with wit, she just made a dismissive arm gesture.

The next day the four of them went to the playground again and once more Joschka failed to show up. This time Wilma persuaded Ernst to stay and demonstrate his admired construction skills. The women sat down not far from the sand while Ernst drew a floor plan onto the ground and began to dig holes and a moat, then began work on a defence wall. Greta was amazed at the logical approach and the far-sighted planning that her son was capable off. As more people gathered around him and watched him, she recognised the man that had to be Joschka. He was standing amongst the spectators, slightly behind everyone else.

She got up and went straight to him, gently tapped him on the arm and introduced herself.

"Hello, my name is Greta. I am the young artist's mother. You must be the famous co-architect Joschka," she said with a friendly and welcoming smile.

"Oh...hello. Yes, that is me. Ehm...nice to meet you," he replied nervously. His head turned anxiously away from her while he said this as if to look for an escape route from the scene.

"I just wanted you to know that I much appreciate you spending so much time with my son. Ernst was devastated yesterday when you could not make it to the playground and help him. I hope you were not ill or otherwise inconvenienced?" she probed.

"No, no. Not at all. I am very sorry but I have to go," Joschka stammered and was just about to turn away when Evka joined the two of them. Unintentionally, she stepped right into his getaway route and made him stop.

"I am Evka, a friend of the family. You must join us so we can get to know you," she said.

"Oh I was just going. Maybe some other time," Joschka replied to the invite.

Evka took him by the arm and whispered in his ear: "You have nothing to worry about with us. Let's get out of sight for a minute so we can talk. Ernst has been waiting for you and you must not disappoint him again."

With that she dragged the poor man behind one of the sheds and said:

"I think I know why you are worried," she said.

"You do?" he asked with disbelief.

"Yes, I recognise the signs. My brother is like you. He moved to Paris to escape the harassment. We are not accusing you of anything. We just want to get to know you, otherwise we would be irresponsible," she assured him.

Joschka sighed with relief. His body had begun to shake when Evka started her little speech, not unlike the onset of one of Wilma's attacks. As the tension was receding he was still trembling all over, his lips shaking until he burst into tears of joy and relief.

"You don't know what this means to me. Thank you. I am so sorry for crying but I have been so lonely. All this time," he said between fits of crying.

"Now, now, let it all out!" Evka reassured him.

"In the death camps we were treated like the worst of the worst. The other inmates seemed happy that there was a class of humans beneath them. We got it from the guards and from the other prisoners as well. In the camp at least we were a group and had each other. Here I am the only one. I have become quite worried that I will be found out. I avoid my living quarters during the day to keep a low profile and to avoid questioning. But it's not easy to keep to myself. So I came to sit by the playground to watch the children because they were leaving me alone. Then I noticed Ernst and how nobody would play with him. He looked so innocent and sad, I felt as if I knew him, as if we were both suffering the same loneliness. With him, I could be myself but I noticed how the women were watching us and I could see what they were thinking. I expected Ernst's mother to come and shoo me away every minute of our time together. I was so desperate for this little happiness that I could not stay away, even though I knew I was running a risk.

Gradually the fear came to dominate my thoughts and all I could see was the hateful looks and the suspicion in everyone's eyes. Yesterday it was so bad that I did not dare come anywhere near here for worry I might be beaten up. I mean no harm, really. I don't like young men or boys like that. I sometimes think I am a little boy myself. Please believe me!" he cried and doubled over again, violently shaking and sobbing on the floor.

Evka kneeled down and hugged him for a long time, then she calmly said to him:

"It is fine. Of course I believe you. I can sense these things. The moment I saw you I knew you were a good soul. You are just like my brother, almost too good for this world, too pure and too soft. We will take care of you my dear. Ernst needs you. Already two of his towers have fallen apart because nobody can hold the wooden planks as professionally as his partner in crime."

At that Joschka had to laugh.

"People are still going to talk. That won't be good for Ernst," Joschka objected.

"Let them talk, because at the end of the day that is what they do anyway," Evka said joyfully. "They won't be happy if they don't. The best defence is always attack. Before those fishwives can get the word about you to Ernst we can give them a different story. How would you feel about acting as my fiancé in front of them? Ernst has already suggested that I marry you because we need a man in the family and you and I are of the same age. I for one have never been the object of gossip but I think that I would rather like to try it."

"That is very kind of you to offer but do you think that anyone will believe us?" he wondered.

"You will have to put some effort into your acting, then. I can't see why not. Just imagine how foolish these women will feel when they realise they have been wrong," she asked.

"Why would you do such a thing for a complete stranger?" Joschka wondered.

"I want my little Ernst to have a friend. I also believe that competition increases business. Maybe if I am seen with you someone else will start to take an interest in me. You never know," she said and giggled.

"Once we get out of this mess and find a permanent place of our own we can untangle all the complications. For now, let us look out for each other and try to get through this time happily and in one piece," she suggested.

Ernst was over the moon when Joschka appeared at the sand area.

"Look at this lay-out," he bubbled with enthusiasm. "Here is a moat with a draw bridge, which is the only way in. Behind the wall there is another moat and another wall. Then there is the front yard, a wall and then the inner yard and finally the castle."

"Well done. I am sure the King and the Queen will be feeling very protected in there," said Joschka.

"Yes, and even better. There is a secret tunnel that nobody knows about, from where everyone can get out well behind the enemy lines," Ernst said pointing proudly at the sand.

"They are lucky they had such a clever architect!" Joshka exclaimed.

Greta had a good feeling about Joschka as well, even though she was still a little bit concerned. She was definitely going to keep an eye on the situation but it would have been impossible for her to deny her son contact with such a great playmate.

Wilma took an immediate and exceptional liking to Joschka. She felt that his gentle mannerisms were a pleasant change. Meeting someone equally nervous made her also feel more at ease herself. Seeing his fear and recognising it as slightly exaggerated helped her recognise how unfounded her own feelings could sometimes be. Their anxieties had come between them and the world, even when there was no threat. It was like looking at herself in the mirror. It was a shame he seemed to have taken to Evka right away or she might have made a move on him. He was frighteningly thin but he had the most adorable eyes she had ever seen.

As they learned about Joschka and his past, Greta became much more at ease. He revealed to Evka that he had come from a small suburb in Budapest and had once been the sole heir to a large factory fortune. Fighting in the Great War, he had met and struck up a 'special friendship' with one of his fellow officers, the handsome Eugene. When their contact continued after the war his already suspicious father hired a private detective and uncovered their 'dirty secret'. He disowned his son immediately and told Joschka to leave the country before his rage got the better of him and he might have killed his shameful son with his own hands.

Almost penniless, Joschka moved to Vienna where he managed to survive as the secretary and assistant to a lawyer. A few years after Austria fell to Germany, the lawyer was arrested for being a Jew and when the Gestapo investigated further to find more Jews associated with the practise, a neighbour voiced his suspicions about the effeminate secretary. Joschka fled and escaped to Brno where he worked as a waiter. Starved of love he started to see one of his colleagues, was caught in flagrante and arrested by the Gestapo only a year before the war ended. His fellow waiter did not survive the camp.

Since liberation from the death camp in Poland, Joschka had no specific idea where to go. His only mission had been to escape the Russians and he was playing with the idea of trying to get to France. The thought of making such a long and dangerous journey frightened him however, and so he had stayed in the camp despite all the problems there, unwilling to trade the known bad situation for an unknown one. The hate he and his people had experienced in the death camp had become so deeply rooted in his thinking that he still expected it at any time from any possible source. His self-loathing was so embedded, he found the idea of living in the gay society of Paris almost as disgusting as himself. He had escaped his prison only in the physical sense, mentally he was still punishing himself. The affection he had received from Ernst and his family overwhelmed him and when they invited him to spend Christmas with them he cried for joy. Of course, there were no presents or a Christmas tree but they were together and had each other.

The New Year started with a rude awakening when the guards read out a list of names that had to report to the train station two days later, to be moved to a different camp near France. There was a huge uproar amongst the communities. Those who had wanted to leave were ordered to stay and so many that were desperate to stay had to go. The gates were open for everyone to try their own luck but outside the camp local citizens were holding guard and threatened everyone who tried to leave back inside.

Announcements on posters explained that the trains would take them to other areas in Germany where fewer refugees had settled and there would be opportunities for work and a new life. It made perfect sense to Greta that the burden of looking after so many new arrivals in the country had to be shared equally between the regions and communities. The soldiers had not made it a secret that only those who had a good chance of returning towards the east were able to stay here – whether they wanted to return or not was immaterial.

It came as no surprise to her that all their names were on the list, apart from Joschka. The soldiers assured Greta that if her father should enquire about her he would find her name on the Red Cross List and would also be informed about her new location. There was no need to worry.

It was hard to believe the officials who appeared to promise everyone anything as long as they were willing to get on a train. Joschka took the news of his new found friend's departure very hard. Evka however would not hear any of it and went from official to official looking for ways to keep him with them. After a lot of queuing to speak to the right people and being sent from one overworked and disinterested bureaucrat to the next, she eventually found out that the only way to take Joschka with them was if he was to be married to one of them. Wilma in her mischievous ways offered herself as bride right away, knowing of course very well that Evka wanted that honour for herself. She was convinced that Evka had a secret relationship with Joschka, or at least would want to have one.

Joschka ignored Wilma's comments, got down on one knee and asked Evka to marry him. There was a lot of uproar about it in their hut. One of the women next to them had overheard the proposal and wasted no time spreading the news around. Within minutes there was a long line of people congratulating them and calling for a celebration. Evka was truly touched by the kindness with which the engaged couple were treated. She had written off everyone in the camp as selfish and untrustworthy. She announced to the onlookers that yes, of course, she had accepted him and without wasting any more time the two of them were on their way to find a priest.

Despite the marriage being one of mere convenience and the ceremony being rushed, Evka did feel emotional on the day which naturally gave everyone the impression that their motive was pure love. They obtained their marriage certificate and only just managed to secure the army's permission for Joschka to join their train a few hours before the scheduled departure. Also just before their departure they received a post card from Luise and Freddie, who had made it to Genoa and were soon to board the Hanna Senesh on their way to Israel. They referred to their boys Heinrich and Adolf as Chaim and Adam. Luise was also pregnant and they would soon have a child of their own.

Despite their general reluctance to leave the vicinity of the border to Czechoslovakia and Jonah, the group was in an optimistic mood after hearing the good news about their Jewish friends. Mail delivery was mainly in military hands and not many private letters managed to get through these channels. Greta regarded this as a minor miracle and a good sign.

All morning, the huts had been searched for people who were trying to hide and those who were to leave were gathered in little groups where they were identified again to make sure that they were eligible for a place on the train. When a Ukrainian man complained about not being permitted on the train, he was told that he was free to leave the camp and go wherever he liked to on foot but the military could not take responsibility for him; it was against the regulations and the International agreements. Naturally, leaving by himself would have been dangerous and difficult with some local citizens standing guard outside.

The soldiers even had to protect the refugees on their march to the station from groups of locals who were worried about their own survival if the floods of refugees kept coming in the same steady way that they had been. Unable to feed themselves properly, they were unwilling to share the little they had with complete strangers. Greta wondered if that would be much different where they were going.

On the train platform she saw that their travels were not going to be easy. She had never seen so many people crammed into such a small area. The station was packed and there were long queues everywhere. Open air freight cars were filled to the brim with 100 deportees each with no space to sit down. It was a mild day for January but the temperatures were still cold enough to add greatly to the inconvenience of the journey. The elderly and fragile people had to travel separately.

It took a long time before Greta and her family got their turn to step onto the train. Their names were crossed off a list and the soldiers waved them on to the next wagon. Evka and Wilma secured themselves a place in one of the corners. The frames of the carriages were so high that only the taller people could look over them and see something of the outside world. Joschka had to lift Ernst so that the little boy could get a good view of the orderly chaos that reigned on the platform. Filling up the train took a good while and their feet were already hurting from all the standing up. At last, the train departed and the journey towards the unknown west began. As they gathered speed, the refugees in the centre of the freight car often lost their balance and fell on to their fellow passengers. The draft from moving so fast bit into people's faces and few had the strength to keep their heads up and observe the landscape outside. What was most fascinating for those who did brave the wind was the contrast between beautiful unspoilt countryside and the extent of destruction that emerged when they passed villages or towns. Nuremberg was one of the worst damaged cities they saw. The train finally stopped for the first time and it was possible for the passengers to relieve themselves. Panic set in when soon after everyone had re-boarded the train was split. The first half was continuing its journey southbound to the nearby Ansbach, the latter half was to carry on for a few more hours to Aschaffenburg. Friends who had boarded at different ends of the train were now to be parted without the chance of ever saying goodbye to each other. Some tried to leave their wagons and join others but the soldiers refused to let them. The Allies had decided that the distribution of settlers to the various communities in occupied Germany should separate local groups to avoid forming enclaves who were unwilling to assimilate and blend in.

When Greta's wagon continued its journey towards Aschaffenburg there were still tears and pleas from people who felt they had been tricked and betrayed. Others complained about their hurting feet. Their misery added to the melancholy about moving further away from their former home. Evka found herself annoyed with the self-pity and moaning. Of course, there was a lot of tragedy in people's stories and reasons for unhappiness. She had experienced a lot of the same dramas first hand. But everyone was still alive and they were cared for by the army of countries whose citizens had not been treated in the same humanitarian manner by German soldiers. The transport was relatively short and less claustrophobic than it could have been if closed train carriages had been used. There was a lot to be grateful for.

She found it also unbearable to utter sympathetic remarks to people who had had a comparatively easy fate when next to her stood a man who had survived unimaginable horrors; a man who could laugh and smile and cheer up a young boy. They should take a leaf out of his book.

Greta was mainly concerned for Wilma and what yet another move and all the misery around them on the train would do to her condition. So far, everything seemed fine. Her fragile sister had been leaning over the edge of the train and appeared completely taken in by the landscape that was rushing past them. Earlier she had joined Ernst and Joschka in their travel games and had clearly enjoyed herself.

At long last they arrived in Aschaffenburg and were allowed off the train. From here it was another hour's walk to reach a former German military ground with large barracks. The last two freight cars had been kept shut. For the passengers of those, separate accommodation had been set up in a former school building.

Space at the barracks was much more limited than in their previous camp. The bunks and rooms were much smaller, there was no playing area or any other recreational facilities for that matter and the guards made it quite clear that once the mass exodus from the Sudetenland was set in motion even these camps were not enough to shelter everyone. Anybody who had relatives or friends on the outside was greatly encouraged to give up their space for people with greater needs.

"Maybe we should go to Paris?" Wilma suggested. "Edith and Esther should be there by now. If father and Alma can't find us in the camps, that is where they will go."

"We better not mention any of this in front of other people," warned Evka. "We might be thrown out to make place for someone else if there is a suspicion that we have alternatives to here."

"But we have alternatives!" insisted Wilma.

"We don't really know that," contradicted Evka. "Do you think we could still cross the border to France? When you were making this plan of meeting up in Paris you were clearly not anticipating the amount of refugees swamping all of western Europe. We were as naïve as the brave soldier Sveijk: 'Let's meet at six o clock after the war.' I wish it was that easy. I would be very surprised if the border was still open. "

"You are right," agreed Greta. "It has become a little bit more complicated than we thought. We should try and stick it out here until we find father and Egon. We have to get registered with that missing people's organisation again and see if they can help us."

Settling into their new environment was very difficult. As a married couple, Evka and Joschka had access to only one single bed, Greta had to share with Ernst, and Wilma was the only one with a bunk of her own. Above her slept another single mother whose four children were sleeping two and two on a different set of bunks. There was one more set of bunks that currently was not occupied and for now it served as room for everyone's luggage, which was not more than a small backpack per person. One of the guards came to inspect the room and made a record of the available space. He wrote an eight at the door outside.

"What does that number mean?" asked Evka.

"Eight more spaces in here," he replied curtly, clearly not in the mood to make explanations.

"But there are only two more bunks!" Evka pointed out.

"Yes, yes I know. This is no luxury hotel. Two spaces per bunk makes four, one bunk becomes free if two of the children share with their mother and then there is space for two more on the floor. I make this eight. You are lucky to have a roof over your head, so shut up and stop complaining."

He stormed away before she could say anything. She had not

meant to sound pushy. She was simply surprised at the harsh conditions she found herself in and was very sorry to have sounded so ungrateful to the soldier.

"It is a different regiment serving here," explained the mother of the four children. "I have heard that we are not far from a concentration camp. The troops here have liberated the camps and they hate anyone who speaks German. I speak a little English and I have heard them complain that the aid organisations are even considering helping us. They think we should be left to starve and any money and food should go to the victims alone. It is nothing like our old place. We had a vacation there in comparison. Mark my words, we will be sorry to have moved."

"We won't be staying here forever. We want to get out of here, find work and a place of our own," declared Evka.

"Of course, we all do. But there are no jobs. There are also not many apartments or houses and the few that exist are already occupied. No one is waiting for us here. We are not only starting from square one, we also have to do that in a place where nobody welcomes us. You better get used to that idea," said the mother, full of gloom.

"You are probably right, but the way I see it is that the people who already live here will need our help rebuilding the country. We will blend in eventually. Once the Russians take back their Soviet citizens there will be plenty of space and a lack of work force, that is what I hope for," Evka said, optimistically.

Only a week later there were further trains arriving at the barracks and another ten people joined the room. Wilma and the single mother, Erika, each had to take one of the children into their bed at night. Four women slept in the empty bunk unit and four had to crowd themselves on blankets on the floor. It was impossible to move without standing on anyone's bed. The four women on the bunk unit were Sudetengermans from Brno and Greta immediately asked them lots of questions about the situation there, trying to find out anything she could that might give her an idea about the fate of her father. The women could only tell her what she already knew: There had been so called wild expulsions of Germans towards the border and the march had cost a lot of people their lives.

As nurses, the four of them originally had been kept behind to help out in the hospital but the hatred towards them was too much for them to bear and they decided to leave of their own free will.

The women who had to sleep on the floor were fairly old and had refused the offer to sleep in the bunk beds. They were arrogant and nasty and did not only complain about everything, they wanted to dictate. The eldest of them, and clearly the ring leader, continuously told the children off for being too noisy and too lively. With nowhere to play to get rid of their energy, the poor little ones became very agitated and frustrated. Added grief from those women about their behaviour made everyone miserable. Evka was the only one with the guts to talk to these women and occasionally she succeeded in putting them in their place. She thought it was outrageous that the children should be kept quiet only so that all day long the entire room would have to listen to their sorrow about their lost homes and fortunes. When Evka pointed out to them that they were lucky to be alive and what horrors had been happening in the death camps, the women responded in two different ways: Either they laughed it off as unconfirmed and made up gossip or – on days when they felt particularly confident – they declared that no one had been put into those camps who had not belonged there anyway.

Ever since they first made remarks of that kind, the room split into the four of them in one group and the rest of them in another. It was bad enough to have those old ladies in their midst but because they were inhabiting most of the floor space that everyone had to use when getting in or out of their bunk, there was continuous moaning about the traffic over their beds.

"If Hitler had managed to get the venom out of your tongues he would have won the war!" said Evka to the ringleader. "You are evil through and through!"

"You can't talk to me like that, you dirty Jew whore. You make me sick!" the ringleader spat at her.

"He is not a Jew and even if he were he would still be ten times more of a human being than you will ever be!" Evka shouted back.

"Not a Jew? How did he get into the camps then? Is he a communist? Well, take him to the Soviets then, they will be glad to have him!" the old woman said hatefully.

"If you were a communist, even then the Soviets would not take you," Evka replied angrily.

"Stop it!" Greta told her friend. "She is not worth your anger. Leave her be."

Evka agreed but it was hard to ignore the four women who never missed the slightest opportunity to nag and start a row. Far too often Evka got angry and replied, which in Greta's view was exactly what the four women had wanted. They needed a vent for their anger and had found in Evka a willing victim that would fight back and give them a battling opponent.

Since every move annoyed the four mean spirited women on the floor, the daily routine of the room revolved around a regime that minimised movement. The nurses volunteered to help in the camp health tent and were usually outside of the dorm all day, giving the rest of the inhabitants extra beds to stretch out a little, but the atmosphere was subdued and depressing.

After a few weeks of what Evka called 'The reign of evil' things took a short change for the better, at least for some of Greta's group. The nasty ringleader slipped on an icy patch outside and broke her hip. Unable to move by herself, she had to be transferred to a small hospital and care tent. The remaining 'three witches' felt suddenly much less confident and from then on kept quiet.

Evka used the situation and suggested to the guards that the extra space in their hut should be made available to someone else. This was followed by an unpleasant row with the three women and the officers, and as a result, not only did the three witches have to move, Joschka had to move as well. His internment in a room full of women had been an oversight and the guards consequently moved him into a men's dormitory. He felt a great deal of anxiety about having to leave his safe haven behind and only reluctantly packed his things and followed the soldier out of the hut. His new 'residence' however turned out to be a change for the better. A former training room had been converted into a floor full of mattresses and his allocated space was right next to a group of three middle aged Hungarians. From what he could understand of their conversations with each other, they had been Jazz musicians in Vienna and only just managed to get out of Austria before the Soviets arrived. On their route to France, they had been stopped at the border between the French and the American occupied sector and eventually found this displaced person's camp.

The sole mission of these new neighbours was to find a way to practise and to rehearse. Initial attempts to do so in the camp had attracted a lot of complaints from mothers with children and some of the elderly who were infuriated by this 'negro noise', although many enjoyed the distraction. Now the search continued outside the camp but so far had proven fruitless. The band members were usually upbeat and cheerfully hummed melodies, many of which Joschka, being a fan of Jazz music, recognised. Within a day, he was talking to them and joined them on their excursions. Gyorgy, Ferenc and Zsigmond were delighted to have found someone who shared their passion and who was not wallowing in gloom and misery. Joschka had made it a habit to avoid speaking about his past in the death camp and was pleased that no questions were being asked. Zsigmond had once stared at the number on his arm but never said anything about it.

The trio was hoping to find steady employment in a night club in Paris or, maybe, Berlin. They were less confident about getting visas to New York since none of them were Jewish, they said, and neither were they young and strong enough to be judged as useful for hard labour. Their chances of emigration were poor they figured, and so decided to get on their feet locally as quickly as possible. They could do with a manager, would Joschka know anything about negotiations and contracts?

Evka was very excited for her 'husband' when he told her about the offer.

"That is perfect for you!" she exclaimed. "All that work as a lawyer's assistant must be really useful."

"Well, it is quite a different kind of work really, but it might help," Joschka replied.

"I can't wait to meet them and hear them play," Evka said.

"You may be able to," Joshka promised. "Zsigmond went to Frankfurt today. There are more entertainment venues in the big cities. Ferenc is talking to the American army later today to see if they have any use for us for their parties. He wants me to come with him to assist in the negotiations. Something is bound to come of it."

"I hope it goes well," Evka said.

"I am glad you are happy for me. I have been thinking about the future a lot since I met the trio. There may come a time when I have to go away with them, either to a big city or, if we get lucky, being constantly on the move. That is what the life of musicians is all about. Would you be happy to let me go or see me as another leaving traitor?" Joschka sounded very concerned.

"You wouldn't be a traitor. If you have such an opportunity you must take it. Hopefully, Greta and I will settle down somewhere and then you can always come and visit your wife. Of course we will be happy for you," she said cheerfully.

"My concern was for Ernst," Joschka admitted. "He will lose another person close to him."

"I know. But he is young and he will learn how to cope," Evka said quickly. "Greta is a very attractive woman and she will find someone who can be a father figure to him. Much more important is whether or not you feel safe with the musicians. You know... the way you are. Will they mind?"

"Jazz musicians have always had a more liberal approach to life. After the Great War when I was seeing Eugene, we usually went to Jazz clubs. The musicians I met there did not mind. They were glad there was less competition for the ladies," he told her.

"Oh good. I hope that it works out for you. I really do," Evka said.

"How is the atmosphere in your hut since the new arrivals?" he asked.

"Still not very pleasant. Two Polish women came with three children. One of them is supposed to sleep with me in my bed but they have managed to sleep all together on the floor. They won't speak to anyone. We think they have been forced labourers because when we speak their heads often turn as if they can understand everything. They are too well fed to have been in a concentration camp and if they were refugees from Poland they would be further north. Their children are not allowed to play with the others in the room. It is very awkward."

"I am sorry to hear that," said Joschka,

"The real shame is that the nurses are likely to move out of the camp, they say they are needed in a hospital nearby and they had enough of living in the camp. If they work for the hospital, they are entitled to living room allocation; that means a proper room to themselves. We still can't move in our dorm, so I am not surprised they are considering it. It won't be long before it all becomes too much for Wilma. Greta keeps going to the Red Cross tent queuing to request information about her father and Egon but they are totally flooded with requests and pleas. I wonder if we will ever find out."

"Maybe you should find some work yourself," Joshka

suggested "We should all try and get out of here."

Before Evka could turn these plans into reality however, a solution to their predicament came from the nurses. They were leaving the camp to work at the local hospital in a few days' time. The woman who had come to interview them had asked the nurses if they knew of any other qualified personnel here in the camp. Recruitment campaigns often proved futile because the desperation to start a normal life made many people lie about their abilities and work experience. It had proven far more successful to use recommendations from already chosen candidates, who would not suggest anyone lazy or useless if they would have to work together with them in the future.

Being aware of Wilma's fragile condition and the need to get her out of the claustrophobic environment, the nurses had tried to get positions for the two sisters and her friend as well. Greta was offered work as an assistant nurse in the hospital while Evka, Wilma and even little Ernst could help out in the hospital canteen and laundry. The work would be hard but there would be food and accommodation, at least slightly more comfortable than here. It was also a steady place for them to wait for further news of Jonah, Alma and Egon. Joschka could always visit his 'wife'.

"What do you think?" Greta asked her friend Evka.

"We would be mad not to take this opportunity," replied Evka immediately. "I am game for anything that brings us closer to normality. I am sick of living on charity, I want to earn my living and I want to get away from the people in here."

"Others are your hell, Sartre said, and he was spot on," Greta said philosophically.

"Very true," Evka agreed. "When I worked in the factory, I was at the mercy of my superiors, the Germans told us what to do for six years; here in the camp the Germans hate me, the Czechs hate me and the Americans can't wait to dissolve the camps so they can go home. I'll never get back to Pilsen and I know I'll never be welcome in Germany. At least we are moving forward, instead of waiting and crying over spilt milk. I'd pack my bag right now if you all decide to come along. All I want is for us to stay together."

"Me too!" said Ernst. "I don't want anyone else to leave."

"Yes, let's get out of here and move to the hospital!" Wilma agreed.

"You are right, Evka," said Greta after a little pause. "This is no life at all. But let's be clear about one thing: The world has not changed overnight, nor have the people. Outside we will meet the same types that we have met in here."

"I know," Evka said, "But let us take our chance and hope for the best. This is as good a place as any to start anew. Who knows what the Allies are going to decide about the refugees next. Maybe they will send them all to Africa or Asia. It would be good if we could be the masters of our lives for a change."

"So it is agreed? We leave?" asked Wilma full of excitement,

"Agreed," said Greta.

They moved out of the camp two days later, into two small rooms that had been confiscated from a German family. Bravely, they endured the resentment by the family. Ernst and the three women soon charmed their way into the family's heart. Their new life in a new country had begun.

Epilogue

Greta soon became a trained nurse, a profession she carried out until her retirement decades later. By alleviating pain in others she felt she could right the many wrongs that had happened. When she cared for a complete stranger she hoped that maybe somewhere another woman was doing the same good deed for her brother and father. Many who tried to learn the profession had to give up because they could not handle seeing all the pain and suffering in the hospital but to Greta, every little bit she could do to help mattered more than all the lost cases put together. With so many dying of hunger and dysentery, it was comforting to save some.

Her own life had begun promisingly by falling in love with a man who she loved and with whom she had shared dreams and ideals, but now her sense of morals and duty ordered her to lead it selflessly for others. Her goal was to keep Wilma sane, get Ernst an education and a future, and learn about her father and her brother. She still longed to read books but there was little time for that and few books survived the war of bonfires and bombings. Patiently Greta went through day after day, doing what needed to be done without complaining. Only long after Ernst had started his own family and television had become the sole entertainment for the rest of the family did she start to read again. Entire evenings and weekends were spent with new and old favourites she borrowed from the local library. For a little while she befriended an invalid who worked there until some of his remarks aroused suspicions that he had been a willing participant in the war. From then on she only looked for books on days when he was not working there.

"There are so many widows and decent men in my church choir. Let me introduce you to some of them," said her daughter-in-law once.

"Leave me alone," was Greta's curt response. "It is too late for me to start dating again and I am quite happy with the way things are. This is my time now. I don't want to become someone else's companion, I enjoy being free. I still have more than enough responsibilities. Thank you, but you would be better off doing your matchmaking for someone else."

Many years after the war, Greta finally received the news that

Egon had been captured near Stalingrad and had died of pneumonia in a prisoner of war camp. There had been no official records from the Soviet administration but one of the survivors – who eventually was allowed to return to Germany – had taken Egon's coat and handed letters and documents that were stashed in one of the inside pockets to the Red Cross. As devastating as that news was to her, Greta was also relieved to at last know the truth. She never had the heart to tell her sister who had stopped mentioning their brother a long time ago. Better to let sleeping dogs lie.

The Red Cross was able to provide information on the Countess. She had been shot by Czech guards right outside Pilsen as they had feared. Her body had been found and she had been identified immediately, but the name had not been added to the lists until a few years later.

Edith and Esther had successfully made it to Switzerland, where they found their lawyer and were also able to retrieve their fortune as well as money that the Countess had deposited for them in a numbered account.

After two years in Paris they gave up waiting for her Highness and took a cruise liner to New York. Once their lawyer forwarded Greta's new address they wrote the occasional letters to their friends but they never set foot on European soil again. In one of the letters, Edith admitted that she still felt guilty for abandoning the boys and for getting everyone into trouble with her old passport.

Luise and Freddie's ship was one of the few that managed to get through the sea blockade and the young family started a new life in Haifa by the sea. Evka found out much later that the ship their friends had taken had made it safely to Israel but they never established contact with the Weissensteiners in Germany.

Wilma continued to be plagued by panic attacks and general anxiety for the rest of her life, but stayed off medication for most of it. The doctors saw many cases similar to hers after the war and were neither trained nor often in a position to do much about it. Some told their patients to just get on with it or to get over themselves; some suggested heavy medication, others recommended therapy.

With Evka by her side, Wilma managed to continue her life

344

without many major attacks. She proved to be a valuable and hardworking asset to the hospital canteen and even though most of her colleagues thought she was a little odd or mad, they respected her for her surprising physical strength and endurance. Only shortly before her retirement age did the nightmares and panic attacks increase again. It started with a visit to the cinema, where Evka and she often spent their Sunday afternoons. When the lights went out Wilma started to shake and whimper, kicked her feet so violently that she caused a panic in the surrounding people and the ushers took her outside immediately. Shortly after that incident she developed a fear of bridges and from then on had to enter the hospital from a different entrance to avoid crossing a little stream on the way she had used before. Any loud noises set her off, and Evka and Greta often found her in the laundry room in the basement of their apartment block, seeking 'shelter from the bombs', but with all the lights on. She annoyed her neighbours by accusing them of spying on her and made them uncomfortable with her obnoxious looks. Twice Greta had to collect her sister from the police station where Wilma had fled to, insisting that someone had followed her. She was unable to describe the person but she could swear she had seen him before. Greta had a hard time keeping her out of a lunatic asylum and had to call in favours from her hospital colleagues to keep it from happening. She knew that any internment would be the end for her claustrophobic sister.

Wilma's eccentric and unconventional mannerisms however made her a huge success with Ernst's children, and grandaunt Wilma was always a sought after child-minder and a popular baby sitter, something which she absolutely adored. After her forced early retirement from the hospital, this new role gave her a new lease of life and helped her to carry on despite her many fears. Then at the age of only sixty she silently died in her sleep of a haemorrhage.

Sudetengermans formed associations in the new Federal Republic of Germany and organised a political lobby to regain 'their homes' in the lost territories, which were now part of Poland and Czechoslovakia. Mistaken for one of these unpopular activists and be-moaners of the past, Greta and her family were regularly subjected to unkind remarks and other minor acts of discrimination. They calmly endured all of it, but it made it hard for them to ever feel at home in the place that had reluctantly allowed them a 'fresh start'. After the many casual anti-Jewish remarks Greta had heard in the refugee camps she was not going to trade that new stigma for the old one. Gradually the communist countries changed their policies and set free thousands of deported and imprisoned Germans from Siberia and other regions, some of them born in exile. The Federal Republic controversially offered them a new home. Greta became very uncomfortable when she heard the same arguments that had been voiced when she had arrived after the war: "There is not enough space.", "They don't even speak German!", "Who is going to pay for all this?"

Greta was disheartened over these all too familiar voices until one day the doorbell rang and a very old woman stood outside her door. The two women stared at one another in disbelief.

Not only had Alma survived the war, she had lived to an old age and found her family. Over several long afternoons, Alma finally told Greta how her father Jonah had escaped both Germans and Russians and had died of natural causes on Johanna's new farm. Greta cried tears of both happiness and sadness at the news. Until the end her father had not lost his spirit to fight and even though he failed to complete his mission to find Egon, he had never given up. That Johanna had fallen on her feet and made a new life for herself with a new man was not a huge surprise to Greta. Maybe it was a little questionable how permanent this happiness would last in light of the communist revolution in Czechoslovakia after the war.

It was horrible to hear about Alma's bad luck and her futile attempt to assist her mentally unstable Ukrainian friend Halyna. Alma had spent over ten years in a Gulag in Siberia and couldn't tell Greta how on earth she had survived that hell. She was very surprised when she was suddenly released. For years she was not allowed to travel. She finally got permission to relocate to the Ukraine but never managed to find her friend or hear anything about her. She convinced an embassy official in Kiev that she was an abducted German. Fragile, ill and useless to the Soviet Union as a worker, there was no resistance to her leaving for yet another camp in Bavaria, where her integration process into German society would begin. The social worker assigned to her case was delighted to find that Alma was able to produce names of potential sponsors, found Greta's address and put her on a train right away before Alma could change

346

her mind or Greta could be contacted and refuse to take her on. Greta took Alma in until the old woman had a stroke a year later.

Greta was living on her own when Alma arrived. For many years Evka had stayed with the two sisters, but had frequently travelled to meet her husband Joschka and his musician friends in concert in cities all over Europe. He had found a special friend in West Berlin with whom he shared a bachelor apartment in one of the more bohemian quarters of the city. Joschka was 'mugged' outside a bar that was known to have homosexual customers and died due to injuries he had acquired during the attack. Evka never quite recovered from this loss and days after Wilma died she took an overdose of sleeping tablets and followed her friend to the other side. She left a short note for Greta, which simply said:

'Sorry my dear but I really want to go home now. Don't be sad, because I am not. Thank you for everything.'

Ernst really did become an architect. When school started again he surprised everyone with an almost genius-like intelligence. He skipped two years and admiration for his clever mind helped him find friends. For once, he was singled out for his achievements and not just his status as a refugee. The three women saved any money they could to help him during his time as a student and before he even finished his final exams he was hired by a construction firm where he had been an intern. He married a secretary who worked at the construction firm and had three children, all raised Catholic according to his new wife's wishes. He also developed a liking for Jazz music, influenced by Evka and Joschka, and learned to play the clarinet in his later life. When the Berlin wall came down, he decided to look for his father and found him still alive in a house just outside of East Berlin. Wilhelm Winkelmeier had survived the war in a comparatively danger free position in Norway. He had remarried and fathered two more sons, who had recently distanced themselves from their father after he had been exposed as a Stasi spy. Wilhelm's brothers, Ludwig and Bernhard, had both fallen in battle and his parents had fallen victim to an air raid.

Ernst's brother Karl had lost his job in a paint factory that had folded and was now working at a bookshop in West Berlin. Ernst and his father had little to discuss with each other apart from the exchange of these facts. Wilhelm offered no apologies or other sentiment regarding their family saga. Ernst, on the other hand, realised how uninvolved emotionally he himself was towards this strange old man. He should have known better than to expect any different. After all, Wilhelm could have tried to contact his son many times himself. Ernst realised with satisfaction that he still had the Weissensteiner optimism and naivety left inside of him after all.

When he met Karl over lunch the two got on very well. They were both amazed and stunned by gestures and idiosyncrasies they shared with each other, despite never having met each other. Ernst offered Karl a job in his office, but the brother refused, saying he could not imagine leaving Berlin now. He wanted to see his mother, but he wondered if she would want to see him after all those years during which he had done nothing to contact her. Ernst told him there was nothing their mother wanted more than seeing her long lost son. The reunion took place two weeks later in Frankfurt, where Greta lay in hospital. She was losing her final battle with breast cancer. Already quite hazy from the morphine, she gathered all her strength to look him up and down. The resentment that Karl had feared was nowhere to be seen. She was full of joy and for that one afternoon managed to pull herself together. She listened to all his stories, about his life in war-torn Germany, in the GDR and his new family. Then her strength left her. She died a few days later a happy woman in the presence of both of her sons.

The End

Did you like the book?

Thank you for reading my book. If you enjoyed it then please let everyone know by posting a review on: Goodreads, your national Amazon your favourite review site about it; it would mean a lot.

If you did like the book then read on and sample the first part of:

Sebastian
(Three Nations Trilogy: Book 2)

Chapter 1: Hospital

"I am afraid I won't be able to save his leg!" the handsome Serbian doctor said shyly to Vera. The tremble in his voice betrayed a discomfort that she had not expected judging him by his dark and hard looking Slav features. She also thought that he seemed far too young for his profession, maybe even only twenty five years of age if that. Was that old enough, she wondered, to be in control of someone else's leg and ultimately their life?

Had this not been the third time in one week that she had been given the same verdict she would have questioned his credibility rather than believed him, clinging to hope that his judgement could be challenged and thereby the outcome altered. Could he be fully qualified with those youthful looks or was he possibly just a student posing as a doctor. She would have liked to argue, and she would not have relented until she had the most senior medic arrive on the scene and explain himself to her but such drama and aggravation seemed futile after once again hearing the same universal and shattering diagnosis.

She sat opposite the young medic in a private consultation room of this luxurious and expensive clinic. Dr Vukovic had dark, moody eyes and strong facial features that did not seem to fit his youthful skin. With both soft and harsh looks showing in the same face, to Vera this man was one moment only a young boy whom she could send on an errand and the next moment he became the representative of the higher fate that she realised she would have to accept for her son.

She had brought her son Sebastian here yesterday morning in the desperate hope that if she paid enough money the verdict would be a different one this time. Dr Vukovic might have been young but he already had the reputation of an expert in the field due to some experience in the army hospitals during the Balkan War which had only just ended. The fact that he was from Serbia did bother her a little but she had no chance of discrediting him on those grounds. Her country had been fighting the Serbs for as long as she could think. Whatever was happening during the Balkans and regardless of which nations were forming a pact at the time, Serbia and Austria seemed always on opposite sides. Just a few years ago the army had been mobilised against them during the Bosnian crisis but at the last minute the government and the Kaiser had decided against military action. Why anyone gave so much about two small provinces like Bosnia and Herzegovina was beyond her but then she had never taken more than a passing interest in politics. She left such musings to her husband and most of what she knew did not even come from newspapers but from comments that she heard other people make.

She did think it odd that a doctor from an almost enemy country was allowed to work in Vienna and she naturally asked herself if he could be trusted. Even a private clinic like this was taking a bit of a risk in her eyes by employing someone like him. Thinking about it she came to the conclusion that he really had to be as talented and professional as she had been promised. Or had she been fooled into accepting a second rate understudy rather than the promised expert in the field?

As if he could read the doubts on her mind Dr Vukovic – after he had given her a little time to digest the verdict – cleared his voice and continued talking with more authority and professionalism.

"The infection has been left unattended for too long." He also sounded cold and bureaucratic now. "Too much tissue has died. The colouring of the wound is a clear indication that the situation is rather severe," he explained to her calmly, obviously glad that the emotional outburst he had feared from the beginning of this conversation had not occurred. Vera remained outwardly composed and in control of her emotions. After all, she had known in her bones that this was going to happen - ever since she finally had seen that horrific wound. The sight of the pus and its smell had almost made her sick and at the time she had to be very careful not to frighten her son by reacting too strongly to it.

She had been utterly furious at Sebastian about it. Throughout his entire life she had told him to be careful with his body, that his health was the most important thing in his life. However, not only had he carelessly injured himself by hurting himself with a rusty nail - he also had not told her about it, too scared that she would put some stinging disinfectant on the wound.

A piece of the nail had been stuck in the wound until he managed to pull it out. Had he not been trying to avoid going to the doctor the injury would have been dealt with quickly and none of this would be happening.

The sight of the injury had soon become badly infected and

had caused him constant pain. He had still been too scared of what a doctor might do and had also wanted to avoid more scolding from his mother, he admitted later.

It was his geometry teacher who accidentally found out about the poor state of Sebastian's leg in the boys wash room and sent him home. Vera knew that part of her son's hesitation was to do with his phobia of needles and medical treatment in any shape or form.

Sebastian was also prone to accidents due to his day-dreaming and permanent lack of attention to his surroundings. He had never been good at sports and so it was no wonder that his slow speed and slight limp had not been noticed at school earlier.

Now there was nothing anybody could do to save the leg. Her beautiful 16 year old son would be an amputee, a target for ridicule and bullying at school as well as in any other sector of public life. Her bubbele a cripple for life, shunned by prospective brides for his handicap and destined to be alone. A tiny error of judgement by an adolescent was going to ruin him forever. The most dreadful pessimistic thoughts started to flood her mind.

"Don't upset yourself too much, Frau Schreiber," the young doctor - who seemed to know what thoughts were going through her mind - implored. "We can cut beneath the knee. That will make the recovery and his future mobility much easier. There are a lot of modern aides available for purchase nowadays. Artificial limbs and other prosthetic designs - a wide range! I bet you have seen people with a wooden leg on the street without ever even knowing about it," he promised.

Vera nodded slowly as she took the news in. She didn't know what she was more afraid of; telling her son or her husband, Franz.

"We will be performing the operation first thing tomorrow morning," Dr Vukovic told her, reversing back into his impersonal manner. "Try to be strong when you speak to him. In my experience it is best not to tell the patient any sooner than absolutely necessary. He will just spend all night being upset and not sleeping a wink."

Vera knew too well that this would be the case. Her son was not very brave for his age, a weak book worm who didn't hold much interest in the adventures his school mates liked to participate in.

"He will probably also keep the other patients awake and bother the night nurses unnecessarily," Dr Vukovic added. "Sebastian seems particularly fearful for his age. In my time in the field hospital I have gained some useful knowledge about men and how to judge their bravery. I have my doubts about your son as to how well he will react to the news."

She nodded in silent agreement, struggling to deal appropriately with the situation. In comparison to this doctor, her son was a late developer.

"Frau Schreiber, are there any questions you have for me at all?" Dr Vukovic asked her, trying to provoke her out of her prolonged silence.

"Could you do the operation tonight?" she finally asked. "Why wait? He drank his morning tea around 7 o'clock but he refused any food since then. He is sober and ready for the operation. He gets too nervous to eat when we go and see a doctor. This is exactly why we are in this mess right now in the first place. Let us get it over with now, Herr doctor. No torturous delay. I beg you! Have mercy."

Dr Vukovic seemed reluctant, which she took as a sign that she had already started to win the argument as long as she pushed him a little more. If there were no possibility to operate tonight he would have come out with it right away, now she just had to find the right angle to persuade him to agree.

"If you could do it now, I could tell and comfort him without dragging the process out unnecessarily," she said. "Sebastian is aware that I am talking to you today and he will expect me to come and see him right after. I have never been able to lie to my son. He can read me like an open book. The moment I enter his room he will know that something is wrong. He is very intelligent. If I don't speak to him tonight at all he will also suspect that I am avoiding him and then he will be up with worry all night just like you predicted. If it has to happen let's get it over as soon as possible. Please doctor!" she begged.

"That is entirely up to you, Madam," Dr Vukovic replied. "It seems a little dramatic, if you ask me. The boy is 16 years old. How many allowances should we make for his lack of courage? At his age I was already...." He stopped himself suddenly. It was obvious that this woman was at a personal breaking point. Adding criticism about her son's character was untimely, even though he felt that someone had to tell her some unpleasant truths at some point. If this was Austria's youth then Serbia had nothing to fear in the future, he thought to himself.

"Never mind," he said. "If you insist I will get the operation theatre ready now."

"I do," Vera said with determination. "I would be very grateful. You have a remarkably good reputation for this procedure I have been told. I wouldn't let anyone else but you operate on him."

The young doctor liked her sudden humbleness. He was very proud with the way his medical career had gone thus far but the speed of his success occasionally made him worry that just maybe he could not live up to the high expectations that came with it. At university he had not been the best of students and had to count himself lucky to be taken on as army physician. When war broke out his talent for certain surgical procedures had been over-rated in his view but very soon he was allowed to work unsupervised and completely by himself. At first he had played down his abilities and credited the army's desperation for his promotion. Then he was offered this position in Vienna - despite his nationality - which was recognition enough for him to turn into an arrogant and self-satisfied human being. Because of his original doubts however he loved reassurances and praise all the same.

Suddenly Vera had a worrying thought flash through her mind: "He will get ether and morphine, won't he?" Her voice was starting to break. "He won't be in much pain? Can you promise?"

"Of course," Dr Vukovic said quickly. "He is in the best of hands. This will be much more civilized than it is in a field hospital. Please don't worry."

Vera thanked him and left the room to go and speak to her beloved son. She took a moment in the corridor to compose herself before entering Sebastian's room.

The moment she laid eyes on him he indeed seemed to sense bad news and he started to shake all over his body.

"What are they going to do? Mother!" His eyes filled with tears.

"Sebastian, be strong now. The doctor will have to operate on you. He will give you a cloth that smells a little odd and then you will fall asleep. There is nothing to worry about and that is all you need to know. When you wake up you will be better. You won't feel anything," she promised him and squeezed his hand as gently as she could. It broke her heart to keep the worst part of the truth from him but there was no need to upset him any more than he already was.

"No needles?" he asked.

"No, you won't feel even one tiny prick."

Fortunately this small deception and the omission of the bad news had worked and Sebastian put up no resistance when the nurses came and wheeled him into the operating theatre. Despite her resolve to stay with her son until he was unconscious Vera failed tragically in that regard and fainted at the first sight of the medical instruments that the nurse was cleaning with hot steam.

When Vera came to, the operation was already under way. When asked about her son the nurses reassured her, Sebastian had been a brave little man. Dr Vukovic had also kindly allowed them to give the patient generous helpings of morphine should it be necessary.

She knew that this was meant to make her feel better but Vera could not see the blessing this news entailed. Her blood circulation had always been poor and she knew she had to take it very slowly before getting up from the chair that she had been put to rest in. Soon she would have to resume control of the situation and she was ashamed for not being stronger for her son.

She blamed herself entirely for this disaster, not only because she had failed to notice the wound when there was still a chance to cure it. No, in her heart she knew that it was her own weak constitution which had to be the reason behind her son's misfortune.

The doctors had always warned her that her body might not easily cope with a pregnancy and in light of her frequent faints and dizzy spells had encouraged her to adopt a child rather than to have her own.

Her husband, Franz, had been madly in love with her and had instantly agreed with the doctors not to take any foolish risks. He would never endanger her life for the sake of a child, especially one whose survival in the womb was in question due to its mother's weakness,

Against all better judgement she had insisted and had become pregnant with Sebastian.

The entire nine months she had been worried and miserable and the doctors had restricted her to bed rest for most of the time. Vera almost died in childbirth and as a consequence was from then on officially forbidden to have any more children, which for the sake of her first born she luckily accepted.

Yet, the damage was done: She had passed on her faulty genes against the doctor's clear warnings and her son was paying the price for her stubbornness by sharing her generally weak physical constitution and her cowardice.

"Frau Schreiber!" One of the nurses woke her from her day dream. "There is a spare bed in Sebastian's room. If you want to rest beside him until he wakes up we won't tell. You won't be charged." The nurse was a big matron type who appeared as if nothing could make her lose her calm. She probably had seen it all during her life in hospitals and Vera felt incredibly safe in her presence.

"Thank you, Nurse Liesl. That is very good of you," Vera said with a brave smile. "I am so sorry for being a nuisance. Please just give me one minute. I have this poor circulation. That is probably why Sebastian is so fragile. I was warned not to have children but I wouldn't listen."

"Don't you blame yourself, Frau Schreiber. You have heard too many modern stories about genetics and evolution. Life and health are all still in God's hands," Liesl said.

Vera was surprised that the nurse seemed to be able to read her mind and that a regular and obviously religious nurse would know about the modern theories which she herself only had heard of by accident.

On the other hand, those words comforted her in this hour of need and so she clung to them happily without questioning. Maybe it was God's will, however horrible it was. Then it occurred to her that she had not informed her husband Franz yet. Although by now he was always busy with work, he might be wondering where she was.

"Do you think you could send someone to my husband and tell him to come to the hospital, or at least tell him about Sebastian's operation?" she asked the lovely nurse.

"Of course, Madam. I will send someone right away."

Nurse Liesl disappeared for a few minutes and when she came back she led Vera to the room where Sebastian was in deepest sleep. He looked so gentle and innocent for his years. Other boys his age looked like men already.

Maybe Franz had been disappointed by his son who was not the strong and virile offspring he might have hoped for but Vera was very proud of him. At least now it turned out useful that Sebastian's forte had always been his intelligence and his speech and not his physical qualities.

Sebastian would never have been any good at manual labour and his contribution to the family shop had never been particularly great. He would have to help out with the desk work and focus on his academic education rather than vocational training.

Vera soon drifted off again having tortuous nightmare visions of the future, occasionally lightened up by more pleasant dreams in which she was flying above the beautiful fields and mountains of Austria.

Hours passed without anything happening. Sebastian woke up only once and screamed with pain but the night nurse almost immediately administered an injection of morphine and he settled back down. He had probably not even been aware that his mother was in the room. Even to the nurses' voices he had been almost unresponsive. Who could blame him, a young man like him was not supposed to be the victim of such a tragedy.

Her husband Franz had not come to the hospital. She had guessed that – without her at the shop - he would decide to stay there to look after the business all by himself. The couple had taken over his father's grocery store four years ago when a heart attack had rendered the old man unable to perform physical labour.

Her in-laws were both unable to help in the store. Rebecca, Franz's mother, suffered from a bad back and spent most of her days in bed in total agony, trying to find a comfortable position. She and her weak hearted husband Oscar could only just manage minor tasks in the household. Vera felt very sorry for her husband to be surrounded by a completely incapable and handicapped family, including herself.

Now his own son would join the league of dead weight dragging the good man down. This hit her particularly badly as Franz had been the first to discourage her from becoming pregnant to safeguard her health. She had lied to him about her cycle to have the baby. What was meant as a gift, given to him under the risk of her life, had instead become another spanner in the works.

Overcome by guilt she curled herself into a foetal position on the bed and hugging the pillow tightly she fell asleep. In her delirium she thought she heard the nice nurse have a long talk with Sebastian about his future and how he had to be strong to beat his new condition. Or maybe she was only dreaming it, she could not be sure. When she got up to assume her role as responsible and attentive parent Sebastian was fast asleep and no one else was in the room. It was almost morning.

Vera had slept in her street clothes and now felt itchy, dirty and unfit to be seen in public. Her short hair was the least of her worries but her makeup had smeared all over the pillow. She left the room to see if there was anywhere where she could freshen up.

A new shift of nurses was on duty now and they were not particularly friendly or forthcoming with help. Of course they might not know what she had just been through. After a few minutes in the ladies toilets Vera returned to Sebastian's room.

She found out that Dr Vukovic was not expected to arrive for another few hours and that the night nurse had only told one of her colleagues about Vera and Sebastian's night. When the said colleague came to see how mother and son were doing this morning Sebastian finally woke up.

He appeared in much better spirits than Vera would have expected him to be.

"Sebastian my brave darling," his mother said stroking his face. "I am so sorry. The infection was too far gone. They had to take part of your leg away," she added, fighting the tears.

"I know," Sebastian said. "Nurse Liesl told me. It's fine."

Vera was surprised by his stoic attitude. It had to be the morphine talking.

"It's too late to cry over spilt milk," he continued. "But I think that I might be ready for more pain killers."

He had directed the last part of his speech towards the nurse in the room. She was much younger than Liesl and she showed much more personal concern for the young man and his fate. Her attitude did not have the assuring effect that was intended. The seriousness with which she treated the patient only frightened mother and son alike.

"Of course my little angel, I will get everything ready. You are a marvellous child," she said with a trembling voice and left the room in a hurry.

Vera marvelled at her son. He had still a bit of his baby fat visible in his face and beautiful vibrant hazelnut eyes. When he smiled her entire world lit up and when he pulled faces he was ever so entertaining. Despite his youthful appearance Sebastian often had the charisma and the air of a wise person about him and now he had managed to use this talent to gain a positive perspective on his health. Maybe it was all the reading or maybe the night nurse had gotten through to him with her speech. Her little prince had matured overnight way beyond his age. Vera was utterly impressed.

She was however disappointed that her husband had not come to see her and had not even sent her a messenger, but that was Franz for you. Always busy with his work and obsessed with providing for everyone. She could not blame him really, he had to shoulder a lot of responsibility and he did it with focus and without ever complaining. If he chose to neglect his family in times of crisis like this, he surely did so out of duty and sense of obligation for the very people he seemed to ignore.

Dr Vukovic came in briefly to see Sebastian. He was pleased with what he saw – however little that was in the short time he spent examining the boy. He confirmed to Vera that the procedure had gone well and rushed off to his next patient.

Around lunchtime, Vera left Sebastian at the hospital. The boy was either asleep for most of the time or in a trance like state. Her presence seemed to make little difference. She thought she could smell the night sweat on her clothes and felt dirty and sticky and in need to freshen up.

Franz had little time for her when she got to the shop. He was busy with customers when she arrived and seemed to avoid her. Well, he knew the big news already and he seemed in no rush to find out any details. She could see the sadness on his face, but there was also anger and fury showing in his eyes.

It was typical of her husband to avoid talking about unpleasant things. If she confronted him about it he would say that he would have known if there had been any complications because in such a case Vera would have sent another messenger to him right away. She could not accuse him of not being concerned. The absence of bad news was confirmation to her husband that everything was just fine. She called that coldness, he called it prioritising.

He was the kind of father who took great interest in his son and under different circumstances he would have liked to take an enormous part in his son's education and upbringing. Yet, with the ill health of his parents and the unstable condition of his wife, he had more than enough to deal with in the shop. Soon he would find out how much the extravagant luxury of going to three well renowned hospitals had cost him. All of which had produced the same results and exorbitant consultation fees. Vera was glad that despite a great dowry which she had brought into their marriage she had still some money of her own that could take care of the hospital bills.

She offered Franz her help with the customers but he told her he'd prefer it if she could look after his parents upstairs and prepare some food for all of them. When he was like that she knew it was easiest to leave him alone until he snapped out of his mood.

At lunch Franz gulped his food down and hardly spoke at all. Vera told him in detail as much as she knew about the operation. Dr Vukovic had reluctantly explained a few details about the way it had all gone and how optimistic he was regarding a speedy recovery of Sebastian.

"Good," was all Franz had to offer on the matter and he rushed away from the table quickly and went back downstairs to the storeroom where the sacks of provisions were in urgent need of sorting.

All afternoon he hardly spoke to Vera while she was serving customers. Whenever there would have been an opportunity to talk he went into the basement to bring up more stock and only stayed with her when she called him for help. In the evening he sat down and went over his accounts so ostentatiously that Vera didn't even ask whether he would accompany her to the hospital. She served dinner and then rushed to see her son.

Nurse Liesl was on duty again and she let Vera into the ward despite the fact that visiting hours had already passed.

"Your son is doing fine. He is a right little angel," the nurse told the concerned mother. "Hardly any trouble at all, and so mature. When I asked him where you were he said that you were busy with work. He never complains. What a lovely boy. You have raised him very well."

"I wish that I had brought him up so he had looked after himself more," she replied with bitterness in her voice. "I am very sad that he injures himself all the time. We would not be here if that was not the case."

"Oh Frau Schreiber, not that again," Nurse Liesl protested. "You must pull yourself together, especially for his sake. Now that he is putting on a brave face I recommend you try and do the same.

Complaining and moaning is not going to get either of you anywhere. Dr Vukovic told you that you were lucky they could cut beneath the knee. Once you go above that point prosthetic limbs become much more noticeable and a real burden to the patient. Count your blessings. Now go and be his mother!"

"It is easy for you to say that. He is not your child!" Vera said outraged at the nurse's impertinence.

"That is true," Liesl admitted, but then she added with little concealed impatience: "Because if he was my son I would be very proud of him, I wouldn't think about myself and how I feel about his misfortune and how it impacts on my own life. I would be delighted that he has this great attitude and life affirming way. He is an inspiration to all of our patients and that is only on the first day after the operation. He is very special, Frau Schreiber, I hope you recognise and appreciate it."

"I am afraid he is only putting on this brave face while he is on the morphine. Normally he is very sensitive and fragile," Vera retorted.

"In that case I have even more respect for him," the nurse said. "Those patients who are already strong usually try to laugh it all away and more often than not they become bitter and full of self-pity after a few years because they have tried to live in denial of the facts. Your Sebastian is facing his future life without illusions or complaints. That is real bravery to me, especially if he is not normally this strong. I also see a lot of cases in here that are far worse. Frau Schreiber, believe me you are very lucky given the circumstances. Try and see it from this angle. Think about what I have said. I only mean to help."

Vera knew that the nurse was right but she found it hard to admit it.

"Can I see my son now?" She said in a slightly reconciliatory tone.

"Of course Madam," Liesl said kindly. She knew that the woman in front of her had a lot to deal with, but nevertheless in her experience it never hurt to start working early on people's attitude before they got wrong ideas into their heads about their future life.

Judging from what Nurse Liesl had seen the family had sufficient money to afford the son a comfortable enough life. Much more than could be said for some of the polio children she had met. Someone just had to help Frau Schreiber to see her life in the right

361

context and maybe the woman might succeed in feeling better.

Sebastian was asleep when Vera came into his room. Someone had been moved into the empty bed that she had slept in the night before and Vera had to sit on a chair and wait for her son to wake up, which he didn't do for another three hours. He woke with a start and immediately called for the nurse and his next shot of morphine in a gentle and quiet voice – but not without urgency and determination.

"Mother, you are here!" He almost got up to say hello to her before he realised that he could not. "Liesl said that this might happen to me," he said.

"That what might happen?" Vera asked her son.

"That I think I still have both my legs. It hurts, but not as bad as before. They will stop the morphine soon, so I don't get dependent on it."

She was very impressed at the way he spoke about the facts, so detached and intelligent.

"Your father sends his love. He is very sorry he cannot come but you know how it is. Someone has to look after the shop and he does not like to give someone else the responsibility," Vera said nervously, worrying that her son might see right through her lie. If he did he never let on.

"Of course I understand, mother. Here, I have made a list of books I would like you to get for me next time you can make it to the hospital. But I know you and father are very busy. You must not put yourself out. I am being looked after really well," he reassured her.

The night nurse came in to administer his next injection and asked Vera politely to leave immediately but to come again at more acceptable hours.

Franz had already gone to bed when Vera got home. She knew how he hated to be woken in the middle of the night and to grant him a good night's sleep she went to Sebastian's room and slept there. Unable to put her mind to rest, she woke up early and made breakfast for everyone. Franz continued to keep a low profile and spoke little. As soon as he could, he went downstairs to prepare the shop for opening.

"You must give him time," Oscar told his daughter-in-law. "Franz always takes a while with the big news."

He was a gentle giant of a man, tall and broad with a wreath of curly grey hair around a growing balding patch on his head. His face was pale with deep lines on his forehead. It was still possible to see how bear like and strong he once must have been but his illness had left him with a pouch for a belly and his shoulders had shrugged forward. Only when he spoke could he achieve the authority and command that used to be his by just entering a room.

"I know," Vera conceded. "I am just sad that Franz does not even seem interested to go into the hospital. I could look after the store for a day. I have done it in the past."

"Sebastian will understand," Rebecca now entered the conversation. Her prolonged bed rest had made her eager to share everything that was occurring in the house. For years she had preferred to mind her own business and had never interfered or offered her opinion without being asked. Now she hardly got out of her night dress, rarely washed or combed her long curly red and grey hair. She spent most of her time complaining about the incredible pain she was suffering. The skin beneath her eyes had formed big bags, her entire body seemed to have sagged and the corners of her mouth were hanging downwards just like her spirit. She had never been bored in her life, always busy and proud of it, but since her back had started to give her this incredible grief she had become one of those nosy women she most despised. "He is not very spoiled," she defended her grandson. "I bet all he wants is his books."

"That is exactly what he asked me to get him: A long list of books. And I know how good Sebastian is but I am afraid for him all the same. What chance does he have if even his own father rejects him now that he has become a cripple?" Vera said, fighting her tears.

"Franz is not rejecting him," Oscar defended his son. "He just finds it difficult to get used to the idea of how life is going to be for all of us. He is working it all out for himself and when he is ready he will go and step up and do his fatherly duty," he promised.

"I encouraged him not to rush things," Rebecca admitted. "He can be such a hot headed person. I told him to work things out in his own head before he goes and says or does the wrong thing."

"How can he say the wrong thing?" Vera said without understanding. "His son is unwell, he should want to go and see him. What could he possibly say that would be wrong?" she asked her mother-in-law.

"We all have to make sure that we do not blame the boy for

363

what has happened to his leg and the consequences this will have for the family. We may not be able to keep the business like this or we may have to hire someone else. I think it would be good if Franz had a plan and then went into the hospital with a big smile and a positive outlook. We must not ruin Sebastian's life with guilt. Don't you agree?" Rebecca said.

Vera had to admit that her mother-in-law was at least partially right.

"That is very thoughtful of you. I just hope that Franz's absence from the hospital is not already provoking those guilty thoughts in Sebastian. You all know how sensitive he can be."

"Nonsense," Rebecca said a little too quickly. "He won't be clear in his head with all the morphine."

"Can I ask you a favour?" Oscar said to divert the tension. "Could you go and get some more of Rebecca's medicine from the pharmacy? We ran out last night."

"Of course," Vera promised.

Over the next few days Vera went back and forth between the hospital and her home. Oscar offered to come with her and keep Sebastian company but they all knew that it was far too risky with his fragile heart - and more recently his lungs - to walk through the current May heat. Last week he had gone down the stairs to get the mail and had hardly managed to come back up again. He had to sit down on the cold stairs several times, unsure whether it was his heart or his lungs that threatened to give up. Rebecca's back was also particularly bad this week. She could hardly lift herself off the sofa on her own and relied heavily on her husband.

Sebastian was happy in the hospital. He had taken a particularly strong liking to Nurse Liesl and she to him in return. Most of his days he spent reading and Vera had to go and buy him more books.

His pain was receding quickly but the wound was not healing as well as the doctors would have liked. Dr Vukovic had been dismissed rather unexpectedly. Due to the continuing war in Serbia, the army had called him back and he had decided to follow his patriotic duties.

Vera had to deal with a Dr Rosenzweig now, a condescending and arrogant established doctor in his fifties whose most prominent feature was a moustache with pretentiously curled end parts. He was not in the least interested in Sebastian and his leg which he regarded as beneath him since the hard work had already been done by someone else. He suggested a quick discharge of the boy to make space for a more interesting and challenging new patient.

Franz still stayed away from the hospital and this - combined with Dr Rosenzweig's hostile attitude - made Vera finally push everyone at the hospital herself to allow her son to come back home soon. Franz was easily convinced once he saw the hospital bills.

The reunion between father and son was cool and distant but on the surface amicable enough to give the impression that relations were fine.

Sebastian was not so much hurt by the negligence but worried that it was a sign of his father's anger and accusation. He felt guilty and worried about the impact of his injury and understood how busy his family would now be because of it. He longed for some kind of absolution from his father which sadly never came.

The young patient was able to walk with a crutch and wanted to be independent from any outside help as soon as humanly possible. Vera had ordered a wooden leg from a supplier of prosthetics but it was too soon to fit it. The wound needed to heal properly first and Sebastian could not wait for that to happen, eager to make his contribution to the family.

Franz occupied himself as much as he could with the business. He was struggling hard to make enough money to feed the entire family. Vera worked in the store whenever it was busy and did as much housework in the evenings as she could. Her weak constitution luckily was stable at this time, playing along with the current need for her increased productivity. Oscar supported Sebastian in his aim to catch up with the lessons he had missed at school and tutored him with the help of study materials supplied by a fellow student.

The three patients upstairs in the flat formed a happy group trying hard not to be in any one's way or make any unnecessary demands. Rebecca could contribute the least in the physical realm but she knew how to run the house and so she took the role of the leader, supervisor and instructor.

Sebastian soon developed a sense of balance with his crutches and could sweep the floor with one hand and do some cooking as well without falling over. Oscar, equally eager to be useful, could do the things that required bending down, which neither Rebecca nor

Sebastian could. Oscar could also perform some light activities when he was sitting.

The trio surprised Vera one day with their first meal and an almost clean flat when she returned from her morning shift at the store. At first the mother was concerned for her son's lack of educational progress if he was involved in the housekeeping but Oscar could ease her mind about that effortlessly. He assured her that there was plenty of time during the afternoon and that Sebastian was a natural when it came to learning, a highly intelligent young man.

Vera did not find that too hard to believe. Oscar gave his grandson mathematical tasks or tested his knowledge of Latin verbs and grammar while the handicapped youth cleaned dirty dishes, dried them and put them away again. Sebastian made good progress with his studies. One of the nicer boys in his class, Philip Federer, came once a week to lend Sebastian his books and notes from class. Oscar copied them and read them out loud while Sebastian balanced a bucket of water or carried logs in to the kitchen, a few at a time of course.

Franz was tremendously happy about this development. It freed up most of Vera's time to help in the shop and her kind manner was of huge importance for the success of the business which faced fierce competition from other merchants in the quarter.

Vienna had inhabitants from all corners of the Austro-Hungarian Empire and their demands for different types of food made the life of a local grocery seller a challenging task. To get the balance right for the varying requests of all ethnic groups that came through his doors demanded foresight and luck. Franz did not want to be seen as favouring one group and thereby miss out on the custom of the others. Being too much of a perfectionist himself to take criticism of his stock lightly, Vera was a natural to distract clients with her charm, placate their frustration and win them round with her empathetic smile.

The current arrangement left his wife free to work in the shop which was a huge help for his overtaxed body. He dreaded the day when Sebastian was back at school and Vera would have to share her time between her family and the business obligations again. He had hoped to use the boy in the store and teach him a few tricks of the trade but that seemed more and more unlikely now. Instead, his son seemed to be destined for university life and maybe a career in academics. The hope that Oscar would help to earn money in the family business rather than incur the costs for higher education was smashed to pieces. Now one had to think in the longer term and hope that by performing well in his exams and taking further studies Sebastian might find lucrative employment that would eventually be enough to feed his family.

Franz worried excessively about the business despite its good shape. He would have preferred a larger profit margin to feel secure against any possible problems in the future.

On the other hand he was pleased that fate had taken the decision to utilize his only son for the family's material short-term situation out of his hands. As proud father he wanted his son to have a better life. Now that it was clear that his son could not run the shop alone, an alternative and maybe better future had to be considered and pursued.

The difficult decision to make was whether to use their savings to hire someone for the store or for the house hold. Franz was by no means stingy but he feared that using up his emergency resources would leave him vulnerable in a world that so often changed and turned against his kind. If only he had some distant relatives whose guilt he could exploit into helping him out.

He remembered one of his customers telling him a remarkable story. The man's wife had been taken to hospital with high fever. A cousin of the wife was sent to help out with the children and the house-keeping. The girl that came turned out to be a much better cook and child minder than his wife had ever been. The wife returned from hospital but the stay of the helpful relative was extended. By the time the family was able to function without assistance, the children had grown so fond of their new 'auntie' and her cooking that it was decided by all parties involved to keep her in the household until a prospective marriage was on the cards. Vienna – so the official justification went - was a much more suitable location to meet a future husband than the small town she had come from and hopes were high for her. The young woman however failed to attract a suitor and left the house many years later, only when the youngest child had reached puberty, much to the client's liking who had managed to save himself a small fortune.

Franz longed for a stroke of luck like that and put word out amongst the families if anyone could oblige him - but no such help was forthcoming. He found it hard to make up his mind also whether the help should be for the store or the home. Having a stranger in the shop and trusting them with the customers and the money was almost too much of a risk but then again leaving the care of his parents and his son to someone who might be either too sympathetic or too little concerned for their welfare was something he felt equally uncomfortable with.

For the time being he was 'lucky': Dr Rosenzweig was not yet satisfied with the healing process of Sebastian's leg and had surprisingly recommended a few more weeks of bed rest at home for the young boy before he thought it was possible for the prosthesis to be fitted and even to think about sending him back to school. The trio of patients could continue their cooking and housekeeping and Vera could remain in the store until Sebastian was fit to leave the house.

Philip Federer continued the supply of learning materials but never stayed long. He was an extremely quiet boy and rarely spoke to anyone apart from Sebastian. Vera and Franz had invited the kind student into their house on many occasions but he had always declined and seemed eager to get away. Sebastian's lot had become the talk of the school and while few had taken notice of him before the incident, now there were many who had offered to bring their study materials to meet the hero with one leg. The class teacher however had insisted that Philip carried on with the task since he had proven so faithful a friend and also because his writing was so neat and his grasp of most subjects was so immaculate. The teacher wanted Sebastian to receive only the best in order to keep his status as star student at the strict grammar school.

Oscar enjoyed a new lease of life that the task of home schooling his grandson had given him. He felt more energetic and alive than he had in years. With every correct answer Sebastian gave him he felt useful again and saw his declining existence a little more justified.

He was aware how much of a burden he and his wife were for his son and hated that there was nothing he could do to alter that. All his money was in the business and he had already given that to his son. Now he felt he was at last contributing again to the future of his family in a constructive way. Exams were another six weeks away and his student would do very well.

"Are you nervous about taking your exams?" Oscar asked his grandson one evening.

"Not at all. If they ask me the same questions as you do I think I can't fail," came the confident reply.

"I think I could take the exam," called Rebecca from her bed through the open door. "You two have gone over everything so often, the mice in the basement could take the exams," she joked. "I wish I could have had this bad back when I was in school myself. Then I would have done better at my exams than I did."

"In those days women did not need education," Oscar put her right. "There were not even spaces for you in the universities. Even if you had passed your Matura with flying colours you still would have lived at home until your marriage."

"Just as well," Rebecca snapped back. "If I had grown up in these times I am not sure I would have married at all. I think it is so exciting that women are finally able to prove themselves and get an education. Of course many of these poor girls are not very successful but they stroll around the streets with pride. So what if they have to sacrifice a lifetime of servitude to their husband and children? They can get satisfaction and a sense of achievement out of their lives that has been the sole privilege of men thus far."

"I am sorry, my dear. I was always under the impression that we married for love and that you wanted this life," Oscar said, playfully pretending to be hurt.

"Stop twisting my words. You will be the end of me one day!" she shouted.

"I love you too," Oscar shouted back with a sarcastic tone but a gentle smile.

Sebastian admired his grandfather who had such a loving and patient manner and he swore to himself that one day he might be just as nice kind and generous as this.

Nurse Liesl had put great ideas into the head of the little amputee when she had talked to him about the importance of his own positive attitude towards his disability. Grandfather Schreiber now was the perfect coach to put those ideas in to practise. He seemed to know perfectly well when to push the boy to try a little harder and make a step forward towards recovery and when to give him a rest.

"If you give up on something, you often give up on yourself as

369

well!" he frequently whispered into his grandson's ears when it seemed as if the latter was about to give up on a task.

Combined with the personal attention and tutoring the old man had become the father figure that Franz always would have liked to be, if only he had had the time for it.

Rebecca loved to see her husband so happy and cheerful and was very proud of his achievements. The old couple managed to almost forget about their own problems as they focused on the boy. Nothing could ever really ease her back pain and it would have been too much against her nature not to complain about it. Yet, witnessing the positive changes in her husband transformed her too and made her life more colourful and fresh and bearable.

Another two weeks went by and Dr Rosenzweig was expected any day now to pay a flying visit to the house and have another quick examination of the state of Sebastian's leg when out of the blue the poor boy collapsed and fell while preparing dinner for the family.

Rebecca heard the thump and called out hysterically to her husband. By the time Oscar had come running from the other room, her calls had turned to screams.

"Calm down, woman!" he scolded her and bent down to examine Sebastian whose face was pale and ashen.

"What is the matter, son? Are you hurt?" Oscar asked.

There was no reply.

"What is he saying?" shouted Rebecca. "I can't hear anything?"

Sebastian was clearly conscious and awake as his eyes were open but avoided his grandfather's glance.

"Speak to me!" Oscar said, gently shaking the boy's shoulders. "You are scaring your grandmother."

Sebastian still said nothing, quite contrary to his usual considerate and open manners. Oscar examined the boy for signs of blood or fractures but all seemed fine.

"Don't get up," he advised the patient. "Stay on the floor. I will get you some water. Maybe it is just the heat," he said hopefully and slowly got up. He almost fainted himself as he did so. He knew he had to be so careful with his heart.

"I'm just getting some water for Sebastian. I think he has fainted in the heat," he called to his wife who – for a patient with a bad back – seemed admiringly flexible in her efforts to get a view of the accident. At this rate she would put herself in even greater agony.

"Go down to the store and get his mother. She will know what to do," Rebecca suggested.

"No, I mustn't worry them during the day. They are busy and Franz will never forgive me if it turns out to be just a minor faint," he cut her short and poured some water from the pitcher into a glass for his grandson.

Sebastian's face betrayed him as he tried to sit up. The second Oscar saw the face he knew it was the leg that was causing the boy pain again and that had been the reason behind the fall. He gently touched the skin above the bandage. Sebastian immediately doubled over in pain.

"Since when have you had pain in your leg again?" he asked calmly but seriously.

"I don't know," Sebastian said. "Maybe since yesterday?"

"Oh you little fool," Oscar sighed out loud. "It has been longer than that, hasn't it?"

He took the silence as confirmation of his fears. "We need to take you to the doctor."

He braved the walk down the stairs to tell his son and daughter-in-law. Vera dropped everything and ran up the stairs to see with her own eyes what her ears refused to accept as truth. When she saw the pain on her son's face she knew it to be true.

More Books by Christoph Fischer:

The Luck of the Weissensteiners
(Three Nations Trilogy: Book 1)

In the sleepy town of Bratislava in 1933 the daughter of a Jewish weaver falls for a bookseller from Berlin, Wilhelm Winkelmeier. Greta Weissensteiner seemingly settles in with her in-laws but the developments in Germany start to make waves in Europe and re-draw the visible and invisible borders. The political climate, the multi-cultural jigsaw puzzle of the disintegrating Czechoslovakian state and personal conflicts make relations between the couple and the families more and more complex. The story follows the families through the war with its predictable and also its unexpected turns and events and the equally hard times after. What makes The Luck of the Weissensteiners so extraordinary is the chance to consider the many different people who were never in concentration camps, never in the military, yet who nonetheless had their own indelible Holocaust experiences. This is a wide-ranging, historically accurate exploration of the connections between social status, personal integrity and, as the title says, luck.

Praise for The Luck of the Weissensteiners: "… powerful, engaging, you cannot remain untouched…" "Fischer deftly weaves his tapestry of history and fiction, with a grace…"

Amazon: http://smarturl.it/Weissensteiners
Goodreads: http://bit.ly/12Rnup8
Facebook: http://on.fb.me/1bua395
B&N: http://ow.ly/Btvas
Book-Likes: http://ow.ly/J4X2q
Rifflebooks: http://ow.ly/J4WY0
Trailer: http://studio.stupeflix.com/v/OtmyZh4Dmc

Sebastian
(Three Nations Trilogy: Book 2)

Sebastian is the story of a young man who has his leg amputated before World War I. When his father is drafted to the war it falls on to him to run the family grocery store in Vienna, to grow into his responsibilities, bear loss and uncertainty and hopefully find love. Sebastian Schreiber, his extended family, their friends and the store employees experience the 'golden days' of pre-war Vienna, the times of the war and the end of the Monarchy while trying to make a living and to preserve what they hold dear. Fischer convincingly describes life in Vienna during the war, how it affected the people in an otherwise safe and prosperous location, the beginning of the end for the Monarchy, the arrival of modern thoughts and trends, the Viennese class system and the end of an era. As in the first part of the trilogy, 'The Luck of The Weissensteiners' we are confronted again with themes of identity, Nationality and borders. The step back in time made from Book 1 and the change of location from Slovakia to Austria enables the reader to see the parallels and the differences deliberately out of the sequential order. This helps to see one not as the consequence of the other, but to experience them as the momentary reality as it must have felt for the people at the time.

Praise for Sebastian: "I fell in love with Sebastian…a truly inspiring read for anyone!!!!" – "This is a MUST read, INTELLIGENT, SENSITIVE, ENGAGING, PERFECT."

Amazon: http://smarturl.it/TNTSeb
Goodreads: http://ow.ly/pthHZ
Facebook: http://ow.ly/pthNy
B&N: http://ow.ly/Btvbw
Book-Likes: http://ow.ly/J4X8M
Rifflebooks: http://ow.ly/J4Xgv
Trailer: http://studio.stupeflix.com/v/95jvSpHf5a/

The Black Eagle Inn
(Three Nations Trilogy: Book 3)

The Black Eagle Inn is an old established restaurant and farm business in the sleepy Bavarian countryside outside of Heimkirchen. Childless Anna Hinterberger has fought hard to make it her own and keep it running through WWII. Religion and rivalry divide her family as one of her nephews, Markus has got her heart and another nephew, Lukas has got her ear. Her husband Herbert is still missing and for the wider family life in post-war Germany also has some unexpected challenges in store.

Once again Fischer tells a family saga with war in the far background and weaves the political and religious into the personal. Being the third in the Three Nations Trilogy this book offers another perspective on war, its impact on people and the themes of nations and identity.

Amazon: http://smarturl.it/TBEI
Goodreads: http://ow.ly/pAX8G
Facebook: http://ow.ly/pAX3y
Book-Likes: http://ow.ly/J4Xpp
Rifflebooks: http://ow.ly/J4XqX
Trailer: http://studio.stupeflix.com/v/mB2JZUuBaI/

Time to Let Go

Time to Let Go is a contemporary family drama set in Britain. Following a traumatic incident at work stewardess Hanna Korhonen decides to take time off work and leaves her home in London to spend quality time with her elderly parents in rural England. There she finds that neither can she run away from her problems, nor does her family provide the easy getaway place that she has hoped for. Her mother suffers from Alzheimer's disease and, while being confronted with the consequences of her issues at work, she and her entire family are forced to reassess their lives.

The book takes a close look at family dynamics and at human nature in a time of a crisis. Their challenges, individual and shared, take the Korhonens on a journey of self-discovery and redemption.

Amazon: http://smarturl.it/TTLG
Goodreads: http://ow.ly/BtKs7
Facebook: http://ow.ly/BtKtQ
Book-Likes: http://ow.ly/J4Xu0
Rifflebooks: http://ow.ly/J4XvR

Conditions

When Charles and Tony's mother dies the estranged brothers must struggle to pick up the pieces, particularly so given that one of them is mentally challenged and the other bitter about his place within the family.

The conflict is drawn out over materialistic issues, but there are other underlying problems which go to the heart of what it means to be part of a family which, in one way or another, has cast one aside.

Prejudice, misconceptions and the human condition in all forms feature in this contemporary drama revolving around a group of people who attend the subsequent funeral at the British South Coast.

Meet flamboyant gardener Charles, loner Simon, selfless psychic Elaine, narcissistic body-builder Edgar, Martha and her version of unconditional love and many others as they try to deal with the event and its aftermath.

Amazon: http://smarturl.it/CONDITIONSCFF
Goodreads: http://ow.ly/
Facebook: http://ow.ly/C0ZqX
Book-Likes http://ow.ly/J4Xzj
Rifflebooks: http://ow.ly/J4XBl

The Healer

When advertising executive Erica Whittaker is diagnosed with terminal cancer, western medicine fails her. The only hope left for her to survive is controversial healer Arpan. She locates the man whose touch could heal her but finds he has retired from the limelight and refuses to treat her. Erica, consumed by stage four pancreatic cancer, is desperate and desperate people are no longer logical nor are they willing to take no for an answer. Arpan has retired for good reasons, casting more than the shadow of a doubt over his abilities. So begins a journey that will challenge them both as the past threatens to catch up with him as much as with her. Can he really heal her? Can she trust him with her life? And will they both achieve what they set out to do before running out of time?

Amazon: http://ow.ly/J4Wt6
Facebook: http://ow.ly/J4Wun
Goodreads: http://ow.ly/J4Ww4
Book-likes: http://ow.ly/J4WxU
Rifflebooks: http://ow.ly/J4WzY

Thanks and Historical Note

I would like to thank the following people who helped me write this book:

Brenda Whitby for encouraging me to write, Daz Smith for pushing me to get this book published, Bettina Weissensteiner for letting me use her name, and to all the people who read the various drafts and gave me invaluable feedback: Andrea Steiner, Sal Andrews and Susanne Weigl. Also thanks to the inspiring figures in my literary life: Madlon Veronika Koepfler, Alois Pfaller, Dr. Eugen Weigl, Saber of Topping & Company Book Sellers Bath, Dal Kumar, Gabriele Nowak, Terry Sandwick and many, many more. Last, but certainly not least, to Deborah Wall and Ryan Cheal for their amazing patience and editing skills. This book is a work of fiction. All characters apart from actual historical figures, such as Heydrich, Benes, Tizo and Hitler, are the result of my own imagination.

The story – apart from actual historical events, such as the events of WW2 and the Brno Death March – is also not based on the lives of any particular individuals.

Bombardment, Communist occupation and later 'rewriting' of Slovak history have made research difficult and some 'facts' are hard to prove or to objectify. For example, the exact use of the Presidential Exemption Papers for Jews is a controversial subject and heavily disputed by some historians.

The description of camp life is based on research but the layout and location of refugee camps have been amended to fit the storyline. I have included a list of recommended further literature; many of these books helped me get a better understanding of the times and make the story as life-like as possible. In some cases however I had to make educated guesses and took liberties in order to make this a story rather than a painting by numbers, fictionalised re-telling of history.

I hope the resulting compromise will please readers either in search of entertainment or those hungry for facts.

I apologise, in advance, for any mistakes and errors that have slipped through the net.

Further Reading

Gilad Atzmon: "The Wandering Who? A Study in Jewish Identity Politics"

Israel Bartal & Antony Polonsky: "Polin: Studies in Polish Jewry, Vol 12: Focusing on Galicia: Jews, Poles and Ukrainians 1772 – 1918"

Gad Beck: "An Underground Life: Memoirs of a gay Jew in Nazi Berlin"

W. Michael Blumenthal: "The Invisible Wall: Germans and Jews: A Personal Exploration"

Gunter Boddecker: "Die Fluchtlinge: Die Vertreibung der Deutschen im Osten"

Michael Brenner & Derek J. Penslar: "In Search of Jewish Community: Jewish Identities in Germany and Austria 1918 – 1933"

Ted Falcon & David Blatner: "Judaism for Dummies"

Joachim Fest: "Not Me: Memoirs of a German Childhood"

Harriet Pass Freidenreich: "Jewish Politics in Vienna, 1918 – 1938"

Peter Glotz: "Die Vertreibung: Bohmen als Lehrstuck"

Vasily Grossman: "A Writer at War. Vasily Grosman with the Red Army 1941- 1945"

Annette Grossbongardt & Uwe Klussmann: "Die Deutschen im Osten Europas: Eroberer, Siedler, Vertriebene"

Mary Heimann: "Czechoslovakia: The State That Failed"

Stanislav J. Kirschbaum: "A History of Slovakia: The Struggle for Survival"

Hilke Lorenz: "Heimat aus dem Koffer: Vom Leben nach Flucht und Vertreibung"

Friedrich Reck-Malleczewen: "Diary of a Man in Despair"

Joseph Roth: "The Wandering Jews"

Shlomo Sand: "The Invention of the Jewish People"

Ben Shephard: "The Long Road Home: The Aftermath of the Second World War"

Gerald Steinacher: "Nazis on the Run: How Hitler's Henchmen fled Justice"

Frederick Taylor: "Exorcising Hitler: The Occupation and Denazification of Germany"

Elie Wiesel: "Night"

A Short Biography

Christoph Fischer was born in Germany, near the Austrian border, as the son of a Sudeten-German father and a Bavarian mother. Not a full local in the eyes and ears of his peers, he developed an ambiguous sense of belonging and home in Bavaria. He moved to Hamburg in pursuit of his studies and to lead a life of literary indulgence. After a few years he moved on to the UK where he now lives in a small hamlet, not far from Bath. He and his partner have three Labradoodles to complete their family.

Christoph worked for the British Film Institute, in libraries, museums and for an airline. 'The Luck of The Weissensteiners' was published in November 2012; 'Sebastian' in May 2013 and The Black Eagle Inn in October 2013. These three historical novels form the 'Three Nations Trilogy'. 'Time to Let Go' was published in May 2014 and 'Conditions' in October 2014. 'The Healer' was released in January 2015 and 'In Search of a Revolution' in March 2015. He has written several other novels which are in the later stages of editing and finalisation.

Twitter:
https://twitter.com/CFFBooks
Pinterest:
http://www.pinterest.com/christophffisch/
Google +:
https://plus.google.com/u/0/106213860775307052243
LinkedIn:
https://www.linkedin.com/profile/view?id=241333846
Blog:
http://writerchristophfischer.wordpress.com
Website:
www.christophfischerbooks.com
Facebook:
www.facebook.com/WriterChristophFischer
Goodreads:
https://www.goodreads.com/book/show/23662030-the-healer
Amazon:
http://ow.ly/BtveY

48836628R00209

Made in the USA
Charleston, SC
13 November 2015